# Of Dawn and Embers

# Kyoko M.

**For my mother, Judy**
Your courage and love get me through my world of embers. I
love you always.

**Of Dawn and Embers**

**Of Cinder and Bone series**
Of Cinder and Bone
Of Blood and Ashes
Of Dawn and Embers

**Other Works by Kyoko M.**
The Black Parade
The Deadly Seven: Stories from *The Black Parade* series
She Who Fights Monsters
Back to Black
The Holy Dark

Visit http://www.shewhowritesmonsters.com for more

Dragons have no darting tongues,
Teeth saw-edged, nor rattling scales;
No fire issues from their lungs,
No black poison from their tails:

For they are creatures of dark air,
Unsubstantial tossing forms,
Thunderclaps of man's despair
In mid-whirl of mental storms.

-"Mermaid Dragon Fiend" by Robert Graves

# PROLOGUE

## FIRST LIGHT

The sky was on fire.

Jack sipped his coffee and stared at the horizon above the line of trees surrounding the property. An explosion of reds, oranges, and pinks assaulted the heavens, made clearer by the lack of a city skyline or smog. It had been quite a while since he'd seen it. There was some, small thing, inside of him that sighed contently at the sight as a wealth of childhood memories welled up. Of stepping out into the crisp air, lacing up his boots, and getting ready for his morning chores. How the grass and gravel crunched as he walked towards the barn. The cool breeze sweeping down through the forest and brushing his perpetually messy dark hair off his forehead. Clean living.

"Colder than I thought," Kamala murmured to him, as she stepped out onto the porch and pulled the front door shut once the screen door had swung closed behind her. She had one arm in her coat sleeve already, so he put his coffee down on the railing and helped her into the other.

"Yeah, most mornings here are." Jack said. "Even in the summer, it's kind of brisk before the sun wakes up."

She sipped her chamomile tea and settled next to him, her dark honey eyes scanning the sky as nearby, a flock of birds took flight. She watched them wheeling about in perfect sync, a part of her envious of them. The wind picked up for a second, brushing her thick, glossy hair away from her neck and making her shiver slightly. They drank in silence for a time.

"That reminds me," Kamala said. "Why don't you have an accent?"

Jack arched an eyebrow. She grinned. "No, I mean it. Greenville, Georgia could definitely be considered the Deep

3

South. I heard some of the locals when we stopped for dinner last night. You don't have a Southern drawl, Jack."

He cleared his throat. "I just never really picked it up. Mom's is pretty mild and she was the one who always read to me as a kid or helped me with my homework. Then, by the time I was old enough to watch television and movies, the kinds of things I liked didn't have many Southern characters in them."

He smiled faintly. "But if it makes you feel better, I can start dropping 'ain't' and 'y'all' into our conversations occasionally."

She snorted. "What's a y'all?"

"Short for 'you all.' It tends to be overused in movies that don't understand how Southerners act, but we do actually use it. *Gone with the Wind* really didn't do us any favors for accurate portrayals, but I guess it didn't bug my mom enough not to name me after Clark Gable's character."

Kamala shook her head. "I still don't understand why you detest your first name so much."

Jack sighed. "It's just...I don't know. You grow up with the name of a guy who some consider the quintessential Man's Man character, and I was a skinny little geek all through school. The literal opposite of the guy. Besides, with the benefit of hindsight, the character was pretty problematic and I don't like to invite the comparison."

He paused. "Though to be fair, I am problematic as hell. Just maybe not in the same way."

She watched him from beneath her thick eyelashes, her voice mild as honey. "I've seen worse."

Something in his chest stung. Jack leaned his arms on the railing, holding the mug between his hands to warm them. "Sorry."

"You've apologized a thousand times since it happened, you know."

"Only a thousand?" he said, chuckling bitterly. "I'm behind on my numbers."

Kamala watched him for another long moment and

then reached out. She slipped her fingers into his hair and brushed them along his scalp, smoothing the messy locks away from his forehead. He shut his eyes and breathed in the scent of her daffodil perfume. She smelled like home to him.

The front door opened again. An older man, roughly the same height and hair color as Jack stepped out, blinking in surprise as he pulled his Braves cap down over his forehead.

"Morning, you two," Jack's father, Richard Jackson, said. "You're up early."

Kamala faced him, smiling. "Rhett told me a sunrise down here isn't something to miss."

"He's right about that," Richard agreed. "I was just about to get started feeding the sheep. Care to join me?"

Jack turned and gave his father a look. "Really? You're gonna put your guests to work?"

"Guest," Richard corrected with a smirk. "I was talking to you, young man, not the lady."

Kamala giggled. "Actually, Mr. Jackson, that sounds lovely. I've always been curious about your profession and I'd love to see the process."

Richard nodded. "Be happy to show you. Rhett, since you're a *guest*, why don't you help your mother cook breakfast?"

"Will do. Play nice, Dad." Jack kissed Kamala's cheek and stepped back inside. Richard offered his arm and Kamala smiled wider as she took it and accompanied him across the yard.

Jack stepped into the foyer and shut the door. He walked around the corner through the den and the fluffy Maremma lying in front of the fireplace, perked his head up, and wagged his tail eagerly. A few years ago, d'Artagnan would have raced to the door and mobbed his owner with doggy kisses, but he was coming up on fifteen years old now, although he was no less enthusiastic when Jack got in range of his affections. Jack chuckled and knelt for a moment, scratching the dog's ears and letting him lick his chin. "Calm

5

down, old man, before you break a hip."

Dart barked happily and trailed after Jack as he headed into the kitchen.

Edith Jackson had her back to him as she stood over the island counter, carefully laying strips of bacon into a rectangular metal pan. Jack kissed her cheek and washed his hands, then walked over to the far counter, squatting as he grabbed a large silver pot. He filled it with water and set it on the stove, flicking the gas on to get it boiling. He grabbed the bag of grits from the pantry and sat it next to the stove, then set about finding a pan for the biscuits.

"Where's Kamala?" Edie asked.

"Went out to see the sheep with Dad," Jack replied, pulling the can of biscuits from the fridge. He eyed it warily as he peeled off the outer wrapping and gave the end a cautionary tap. It popped and he jumped a bit, sighing. "That scares the bejeezus out of me every time."

Edie smiled as she went to wash her hands. "Been doing that since you were a kid."

"Can you blame me?" he groused, peeling the dough away from the can. "It's too early in the morning for surprises like that."

He popped the biscuits in the oven. Edie nodded towards the grits. "Is all this going to be filling enough for her? I can make some hash browns too."

"No, she's not a big eater. She's got the cinnamon toast, the grits, the biscuits, and tea. She'll be good to go."

Edie's hazel eyes flashed playfully. "My son, in love with a vegetarian. What is the world coming to?"

"Trust me, it caught me off-guard too."

"You never told me how it went when you told her."

Jack blushed and rubbed the back of his neck. "Uh."

Edie pursed her lips. "Uh-oh. What? Did you pick an inopportune moment?"

He coughed slightly. "You could say that."

Edie shook her head and grabbed a Teflon pan. "My son, the lady killer."

"Hey, we can't all be as smooth as Clark Gable."

"Having good timing isn't the same as being smooth, kiddo. Was it at least a memorable time?"

Jack winced. "You could say that."

Edie eyed her son. "You did it while you were in mortal peril, didn't you?"

"...no?"

Edie sighed. "Come, help me cut the fruit, you hopeless case."

Roughly half an hour later, the four of them sat at the dining room table, their breakfast finished, the conversation, light and pleasant, as it had always been. Once it lapsed into a natural, comfortable silence, Kamala slipped her hand under the table and gently took Jack's hand, squeezing it. He took a deep breath to center himself before he spoke.

"Thanks for breakfast, guys," Jack said. "And thanks for having us over and welcoming Kamala. I really want her to get to know you two."

"It's no trouble at all," Edie said. "She's absolutely wonderful and we adore having her around."

"Good," Jack said, smiling weakly. "Because we have some news for you."

Kamala also took a deep breath, willing her voice not to waver. "I'm pregnant."

Thick, suffocating, awkward silence fell.

"Holy hell," Richard whispered, his eyes wide. He ran his hand down his face and cupped his chin, glancing between them both in shock.

Edie didn't move for a moment or two. Then she crossed her arms, all emotion wiped from her features. "How many months?"

"Almost two," Kamala answered.

Edie flicked her unnerving blank gaze over at Jack. "Then I take it this wasn't planned?"

"Let's call it a happy accident," Jack said.

"That's one word for it," Richard said, licking his lips.

"Well, congratulations. But you both understand what a

sucker-punch this is, right?"

Jack snorted. "How do you think we felt?"

"And what's your plan?" Edie asked quietly. "Are you going to get married? Are you going to move in together? Have you started saving for the hospital bills and day care and college?"

"Ma," Jack said, his tone soft. "Don't do this. We didn't come here to start a fight."

"You didn't come here to start a fight?" Edie repeated. She pushed up from the table and Richard rose with her, murmuring her name and touching her arm. "First, you run off to Tokyo to steal your dragon back from the Yakuza. Then you storm off into a haunted forest to bring back a dragon the size of a Tyrannosaurus Rex, nearly getting yourself, as well as Kamala, killed in the process. Now, you tell me you're about to bring a child into this world when you're unmarried and you've only been dating each other for barely two months?"

She turned away for a moment, a bitter chuckle in her voice. "What response did you think you were going to get, Rhett? Please, I'm genuinely interested to know."

"Not far off from what I got," Jack said. "But I love you and Dad and you needed to know. What you do with the information is up to you. I can't stop you from being any angrier than you've already been since this all started."

"I'm not angry," Edie retorted. "I'm disappointed. I never doubted that you would fall in love and start a family someday, but I didn't think you'd do it in the middle of the most chaotic part of your entire life. There are people out there looking for you, for both of you, who want to hurt you. Now you're bringing my grandchild into that equation."

"Edie," Richard said. "They didn't come here so you could be their judge and jury. You know as well as I do that they're not taking this lightly. Rhett's not a little boy anymore. The best we can do is stand by him."

"Stand by him, huh?" Edie ground out. "That's the tune you're playing now, is it, Rick? Like you didn't break

8

my son's arm and lie to my face about it for ten damned years."

Richard clenched his jaw. "Yeah, I did that. I can't take it back. I'm an ass and a shitty father for making him lie to you too. All I can do is try to make up for it by supporting these two when they need me. They need us, Edie. That's the only way we all get through this. Together."

"Yeah," she said. "Because you know what's best for our family."

Edie turned and walked out, the screen porch door slamming shut behind her.

# CHAPTER ONE

## UNTETHERED

"Jack...why is there a dragon in our backyard?"

Dr. Rhett "Jack" Jackson spit out his coffee and gaped at his pregnant girlfriend. "Wait, *what?*"

He pushed his chair out and stumbled to Dr. Kamala Anjali's side. She had the curtain drawn to one side, her jaw hanging open slightly, her brown eyes wide as they beheld the mythical beast that was calmly sniffing the red snapdragons in her garden. Jack rubbed his eyes with his palms just to be safe, but there was no mistaking it. He ripped the sliding door open and padded out onto the neatly cut grass in his faded grey MIT t-shirt and black pajama bottoms.

"Pete? Is that you?" The scientist asked, of course, knowing the creature wouldn't answer, but he just couldn't help himself.

Pete hadn't changed much since the last time he saw her. She stood at the height of the average horse with long limbs and a muscular, streamlined body covered in leaf-green scales aside from her belly, which was a pale cream. Her wings folded along the groove of her spine, rustling slightly as she lifted her head as he approached. She blinked large golden eyes at him and her tail lashed in the rose bushes behind her, scattering pale pink petals. Her long, sharp fangs protruded down over her lower jaw, which was closed as she was muzzled. She flared her nostrils as he cautiously extended his hand towards her snout, palm flat. The dragon sniffed it and a soothing vibration filled the air.

"Goddess above," Kamala whispered as she reached Jack's side. "It is her."

The dragon chittered slightly in delight and nuzzled Kamala's cheek, then blinked in confusion at her protruding belly. Kamala laughed slightly in spite of her puzzlement and rubbed the bumpy crown of the dragon's head as she sniffed her enormous stomach. "I guess introductions are in order. Pete, meet the baby. Baby, meet Pete."

"Kam...how the hell is this possible?" Jack asked, pushing one hand into his dark brown hair. "How did she get here? How did she even find us?"

"Excellent questions," Kamala agreed. "Which we will answer momentarily. Do you think we can sneak her into the house?"

"I don't know," he said, scanning over their eight-foot wooden fence to see if anyone had spotted them yet. It was still early, barely past seven o'clock in the morning. Cambridge tended to wake up on the early side, as both the MIT and Harvard students as well as alumni would be flitting about getting ready for the day. "She's kind of skittish about small spaces. Let's try to get her into the garage."

Kamala clucked her tongue. "Come along, Pete."

She walked back inside and the dragon followed with slow, steady steps, ducking her head beneath the threshold. Pete's forked tongue darted in and out, testing the air, as she glanced about the two-story house. The den had vaulted ceilings, so she had no trouble standing on all fours. She sniffed the couch as Jack pulled the sliding door shut and tugged the curtains together. He gave the dragon a nudge and she got moving again, following Kamala to the two-car garage. Jack's trusty old Mazda Protégé and Kamala's powder blue Volkswagen Beetle were already inside, but it wasn't too cramped. Kamala led the dragon between the two cars and gently pushed on her shoulders until the creature sat on its hind legs.

"Did anyone see us?" she asked.

"Not that I noticed, but if she flew in here, there's got to be somebody who saw her," Jack said, taking his phone out of his pocket and Googling dragon sightings in the last hour. He noticed quite a few hits, mainly a blurry picture, or a short video of a shadow sweeping over someone's backyard. Neither he nor Kamala had any social media accounts, so he had to check to see if dragons were trending, and they were at the moment. Plenty of people were trying to prove or disprove the sightings, but no one had convincing evidence, yet.

"I don't get it. The government shut down our project almost six months ago and seized her as well as our other dragons. How could she possibly have gotten loose?"

"Dunno," Jack said, pacing between the cars and rubbing the five o'clock shadow he hadn't shaved off yet. "Maybe they were transporting her somewhere and she busted out. Does she have any abrasions or injuries?"

Kamala flicked on the overhead light and examined the dragon. "No injuries, but look at this."

Jack stepped next to her and peered at where her fingers rested on the dragon's neck. He could see one of her scales had been removed, so there was just smooth pale skin beneath it. The species of dragon that Pete was, *varanus lacerto*, had multiple epidural layers, thick outer scales about the size of a quarter, and then a protective layer of fat over the muscle. Someone had removed the first layer by force, it appeared, and there was a small scar as if she'd been sewn up after an incision.

"Shit," Jack muttered. "Dollars to donuts that's where they placed a subcutaneous tracker."

Kamala shut her eyes for a second. "Which means the bastards are on their way right now."

"More than likely," Jack sighed. "Dammit. Ten bucks says they'll find some way to blame this on the two of us."

"I'll take that bet," she complained, stroking the dragon's swan-like neck. "That still doesn't explain how the hell she found us. She's never been anywhere aside from MIT campus. Is her sense of smell truly powerful enough to locate us from literal miles away?"

"In theory? Yeah, I guess so. She imprinted on us at birth, and dragons' senses are sharp as hell. Even though we're indoors, we've lived here for a good while, so our scent's on everything around here by now. Still, this is insane."

Kamala smiled a bit. "Yes. But in spite of it all, I...missed her."

Jack rubbed the bumpy scales over Pete's right eye and listened to her purr. "Yeah. Me too, Kam."

The doorbell rang.

Jack shut his eyes. "And here comes trouble."

"I'll stay with her," Kamala said. "Make sure they show you a bloody warrant first."

Jack shuffled back to the door, snorting. "Like that'll matter."

He shut the garage door, grabbed his coffee from the dining room table, and then opened the front door.

"Morning, assholes!" Jack said brightly. "What would you like to steal from us this time?"

Two men stood on Jack's welcome mat. The one on the left was tall, sturdy, and had brunette hair and deep frown lines with a no nonsense expression on his face. He wore sunglasses, a black suit, black tie, a white dress shirt, and polished shoes. The one on the right was slightly shorter, pudgy, and had curly brown hair and a beard. He wore a lab coat over a stained *Firefly* t-shirt, khakis, and sneakers.

"Climb down off that cross, Dr. Jackson," the man on the left said, folding his sunglasses and tucking them in the pocket of his suit.

Jack stared at him and then pointedly tilted the mug enough to spill coffee on the man in black's shoes. "Oops. Clumsy me."

The man sighed laboriously and shook his feet. "So infantile. You know why we're here. Where is it?"

"What?" Jack asked innocently. "Oh, your hairline? I think it's on the back of your head."

"The *dragon*," the man snarled. "Where is the dragon?"

Jack leaned against the doorjamb and purposely slurped his coffee before answering. "Oh, I'm sorry. Have you lost one of our dragons? What a pity. It's almost like you two chuckleheads and the rest of your department have no

13

idea what you're doing."

"It wasn't my fault," the pudgy man insisted. "The handler was careless."

Jack glanced at him. "You're really not helping your case here, buddy."

"Dr. Jackson," the man on the left said through his teeth. "Where. Is. The. Dragon?"

Jack leaned in, pronouncing every word slowly. "Up. Your. Ass."

The man stared at him with his dead brown eyes for a long moment before smirking. "You know, if you weren't so high-handed and pretentious, I'd probably like you. Fine. We'll do this by the book."

He reached into his suit jacket and withdrew a document, slapping it against Jack's chest. "Here's the warrant you're about to ask for. Not that it matters."

He jabbed a thumb at the man beside him. "Dr. Whitmore's got the tracker to prove the asset is within these premises. So scurry along and go get it before I call local P.D. to kick the door down."

Jack scowled and flipped the document open, again slurping his coffee obnoxiously loud and reading it as slowly as possible. "Well, seems everything's in order here. If you'll excuse me, I'll see what I can do about facilitating the evidence of your complete and utter ineptitude."

"It wasn't my fault!" Dr. Whitmore whined, but by then, Jack had slammed the door in both their faces.

Jack returned to the garage and handed Kamala the letter. She growled and crumpled it in her small fist. "Four hours. She's been missing for four hours according to this nonsense. They couldn't pour piss out of a boot if the instructions were on the heel."

"Agreed," Jack said. "But this is a fight we can't win right now. Maybe we can use it later, but we have to turn her over to them."

"Bastards," she spat.

"Hey," Jack said gently, kissing her temple. "Stress

14

levels, remember?"

She exhaled, rubbing the top of her swollen stomach. "Right. Pete won't go willingly. Find out if they have a tranquilizer first. I'll administer it so she doesn't get upset."

"Will do angel."

Jack opened the front door again. "Agent Shannon, I assume you have something that can subdue the dragon."

"Yes," he said. "What about it?"

"Mind handing it over? I'm pretty sure she'll rip your face off if she sees you coming at her with one."

Agent Shannon lifted a thick eyebrow. "You want me to hand you a tranquilizer gun? So you can knock me out, take the asset, and run?"

Jack rolled his eyes. "Actually, I don't want your big, ugly body on my driveway. You'll scare my neighbors and cause the property value to plummet."

Agent Shannon sucked his teeth and glanced at Dr. Whitmore. "Doc?"

"He's right. The dragon is, uh, rather averse to your presence. It imprinted on the two of them and should allow them to inject it."

The government agent gave Jack a long stare before walking over to the large unmarked truck with a long, metal trailer attached. He unlocked it and pulled out a silver briefcase. He popped it open and withdrew a tranquilizer gun.

"Any funny business," Agent Shannon said, slapping it into Jack's hand. "I take you down."

Jack smiled. "Yeah, because that worked so well last time."

Agent Shannon sneered. "It was a cheap shot, Jackson. Want to try me again, when I'm paying attention?"

"No, I think I'll just let you live with the shame of knowing a civilian put you on your ass." Jack slammed the door shut a second time and headed into the garage.

Kamala took the tranquilizer gun and gave it a detailed once over, checking that the dosage looked correct and would subdue the dragon. She sighed and pressed her forehead to the dragon's, her voice slightly hoarse. "I am so sorry, *meri priya*. We will save you. I swear it."

She injected the sedative. The dragon flinched slightly when the tiny needle pierced her skin. The effect was almost immediate. Pete swayed and Jack caught her upper body, lowering her to the ground as gently as he could. A thin green film slid down over her golden eyes and she fell asleep in minutes. She even snored, which they both thought was cute.

Jack heaved another sigh and walked over to the garage door. He hit the switch and the door rumbled and roared as it slid up from the ground. Agent Shannon and Larry were already standing there with an altered version of a hand truck. It was collapsible and about eight feet long and a couple feet wide. Agent Shannon smiled as he spotted Kamala.

"Dr. Anjali," he said politely. "Don't you look radiant."

"Don't you look smug and unintelligent." she replied, and swept back inside the house without another word. He chuckled and helped the chubby scientist load the dragon onto the carrier. They wheeled her up into the trailer and locked it shut. Dr. Whitmore got inside the truck and Agent Shannon slid his aviator sunglasses back onto his face.

"Thank you for your cooperation, Dr. Jackson."

Jack smiled again. "I hope you step on a Lego. Barefoot."

Agent Shannon bared his teeth in a grin and climbed inside the truck. He backed out of the driveway slowly and then pulled off into the street. Jack spat the sour taste in his mouth out into the bushes and returned inside.

Kamala stood in the kitchen, furiously stirring her chamomile tea. "This is unacceptable."

"Yep," Jack agreed, pouring the remainder of his coffee down the drain.

"Who do they think they are? They lose our dragon -- they risk her life with their idiotic inability to comprehend

16

her abilities -- and then demand that we return her to them without any consequences whatsoever? I have never heard of anything so ridiculous in my life."

"Yep," Jack agreed, rinsing out the mug.

"What if someone had gotten hurt, eh? What if some gun-toting moron with a twitchy trigger finger spotted her before she came to us? She could be gone, just like that, taken from this world through no fault of her own."

Jack stepped up behind her and slid his arms around her shoulders. Kamala's stiff spine slowly relaxed against his chest. Her eyes drifted closed, as he ran his large hand over her belly in soothing circles. He kissed her ear, his voice low and soft. "I know. But, we're not going to let them get away with this. We're going to give them hell. We're not going to give up on the fight until our dragons are back where they belong, safe and sound."

She shook her head slightly. "You always know just what to say."

"Hardly," he said. "You were stirring that tea pretty hard, Dr. Anjali. I just didn't want you to break my favorite mug."

Kamala turned in his arms. "Yes, we both know you're terrified of my superhuman maternal powers. I'll try not to scare you so much."

"You kidding me?" he said, lacing his fingers over the small of her back. "I'm counting on them to save us someday. You should be wearing a cape instead of stretch pants."

She sighed. "Oh, don't bloody remind me. I went up another size this week. I need to get this blasted child out of me before I become a manatee."

Jack choked on a laugh. "Stop it. You're gorgeous no matter what size you are."

She pursed her lips. "Don't try to get back on my good side, Dr. Jackson. Remember, it's all your fault that I'm like this."

"Oh, lest we forget. The rug rat was conceived the first time we, uh, *fondued*, and I believe you were the one who initiated that."

Kamala blushed. "Point taken."

She pressed her forehead against his and sighed. "This sucks."

"Yes," he said softly. "It does. But you know what doesn't suck?"

She glanced up at him. "What?"

Jack leaned in and kissed her gently between words. "Slow..." *Smooch.*

"Heartfelt..." *Smooch.*

"Intimate..." *Smooch.*

"...oral sex."

Kamala collapsed into stunned giggles. "You are an idiot, Dr. Jackson."

"What? I mean, am I wrong?"

Her smile turned a bit wicked. "Not in the slightest. It would be an excellent distraction from the chaotic morning we both just had."

She eagerly gripped his hand ready to drag him into their bedroom, but then her cell phone rang. She sighed and answered it with a brisk, dismissive tone. "Yes?"

"Kam," Faye Worthington's resigned, annoyed voice said. "I'm in jail."


Jack and Kamala had gotten rather familiar with the Cambridge Police Department over the past year. It had all started when nearly eight months ago, yakuza lieutenant Kazuma Okegawa stole their dragon and murdered Detective Colin Stubbs on his way back to Tokyo. The case had escalated to the FBI as well as the CIA. After their yakuza-funded rival scientist Dr. Yagami Sugimoto cloned the world's deadliest dragon, Baba Yaga, who escaped and tore through the streets of Tokyo, killing over twenty people, Jack and Kamala had returned to Japan to capture the dragon. They were successful, but Baba Yaga's reign of terror caused the U.S. government to issue a cease and desist on all

18

dragon cloning, closed down their grant, and took custody of all the dragons they had cloned. Jack and Kamala did everything they could to fight the order, but as of right now, the government refused to budge. Their entire lives' work shutdown, packed away in some shady government lab of unknown location.

They had also become acquainted with the Cambridge Police Department on account of Faye Worthington. Six months ago, Aisaka Tomoda, Okegawa's second-in-command, ordered her abduction while Jack and Kamala were en route to capture Baba Yaga. They later found out Aisaka had no intention of ever ordering Faye's release, but rather intended for the hitman to torture and kill her as revenge for Jack and Kamala putting Okegawa in a coma. Faye had been clever enough to escape her captor, but he escaped from police custody and issued her a challenge. That he would be back one day to settle their account. Faye spent the next six months working with the pair of detectives who had rescued her trying to find any links to his whereabouts, but after months of grueling investigation, they'd hit a dead end after dead end.

Unfortunately, Faye decided to take matters into her own hands.

Jack and Kamala signed in at the front desk and filled out the appropriate paperwork before heading into the bullpen. They knew exactly where to go, walking over to two desks facing each other near the middle of the room. A large black cop with a bit of grey at his temple and in his goatee glanced up as they approached and offered a weary sigh.

"Doctors," Detective Ernie Houston said politely.

"Detective Houston," Kamala said, nodding to him. "What has she done this time?"

Houston sighed. "They caught her breaking and entering into a property that she claims is one of the safe houses that Winston the hitman might have used while he was in town."

Jack rubbed his sinuses. "Great. Just great."

19

"Tell me about it," Houston agreed. "The woman's like the Terminator of being impulsive and not listening to reason. I assume you bailed her out?"

"Yes," Kamala said. "They said they just buzzed her out of holding. Have you had a chance to verbally chastise her yet?"

Houston nodded. "Oh, I laid into her when they brought her in, trust me. Please, have at it. Maybe you'll have better luck."

A moment later, a tall, statuesque blonde woman came around the corner with a uniformed officer at her heels. She wore a black sweater, blue jeans, and boots. Her golden hair pulled back in a ponytail at her nape. A few heads in the bullpen turned to watch her walk past, that was nothing new. She was stunning, even in such casual clothing.

Faye walked up to the pair of scientists with her hands up in a placating gesture. "Look, I can explain--"

"Explain what?" Kamala snapped. "How I just had to spend money, I could be saving for my child, on bailing you out of jail, Faye?"

Faye winced. "Jesus Christ. Not pulling our punches today, are we?"

"Save it. You're lucky I even bothered showing up at all. I wanted to leave you in there for twenty-four hours and let you stew in your own juices with the rest of these criminals. Do you have any idea what you've put us through? Any idea at all?"

Faye scowled. "Look, it was a solid lead and the higher ups wouldn't give Houston and Carmichael clearance to check it out. If I had found something, I might have been able to convince them to--"

Kamala stepped closer. Faye was a full five inches taller than her girlfriend, but she still flinched regardless. "Are you a police officer, Faye?"

The blonde worked her jaw. "No."

"No. You are not. You are a civilian. You may be smart as a whip and a hell of a fighter, but it is not your job to risk

20

your life obtaining this kind of evidence. The criminal justice system is in place for a reason--your protection. If I ever catch you doing something this reckless again, I will leave you to rot. Do you understand me?"

Faye's shoulders slumped a bit. She glanced obliquely at Jack, hoping for sympathy, but he had the same stony, frustrated expression as Kamala. Faye exhaled and nodded. "Alright, fine. I get it. I was out of line. I'm sorry."

She glanced at Houston. "You too. Sorry if I got you in trouble."

Houston crossed his arms and smirked. "Oh, no need to apologize. Just getting to witness the little missus issue a verbal beatdown is payment enough for what you put me through."

Faye rolled her eyes. "Thanks, Houston. Did you get the photos I sent?"

The detective shook his head in disbelief. "Yes. I'll go through them and see if anything is the kind of proof we need. Now go home, you hard headed woman."

She flashed him a tired smile before facing Kamala again. "Really, Kam. I'm sorry. I swear, I didn't mean to upset you, either of you."

Kamala stared her down for another moment and then nodded. "Apology accepted."

She gripped her hand. "Now then, are you alright?"

"Yeah, I just got busted on the way out by the neighbors. The uni who caught me was nice enough and I didn't resist arrest or anything."

Jack arched an eyebrow. "That's what happens when blonde supermodels sneak into drug dens looking for murderers. People kind of notice."

"Everyone's a critic," Faye grumbled. "I'm fine, alright. Just hungry."

She rubbed Kamala's tummy, kissed her lips, then Jack's, and walked ahead of them. Houston snorted and shook his head again. "Boy, I'm still not used to that. You millennials and your polyamory."

Jack laughed shortly. "Yeah, chalk that up to the whole generation, why don't you?"

Houston shrugged. "Hey, I'm a baby boomer. We get off on blaming you guys for everything."

Jack chuckled and shook his hand. "Right. Later, detective."

Kamala waved as well and the three of them headed back to Jack's Mazda. They grabbed Faye some drive thru on the way back to the house.

"So, what'd I miss?" she asked through a mouthful of Croissanwich.

"Oh, nothing much," Jack said casually. "Pete showed up in our backyard."

Faye wheezed in the middle of sipping her coffee. "*What?*"

"Yep. Sounds like she busted out mid-transit of wherever she was going and she somehow flew all the way here to find us. But Heckle and Jeckle were right behind her."

Faye frowned. "Oh, you mean those dickheads Agent Shannon and Lackey Larry?"

"The very same."

"Shit. Well, this has got to be better ammo for the appeal, right?"

"Yeah, but you know the good ole gubment," Jack said bitterly. "They'll make up an excuse."

"True. That's all they run on, after all. Did she at least seem healthy?"

"For the most part, just seemed like she missed us. Feeling was mutual."

He glanced at her in the rearview mirror. "What did you find at the safehouse?"

"Not a lot, but word is that Winston was on an assignment in town recently. Based on what I've heard, hitmen often rent properties that drug runners own and just pay them to stay, like an illegal hotel business. As long as they're quiet and discreet, it doesn't bug the drug dealers any for them to stay there until the job is done. Plus, it's good money for them. The place had a similar set up to the one he took me to, so I think chances are good he's been there recently."

Jack shared a look with Kamala, who seemed equally nervous. "So you think he's back?"

"Maybe," Faye said. "He hasn't contacted me since that day in your old apartment. If he was gonna come after me, now would be the time."

Kamala licked her lips. "Then shouldn't we be requesting the police to have a stakeout at our place?"

"No, not your place," Faye said. "I'm gonna rent a hotel room for a few days. One with cameras in the lobby and plenty of security. He'll have to work for it."

Jack gritted his teeth. "So you want to use yourself as bait?"

Faye narrowed her eyes at him. "What other choice do I have Jack? It's been nearly a year with almost no leads. I can't just sit around on my ass, waiting for him to show up."

"God, Houston was right. You really are the Terminator of not listening to reason."

Faye scowled. "I'm going to give him such a pinch the next time I see him."

"This is serious, Faye," Kamala said, turning her head enough to glare at her. "You can't take that man on alone. This is foolish."

"Look, I'm not going to drag the two of you into my mess--"

"It's not just your mess," Kamala said. "We're in a relationship, Faye. You don't get to just decide that your actions won't affect us, because they will. You are not going to go off on your own to face this man. Winston is a professional. We live in a gated community, so he won't want to risk being seen. Houston and Carmichael will know what to do if they confirm that he is back in Cambridge. Until then, you will lay low and you will not do anything else to endanger your life."

Faye crossed her arms. "So you just get to make these

kind of calls for me, huh? Like you own me?"

"Faye," Jack said in warning. "This is not about ownership. Kamala's right. Cutting yourself off from help and safety isn't the way to get this done."

"And what about you two? What about the baby? What if Winston does come for me?"

"Then we'll face him together," Kamala finished for him. "This baby doesn't make me some kind of invalid, Faye. I am fully capable of protecting my child and the ones I love as well. You're staying with us and that's final."

She faced forward. Faye swallowed hard. Tears stung in the back of her eyes. She glanced out the window as the city passed by, a welcome distraction from the conflagration of fear, hope, and gratitude that flared through her.

Jack pulled up to the curb of their house and parked to let the ladies out. Kamala struggled to unbuckle her seatbelt over her tummy and sent her boyfriend a sarcastic smile. "Enjoy furthering your profession simply because there is not a fetus inside of you right now."

Jack snorted. "Gee, at least you're not bitter about the whole thing, hon."

Kamala pursed her lips. "Maternity leave is excruciating. Almost as much as the constant headaches, nausea, and frequent trips to the bathroom."

Jack held up one hand. "I solemnly vow that God-willing my next research project will be how to artificially inseminate men with children."

Faye scoffed. "Please. Remember how utterly ridiculous men are when they catch the flu? No way should you ever be allowed to carry a child."

Kamala nodded. "Point taken."

She leaned in and kissed him. "You still owe me from this morning."

He just grinned at her and then waggled his eyebrows twice. She giggled and climbed out of the car. "Have a good class, my dragon."

"Have a good morning, angel."

Faye leaned over the glove compartment with a sly look. "Have a good class...*daddy*."

Jack visibly shuddered. "Oh God, Faye, that is *not* funny."

She chuckled and kissed him. "No, it's hilarious."

Faye shut the rear passenger door and waved as Jack pulled back onto the street and disappeared in the direction of campus. She took out her key and let the two of them in.

"Need anything?" Faye asked, kicking off her boots by the little area designated for shoes.

"Not at the moment," Kamala said, sliding out of her flats and into a pair of slippers. "I was going to add some final touches to the baby's room. Care to join me?"

"Yeah, I could go for that right about now. Sounds relaxing." She followed Kamala around the corner across from the master bedroom.

Kamala opened the door to a large bedroom the color of the inner petals of a daffodil--a pale yellow with white trim around the windows and at the baseboards. The carpet was a shade of green that emanated fresh grass, but only more muted to match the soft tone of the walls. The crib was against the far left wall, done in white as well, and already had the proper cushions and folded blankets waiting for its occupant. The diaper table sat next to it, and there were two tall, wooden dressers lining the opposite wall, already full of baby clothes. The closet had enough diaper bundles for the next six months, if not more. Kamala's mother Sahana had gone overboard, stocking up on them when they went shopping together a couple weeks prior.

"We decided to compromise with the decorations," Kamala said, gesturing to the framed photos lying carefully atop bubble wrap. Some were 18 x 24 and others were regular 8 x 10 or 3 x 5 photos of friends, family, events, and even a couple candid shots of the dragons they had cloned. "Two walls per person, and then you fill in whatever you like with the remaining space. That was the only way we could feel like it was fair."

Faye glanced at the nearest 18 x 24 framed poster. "Gee, I wonder who the *Pacific Rim* poster came from out of the two of you."

Kamala rolled her eyes. "I fell in love with a complete dork, didn't I?"

"You really did." Faye picked up the yardstick. "So did I, God help me. So how's this going to work? You want me to make them all level, right?"

"Yes," Kamala said. "I figure we put the large ones up all spaced out equally and then fill in the gaps with smaller photos until the space is full."

"Will do." Faye started measuring up from the floor and marking the spots with pencil while Kamala instructed her how far apart to space the larger frames. Then Faye took the nails and knocked them in one at a time. Kamala took her place in front of each one while Faye handed her the frames, since poor Kamala couldn't really bend down to pick anything up in her state.

"So," Kamala said. "Do you want to talk to me about what's going on with you?"

"Such as?"

"You've been to work less and less. Almost to the point of being part time."

Faye shrugged. "My programming isn't really holding my attention as much as it used to."

"Are you thinking of changing careers?"

"Not sure yet."

"What would you want to do if you did change careers?"

Faye narrowed her cornflower blue eyes. "Don't say modeling."

Kamala laughed. "I'd never. You get up on that runway and pants someone."

"Damn right I would. I don't know. Everything's just sort of shifted perspective for me ever since..." She winced, not wanting to finish the sentence. Kamala watched her obliquely as she balanced the photo of them at Clearwater

26

Beach.

"Ever since Winston?"

Faye licked her lips. "Yeah."

Kamala walked over and sank into the black bean bag chair near her. "Talk to me. How has it been going in your therapy sessions?"

"Kam, come on--"

Kamala lifted the slipper off her right foot in warning. "Don't make me use this."

"I haven't been going, alright?"

Kamala blinked at her. "What? Why?"

"Because I don't feel the same way that I did when I first went in. I was..." She ran a hand through her hair, searching for the words. "Scared. Hurt. Confused. I'm not that anymore."

"What are you now?"

"Angry," she said, her eyes flashing. "Because after all this time, that murdering bastard is still walking around a free man."

"You know the police are doing all they can."

"I know. It's not Carmichael and Houston's fault that they're bound to a system that doesn't always work. But, I can't stop thinking about how many contracts he's taken since he left Cambridge. How many people are dead because he's not in jail or six feet under. And I can't help wonder if I made that all possible by not killing him when I had the chance."

"You are asking too much of yourself, Faye. It's not your responsibility to put him away, to hold yourself accountable for the lives he's taken."

Faye just shrugged. Kamala sat back slightly, thinking it over. "Jack and I watched this animated film some time ago when the baby was keeping me up at night, *Batman: Under the Red Hood*. Towards the end, the Red Hood challenged Batman to kill the Joker, saying that he didn't understand why he couldn't do it. Batman explained that it wasn't that he couldn't do it. He *wouldn't* do it. Batman admitted he thought about killing the Joker every single day. However, he wouldn't stop there if he did. The dominoes would begin to fall and his values would change, until he became the very thing he first set out to stop."

Faye stared at her in amazement. Kamala just shrugged. "Not much of a comic book fan, but the movie struck a chord with me. My point is that killing is a choice that changes you forever. Even if you had done it for the right reasons, there would come a time where you would find that killing became easier, seeming more rational and less horrifying to you if you ever found yourself in danger again. Taking a life is a weight you can never get rid of. I wouldn't want that for you."

Faye smiled faintly at her girlfriend's wording. "*I wear the chain I forged in life.*"

Kamala matched her smile as she finished the quote. "*I made it link by link.* You are stronger than Winston, Faye. Don't become that which you fight. That is all that I ask."

The blonde sighed in resignation. "You're too smart for your own good."

"No such thing. Now, help me out of this ridiculous chair. I have to pee."

Faye headed into the kitchen to make herself some coffee — Kamala some more tea, as hers had gone cold when they went to bail her out — when her phone rang. Something near her navel instinctively jerked whenever she heard her phone ring with an unknown number. The important people in her life all had personalized ringtones, so she always knew who was calling. She hated the paranoia her kidnapping had injected into her brain.

Faye exhaled through her nose and answered. "Hello?"

Silence… Then a growling male voice with a Boston accent spoke. "So I hear you're looking for Winston."

Of all the multitudinous things in Jack's life that

required his attention, teaching was surprisingly the easiest one.

He'd been doing guest lectures ever since he first submitted his project and research for the dragon restoration grant and his teaching opportunities only grew more numerous over time. Jack didn't get nervous in front of crowds for reasons unknown to him. He didn't even try to question it any longer. Put him in a room with close friends and he'd sweat bullets. In front of a class of a hundred students. Not a drop. He chocked it up to the idea that maybe he didn't care about random students' opinions of him and he cared deeply about what his friends and family thought of him. Though, the latter part had been tearing him up for months now. He hadn't spoken to his mother since their epic fight at the house six months ago.

Jack didn't even have to pay attention to setting up the powerpoint presentation by now. He could hear the students chit-chatting as he worked and kept an eye on his watch until the clock struck eight o'clock on the dot.

"Morning, class," Jack said, giving a quick sweeping look over the auditorium and a smile. "Hope you guys all had a good weekend. We're going to dive right back in where we left off in the anatomy section of the *varanus lacerto*, so flip on over to page fourteen of your packets and we'll get started."

He hit the remote and the power point switched to a detailed hand drawn diagram of the head and neck of the dragon with the outer edges filled in with scales, then the lower layers of the epidermis, down through the muscles, veins and arteries, nervous system, and finally the bones.

He aimed a laser pointer at the soft palate of the dragon's head. "Recently, it's been discovered that this species' scent capabilities are in tune with that of bloodhounds, except amplified to a ridiculous extent. *Varanus lacerto* are pack hunters, and while they mainly feast on bugs, fish, and leftover kills from larger predators, when food is scarce, they band together and track down live animals using their superior sense of smell. They corner the target and attack together.

A single bite alone isn't enough to take down anything larger than perhaps a possum, but when combined among maybe four or five dragons, they can kill prey as large as a human being. They can strip a corpse down to the bones."

Jack switched to a slide that showed more of the dragon's skull, including its jaws. "*Varanus lacerto* consume meat like any other reptile, for the most part, tearing out chunks and swallowing them whole. The shape of the fangs is similar to your average snake, to hook into the skin and pull the meat down into the throat. If you've ever seen anyone get bitten by a python or an anaconda, that's why it's so brutal — the teeth are designed to catch and hold, so pulling away will rip entire chunks of flesh out if done incorrectly."

He saw a few students wince and grinned toothily. "Hey, want me to look up some Youtube videos on the subject?"

A resounding "NO!" came from the students and he chuckled good-naturedly. "Anyway, let's get a little deeper into the feeding processes."

Class flew by at light-speed once he delved into the digestive tract and paused every so often to let them ask questions. He shut down the equipment as the students began filing out of the auditorium. One small comfort he'd found was that the MIT students weren't nearly as hard on him for the project as the rest of the world seemed to be. He still got the occasional hate mail in his Inbox or a rude comment from a passerby here or there because of the Baba Yaga, Tokyo attack, but over time he came to accept the consequences his actions inadvertently caused.

"Dr. Jackson?"

Jack turned to see a tall black man in his thirties standing there. He had a neatly trimmed goatee and wore a black dress shirt and slacks, no jacket, with a cobalt tie. There was a manila folder tucked under his elbow, his other arm

30

extended. "Hi, I'm Bruce Calloway."

"Nice to meet you, Mr. Calloway," Jack said, shaking his hand, before slinging his briefcase over one shoulder. "What can I do for you?"

"I'm here on behalf of the U.S. government. We'd like to hire you to help us break up a dragon fighting ring."

"...a *what?*"

# CHAPTER TWO

## REFUGE IN AUDACITY

"Okay," Jack said, once he and Calloway were safely shut inside a smaller classroom with no occupants. "Let's start with the first and most important question. What the actual *fuck?*"

Calloway nodded sagely. "That *is* the most important question. I'm afraid I can only give you the abbreviated version. I'm under orders not to spill the beans unless you agree to help, as this is a matter of national security."

Jack ran a hand through his hair and shook his head. "Can I just have a normal Monday for once in my life?"

"I'm pretty sure that's no longer an option for you, Dr. Jackson."

He sighed. "Yeah, you're probably right. Okay, so what can you tell me?"

Calloway offered him the manila folder. "Remember this morning when Agent Shannon and Professor Whitmore showed up on your doorstep to get the dragon back?"

Jack scowled as he flipped the folder open. "Vaguely."

"Well, that was their cover story. Pete didn't escape. She was released."

Jack frowned. "Why?"

"It was a test to see if she could track a scent over an extremely long distance. Check the file."

Jack read the report for a moment or two and abruptly paled. "You're telling me she was all the way in Washington D.C. when she was released?"

Calloway nodded. "That's right, Dr. Jackson. The girl has mad skills."

"No shit. But, why would they have let her go? She's a valuable asset. She could have gone off course or been sighted or tried to hurt someone."

"This was a controlled experiment. Shannon and

32

Whitmore were trailing her closely the entire time to see if she stayed on course to find you and Dr. Anjali. She was never out of their sight and thus wasn't in any immediate danger."

"Look, the data on this discovery is phenomenal, but why were they doing it in the first place?"

"Long story short, they want to use Pete to help track down the other dragons that have been smuggled into the United States for these dragon fighting rings. So far, the organizations responsible have flown so far under the radar not even the FBI and the CIA can catch their scent."

Calloway paused. "Sorry, no pun intended. Both agencies have only caught glimpses of these fights in the carnage they've left behind. The dragons' remains are then sold for millions on the black market, and when the agencies tried tracking it back to the source, they couldn't get anything. All they know is that someone is out there is forcing these animals to tear each other to pieces for profit. You know as well as I do, the risk we run if even one of them gets loose."

Jack swallowed hard. "Please tell me these whack jobs didn't clone another Baba Yaga."

"No, not as far as we can tell. Whoever cloned her had access to technology that these people can't replicate."

The scientist let out a hissing breath of relief. "Thank God. So why the hell is the government knocking on my door? Last time I checked, they barricaded the damn thing and electrified the doorknob."

"Times change. The original plan was to use Pete to track the dragons, not the criminals. However, she won't cooperate with any of our handlers despite numerous attempts to placate her. She reacts violently in anyone's presence but you and Dr. Anjali's, as far as we know. That's why she flew straight to you, no delays, no attempts to hunt for food, nothing. To her, you're the next best thing to her pack and she'll protect you or obey you without question."

Jack gritted his teeth for a moment. "Yeah, it's almost

as if the government shouldn't have just snatched her up without further consideration of the consequences."

Calloway held his hands up. "Don't shoot the messenger, man. I had nothing to do with it. I'm just here to get an answer from you."

"Great, then that's the easy part. No."

Calloway blinked at the bluntness of the answer. "No?"

Jack handed him back the folder. "I can add in an extra 'hell no' in there if it makes it any easier. The government stormed into the middle of my project, seized everything, and shut down my life's work in the blink of an eye. And, now that you can't understand these creatures, you want to come crawling back to me for help? After humiliating Dr. Anjali and me, after we had risked our lives getting Pete back and capturing Baba Yaga. Sorry. I've had enough. I'm not cleaning up someone else's mess, not after Tokyo and certainly not after Aokigahara. Consider me retired."

Jack had headed for the door when Calloway spoke again. "We've found seventeen dead dragons so far, Dr. Jackson."

The scientist froze with his hand on the doorknob. Calloway sighed. "Look, man, this is off the record. I think what the higher ups did to you and to Dr. Anjali is sixteen shades of fucked up. No one really understood the magnitude of what you did when you cloned that dragon. They were looking for some semblance of control, so they just snatched it all and figured they could work it out in the aftermath. They were wrong. That's why they sent me."

Calloway walked over to face him. "Now you want to know why I'm actually here? Because this is wrong. Because these animals have seen nothing but torture and death throughout the centuries and you were the only chance the species would have had to coexist with mankind and help us understand something extraordinary. Now we're back to square one. I think these creatures deserve better than that.

And I think that you do too."

He held the folder out to Jack. "Read the file. If you change your mind, I'm in town until nightfall. You have every single right to be pissed off and say no, but just know that there's at least someone out there who's a part of this and actually gives a damn about the dragons."

Jack stared at him evenly, slowly accepted the folder, nodded and left the room.

"Jack?"

"Yeah?"

"What is the most non-violent thing a pregnant woman can do to express her complete and utter rage?"

Jack thought about it and then silently handed Kamala a throw pillow.

He winced as he heard the seams popping in the pillow she had clutched between her ringed fingers. She let out a single grunt of effort and ripped it right in half, scattering bits of fluff and scraps of cloth in random directions. He waited patiently as she shut her eyes and practiced her Lamaze breathing for a moment or two. He knelt in front of her, picked the synthetic cotton bits out of her thick, glossy hair, and smiled at her.

"You okay now, warrior woman?"

Kamala touched his wrist, her copper eyes molten with anger. "Not even close, my dragon."

"Good. Then we're on the same page. Speaking of which..." Jack sat the file folder in her lap and headed towards the linen closet to grab the vacuum cleaner. He tossed the remains of the shredded pillow and cleaned up its remains while Kamala read the report.

"Seventeen," she muttered. "Seventeen dead dragons in the last three months of their investigation. Think of it in percentages, Jack. How many have these bastards cloned if we're finding dead ones in the double digits?"

"Exactly," Jack said, plopping down next to her on the

couch and almost instinctively reaching for her bare feet. Kamala suppressed a pleased shudder as his strong fingers fell upon her instep. He'd done it so many times, it had become second nature to him. "We could be talking about over a hundred dragons by now, for all we know."

"But this can't be Yagami Sugimoto's work," she said. "He'd never allow such a thing to pass. He may be an arrogant, spoiled know-it-all, but he would never condone something like a dragon-fighting ring."

"Yeah," Jack said, narrowing his eyes. "This has the Yakuza written all over it. My guess is they were ground zero for this insane idea. The Red Fist weren't able to capture Baba Yaga when we were in the Suicide Forest, and so this would be the next best thing. Train these creatures to be vicious, cold-blooded killing machines and then release them out into the world. The dragons cause chaos and become public enemy number one, and then suddenly it's up to the modern day dragon hunters to kill them and save the day."

Kamala grimaced. "I have seen this kind of scheme before. Invent the disease and then sell the cure. They've been obsessed with returning to their former glory for decades."

She glanced down at the folder again. "However, I think you're right. They are the epicenter. There is no way they could have engineered as many dragons as we think they have. There is a larger scheme at work here, which is what we always feared. The government's seizure of our life's work has fallen into the hands we've wanted to keep it from all along."

"And that's exactly why I told them to piss off," Jack growled.

"You said no?"

Jack snorted. "Of course I said no. They can kiss my ass. I'm done with this, all of it. They want to take over the project, then they can clean up the entire mess on their own."

Kamala slid her legs out of his lap. He glanced at her and saw strained patience on her lovely features. "So why am I getting a look right now?"

"Jack," Kamala said. "Have you considered this proposal completely?"

"Kam--"

She narrowed her eyes slightly. "Jack."

He sighed, a frustrated sound, and pushed a hand into his hair. "I've almost gotten myself killed multiple times over this project, not to mention you and Fujioka and now Faye. Every time I say yes to one of these suicide missions, someone gets hurt or worse."

Kamala winced. "You're thinking of Detective Stubbs."

Jack tightened his jaw and nodded. "It's nothing but chaos and pain for all parties involved. They can catch the bastards responsible on their own. I'm not jumping back into the fray, especially not with your due date only a month away."

"You're right," she said. "You're absolutely, completely right."

Jack eyed her. "But?"

"But," she continued. "Tell me how many sleepless nights you've had since they shut down our project."

Jack crossed his arms and shrugged. "A few."

"Try fourteen," Kamala replied. "You have a guilty conscience, Jack. You pretend that you're fine, and maybe you are on some level, but it still bothers you that these animals are out there being abused. Someone has offered you the chance to possibly put a stop to it for at least some of the dragons, but they are the same people who angered you to begin with. So you're being defiant. I'm not saying it's the right thing to do, but I want you to take it into more careful consideration."

"But when does it end, Kam? How many more times are they going to ask me to do this? If I keep saying yes, you'll never see me. I won't keep getting as lucky as I did the last two times we went on a mission."

A lump formed in his throat as he glanced down at her stomach. "And I've got a damn good reason to stay right

37

where I am."

"I know," she whispered. "But perhaps there is a middle ground here."

Jack stood and started pacing. "How so?"

"I'm no expert, but I'm certain that you weren't their first choice after the way things ended with them shuttering our project. They probably have asked other relevant parties, and because things ended so violently in Tokyo and Aokigahara, those relevant parties said no. Now they are forced to come to you because you're the only one with the conviction and the skillset to get the task completed."

Jack paused. "So you think we have an advantage?"

"Yes. They're over a barrel and they don't have a choice. If they don't have a choice--"

"--then they can't negotiate," Jack finished for her.

"Exactly. You would be able to set the terms of this arrangement because if you say no, odds are they'll fall so far behind in the investigation that it would be too late to do anything to stop the smugglers from expanding."

He resumed pacing. "That would mean I could tell them no fieldwork, under any circumstances. No fieldwork means I don't get shot at by yakuza."

Jack absently touched his left side where there was a relatively fresh scar beneath his dress shirt. "Or by ornery descendants of dragon-hunters."

Kamala nodded. "If you were to say yes, then that's exactly how you could help without getting yourself perforated with bullets again. Consultation only. Low risk and you get to sleep at night for once."

He cut his eyes over at her. "It's still weird that you counted, Kam."

She shrugged. "Ex-physician. I can't help but notice things of that nature."

"Point taken." He raked his messy hair back again. "I still don't think this is the right call, Kam. What if you go into early labor? I'd be states away from you and I swear to God, if I miss the birth--"

"Impossible," she said frankly. "If you go, I go."

Jack gave a start. "What?"

Kamala stared at him flatly. "The last two times we got separated, you were kidnapped, drugged, shot, and left to die in a possibly haunted forest. All I've been since then is knocked up. Clearly, without me, you're liable to get yourself killed."

"But--"

Kamala crossed her arms. "But what?"

Jack licked his lips and hastily restructured his sentence. "But what about Faye? She'll flip her shit if we both run off to help the assholes who shut down our project."

She grimaced. "Oh. She will be rather upset, and for good reason."

"And after the shit she pulled this morning, she's not in a state where either of us should be leaving her alone."

Kamala sighed. "True. I suppose we'd need to have a talk with her. She'll be upset, but perhaps she'll understand we won't be in the line of fire this time."

"You're not leaving much room for debate here, hon."

"Don't misunderstand. Does it bother me? Absolutely. Under different circumstances, I'd join you in telling them to kiss our asses. But seventeen dead dragons in only three months?"

She shook her head. "My heart tells me I cannot abide that. And I don't think yours can either."

"Kam, it's not safe."

She held his gaze without wavering. "And if we do nothing and these dragons get loose...we could be in even worse danger. We don't know how many of them are out there. We don't know if the Red Fist and other interested parties are just biding their time waiting to unleash hell upon us all. Then where will we be? How would you feel knowing we could have done something to prevent it?"

She stood and walked over to him, touching his cheek. "If we do this, then it won't be like Aokigahara or Tokyo. We will be safe. We will be smart. We will not endanger our lives

39

to meet their ends. You and I will set the parameters of the deal and if they disagree, we walk away."

"I don't--" Jack shut his eyes as an overwhelming wave of emotions flooded through him. He gripped her upper arms and forced himself to speak past the lump in his throat. "I don't want to lose you. I don't want to lose our daughter. I'm not strong enough for that. We just reached a place where this relationship is working. It was rocky at first, but it works. If we do this, all of it could go away, just like that."

"You are underestimating us," she said gently. "We are both capable people. We're survivors. Nothing can tear our family apart because neither of us will allow that to happen. I know you are afraid, and for good reason, but you have to trust me."

"I can't let anything else happen to you," he murmured. "I already failed you once. What if I fail you again?"

Kamala met his eyes and the surety in her words made him shiver. "You won't."

She settled her hands on either side of his face, drawing him down to her height, and pressed her forehead to his. "We will win this fight together. Are you with me, my dragon?"

"Always, angel."


"Man, I'm getting a flashback right now," Detective Robert Carmichael mused from around his third coffee of the morning, his blue eyes amused as they stared across the cup at the blonde in front of him.

"Do I even want to know?" Faye asked, arching one perfectly plucked eyebrow.

"I was a hot young thing in my day, you know," Carmichael said, puffing out his chest. "Girls used to clamor to buy me a coffee. Then I met the old lady and I had to give up the single bachelor life."

"I didn't realize we'd entered the Twilight Zone,"

Detective Houston said with a snort. "Since when were you ever a lady killer, Rob?"

Carmichael sniffed. "You're just jealous, old man."

Faye shook her head. "My God, it's like watching *Lethal Weapon*."

Carmichael eyed her. "The movies, or the show?"

Faye wrinkled her nose. "The movies, of course."

"Good. Was afraid I'd have to shoot you if you were talking about the TV show."

Houston elbowed his partner and he chuckled. "Stop flirting and get on with it."

Carmichael sighed. "You just want to suck the joy out of everything, Ern. Alright, Ms. Worthington, why did you call both us handsome gentlemen out from the comfort of our precinct?"

Faye took a deep breath. "About half an hour ago, I was contacted by someone who claims to have information that could lead us to Winston."

Both men's expressions sobered simultaneously. They shared a look and leaned in a bit closer.

"Alright, Faye, you got our attention," Houston said. "What else did he say?"

"Not much," she admitted, keeping her voice low. "He knew about me poking around that drug den looking for evidence. He's definitely in the inner circle, because that happened barely three hours ago and it's not as if it's in the papers or something. He told me he wants to meet to exchange some info."

"Did he say why?" Carmichael asked.

"Apparently, he and Winston had a falling out of some sort. Maybe he stiffed him on a bill or Winston pulled out of a hit. The guy says he wouldn't mind seeing Winston behind bars if he were persuaded in the right way."

Houston frowned. "He wants money?"

"Yeah."

"How much?"

Faye sighed. "Twenty grand."

"Fuck that," Carmichael said bluntly.

Houston elbowed him again. "Watch your language in front of the lady."

Faye almost smiled. "You should hear me at home, Houston. The fact remains that this is a lead. However, with all the friction you guys are getting from the top brass, I didn't want to go running into the precinct to tell you that a criminal wants to rat out a hitman. I don't know who could be listening and that's not the sort of thing you broadcast."

"Right," Houston agreed. "But he's got to know you can't just pull that kind of money out of thin air. Our precinct can barely pay to get the copier fixed once a month."

"Exactly," Faye said. "So what do you think? Is he just some opportunist who overheard about my B&E or is he legit?"

"He say anything else?" Carmichael asked.

"According to him, he has the weapon that murdered the driver of the car Winston was in when he shot at me and Jack outside of the burger joint six months ago."

"The guy we found floating in the freaking Hudson with one to the back of the head?" Carmichael said, not hiding his skepticism. "Like hell he does. Ow! Ern, you're gonna crack a rib!"

"Rob's right," Houston said, ignoring his partner. "If the guy's a pro, he'd have tossed the gun into the river with the corpse. He's trying to lure you out. Maybe Winston's the one pulling this guy's strings to get you to play into his hand."

"That also occurred to me," she said, and her blue eyes gleamed. "And that's a shot I'm itching to take."

"Faye," Carmichael said carefully. "We know you're angry. You have every right to be. But, this is reckless. The evidence isn't pointing towards your man. It's pointing towards a trap."

"But we know it's a trap. This is something we could prepare for--"

"There is no we," Houston said. "You are a civilian,

not a cop. You don't walk into the line of fire to catch a killer. We didn't spend all those years at the academy to let you endanger your life."

"I can take care of myself."

"And we know that better than anyone," he said. "But this isn't going to get us Winston. He wants you and he knows how to play you. Don't let this guy get under your skin."

Faye stared between the two of them, the realization pouring over her. "Guys, this is a solid lead. I'm not saying this is everything we need, but we haven't gotten anything else in nearly six months."

"Investigations aren't like on TV, Faye," Houston said gently. "We don't clear homicides in a week like Castle and Beckett or Mulder and Scully. It takes time. It takes being careful and thinking with your head on straight."

She crossed her arms. "And you think mine isn't?"

Houston licked his lips, his wording careful. "I think you're frustrated and this looks like an offer you can't refuse. I think that's what Winston is banking on. You are a smart, tenacious, strong young woman and this is a challenge he wants you to accept. If you take a step back, you might be able to see that."

"Take a step back from what? The night he kidnapped me and chained me up like some animal? He could have done anything that he wanted to me that whole time, and he didn't. Do you know why? Because he was making a statement. He had the power and I didn't. He took any semblance of control that I had, away from me. He could be standing on the corner outside right now with crosshairs aimed at my forehead and there isn't a goddamn thing I could do about it. Is that how you want me to live the rest of my life? Looking over my shoulder, thinking he's right there behind me, laughing at what a helpless little girl I am?"

"Faye," Carmichael said. "You know that we want this scumbag behind bars. We're on your side. But, we can't jeopardize your safety when there isn't enough to go on from an anonymous tip some creep gave you. There are a million ways this can go wrong."

She shut her eyes, quelling the fury inside her. "Then what would you have me do?"

"Take some time off," Houston said. "Go up to a cabin on a lake somewhere. Get a nice tan on a beach. Get out of this city and clear your head. When you're ready, we'll move forward with whatever we have. Look at me, Faye."

The blonde finally opened her eyes and she was met with unwavering mahogany. "We are not going to give up on you. Okay?"

She glanced away quickly, pretending to sweep a lock of blonde hair away from her ear; her thumb brushing away what she refused to admit was a tear. "Okay."

"Where's the guy's number?" Carmichael asked.

Faye dug into her purse and handed him her phone. He cocked an eyebrow upward and then grinned. "Now, I'm not gonna find any naughty pictures on here, am I? Ow! Dammit, Ern!"

Faye laughed in spite of herself. Carmichael copied down the most recent phone number of her Recent Call list and handed it back to her. "Hey, a man can dream. She has a boyfriend *and* a girlfriend, for Christ's sake. You can't blame me for wanting to check those photos out."

"Shame on you," Houston said, shaking his head.

"Exactly," Faye replied, pushing to her feet. "Besides, it's not pictures."

She leaned over Carmichael, her hands flat on the table, using her best Michelle Pfeiffer Catwoman purr. "It's video."

The blonde winked and sauntered towards the door. "Later, fellas."

The last thing she caught before the coffee shop door closed behind her was Carmichael's weakened voice saying. "Marry me?"

Jack was in the kitchen making two Scooby Doo-worthy giant sandwiches when Faye walked into the house and stepped out of her flats. She'd texted him that she was on the way home and he only had two classes to teach on Mondays, which left him enough time for a mid-afternoon lunch. It had become a ritual of sorts between the three of them as of late.

Faye got up on her tiptoes and kissed him. "Hey, Stilts. Where's Kam?"

"She's at the OB-GYN. Her latest checkup's today."

"Ah. I should get better at memorizing these things if I'm ever going to be a decent fake parent someday. We still haven't decided what the kid's going to call me once she starts talking. Auntie would be sort of...odd."

"Agreed," Jack said. "But there's enough time to get that figured out."

"Ha," she said, taking the plate and grabbing two small bags of chips from the pantry. "Knowing you two eggheads, she'll be talking at six months and have a scholarship to MIT by the time she's five."

"One can only hope," he replied, following her to the table. "How'd it go with the detectives?"

Faye just frowned at him. Jack nodded. "Ah. They don't want you to go through with it."

"No," she grumbled, biting harder than necessary into her pastrami, ham, and roast beef sandwich. "Some nonsense about it not being safe."

Jack sent her an even look. "Imagine that."

Faye rolled her eyes. "Don't start, beanpole. You have no room to talk."

"Yeah, but I'm a useless *pagal*. What's your excuse?"

"The whole kidnapping thing," she said in the driest possible tone. "Kind of left an impact. I'm not the kind of girl to sit around and wait for someone to save me."

"No one's asking you to, Faye. You saved yourself. You pulled off something that only a tiny percentage of people would have been brave enough and competent

45

enough to do. Why isn't that enough for you?"

Something akin to a chill brushed through her. She set her food down and wiped her mouth, her appetite suddenly gone. "I don't know. Maybe...it was the challenge he made before he left. He told me he wanted me to evolve into what he thinks I was always meant to be."

"And who gives a damn what some cold-blooded killer thinks?" Jack asked, but he'd made the question inquisitive rather than accusatory.

"Nobody but him. And yet part of me wonders what he meant. Who am I supposed to be? It's like that whole incident just shook my entire life apart and I'm picking up the pieces to the puzzle, but I don't know where any of them go anymore."

"Makes sense, you know," Jack said, setting his own sandwich aside. "This whole time you thought you were safe and when he showed you that you weren't, it changed your entire perspective about life. When you walk down the street, you're no longer seeing people. You're seeing threats. You're constantly analyzing what could go wrong and how you should respond. Faye, that's a hell of a way to live."

She shrugged. "Good way not to die."

"Being ready is always a great idea, but being paranoid can make it worse. That's what Carmichael and Houston were trying to say when they told you not to go after that lead. Push too hard and it all might come apart again."

Faye shivered slightly, rubbing her arms. "I hate feeling this way."

Jack rose and knelt by her chair, smiling softly. "I know. However, you won't always. Storm's gotta pass sometime."

She pressed her forehead against his. "You're super good at this boyfriend shit, you know."

Jack snorted. "Only reason why is I've gotten it wrong enough times to know better."

His smile faded. "Besides, I'm about to screw it up in

46

just a second anyway. We need to talk."

An irrational icicle of fear speared Faye through the chest. Jack seemed to recognize the look on her face and caught her hand. "Whoa, easy, easy. Not that kind of 'we need to talk,' I swear. It's just…"

Jack licked his lips and stood up. "Remember when I said Pete showed up this morning?"

"Yeah, why?"

"Well, it turns out it wasn't what it looked like. The feds were testing her scent tracking skills."

"Why the hell were they doing that?"

"Because apparently, someone's been smuggling dragons into the U.S. and forcing them to fight each other to the death."

Faye's jaw dropped. "Holy shit."

Jack nodded. "A guy named Calloway showed up after my class and told me they want to hire us to find these dragons and disband the illegal fights."

Faye stilled. "Us?"

Jack took a deep breath and steadied himself for the incoming tsunami. "Yeah. Us."

Faye stood up and walked to the back porch window, staring out into the garden for a long moment. Jack stayed silent as he watched her cross her arms beneath her chest and take deep breaths to keep from screaming at him.

"So let me get this straight," Faye said, her voice cold and hard. "You want to take your pregnant girlfriend along on a mission sanctioned by the same government who shut down the project you've worked your entire life to make successful. A mission that requires you to search for a bunch of dragons trained to slaughter each other, who also happen to be in the company of the criminals who shot you recently. Do I have that right, Jack?"

He attempted a shrug. "Well, I did mention the whole 'useless *pagal*' thing."

She whirled on him. "Really? You're making a joke right now?"

"Faye—"

"Next question." She stomped towards him. "How do you stop me from tying you and Kamala to the bed and never letting you see the light of day again until you get some goddamn common sense?"

He tried to speak, but she sliced her hand through the air. "Rhetorical question, Jack. You are not going on this mission. You are going to tell those assholes no and you are going to have this baby and be in one piece long enough to raise it into an adult that I hope isn't as idiotic and altruistic as her parents."

"Faye—"

"Save it, Jack. This is not up for discussion. You're not going."

He gripped her upper arms. "Faye, *listen to me*. I didn't just decide this lightly and I didn't do it on my own. Kam and I talked. We didn't say yes. We're going to tell them that we won't do fieldwork. Just consulting. She won't be in harm's way and neither will I. We learned our lesson from Tokyo and Aokigahara."

Jack paused for an additional second and brushed a lock of hair behind her ear. "And we're not abandoning you."

"You're right. Other way around, Stilts. I'm out."

Faye brushed his hands off her and marched for the door. She got about five steps before Jack's long legs brought him over to her and he caught her wrist. "Dammit, Faye—"

She whirled and threw a stunning right cross at his face, but he knew her. Hell, he'd taught her how to fight. Jack tossed his head back enough that the blow missed and then picked her up around the waist, dropping her into the couch cushions in a body slam so quick she didn't even have time to catch herself. He pinned her arms and gave her a sharp look.

"My turn."

"Fuck you!" she snarled, twisting, but his legs had hers pinned between them and she couldn't push herself up

off the couch under his weight. "Let go of me, you piece of
—"

"If you want to run," Jack said, staring straight down
into her eyes, completely fearless. "Then you'd damn well
better have a good reason. Kamala and I aren't one of your
male model boy-toys that you pick up at the club on a
Saturday night and toss them in the trash by Sunday. I'm not
scared of you, Faye. Maybe all your other boyfriends have
been, but I'm not. I care about you. So does Kam. You're not
a third wheel in this relationship. What you say matters to
me, and it matters to her, and I'm not going to just let you
throw a tantrum and end everything because we've done
something to upset you. I'm sorry. I'm sorry that we've been
asked to do something that is scary and awful and it means
we have to be apart for a while. I'm sorry that I can't take
you with us, because you're damn right it's the first thing
that I thought about. I *know* you, Faye. You're running
because you're scared, not just because you disagree with us.
This whole time you've had one foot out the door, looking
for an excuse to bail since you've never had a relationship
last this long before. If we ever do break up, then I want it to
be for a real reason, not because you're chickenshit."

He let go of her arms. "If you want to hit me, I'll hold
still. When you're done kicking my ass, then we'll talk and
we'll work this thing out. I'm not going to run out on you,
Faye. Neither is Kam. Do you understand that now?"

Faye wanted to hit him. Hard. Possibly hard enough
to chip a tooth and mess up that perfect smile of his. Her
hands ached with the urge to just rip him to pieces, but she
couldn't look away from the infuriating patience in those
brown eyes of his. She couldn't breathe. Why the hell
couldn't she breathe?

Finally, she just buried her face underneath his chin
and wrapped her arms around his neck, squeezing him to
her so he couldn't see that she'd started crying. "You stupid,
stubborn, asshole prick."

Jack held her. "I know."

"Jack, I swear to God, if you die, I'll—"

He kissed her. Gently. So gently, something inside her screamed that she didn't deserve it. He pulled away after a moment and smiled at her. "Come on, I'm the good-looking white guy in the story. Of course I'm not gonna die."

She choked on both a sob and a laugh and kissed him again. There was something desperate and hungry in it. Jack slipped his arms beneath her legs and carried her to their bedroom.

"You're a sneaky bastard," Faye purred a while later, her hair sweaty and mussed, curled around Jack's left side like a well-fed cat.

"How's that?" Jack asked innocently.

"That's why you didn't go with Kam to the OB-GYN. You knew I'd get angry and I'd be less pissed off after three consecutive orgasms."

"I mean, really, who can still be mad after that sort of thing?"

She hit him with her pillow. "Me. But I do admit it took the edge off."

"Angry sex will do that," he said sagely. He paused and felt his neck, noticing a telltale welt, and then blushed.

"Goddammit, Faye, did you give me another hickey?"

She batted her eyelashes. "Who? Me?"

He groaned and fell back against the pillow, massaging the bridge of his nose. "I hate you."

"I had to get payback somehow, Stilts." She settled in beside him, lightly running her fingers over the puckered scar on his left side. It reminded her of a tiny comet with its odd shape drawn over the firm skin of his ribs. A couple inches lower and the bullet would have shattered his hip, giving him a permanent limp, or worse. If it had been higher and to the right, it would have cracked his rib cage open like an eggshell. She shuddered just thinking about it.

"You can't solve every problem with sex, you know," Faye said in a mild voice. "Eventually, we're going to have to deal with it like adults."

50

"I wasn't trying to distract you," Jack said. "I promise. If you want to talk, I'm here for that too."

"You can't keep doing this," she whispered, her throat growing tight. "Throwing yourself into danger for the sake of others. Maybe this is your fault and maybe it isn't, but you're going to get yourself killed if you keep it up. I'm not ready to be this kid's godmother, okay?"

"I know it feels like history keeps repeating itself. It's not like I went looking for trouble this time. It just always seems to find me. I liked my life better when it was just labs and theses and Petri dishes. I'm not an action hero. Things just ended up this way somehow."

"And when is it going to be enough?" she asked, hardening her voice. "If you keep saying yes, it'll never stop. You'll never get to settle down and you'll miss raising that kid."

Jack swallowed. "That's a very valid point. And believe me, I hate this track that we're on right now."

"Don't say this is the last one. That's pretty much a death sentence in these situations, good-looking white guy or not."

"No, it's not that simple. I can still do what I think is needed if I stay in this teaching position they gave me. The baby's going to keep us both busy day and night for the first couple years, and I'm not keen on leaving her with a babysitter. I want to be around for everything. I don't want to miss it."

"Then you're going to have to make a hard choice soon, Jack. The world or your family. You won't get the chance to straddle the fence."

"I know," he murmured.

She touched his cheek and kissed him. A moment later, his phone belted out "Son of a bitch!" in a pudding-thick Southern accent accompanied by rhythm and blues music. Jack groaned. "That's probably Calloway."

"Let him wait," Faye said, tossing one long, toned leg over his lap and leaning across his upper torso with a

51

mischievous look. "I'm still mad."

"Fine, but no hickey this time."

"Whatever you say…daddy."

"Ugh, for the love of God, Faye!"

# CHAPTER THREE
# THEM THAT GOT

"So here's how this is gonna go," Jack said. "No fieldwork. We stay at a secure location and we help you find the dragons. If this goes south, we're out the door. I've done this enough times to know that I'm not going to risk my life or my family's lives to right a wrong that's not even mine to right. We want to help, but everything went beyond our control a long time ago and we have other responsibilities now. Those are the terms. They are non-negotiable. Take it or leave it."

Calloway smiled faintly. "They told me you had a flair for the dramatic sometimes."

Jack shrugged a shoulder. Calloway sat back in his chair. "First, answer this, how is this going to be consultation only if the dragon won't cooperate with any handler besides you and Dr. Anjali?"

"Before you took her, Kamala and I were testing out a method to get Pete social with people other than the two of us. We had at least one successful run. We'll implement that and get the dragon used to the field agent enough that she'll be helpful in tracking the other dragons."

Calloway mulled it over. "I can tell you from my experience that your demands aren't unreasonable. Baby on the way changes a man."

Jack almost smiled. "Kids?"

"Nah. But, I pretty much raised my baby sister, so I can sympathize." He sipped his coffee, glancing down in amusement as he noticed the Captain America logo on the front. "If you don't mind me asking, what changed your mind? You seemed pretty set on 'no' the first time."

"Kamala and I had a..." Jack licked his lips. *"...conversation* at length about it. She's the boss."

"Smart man. How long have you been together?"

"Coming up on eight months."

Calloway nodded. "Well, you've already got the hard part figured out. Happy woman, happy life. You've definitely got your work cut out for you, but it sounds like you two are heading in the right direction."

He sat the mug down. "Here's our next steps, then. I can give you a brief summary of what we need from you in the next few hours and then we'll fly you and the missus out to headquarters in the morning. They'll put you up in a hotel until we get things up and running."

"What do you need from us?"

Calloway handed him a second manila folder, and this one was significantly larger and heavier than the other one. "These are the dragons we've found left behind by the smugglers. This is all the data we have collected on what's known about the species, but there are going to be anomalies that our limited resources can't analyze. With your experience, we're hoping you can grant some insight into how we would subdue the dragons once we find them. The problem isn't that we don't have the equipment--we just don't know what works with each species. They're all different, and we have to assume that like Baba Yaga, they're all, at the very least, mutated. In order for someone to have cloned them in six months or less, we're talking seriously heavy science. Someone's taken your work and put it on steroids. The other problem is that if they've goaded these dragons into killing each other, there's a good chance the dragons attack anything on sight. It'll be highly dangerous for the field agent to subdue them."

Jack snorted as he undid the rubber band holding the files together. "So what psychotic death-wish-having lunatic decided to take that job?"

Calloway grinned toothily. Jack stared at him. "You're kidding."

He shrugged. "What can I say? I'm an adrenaline junkie."

Jack sighed. "You really should reconsider. I've seen

these things up close and personal and it's not a fun experience."

"You ain't lyin'," Calloway admitted. "Pete is no joke. She's a fighter. She gave Agent Shannon a nice set of scars not long after we brought her to the facility."

Jack frowned. "And that doesn't count as some sort of conflict of interest?"

"The department is tightly regulated. Cameras everywhere twenty-four seven. The subcutaneous microchip under Pete's skin monitors her health at all times, so if she is in distress, we'd know immediately." Calloway paused and then added more softly. "And I take personal responsibility for each of the dragons. Let me find out he's ever done anything to hurt her. I'll follow up on that black eye you gave him that day they took the dragons from MIT."

Jack flashed him a grim smile. It was still a vivid, bitter memory he didn't like to revisit. "How'd that prick even get assigned to your department?"

"Shit," Calloway snorted, crossing his arms. "How does anything happen in government? Pulling strings, favors, brown-nosing, and pay offs. Prick or otherwise, he's effective. Everything runs smoothly, because he has no life and he makes sure every rule is followed to the T. He's a damned bloodhound out in the field. He'll track anything down and seize it by the throat."

"Gee, that bodes well for the guy who punched his lights out," Jack said as he flipped pages.

"You do live dangerously, doc."

"So much so that I'm surprised I got tapped for this assignment."

"To tell you the truth, you weren't. Before they found out she was pregnant, my superiors wanted Kamala and not you."

Jack blinked. Then he thought it over. "Makes sense. I mean, it hasn't even been a year and I've been shot twice. She doesn't have a scratch on her and she's ten times smarter than me."

Calloway grinned. "That is almost verbatim what Agent Fry said in his recommendation report."

Jack scowled. "Why does that not surprise me? And where is he, anyway?"

"He's on an assignment in Australia that they couldn't pull him out of, otherwise he'd be out here with us since he's familiar with the Baba Yaga case. He wasn't your biggest fan, but he agreed that your consultation would help the case as well as Dr. Anjali's. He also said you were crazy as a fruit bat, but your heart's in the right place and you're trustworthy. He compared you to Sir Gawain, if I'm not mistaken."

"Sounds like him," Jack grunted. "We should have something solid to present in the morning off of all this info. Now, about our fee."

Calloway arched an eyebrow. "Oh, this I'd like to hear."

"Three times *both* our salaries or no deal."

Calloway chuckled. "Exactly what I expected. Deal."

"Not even going to haggle over it, huh? You guys must be desperate."

"Doc," Calloway said, all traces of humor gone. "You have no idea. The sharks are closing in. We're thinking there's no less than at least six former dragon-hunting clans involved."

"Shit," Jack muttered. "What theories do you have on the end goal?"

"Hard to say. Different things. Money is the most obvious motive. The bets these scumbags are making run in the millions. Then there's the purchase and sale of the dragons, not to mention the working theory that if they've perfected the creation process, then people are ordering dragons like they're some kind of pedigree breed of dog."

"How the hell are they getting access to the DNA samples to even clone this many dragons? There should only be a limited number of remains that are viable for the cloning process."

"My thoughts exactly. We launched an investigation

on every known source of dragon DNA stateside and we're pushing hard to get as many as we can overseas, but not everyone wants to cooperate since a lot of them probably know people in their organizations are guilty. It's not hard to pay off some intern at a museum to sneak you a piece of bone or other genetic material. It doesn't take much to be able to get it done and unfortunately our criminals have a lot of options. Dragons lived on damn near every continent before they got wiped out and their fossils and remains have been excavated all over the place. Without some kind of international taskforce, we'll never be able to shut it down at the source. Right now, all we can do is put out enough fires to cause a setback and then we can take down the real problem."

"Maybe the samples are out of your control, but what about the facilities for upkeep and storage of the dragons? They're going to have very specific needs in order to thrive, regardless of whatever kind of mutations they might have undergone."

"I was hoping you and Dr. Anjali had some ideas on that front."

Jack nodded. "My research had a lot of the items and methods we used, but it didn't have everything there. I can come up with a list of what you guys should be looking for. Your other best bet is finding someone with loose lips."

"We're coming up short on stoolies," Calloway admitted. "Anyone in the inner circle of these clowns know it's a death sentence if they talk."

"Have you made contact with any of the dracology societies?"

"Some. Why?"

"Well, I'm subscribed to quite a few of their newsletters and I've been to a meeting or two for some local chapters. I'd say a good eighty percent of them are just excited dorks who love to study dragons, but that remaining twenty percent is full of complete nutjobs. If anyone would know about the when and where of the dragon fighting ring, it'd be them. Granted, you probably couldn't get them to talk, but the remaining sane people in their groups would likely help out if they can."

Calloway made a note in his phone. "What else you got?"

"What about the people who bet on the dragon fights? If a bet went sideways and they lost a ton of money, they'd be hard up for more and might take a bribe."

Calloway eyed him. "That's illegal."

"Hey, do you want to catch these assholes or not?"

He blew air out between his lips, rubbing his scalp. "I'll run it past my superiors. They only like to side-step the law when it suits them. Directly funding criminal activity is frowned upon unless it has to do with Washington."

"Speaking of corruption, any chance you guys got a bead on Dr. Yagami Sugimoto?"

Calloway grimaced. "I take it the feds cut you out of the loop, huh?"

"Much to my annoyance."

"Yagami's still in the wind, but we've gotten whispers since his father passed back in December that he and his sister Keiko combined forces. We're thinking he's the one engineering the dragons with the eventual plan to announce to the world that they've got some kind of screwed up version of Jurassic Park. Not an amusement park, mind you, but some kind of reservation where they'll claim they're just studying the animals, but that's not all there is to it. Cloning the dragons might eventually lead to learning how to clone other extinct species. Sugimoto Pharmaceuticals is already worth a cool couple billion dollars, but with this avenue they can all but double it in a short amount of time."

"If they do that, wouldn't that open them up to prosecution from the theft of my research?"

"Depends. If all they did was use your work as 'inspiration,'" Calloway said, using air quotes. "Then technically we can't do anything from a legal standpoint. We'd have to have Japan literally ban the cloning altogether

58

and then we could move in on them. Same for these other clans. That kind of effort takes time. Now, granted, Japan is already moving towards the banning law after Baba Yaga sent a chunk of Tokyo up in flames, but you know as well as I do that it won't stop them. They're intent on this endeavor and the law won't matter. However, it would give us the authority to pursue the Sugimoto siblings with the full force of the agency. We wouldn't have to keep playing nice and making overtures to get shit done."

"About damn time," Jack said. "Enough innocent people have died over this thing. With hindsight, had I known any of this could even happen, I wouldn't have started the project to begin with."

Calloway regarded him for a moment. "With all due respect, doc, I think that's ridiculous. You couldn't have possibly predicted things would go this wrong, this quickly. In a perfect world, you'd have been able to open that dragon reservation and people would have been educated and delighted for decades, by all the new information we'd have learned about them. I've read your file, man. You and Dr. Anjali are conservationists at heart. The world needs people like you to open their eyes, and it needs you to still be there after the dust settles and it's all over."

"It's not that simple," Jack said, shaking his head. "No one was supposed to get hurt. No one was supposed to die because of what we started."

"The world's an imperfect place. Doesn't mean you should give up on it." Calloway stood and offered his hand. "Plane leaves in the morning. I'll forward you the tickets once they're bought and get you clearance into the facility."

Jack stood as well and shook his hand. "Thanks. We'll see you there."

He walked Calloway to the door and locked it behind him, sighing to himself. "Time to get to work."

"Dr. Anjali, have you been smoking crack?"

Kamala sighed. "No."

"Are you sure about that?"

"Yes."

"Then would you like to explain what else makes you think I'd ever clear you to fly to Washington D.C. while eight-months pregnant to help the government catch killer dragons?" The acidic tone of the short, elderly OB-GYN no longer had the same effect as it had when she first heard it. Dr. Farris was one of the best doctors money could buy, and Kamala had to admit she was excellent, even if her bedside manner resembled that of a honey badger. Nearly all of her prenatal visits started or ended with the two of them arguing. Kamala had anticipated it going in. She came from a family of physicians, and everyone in the medical world knew that it was impossible to get doctors to go to a doctor without there being friction. "Hell, how did they even clear it since you're already on maternity leave?"

"Because this is more like contract work," Kamala said. "I'm not going to be out in the field. I'll be in a secure location advising the response team. Nothing more, nothing less."

Dr. Farris stared at her hard over her glasses. "Yes, because it has gone exactly to plan the last two times you attempted this sort of thing."

Kamala folded her arms over her belly. "You're going to clear me to go."

Dr. Farris snorted. "Am I, now?"

"Yes," Kamala replied. "Because now I know the truth."

"Which is?"

"You're not as scary as you want me to believe," she continued. "There isn't actually a black hole in the middle of your chest. There's an actual heart in there, contrary to what people believe."

"Is that right?"

"You've been with me this long without reassigning me to another OB-GYN, even after all the squabbling we've done. You rushed right in when we had that false alarm last month. It was your day off."

Dr. Farris scowled deeply and lifted one snow-white eyebrow. Kamala grinned. "Your secretary told me. You can fool all of them, but you can't fool me. You care about my well-being, whether you want to or not, and you're going to clear me to fly to D.C."

"If I gave a rat's ass about you," Dr. Farris said, snapping on her purple gloves. "Then that's exactly why I would refuse to sign those papers. The first thing about all pregnancies is that you should avoid all undue stress, and putting yourself in the middle of a government-sanctioned manhunt for a bunch of criminals is the exact opposite of that. You are about to start one of the hardest journeys any woman can embark upon and yet you want to say yes to this ridiculous assignment. You swore to me that you would put the child first after that fiasco in the Suicide Forest. Is this your idea of doing that?"

Kamala glanced at the door, making sure it was shut all the way, but still lowered her voice anyhow. "This is exactly how I protect my child. If we don't help them get a handle on the massive expansion of dragon cloning, there is a very real chance that we'll see more of what happened in Tokyo. Wanton destruction, lost lives, and panic. We have to get ahead of this storm, and Jack and I are the only ones willing to help right now."

"Because everyone else has common sense," Dr. Farris growled as she began to feel around Kamala's stomach. She located which side the baby had settled against and did some estimates before grabbing a small roll of tape measure. "There is a reason you were a last resort. You and that toothpick you call your boyfriend are clinically insane. I have half a mind to call your psychiatrist."

"It's prevention, not insanity. The decisions we make now will affect what happens to this country, possibly to the rest of the world. Would you be able to simply sit back and hope for the best?"

"I can see the big picture."

"This is the big picture. Baba Yaga sent Tokyo up in flames in less than an hour. What if there were more of them? How long would it take to burn Cambridge to the ground? How about Boston? New York? Shall I keep going or do you get the big picture yet?"

"That's a hypothesis," Dr. Farris mused, tossing the tape measure down and scribbling something on one of her charts. "What proof do you have?"

"They've already found seventeen dragons ripped to shreds."

Dr. Farris' pen paused for a moment. She glanced up at Kamala, but the surprise was quickly hidden beneath another disapproving frown. Kamala pressed forward. "If they've found that many dead, how many more are alive?"

"Why is it your job to do this? Tell me that."

Kamala swallowed hard. "It's not my fault that this happened. I know that now. Someone stole our work and perverted it from its original purpose. But, a mother is not all that I am. My daughter's safety is absolutely my first priority. Nothing will change that. If I can make her world safer as she grows up, then I will do it by whatever means necessary."

She bit her lower lip. "Honestly, I am hoping to start a movement. It's disheartening to me that whomever they approached first for help said no and we are their last resort. I understand why the others wouldn't want to do this, but perhaps our involvement might motivate more of the scientific community to lend a hand. It all has to start somewhere. If we stay silent, then we can't complain if the world around us burns to embers."

"A world like ours and you're still somehow an optimist," Dr. Farris said, shaking her head. "Unbelievable."

Dr. Farris pushed a small plastic cup with a lid into Kamala's small hands and nodded towards the bathroom. "Off with you."

When Kamala returned, Dr. Farris had less of a scowl and more of a contemplative expression. "You said that you were the government's last resort. If that's the case, then you could set the terms of the assignment. Why is consulting over the phone not good enough for you?"

"There might be lab work that they'd need me to conduct. Jack and I work perfectly in sync, but there is a reason we're partners. We make up for each other's shortcomings. There are things that occur to me that don't occur to him and vice versa. Besides, if they had to stop and call me every time they had a breakthrough in the assignment, it might waste too much time. The investigation is already behind."

Dr. Farris eyed her. "I don't fully believe you. My gut tells me you want to stay close to the toothpick."

Kamala rolled her eyes. "Would you please refrain from calling him that?"

"Scarecrow, then," the old woman said. "Fits better anyway, since Jonathan Crane's a doctor."

Kamala's jaw dropped. "You're a Batman fan?"

"Don't read too much into it." The doctor folded her hands and gave Kamala a level look. "This is a bad idea, Dr. Anjali."

"I'm fully aware."

Dr. Farris sighed. "You're going to get a second opinion if I say no, aren't you?"

Kamala widened her eyes to look innocent. "Would I do a thing like that?"

Dr. Farris snorted. "You got grit, kiddo. You're annoying as hell and reckless, but you've got grit. Here's what I'll do, I'll send your medical records over to whoever is in charge of this nonsense. You will be allowed to work six hours a day and no more. Every other hour, I expect you to be resting comfortably in some ludicrously expensive hotel suite doing research. You will have them sign off on a timesheet for the hours you worked to confirm that you adhere to the rules. If at any time you or your Scarecrow notice that you're becoming stressed, you will hop on the first plane back to Cambridge and come see me. This will not be up to you. If any of the staff there notice your distress, you will be bodily removed from the site and brought to this hospital and chained to a stretcher until that little girl pops out of you. Those are the conditions, they will be in writing, and you have to sign them. Do you understand me, Dr. Anjali?"

"You're impossible." Kamala offered her hand. "Done."

Dr. Farris popped her gloves off and stood, nodding to the little scientist. "Godspeed, Dr. Anjali."


Kamala returned home to find Jack and Faye in the kitchen cooking dinner, two ribeye steaks, three baked potatoes, sautéed spinach, Greek quinoa salad, and fresh French bread. She stood in the doorway to their kitchen, passing a scrutinizing eye over the two of them.

"So," she asked. "How did it go?"

Jack popped a grape tomato into his mouth. "Faye tried to break up with us. I body-slammed her into the couch. Angry sex happened."

Kamala shook her head. "It's sad that I know you're not joking."

Jack grinned and winked, offering her a little tomato as well. "Yup."

She accepted it, as well as the tender kiss he planted on her lips next. He stooped and kissed her stomach, he always did when she got home. "How was your check up?"

"Oh, the usual," Kamala said, kissing Faye's cheek as she walked over to the cupboard to gather the plates. "Dr. Farris threatened to tie me to a stretcher until the baby is born."

Faye glanced at her girlfriend mildly. "Why does that sound familiar?"

"Oh, hush. Don't throw stones in a glass house, Miss Broke-into-a-Drug-Dealer's-House."

Faye winced. "Dammit. You're gonna throw that in

my face until we're both old bisexual biddies in a retirement home, aren't you?"

"Most likely," Kamala agreed, placing the plates and bowls on the counter. "What decision did we land on?"

"I'm going on vacation," Faye said, spooning the quinoa salad into the bowls. "Get my head together. Keep my mind off of the investigation."

Kamala nodded. "I like that idea. It's a good time of year to get a tan on a beach in Florida."

"Yes. While I'm there, I can contemplate how I managed to fall for either of you self-sacrificing eggheads."

"You kidding me?" Jack asked, jerking a thumb at Kamala. "Look at her. Aphrodite ain't got shit."

Kamala snorted. "Mostly because she'd die if I sat on her in my current state."

"Whatever. We both know you're a goddess. Go set the table." He gave her a playful swat on the backside that made her laugh and they brought the food over to the dining room. Kamala filled them in on what terms Dr. Farris agreed to and Jack told her what he'd learned from Calloway. He and Faye had spent the post-coital hours packing a week's worth of clothing for the D.C. trip.

Once they were all fed, showered, and packed, the three of them piled onto the King-sized mattress of the master bedroom. Kamala sunk down into her enormous body pillow and Jack and Faye huddled next to her on either side. Jack picked up the clipboard that had been sitting on the nightstand and asked. "Ready for today's list?"

"Go for it," Kamala said.

"Alright," Jack replied, lifting his pen. "Farah?"

"Hmm," Kamala said. "Put it in the Maybe column."

"Noted," Jack said. "Jiya?"

"I like that one. Keep it."

"Mina?"

"No, too many girls have that name already."

"Nikita?"

"I love it, but people will shorten it to Nikki and I

don't care for that nickname."

"Sameera."

"No."

Jack moved to the next column. "Next up, we have Inaya."

Kamala wrinkled her nose. "I'm pretty sure that means 'concerned' in Arabic. Skip it."

"Jasmine?"

"Cute. Keep it."

"Naila?"

"Keep it."

"Nazia?"

"Skip it."

"Laila?"

She paused and smiled. "Laila Sahana Anjali. Definite yes."

"Excellent," Jack said, putting an asterisk next to that name on the list. "Whose turn is it tomorrow? Mine or Faye's?"

"Mine," Faye said, settling into Kamala's side and rubbing her belly. "Now then, let's pick up where we left off yesterday."

Jack set the clipboard aside and picked up a relatively heavy book, cracking it open against his knees. He carefully placed the bookmark on the nightstand and located the place they'd stopped previously in reading to the baby *Alice in Wonderland*. "*When I used to read fairy tales, I fancied that kind of thing never happened, and yet here I am in the middle of one…*"

# CHAPTER FOUR
## THE ROAD LESS TRAVELED

Jack and Kamala's eight am flight put them in Washington D.C. at half-past ten o'clock, and upon arrival, they were met with a limousine, that drove them to the Hilton hotel. Once they had dropped off their luggage in their room, they returned to the limo and drove a couple miles to the facility on the outskirts of D.C. The security guy at the guard tower checked both the driver's credentials as well as their own, before waving them through to a huge concrete building with four floors that had blacked out windows. They checked in at the front desk that had a metal detector and another set of security guards before they were escorted to the elevator where Calloway stood waiting for them, sipping coffee from a paper cup.

"Dr. Anjali," he said warmly, extending his hand. "Good to finally meet you. Bruce Calloway."

"Same," Kamala replied, shaking it. "Thank you for meeting us."

"Happy to." He glanced at her stomach. "Any chance I can introduce myself to your passenger?"

Kamala chuckled. "Her name is still undecided. We're whittling them down. It's surprisingly difficult to find a name that feels right when you haven't officially met. It's not like when you get a cat or a dog and their personality helps you pick the name."

"True. I think lightning just strikes sometimes when it comes to baby names." Calloway hit the Doors Open button and swiped his badge before choosing the basement level. "How are you coping with all the ridiculous pregnant lady shenanigans?"

Kamala grunted. "I just have Jack follow me around and punch any stranger who tries to touch my belly. He's quite good at it by now."

"It's true," Jack agreed. "I have warrants out for my arrest after that one old biddy at the supermarket tried to cop a feel last week."

Calloway laughed as the elevator doors closed. "I believe it. I don't know why people don't know how to act around pregnant women."

He reached into the inner pocket of his suit jacket and handed them their badges, which they clipped to the front of their shirts. "You'll need these for access in and out of the various floors as well as around the grounds in general. We've got transportation to and from your hotel set up, so as soon as you sign out, the girl at the front desk will call your limo around. There's a hospital about a block and a half from here, so if for some reason Dr. Anjali goes into early labor, we can get an ambulance here lickity-split. Cafeteria's on the first floor. Meals are all comp'd, so just swipe the badge and you're good to go. We'll meet up with everyone for a briefing and then I'll take you guys over to see Pete."

The elevator opened to reveal the shiny linoleum floors and white walls of a long hallway with eight grey doors on each side. The pair of scientists followed Calloway halfway down, before he swiped his card to open a door to their right. They found themselves inside a large laboratory that had been split in half, on one side was a conference table with ten chairs and a whiteboard on the far wall, and the other half had black-topped counters with stools and various lab equipment on them.

Dr. Larry Whitmore stood at the far end of one table, glancing up as they walked in. He flicked a nervous wave at them and kept typing on the computer.

Agent Shannon sat at one end of the conference table sipping his black coffee, his dark eyes fixed intently on Jack as he shut the door behind them. The agent still wore a black suit and tie, but he had a lab coat on over it, which highlighted the gun-shaped bulge on his waist.

The last occupant of the room stood near the table across from the whiteboard, fiddling with the projector. She was a young black girl with a short, bright pink afro and tattoos peeked up from beneath the collar of her t-shirt. Like Kamala, she had a gold stud in her nose and her ears were pierced from the lobe to the shell. She wore all black beneath her lab coat and a wide, pretty smile split her mouth as they walked over to her.

"Dr. Jackson, Dr. Anjali, this is Libby," Calloway said. "She's our equipment specialist."

Jack offered his hand first. "Nice to meet you."

She tilted her head slightly. "You're cuter in person."

Jack gave a start. "I'm sorry?"

She giggled as she let go of his hand. "I saw you on *The Late Show with Stephen Colbert.*"

"Oh," Jack said. "Yeah, I had a serious flop-sweat problem that night. Not every day you meet your idol. Also, it's really hot under those studio lights. I ask Kam to do most of the PR stuff because I'm so awful on camera."

Libby shook Kamala's hand next. "Agreed. You looked way better, Dr. Anjali. I almost turned your interview off because my boyfriend wouldn't stop drooling over you."

"Your what-now?" Calloway said, eyeing her.

Libby coughed. "Oh, gee, I think I hear Dr. Whitmore calling me…"

Calloway crossed his arms and just glared. Libby's impish grin widened. Jack's eyebrows lifted as he stared between them and then noticed the resemblance. "Holy shit. I take it this is baby sister?"

Libby scowled. "Baby nothing. I'm legal as of a year and six months ago."

She glanced at Jack and smiled again, a bit flirtatiously this time. "You know, in case that's important."

He jabbed a thumb at Kamala. "Sorry. Taken. Also, ew. I'm almost an entire decade older than you."

Libby rolled her eyes. "Oh, so you really are as earnest as you seemed in that interview. Damn. There goes all my plans for Saturday night."

Calloway buried his face in one hand. "Great first

impression there, sis."

"What?" she said, finally clicking the projector onto the correct input. "Just because you're stuffy doesn't mean I have to be. We're going to be spending a lot of time together. Might as well get the awkward stuff out of the way."

"Speaking of awkward," Calloway said, exasperated but recovering. "Agent Shannon, we weren't expecting you for another hour. Why are you here early?"

"Just checking up on things," he said, still staring at Jack.

"Take a picture," Jack groused, his eyes narrowing. "It'll last longer."

Agent Shannon smirked. "Dr. Anjali, how are you this morning?"

"Fine," she said in a clipped tone that edged on suspicious.

"Still lovely as ever, I see."

Jack's jaw clenched. Libby glanced between the two men and shook her head. "Oh no. We're in the middle of a dick-measuring contest, aren't we?"

"Afraid so," Kamala sighed. "Shall I get the tape measure or do you have one handy?"

"Hey," Jack said, offended. "He started it."

Kamala cut her eyes over at him without saying anything. He grumbled something under his breath and went to grab them two of the lab coats hanging on a rack nearby. Libby smothered a giggle behind one hand. "Got him trained, huh?"

Kamala winked at her as she slid into her lab coat. "Of course."

"I heard that."

Everyone but Calloway took a seat as he plugged a flash drive into the PC beside the projector and brought up a presentation. "Alright, we'll start with a quick briefing and then Dr. Anjali and Dr. Jackson will give us what they came up with as of last night."

He brought up an image first. It showed a loading

area. The closed garage door left a space similar to a pit that was the size of a two-car garage. Dark brown stains of dried blood caked the concrete. There were scratches furrowed into the concrete all over, with cracks and chunks missing in its walls. "This is the latest crime scene we've found. It's the closest we've gotten to the culprits thus far. We got a noise complaint from the neighboring steel mill where some construction workers were on overtime when they heard the ruckus. Blood was still fresh when it was discovered by the uniform who answered the call, which means we were barely an hour behind them by our investigator's estimate. They reported seeing two different semis roll up and unload some steel crates, then the match went down, and they loaded up again and drove off. Confirmed at least twelve occupants inside during the ruckus. However, no fingerprints have turned up yet on the site and the concrete means we can't take any reliable foot impressions. Too many trucks load and unload at that site, so we couldn't do the treads either. These guys are extremely careful, for the most part, but we know that they're not local since they didn't know about the OT workers on this particular night."

He switched to a new photo. It showed a bloody, dismembered hind leg with black claws and bright reddish-orange scales left along a blood trail in the driveway. "They had enough time to load the corpse, but I'm guessing the police sirens spooked them so when this limb came loose, they panicked and didn't go back for it. By our analysis, this unfortunate Chinese dragon was in its adolescent stage and was probably about the size of a bullmastiff. Based on the leftover blood, we've at least narrowed his opponent to be a Highlander dragon."

Jack snorted. "So I guess there could be only one."

Kamala rolled her eyes, but smiled nonetheless. Agent Shannon sipped his coffee, impassive. Calloway chuckled. Libby just looked confused.

"Dammit," Larry grumbled, crossing his arms. "Beat me by one second."

"Anyway," Calloway continued. "The match lasted around twenty minutes. That's part of why it's been so tough to catch them in the act—these people know the average response time for the police is at least half an hour in most areas of the country. We got lucky this time because there was a patrolman who picked up the call and we got tipped off since the warehouse fit the profile for where they hold these fights."

He flipped to a map of the city. "We canvassed and got a couple sightings of the two semis that brought the dragons in and we're retracing their steps to see if they picked the dragons up en route or if they've been carting them around cross-country. It's slow going, but something might turn up. We've got local PD keeping an eye out for the semis leaving town, but my guess is they know to avoid major highways and weigh stations. We're hoping you two might be our Ace in the hole by getting Pete to track the other dragons—either the one that lost or the winner, if Pete's senses are sharp enough to track its blood."

Calloway nodded to them. Kamala stood and took over with her own flash drive. "Jack and I took a look at the case file and we were able to draw some conclusions on the information you gathered."

She brought up an anatomy chart for the Chinese dragon. "This particular species of dragon used to live in one of the harshest climates imaginable—in the mountains. There are records of sightings at Mount Everest, Mount Gongga, Jengish Chokusu, K2, and Kawagarbo. They are part of the solar species, as some people call them, dragons that live in cold climates who sunbathe in order to absorb energy and warmth, and store it for hibernation. They would dig caves into the mountains and they laid their eggs in them, leaving only for food and procreation. They are among the species that were solitary, relying on themselves rather than being in a pack. The lack of social behavior could make some of them rather violent when provoked, but for the most part, they kept to themselves. The first records of dragons that sing came from Chinese dragons, who emit a call that can be heard for miles to attract their mates."

Kamala gestured to Calloway. "It's very dangerous to transport a Chinese dragon without the proper climate. The animal can overheat in certain temperatures and then collapse, making it useless to its handlers. They would have to transport it in a refrigerated container and monitor the conditions closely. Your run-of-the-mill criminal isn't going to know how to do that, so it's likely the dragon had a personal handler. It couldn't hurt to recheck the list of dracologists and dragon-hunting historians you asked prior to hiring us to see if they've made any major lifestyle changes--moved overseas, left jobs they've been at for long periods of time, or seem to have come into a lot of money in a short amount of time. It might lead us to a few suspects."

"Noted," Calloway said, scribbling something on a small pad he'd withdrawn from his pocket.

She changed over from the photo to a folder with a video in it. "Now we'll switch gears. This is some footage we kept of our first successful attempt to socialize Pete with someone aside from us."

She hit the Play button. "Watch closely."

The video showed Pete's enclosure, a fenced area with a large tree at the center where the dragon stood beneath its canopy. The dragon had a collar with a heavy metal chain that had been carefully secured to the thick trunk of the tree. She also wore a muzzle. Jack stood next to her, one hand on the dragon's neck, the other beckoning the veterinarian who nervously stepped towards them. The veterinarian was small and blonde. The lab coat she wore was nearly three sizes too big. She had her phone out in one trembling hand as she approached.

Pete's golden eyes fixed on the woman and a low hiss spread through the air. Jack nodded towards the woman. "Go ahead."

The woman's finger came down on the surface of the phone.

73

And Tupac Shakur's "Untouchable" filled the air.

Everyone at the table except Jack and Kamala did a double take.

The dragon's posture immediately changed. She had been standing with her back to the tree, nearly pressed up against it, at first. Pete cocked her head to one side and her hind legs settled in the grass. She flapped her massive wings once and then cautiously extended her long neck until her face was about a foot away from the veterinarian. Her nostrils flared once, twice. She shut her eyes and leaned forward enough to allow the vet's hand to brush her snout. The vet's face lit up with a pleased grin and she gently petted the majestic creature.

Kamala stopped the video, unable to keep a smug tone out of her voice. "Questions?"

"Bruh," Libby said in total disbelief, her jaw to the floor. "How the hell did you do that?"

Kamala chuckled. "After rigorous testing, we've discovered that Pete's trigger for socializing is based on scent and sound. First, Dr. Middleton is wearing Jack's usual lab coat. Her scent mingled with his and its familiarity broke through the first defensive barrier in Pete's behavior. Second, we've discovered that dragons respond positively to music. We tried out literally dozens of songs until we found that 'Untouchable' is the song that relaxes Pete enough to be social. It can be any number of combinations based on the dragon, of course, but this was a successful run. Dr. Middleton was even able to feed Pete using this method."

"But why?" Calloway asked. "Pretty sure Tupac wasn't alive in the 15th century."

"Dragons that lived in packs sang to each other as a method of location and as a method for mating season. Pete's mother would have sung to her while she was in her nest, so the music mimics whatever sensation she would feel when she was with her pack. The sound doesn't have to be exactly the same as what she would have heard from the other dragon. Like people, every dragon is unique. For example,

74

Baba Yaga responded positively to just a simple ballad from the 1900's. It's the rhythms and the vibrations that appear to trigger social behavior in dragons."

"So what are you suggesting, doc?" Agent Shannon said, his voice thick with sarcasm. "We throw Coachella every time we try to apprehend one of these things?"

Kamala scowled at him. "No. My point is that once the dragons have been reclaimed from the fighting rings, we might have a method to keep them from going berserk. It's also important for how we will introduce Pete to Calloway. We'll start trial runs to get her used to him."

Agent Shannon lifted a shaggy eyebrow. "And what about me?"

"Calloway made it clear that you're here for security purposes," Jack said. "You don't need to interact with the dragon unless in the case of an emergency. Besides, from what we've been told, the dragon already associates you with a traumatic negative interaction. It's likely she'll never warm up to you after whatever it is that happened."

"Yeah, well, the feeling's mutual. In that case, the muzzle and the chains stay on while I'm out in the field with her. I'm not giving the beast a chance for round two."

"You really shouldn't be so down on yourself, Agent Shannon," Jack said mildly. "I mean, beast? Come on. You're at least a mongrel."

Agent Shannon sneered at him. "Better a mongrel than an insect."

"Children," Kamala interrupted. "If we can focus, please."

"Why?" Libby asked, her brown eyes bright with interest as they flicked between the two men. "This is hilarious."

"Libby," Calloway said in warning.

"Killjoy."

"In any case," Kamala continued. "We have something to go on for the dragons we capture. Sedation at first, but there is always a chance of rehabilitation, much like dogs that are rescued from fighting rings can be taught to re-enter a home healthy and healed. They aren't monsters. They're just animals. Figure out their quirks and it's all downhill from there."

"That's pretty solid," Larry said, scratching his beard idly. "But until then we need better than that if we're ever going to shut the smugglers down. The dragon tracker--"

"What?" Jack asked. "You mean the one Faye designed whose patent you stole?"

Larry cleared his throat. "--the tracker your friend designed can't locate anything outside of two miles. The asset can track long range in theory, but we need to be able to see where we're going for when Calloway and Shannon take down the smugglers."

"We had some thoughts about that," Kamala said with a sharp smile. "Give the tracker back to Faye to reprogram. Problem solved."

"Absolutely not," Agent Shannon said. "We're not depending on some civilian for high tech equipment."

He jabbed a hand at Libby. "Can't the kid fix it?"

"I'm a genius in a lot of areas," Libby said, idly picking at her silver nails. "But that thing is outside of my area of expertise."

She flicked an annoyed look at him. "Kid."

He worked his jaw and glanced at Larry. "What about our tech team?"

"It was there for weeks before we used it yesterday. They don't have a clue how the civvie--"

"Her name," Kamala said tersely. "Is Faye Worthington."

"Er, how Ms. Worthington," Larry said. "Got it to work when it malfunctioned."

Agent Shannon massaged the bridge of his nose. "Fine. Send it out to her, but I want an NDA sent out before she gets her hands on it. I take it she's still in Cambridge?"

"Not right now," Kamala said. "She's in Clearwater Beach on vacation. I can call once her plane lands and let her know we need her help."

Agent Shannon glanced at Larry. "Have someone FedEx the thing to her hotel room."

Larry grabbed one of the lab phones and made a call, then returned to his seat. Agent Shannon gestured towards Kamala. "Continue."

Kamala switched the slide to a diagram of a jet-black dragon with a human silhouette beside it for scale. The dragon stood at waist-level with a long, streamlined body not unlike a crocodile. It had fangs that protruded down over its lower jaw and muddy amber eyes. Its limbs were shorter as well, but its wings were nearly twice the size of the rest of its body. It had a powerful tail ended in spikes with faint bluish tips,

"This is the Highlander dragon. Though most people think it was named after the movie, it's actually because they are native to Scotland. Based on the scales and the blood left behind at the crime scene, it was determined to be roughly around the same age as the Chinese dragon that it fought. Highlanders came from a similar line of evolution as your average crocodile, so they dwelled in rivers and lakes and helped contribute to some of the Loch Ness Monster sightings in history. They fed mainly on fish and livestock. They tended to only use their wings when food ran scarce and they needed to scavenge in the hillsides and forests for sustenance. They are incredibly accomplished diggers and created entire networks of caves near their water sources."

She pointed to the spikes along the tip of its tail. "It's also one of the few species of dragon that has external venom secretions from its tail. It only takes one hit for it to kill anything its own size or smaller. It can kill a full-grown man in two hits and there is no antidote. Typically, the Highlander dragon grabs its victim and drags it into a body of water to drown it, but when on land, it uses its tail to wound and poison its prey and then eats the remains. It can digest hooves, bones, cartilage, and pretty much anything short of metal. They also have particularly tough hides. From my estimation, it could stop a few kinds of small caliber bullets or at least survive being shot with them."

"So, in theory," Calloway said. "If we want to take one alive, what's our best bet?"

"I would hearken to what crocodile hunters tend to do," Kamala said. "Use a net. Blind it. Tie its limbs together. However, the tail must be taken out of play first. If it even nicks you, then you're down for the count and there is no telling what kind of treatments we'd have to try to revive you."

"Goody," Calloway said. "How fast are they?"

"On land, they can reach up to about ten to fifteen miles per hour. If you have the room, yes, you can outrun it, but in close quarters, it would be extremely difficult since it can fly. Long distance is the preferred method of capture, according to the history books. However, the dragon's strength is off the charts. It's a lot more powerful than a crocodile in terms of both bite-force and limb strength."

Calloway glanced at Libby with a small smirk. "You're up, sis."

Libby beamed as she hopped to her feet and scurried over to her desk. She returned with a black canvas bag and withdrew what looked like a folded-up obsidian net. She placed it on the table. "Check it out. It's a modification of diamond wire. The edges are dulled to prevent from cutting into its captive and it can stretch ten times its original length without snapping. Ends are weighted with steel balls to help it wrap around its captive. Oh, and there's also this—"

She fished a small remote from the same canvas bag and pressed the button in the center. When she'd put it on the table, the wad of net was the size of a large book. After she hit the button, it shrank down to the size of an apple.

Jack whistled and prodded it with a pen. "Nice. How long did it take you to develop it?"

"Mm, maybe a week?"

He blinked at her. "Wow. The military would kill for that kind of turn-around."

"There's less red tape to go through here. That's why I said yes to this position. Well, that and to keep an eye on my big bro. He's pretty useless without me."

Calloway rolled his eyes. "Whatever, little bit. If you're done showing off, we can go see Pete and try out that Tupac thing."

They all stood and headed for the door. "How the hell did you figure that out, anyway?"

Jack grinned. "I just sat with her in the enclosure for like four straight hours until I found something she liked. Phone was on Shuffle. Dragons always surprise you."

"Tell me about it. Are you telling me you think that music might work on all of them?"

"Well, it's honestly a completely new method of capture. There's no certainty, but if you let us test it on the other dragons here on the site, we can find out."

Calloway sent a wary aside glance at Agent Shannon. "Not up to me on that one, doc."

"The two of you are only authorized to interact with the main asset," the dark-haired man said. "If the information you presented proves useful, then we can talk about the other dragons."

"If?" Jack demanded. "And what's the alternative if we don't produce the results you want?"

"They're killer dragons, Dr. Jackson," Agent Shannon said. "If you can't control them, then they need to be put down."

"Where have we heard that before?" Kamala growled, her gaze straying over to Jack's.

"Be grateful we're trying to capture them at all. Wasn't my call."

"What a shock."

"In case you can't tell, I want things neat and clean. Everything about dragons is messy. You ask me, that's why they went extinct to begin with."

"Good thing no one's asking you," Jack replied.

"Kamala, where's that tape measure?" Libby said

innocently. Jack gave her a look. She batted her eyelashes. He sighed and shook his head in resignation.

The group rode the elevator up to the lobby and then piled into a tour-sized golf cart parked out front. Calloway drove them across the grounds to another sector that had a security gate just like the one at the entrance.

"Tell me," Kamala said once they'd passed through. "Where did they dig you up?"

"Oh, nowhere special," Calloway said. "I was sweating it out in the Amazon when I got the call."

"Doing what exactly?"

"I'm a zoologist. Well, I was one. After I got my feet underneath me career-wise, I started taking contract work dealing with predators."

"Really?"

"Yeah. Whenever someone needed a particularly tough S.O.B. captured for documentation, they'd call me in. Been at it since I graduated."

Kamala glanced behind her where Libby sat, texting someone and surreptitiously sneaking looks at Jack. "How did your sister wind up here?"

"Libby was pretty much a child prodigy. She finished high school at fifteen, finished college at eighteen, and then she wanted to tag along to watch my back out there. I said no at first, of course, like any responsible older brother would, but the gear she made to help me trap the predators was out of this world, so I let her stay close by. We're a package deal, so they scooped us both up."

"How long have you worked in this department?"

"Coming up on six months. They had already hired us when they came to, uh, *collect* your dragons from MIT."

"You've been working with Agent Shannon the whole time?"

"Yeah, he's..." Calloway cleared his throat. "Interesting to work with, I'll say. There's a reason that Dr. Jackson didn't get in trouble for cold-cocking him that day at MIT."

"And that reason would be?"

Calloway's brown eyes sparkled briefly. "No witnesses."

Kamala arched an eyebrow. "Shannon had a partner that day."

"Yep. The agent he was partnered with said he didn't see anything. I'm guessing Shannon's pride couldn't stand admitting that Dr. Jackson dropped him in one hit, so when his superiors asked what happened, allegedly he said someone attempted to mug him while he was in Boston."

"I guess that sort of thing happens when you're an arrogant, swaggering jackass."

"Definitely. Guy's got enemies all over the place due to that charming personality. Still, he's a hell of an agent in the field. I've seen him do a few take-downs of suspects. He doesn't play around."

He paused. "Mind if I ask you something?"

"Not at all."

"Why'd you say yes? Dr. Jackson sounded vehemently against it."

"Two wrongs don't make a right," she said. "Don't think that I'm not as angry as he is. I certainly am, but allowing that emotion to prevent me from helping isn't something I'm willing to do."

He nodded to himself, seeming satisfied with her answer. He parked the golf cart to one side of a long single-story building with metal walls that put Kamala in mind of one of the sheds on the Jackson family farm. A little chill went through her as she recalled the nuclear explosion of a confrontation they'd endured during their visit. Almost immediately, she felt the baby shift to one side of her stomach. Kamala almost smiled. Good to know she alone wasn't entirely unaffected.

"This way, folks," Calloway said after climbing out. The group walked over to a side door and he swiped his card to let them in. Jack and Kamala found themselves in a huge open hangar that had been converted for the current needs of its occupants. People in coveralls were moving back and

81

forth building metal stalls along the walls. Several of the stalls on the end had already been constructed, featuring thick scratch-proof glass for observation purposes. Most were the same length, width, and height; the size of a large cubicle in an average office building.

"This is the temporary storage facility for the dragons," Calloway said. "The short term plan is to move them here, analyze their needs, and then ship them out to a permanent home on an appropriate reserve. It wouldn't be the best idea to have them all in the same place in case someone decided to storm the facility. Right now, there's just Pete and the diamondback dragons you bred."

"Where are the dead dragons being stored?" Jack asked.

Calloway pointed back towards the main compound. "We've got something of a morgue set up in the lab building. I can take you through there before I head out, assuming your music idea works."

He winced. "Though I wouldn't recommend you eat lunch between now and then. It's not a pretty sight, trust me."

Calloway led them through the hangar to the end where two of the largest stalls had been constructed, nearly three times the size of the others. They faced each other from across the space. The one to the right held Pete and the one on the opposite wall held the diamondback dragons.

Jack and Kamala immediately walked up to Pete with matching eager smiles. The dragon lay curled in on herself like usual, nesting in what appeared to be a combination of hay, pine needles, and artificial grass. She wore a muzzle and had a metal collar around her neck that had a heavy chain secured to a bolt in the concrete floor. Her nostrils flared and she opened her eyes. Her forked tongue flicked out a couple times and she stood up, shaking out her wings before shuffling over to the edge of her enclosure. Pete let out a short chirping sound and rubbed her cheek where their hands rested on the glass.

Kamala sighed happily. "I never get tired of seeing her."

"Me neither," Jack grinned. "She's a thing of beauty."

"Get on with it," Agent Shannon said. "We haven't got all day."

Jack rolled his eyes. "Got a key?"

Calloway unhooked a ring from his belt and picked one, holding it out to him. "Sure you'll be alright?"

"Yeah, we're good." He and Kamala started forward, but Agent Shannon intercepted them.

"Dr. Anjali, may I remind you that you are pregnant?"

Kamala stared at him in disbelief. "I'm pretty sure I noticed that, yes."

Agent Shannon's eyes narrowed. "Then why are you going into an enclosure with a killer dragon?"

Kamala's small ringed fingers balled into fists. "Because she is *my* dragon."

"She's unstable."

"Yes, around you," she hissed. "Because she doesn't know you. She knows me. I'll be fine."

"Correct me if I'm wrong, but the form you signed, which is *legally binding*, says you are not to perform any tasks that can cause undue stress that will exacerbate your condition."

Kamala stepped forward, prompting Jack to touch her arm gently and murmur her name, but she didn't back down. "You are not my bloody doctor. The dragon is not dangerous to me and she never has been. The only thing causing me undue stress is you."

Beside them, Pete's golden eyes locked on Agent Shannon and her pupils contracted into thin lines. Her upper lip curled back from her sharp white fangs and she hissed at him, the dark-green spines along her back stiffening in warning.

He scowled and pointed at the dragon. "You're telling me *that* doesn't look dangerous to you?"

"That," Jack said. "Is a defense mechanism to the

83

dragon's territory being encroached upon and a response to a threat being presented to a member of the pack. The problem is you, not Kamala. Do you need me to speak slower or should I go find someone who speaks fluent asshole?"

"She's not going in there. End of story."

Jack stepped forward as well, but Calloway darted between the three of them. "Hey, hey! Take it down a notch, will you?"

He turned to Agent Shannon. "They raised this dragon from birth. I've seen the footage. Dr. Anjali has even ridden on the dragon's back, for God's sake. She's in no immediate danger, especially not with the dragon's muzzle on and she's chained up. You need to chill out."

"We've had enough trouble thanks to that thing and I'm not trying to lose my job over it, Calloway," he responded. "Either she stays outside this cage or she goes home."

"You son of a bitch!" Jack caught Kamala's arm and dragged her back several feet away as carefully as he could.

He stood in front of her, blocking her view, and rested both hands on her shoulders. "Easy, easy. Look at me."

"You're just going to let him do this to me?" she demanded.

"Kamala, I'm in this for the long haul. Ride or die. If you tell me to, I'll turn around and take his fucking head right off his shoulders."

He ran his thumb along her cheekbone. "But I don't think that's what you really want. He wants this thing run his way and he's going to do everything in his power to frustrate us until we bail. We're parents now, what we do no longer affects just us. We have to think about our daughter too. If we're going to stick it out, we have to be on the same page. It's now or never, angel."

Kamala stood there, fuming, and then shut her eyes for a moment. "The one time I actually want you to punch someone and I can't even bring myself to say the words."

"Life's a bitch that way," he agreed.

She touched his wrist and lowered his hand. "Fine. Do not punch his head off."

"That is a very wise and mature decision." Jack paused. "And to be fair, I did get lucky last time and he's been caressing that Beretta ever since I walked in the door. I really don't want to get shot a third time. It kind of sucks."

She let out a hollow little laugh. He kissed her forehead and straightened as the two walked back toward Pete's enclosure.

"For the record," Kamala said, smiling sweetly up at Agent Shannon. "If you mention my pregnancy to me one more time, I'll stick my foot so far up your ass that you'll cough up my ankle bracelet. Do you understand me, Agent Shannon?"

The older man snorted. "You know I could haul you in for threatening me, right?"

"Barking dogs don't bite."

Libby shook her head, a wistful sigh escaping her lips. "God, I wish I had some popcorn right now. Ow!" She rubbed the spot where her brother had elbowed her in the side.

Kamala nodded to Jack. "Go on, you useless *pagal*. I'll be alright."

Jack gave her a little bow. "As you wish."

He sent a quick filthy glare at Agent Shannon and took off his lab coat, handing it to Calloway. "Here, put this on."

Calloway eyed him. Jack scowled. "Hey, I bathe, alright? No cooties, I swear."

Calloway donned the lab coat as Jack unlocked the door on the right side of the cage and stepped inside, locking it back behind him.

As soon as he crossed the threshold, Pete's behavior immediately changed. The low bubbling hiss ground to a halt and her posture relaxed into what it had been a moment ago. Jack offered his hand, palm flat and facing upward, and the dragon sniffed it. Then she butted her large head into his

85

chest, nearly bowling him over.

"Nice to see you too," Jack laughed, rubbing her long, scaly neck. "Any chance you're feeling friendly today?"

The dragon propped her chin on the top of his head and chuffed. "I'll take that as a yes."

"Is he talking to the dragon?" Libby asked, stifling a giggle.

"It's no different from the way you talk to your cat," Calloway said.

"Yeah, except the cat isn't seven feet tall." Libby tilted her head. "Though the cat does hate everyone and everything, so maybe you have a point."

Jack fished his phone out of his pocket and brought up the music player. The bass to "Untouchable" dropped and Jack set it on Repeat before placing it in the corner. The dragon sat and her eyes fixed on the small device as if mesmerized. Jack looked her over carefully and then strode to the door to unlock it for Calloway.

"Move slowly," he said. "Just a step at a time."

Pete lifted her head as she spotted Calloway. He stood still, hands at his sides, letting the dragon get a good look at him. She sniffed the air a few times, but made no move one way or the other.

"Well, we're off to a good start," Calloway muttered to Jack. "This is usually the part where she bum-rushes me."

Jack patted his shoulder. "Animal magnetism, my friend."

Calloway sucked his teeth. "Smartass."

Jack chuckled and nudged him forward. "Alright, let's get a little closer. Easy does it."

Calloway edged his way over to the dragon until he was an arms' length away. She lifted her snout to just below his elbow and sniffed. Her golden eyes flicked up to his face and he couldn't help swallowing a bit hard as he watched her pupils contract. "Any chance she's related to a Velociraptor?"

"Not as far as I know," Jack said, patting the dragon's

bulky shoulder. "Alright, Pete, this is Calloway. He's a good guy and he wants to help us out. So I need you to not eat him."

"Ha-ha," Calloway said.

The dragon eyed him one more time and then nudged his hand. Jack smiled. "Excellent. You can pet her, if you want."

Calloway cautiously ran his fingertips over the bumpy ridges of the dragon's snout. She didn't snarl or lunge for him. She sat there staring up at him, blinking occasionally.

"Wow," he muttered. "This is seriously weird."

"Welcome to my world," Jack said. "Kam, your thoughts?"

"Her body language is pretty consistent with what we saw during the initial trial," she said, one hand on her chin. "Perhaps we could find some kind of wireless headphones to keep the song playing while the two of them get used to each other. Then once the relationship is established, there should be no need for it as she should associate him with positive interactions."

Calloway glanced at Agent Shannon. "Satisfied?"

"Not hardly," he said, crossing his arms. "Stay in there. I want to be absolutely sure it's not a fluke before we take it out into the field. In the meantime, Dr. Whitmore and I will take Dr. Anjali to the morgue to see if she can find anything the coroner couldn't about the dead dragons. If you're still alive by the time we come back, we'll give the scent-tracking a try."

"I enjoy these special chats we have," Calloway replied dryly, scratching under the dragon's chin. He glanced at Kamala. "You gonna be okay with Larry and Moe?"

Kamala arched an eyebrow quizzically. "Three Stooges reference, hon," Jack said helpfully.

"Ah. I suppose I'll survive."

"Good," Calloway said. "Libby, now that me and Pete are acquainted, think you can figure out the best way for the two of us to travel while she's tracking the other dragons?"

Libby's face split in a wide grin. "Oh, I've got some ideas alright."

"Meet us back here once you've got something. We need to get moving yesterday."

She saluted him and they headed back to the golf cart. Larry drove it back to the main building and Libby headed to the lab while the three of them went to the morgue.

"There's not much to tell," Larry said, swiping his card in the access port. "Pretty obvious that the dragons tore each other to pieces in the ring."

"Doesn't hurt to take a look anyway," Kamala said, slapping Agent Shannon's arm away as he tried to open the door for her. She stepped through it first and found herself in a room that had gurneys lined up in a grid formation. She spotted a cold storage locker to her left and an exam table to her right as well as a desk that had a monitor and personal computer tower.

She scooped her shoulder-length black hair into a bun, washed her hands in the small sink beside the locker, and grabbed the necessary materials, gloves, a mask, coveralls, and booties. Agent Shannon leaned against the far wall with his arms crossed, apparently content to oversee the process. Larry followed Kamala's lead and then wheeled the Chinese dragon's corpse over from the storage locker. He dumped it onto the exam table and turned on the microphone clipped to the lampshade above the table. He read off the date, time, subject number, and gave their names.

Then he gestured towards the bag with a slight smirk on his lips. "After you, doc."

"Thank you." Kamala unzipped the body bag and spread it open.

Calloway had been right. She was glad she hadn't eaten anything yet.

The Chinese dragon's scales when it had been alive would have been a brilliant scarlet, but now they were a dull reddish-brown. She saw the marks where it had been vivisected for the autopsy, but there were only a few markings. The dragon's throat had been torn out. She could see gouge marks in its back, side, and at least half of its tail was missing. It had all four limbs, meaning it hadn't been the most recent dragon they'd found. Its jaws lay open, locked in an agonized death scream, and the eyes had been removed, leaving behind vacant black holes in its skull.

The baby pressed its hands against one spot near the bottom of Kamala's belly. She shuddered and touched the spot absently. It gave her some small amount of comfort.

She took a deep breath to steady herself and asked. "How long ago did you find this dragon?"

"Three weeks ago. We were in Orlando."

"Risky," Kamala said, peering into the dragon's open maw. "Dragon could have died of heat exhaustion if they weren't careful."

"Right," Larry said, scratching his protruding stomach idly. "Maybe that's why it lost the fight."

"Did you find anything on the X-rays?"

"Nothing unusual, no."

She grabbed a penlight and examined the dragon's chipped teeth. "Contents of the stomach?"

"Bits of the other dragon, but the stomach acid pretty much made it unidentifiable."

"Did any of its teeth break off on the Chinese dragon's hide?"

"No."

"Hmm."

Larry frowned. "What?"

"This dragon has two sets of teeth."

"What?" he sputtered, walking around the exam table. "Where?"

"Not in the mouth," she said, reaching her arm down into the dragon's throat. "Do you see this opening of the esophagus? It's similar to the epiglottis, but this outer ring of muscle that closes the esophagus and windpipe has teeth around it to catch anything the mouth and tongue didn't."

She pulled the slimy pink membrane down until he

could see the sharp, thin circle of teeth. She plucked a chunk of brown flesh free. She held it up to the light and nodded. "This might belong to the Highlander dragon. Send it out to labs for analysis."

"Y-Yeah, got it," Larry said, tucking it into an evidence bag and shuffling out of the room in a hurry. Kamala continued her exam in silence for a while before she heard Agent Shannon break it.

"Why him?"

She exhaled through her nose. "Why who?"

"Jackson," Agent Shannon clarified. "Why him?"

"That is none of your business." She continued her exam.

"He can't protect you."

"I'm not a princess locked in a tower somewhere," she snarled. "He doesn't need to protect me."

"You know they'll come after you eventually," he said in a disturbingly placid voice. "I've read up on this case. As long as you're still out here trying to stop them, they'll come for you. You really think he can handle that?"

"He's handled it well enough so far. Now be quiet. I'm trying to concentrate."

"I've known men like him before, you know. Good men. Good agents. But they're not the ones who get the job done. They can take a hit, give as good as they get, but eventually they crack. Collapse. And you're left holding the foundation up by yourself."

She finally glared at him. "Remind me which part of that is your concern?"

He shrugged. "Figured you deserved a warning, that's all."

"From the man who has known us a grand total of —" She checked her watch. "Forty-five minutes. A very accurate and unbiased opinion, I'm sure. Now shut up and let me work."

He adopted a cold, confident smile and fell silent, his dark eyes settling on her. Her skin crawled the whole time

she worked, but she didn't quit.
She never would.

# CHAPTER FIVE

## OF MONSTERS AND MEN

"I know this song's keeping her from tearing my head off, but I have to admit it's getting kind of tedious after the twentieth go around," Calloway admitted as he eyed Jack's phone.

"Believe me, you learn to drown it out after a while," Jack said as he plopped down onto the artificial turf where Pete had nestled. The dragon laid her head down on her crossed arms and shut her eyes for a nap as Jack leaned against her scaly side as if she were an enormous, living bean bag chair. Calloway stared at the scientist in disbelief as he withdrew a small notepad from his pocket and started jotting down notes with a pen.

"No offense," Calloway said, leaning his back against the wall of the cell and tucking his hands inside his pockets. "But what's Tupac doing on your playlist in the first place?"

Jack glanced up at him and narrowed his eyes, replying in perfect deadpan. "That's racist."

Calloway laughed. Jack grinned and then shrugged once he was done. "Actually, you can thank my first girlfriend for showing me the light. Gina was a huge Tupac fan and his music was on pretty much every time I drove her anywhere back in high school."

"Stranger things have happened, I admit. You're just sort of hard to read, to be honest."

"Seriously?"

Calloway shrugged. "Maybe it's working with the government for a while, but I tend to get people figured out pretty quickly after meeting them. I thought you'd have jumped at the chance to work with your dragon again, but you said no, and I get the impression you'd have stuck with that answer if not for Dr. Anjali."

"And that surprises you?"

"Hell yeah," Calloway said. "I read your file before I headed out to Cambridge to meet you. This project has pretty much defined you, at least on paper. So much so that it's left an impression on pretty much the entire scientific community."

Jack frowned. "How so?"

Calloway glanced aside at the thick glass wall behind him just to be sure no one was standing there. "Alright, this stays between the two of us, but the people that we approached before you and Dr. Anjali didn't just say no because of the inherent danger in what we're doing. Agent Shannon's not a people person, so they sent me to recruit instead. Most of the people that I offered the job to, said no out of solidarity with you and Dr. Anjali."

"Holy hell," Jack said. "Really?"

"Yeah. Some of them had a lot to say about you cloning dragons and not understanding the ramifications, but they also asked if you were working on recovering the dragons, and when I told them no, that's when they turned the offer down. The ones that knew you personally said it was a matter of integrity, that if it had been the other way around, you'd have said no out of respect for their work. They agree that it's messed up the government shut you guys down and took over without offering to keep you on since you're the ones that made it all possible. They appreciate the fact that the money you've made from all your public appearances has been going to the charity you two set up for the victims of the Tokyo attack. They seem to trust you, Doc. That's pretty powerful."

"Wow," Jack said, running a hand through his dark hair. "Thanks for telling me that. I never would have thought it was the reason why a lot of them said no."

"Well, my sister wasn't off when she said you were earnest. I've heard a lot about you, but no one's ever said you did wrong by them personally. In this day and age, that's rare."

"Don't be too impressed," Jack grumbled. "I've got my

share of enemies, trust me."

"That's true enough. I had to put in a call to Juniper Snow before I came out to see you."

Jack groaned and leaned his head back on Pete's spine. "God, that woman."

Calloway chuckled. "Yeah, she had a lot to say about you. Mostly four letter words."

"It's reciprocated, trust me. I'm still amazed we didn't kill each other on the way out of the Suicide Forest. Not for lack of trying. She tell you that she shot me?"

Calloway gaped. "Jesus Christ."

Jack scowled. "To be fair, she shot the woman holding a gun on me so it *technically* saved my life, but she still shot me."

"I can see that making you feel some type of way."

"Eh, well, I saved her life first, so we're even. I just pray that Baba Yaga stays in cryo-sleep so I don't have to associate with that woman ever again."

Calloway shuddered. "I watched the footage of the Tokyo attack. I've pretty much hunted down and trapped every apex predator you can think of short of maybe a polar bear, but Baba Yaga scares the living shit out of me. I'd still have gone out there to Aokigahara if I'd have gotten the call, but I wouldn't have been happy about it. Neither would Libby. She'd probably have hogtied me and left me in a closet somewhere."

Jack smiled faintly. "Siblings get like that, I imagine." He checked his watch. "When's the last time Pete was fed?"

"We keep her fed every four hours. Why?"

"I think if you feed her, you might add some extra good will in your favor."

Calloway stared. "You want me to be in the same room with her without a muzzle on?"

Jack widened his eyes to look innocent. "Calloway, I'm offended. I asked her not to eat you. Isn't that enough?"

He rolled his eyes. "You are trying to get me killed."

"You don't have to do it. It's just a suggestion. It's okay

if you're chicken."

Calloway pursed his lips. "Gee, that's some subtle reverse psychology there."

Jack grinned. "Well, I am a doctor."

"Wrong kind of doctor, dude."

"Says you."

Calloway shook his head and headed for the door. "Good thing I have no sense of self-preservation."

He returned several minutes later with a large bucket of fresh fish. As soon as he stepped back inside, Pete's head perked up and her tail thumped along the floor in a gesture similar to a dog wagging its tail. Jack stood up beside her as Calloway brought the bucket over one careful step at a time.

"You good?" Jack asked, his hand hovering over her muzzle.

"Nope," Calloway said. "But do it anyway."

Jack undid the dragon's muzzle and slipped it off carefully, rubbing her jaw. Pete sniffed the contents of the bucket, eyed Calloway, and then dug in. Calloway looked a bit green in the gills as he watched her sharp, white fangs slicing the trout carcasses in half in quick bites, but he didn't say anything until the dragon had finished her meal.

"Well, I'm not dead yet. Must be a good sign."

Pete swallowed the last mouthful of fish and butted her head underneath Calloway's chin, which made him jump. "It's an affectionate gesture," Jack assured him. "Relax. She's a pack animal, remember?"

"Right." He patted her awkwardly and then set the bucket aside.

The dragon yawned and resumed her spot by the glass wall. Jack sat down again and this time Pete settled her head in his lap before she resumed her nap.

"How the hell did you learn all this stuff?" Calloway asked. "I've studied up on the species and I don't know half the stuff you seem to know about her."

"That's the thing about academic projects," Jack said. "Not everything we observed went into our notes or into the paper. We can draw conclusions based on some of the stuff we've seen. For example, they had Kamala and me do a write up of what we saw in the Suicide Forest with Baba Yaga, but not everything we saw from her was something you'd put in the books. She's still a living miracle, terrifying as she is. There are things we understood through intuition and not just based on the recorded history or science."

"Makes sense," Calloway said. "A lot of people try to pick my brain for how I've been able to successfully trap so many predators without losing a limb or two. I tell them it's not about the animal. It's about you."

Jack nodded. "Yeah, that's exactly it. What you put out there, is what the animals pick up. It's all about attitude. So what's the biggest thing you've ever managed to trap?"

"Kodiak."

Jack's jaw dropped. "No fucking way."

Calloway grinned. "Hand to God. About a year and a half ago up in Alaska."

"Fully grown?"

"Yeah, she was about twenty years old. Cool seven-hundred pounds."

Jack shook his head in disbelief. "And why'd they want her captured? Did she attack someone?"

"No, it was a catch-and-release. She'd wandered into someone's home and smashed up the place looking for food, so they wanted to tranquilize her and move her further out into the woods so she wouldn't be tempted to do it again. After all, the average door ain't shit to a Kodiak. She could push it down and waltz in there at any time, and the house owner had kids to worry about. Thankfully, no one was home during her little visit."

"Geez. How'd you manage it?"

"We lured her in with drugged meat. We gave her plenty of room, but she got wise to us." Calloway scratched his beard. "You never know how much you appreciate your own mortality until a Kodiak lifts its head and stares you dead in the face from fifty yards out. I mean, hell, we were

96

well hidden, for God's sake. But somehow, old girl just looked right at me. It was unforgettable."

"That's a word for it. What'd you do?"

"Stared her ass down. Thing is, Kodiaks aren't known for killing people. Sure, every other year or so they rough somebody up, but they're not known for mauling people to death like other species of bear. They tend to keep to themselves. But, that's what they say in the books. It's one thing to know that and another to be staring death in the face. If she'd wanted me badly enough, I'm still not sure if I could've done something to stop her. If she'd charged, it still would've taken a while for the tranq to kick in. Bears are pretty damn fast. If you ask my crew, they'd tell you her hunger overrode her instincts and that's why she gave in and ate the meat."

"And what do you think happened?"

Calloway smiled. "She was tired. Tired of running from whatever. She wanted to be somewhere new for another adventure out there in the wilderness. I think she let us take her."

He glanced at the sleeping dragon in Jack's lap. "And that's not hard for a man to understand, if you ask me."

"No," Jack said, feeling the faint rumble of Pete's steady breaths over his legs. "It's not."


"Well, angel," Jack said as he strode into the lab where she sat cataloging what she'd learned from the autopsy into her laptop. "You want the good news or the bad news first?"

"You should know by now that I prefer the bad news first," Kamala said.

"The lab's run into some kind of catastrophic failure. They're not going to be able to get the results for the sample that you found in that Chinese dragon until tomorrow. If we're going to get anything done today, it's not going to be on that front."

She sighed. "Great. What's the good news?"

Jack checked his watch. "Four solid hours and Pete didn't try to eat Calloway. I even stopped the music for a brief period and she was still friendly. The method's looking promising. The real test will be after Libby figures out the best way for them to travel together. Plus, I checked out the schedule for the local chapter of the National Dracology Society and they've got a meeting tonight at six o'clock. We might be able to catch a lead that way instead."

"Perfect," she said, saving her work and pushing the stool back. "I was starting to get antsy."

Jack winced. "Uh."

Kamala eyed him. "What?"

"You just hit the six hour mark on your shift for today. They're sending you back to the hotel."

Kamala shut her eyes and let loose a rather foul string of curse words in both Hindi and Kannada. Jack offered her a helpless smile. "I know. This sucks and I'm sorry. However, it's just some boring meeting. I'll text you everything that happens, I promise. Calloway won't scratch his nose without you knowing about it."

She sighed. "No need to apologize. I agreed to the terms. I'll waste energy gnashing my teeth over them. To be honest, I'm exhausted and that stool was terribly uncomfortable anyhow."

"Can I walk you out?"

"There is more work to be done. No need." She offered him a challenging smirk. "But you most certainly may kiss me goodbye."

Jack waggled his eyebrows before he laid one on her. She sank into it, slipping her fingers into his thick hair, until she heard someone in the doorway clearing their throat. Kamala glanced around Jack's shoulder to see Agent Shannon standing there. He glared and tapped his watch. Kamala flipped him off and kissed Jack once more for good measure before gathering her things.

"I'll walk her out," Agent Shannon said as he held the door open.

"I have legs," Kamala said tartly. "And clearance. Do us both a favor and get back to work."

"God, I love you," Jack said wistfully. "Travel safe, angel."

"Work hard, my dragon. I'll see you tonight." She left.

The driver took her back to the hotel. She took a shower, washed her hair, made a nest out of the pillows on the bed so she'd be comfortable as she climbed onto the mattress, and then painted her fingernails.

She frowned when she noticed Faye that still hadn't called or texted her back since her initial voicemail that morning, but she also knew it wasn't unusual for that to happen. Faye tended to be the kind of girl to spend the whole day out on the beach with her phone safely buried in the sand beneath her towel so it wouldn't be stolen. After her first day soaking in rays, she'd hit Instagram with pictures of her tan-in-progress to get her thousands of fans drooling. Kamala figured she'd get a reply around dinnertime once Faye was done hitting the town.

Kamala took a deep breath, briefly prayed for forgiveness, and made a different phone call.

"Good evening, Fujioka."

"Kamala," the older woman said smoothly. "How goes it?"

"I'm in D.C. in our hotel room," Kamala said. "I can only work six hours a day."

"That sounds like torture for a busybody like you."

"It is," Kamala sighed, flopping back on one of the oversized pillows and rubbing her sensitive stomach as she felt the baby beginning to roll to one side. "But it's my cross to bear. How are you?"

"I'm walking again, thank God," Fujioka said. "If I spent another goddamn month in that wheelchair, I was going to murder the entire hospital's staff. Still only walking with assistance, but it's the most improvement I've seen since it happened. Prognosis looks decent, at least, but they're keeping an eye on the recovery rate."

"That's wonderful, Misaki."

"Come off it," Fujioka said. "You didn't call to check up on me and we both know it."

Kamala rolled her eyes. "Porcupines are less prickly than you, just so you know."

"I've earned my prickles, thank you very much. Now then, where did we leave off last time?"

Kamala took a deep breath and let it out to soothe her nerves. "You had told me about the guy in Shinjuku. What did you find?"

"He wouldn't talk, not even after a substantial amount of persuasion. However, searching his place gave us a new avenue to explore. He had a contact in his phone of a former associate. Name's Ido. I've had my guy doing regular sweeps to see if we can track him down."

"Good. Any luck with the Sugimotos yet?"

"Ugh," Fujioka grunted. "Those assholes are locked down tight. He's been tracking Keiko's movements for months with nothing indicating that Yagami has been meeting with her in person. They've been smart. My hunch is they're waiting until the heat's completely off after the Baba Yaga incident. Communication via phone calls, I'm guessing. I'll let you know if anything changes, but the two of them are still a dead end unless the feds turn something up."

"Doubtful," Kamala said. "They have their hands full with this dragon-fighting ring. I doubt they're even looking for Yagami any longer."

"They should know better. Misdirection wouldn't be completely out of the realm of possibility."

Kamala shifted on the bed. "You think so?"

"It would mean losing a lot of assets, yes. However, this entire dragon cloning deal is one massive chess game. Sacrifice your pieces to get the attention away from where you don't want it. It's unlikely the Sugimotos would let something this sloppy happen under their control, but I wouldn't be surprised if Keiko suggested that they slip the yakuza some technology to go start a fire while they work on

100

their end game."

"I'll keep that in mind." She exhaled again to keep her voice steady. "And what of Okegawa?"

"Still no sightings," Fujioka said, her voice sharper and harder edged than before. "The nursing staff won't talk. I couldn't find any hospital records either. They paid off the cops that were watching him when they took him out of there. If I had more pull with Kyoya's former colleagues, I'd ask them to search their financials, but it's been too long since I lost him. They started asking questions and I had to bail."

"Dammit," Kamala hissed. "Why do you think he's biding his time so long?"

"Recovery," she said frankly. "The man was in a coma for nearly two straight months. All that cognition doesn't snap right back without consequences, even if Yagami's people pulled some kind of crazy science experiment to bring him out of it. Muscles get weak. He's not all there and he'll need time to adjust to the changes."

"Why send the threat, then?"

"To put you off-balance. You wounded his pride. He wants you scared. Yakuza don't forgive and they don't forget. He wants you to know you're on his shitlist and once he gets his legs underneath him again, he'll be gunning for you."

Kamala clenched her jaw. "Only if he finds me first. I won't let that happen to my family. Not again."

Fujioka paused, and when she spoke again, her voice had lost its edge. "Kamala, I'll only ask you this once. Are you sure you don't want to tell Jack about all of this?"

"No," Kamala said fiercely. "If he knew what I did, what I said in that hospital room, it would make him worry about me, about us. He doesn't need that burden. He's barely keeping it together as is with the stress of being a father and now this assignment. He can't know what we're doing, Misaki. Promise me that you won't tell him."

"*Chikushō*," the older woman muttered. "I knew you were going to drop the damned P-word on me. You understand what will happen if he finds out on his own, don't you? You spent the last few months slowly learning to trust one another again. It'll undo it all."

"I want him safe. I want my daughter and my lover safe as well. I will do anything to make it happen. Anything."

Fujioka sighed. "Very well. Then I guess I've got to see about a man named Ido."


"You do realize this directly violates the agreement we put in the contract you signed, right?"

Agent Shannon stared unblinking across the car at Jack as he offered him an earpiece and a lapel mic. "Uh-huh. You mentioned it about a thousand times already."

Jack scowled and snatched the items from him. "If anything happens to me in there, we're suing the pants off of you."

Agent Shannon arched an eyebrow. "Suing the U.S. government. I'm sure that'll go well."

"I know a few good lawyers, trust me." Jack sighed and eyed the Hilton hotel across the street. "This had better be on the up-and-up, Shannon. Dislike me all you want, but it's your damned job to make sure it's secure."

The agent rolled his eyes. "There is no immediate threat to your ridiculous person, Dr. Jackson. Any useless egghead could get this job done, hence why we asked you to do it."

"It is the literal opposite of that, you giant toehead," Jack said. "The reason Calloway's not doing this is that he doesn't have a background in dracology and I do."

"Give yourself a pat on the back on your way out the door, doc. Let's go. We don't have all damn night. I want a lead sometime this century."

"Play nice, children," Calloway reminded them over the radio link. "We're on the same team."

Jack grumbled more insults as he climbed out of the car and crossed the street. He entered the hotel and took the

102

elevator to a lower floor where the ballroom had been set up for the meeting. There was a sign-in sheet out front on top of a small podium and Jack spotted a few members outside wearing their forest-green blazers with the gold insignia of the National Dracology Society on the breast. As he stooped to sign the ledger, he noticed them pause to stare.

"Wait, are you...?" one of them asked.

"Dr. Jackson, yeah," he said. "Nice to meet you."

"What the hell are you doing out here in D.C.?"

Jack offered a weary sigh. "Long story, trust me. I'm in town on business, but I wanted to stop by to see where the NDS is these days."

"Are you one of the speakers tonight?"

"Hadn't planned on it, no."

The girl smiled at him over the rim of her sparkling grape juice. "If I were you, I'd prepare something anyway. There is no doubt in my mind Swati's going to yank you up there. She's your biggest fan."

"Oh boy," Calloway sighed over the radio. "Don't like where this is going."

"Ah," Jack said nervously. "That might be a problem. I'm not exactly here to make a scene or anything. I was just genuinely interested in current events."

"You're kind of a rock star in our circles, Dr. Jackson. It's inevitable."

"Point taken. Any chance you want to give me a heads up of what she looks like so I can avoid her?"

"Too late." She pointed behind him. Jack turned and nearly got bowled over by a short dark-haired Indian girl who wrapped him in a rib-cracking hug.

"Oh my God!" she shrieked. "I can't believe you actually came!"

"What?" Jack wheezed.

She let go and bounced up and down, nearly shaking her ponytail loose. "This is the best day ever! Come on, let's get you inside to meet the gang."

She grabbed his hand and yanked him into the

ballroom with what felt like the force of several NFL linebackers. Jack caught his breath and tried to get his arm loose to no avail. "Wait, wait, what's happening? I did what?"

Swati hauled him onto the small stage at the end of the room and tapped the mic, her grinning ear-to-ear as she tugged Jack up to her side. "Everyone, I am absolutely delighted to say that Dr. Jackson accepted our invite to speak tonight on the subject of reintegrating dragons into the world's ecology."

The forty plus attendees clapped and cheered enthusiastically. Jack slapped on a smile, sweating bullets as all their gazes fixed on him.

"What the hell is going on?" Agent Shannon demanded.

"Don't know," Jack said out of one side of his mouth as he waved at the crowd. "Either she's nuts or I'm a lot more forgetful than I thought with my own event planning."

Swati turned and patted his chest. "Please, take your time. We have the room for a whole two hours. Why don't you start your lecture and we'll do a Q&A session afterward?"

"But—"

She flounced off stage and whipped out her phone to start live-streaming on Facebook. Jack cleared his throat and stepped up to the podium. "Uh, good evening, everyone. Thanks for coming out tonight. I'm pretty sure most of you know who I am, but just in case, I'm Dr. Rhett Jackson. I am —" He winced. "—*was* responsible for the dragon resurrection and conservation project at MIT this past year."

He forced himself not to run a hand through his hair—a perpetual nervous habit—and started gathering his thoughts before the dead air got too long. "The reintegration of dragons into the world's ecology is a bit of a complex subject. It's a very delicate balance to introduce a major apex predator back into an environment where there's been such a large absence, especially considering it would have been near

104

the top of the food chain during the time before it went extinct. The original purpose of the project was to rebuild a small population of dragons that wouldn't cause a great deal of harm not only to people, but also to the ecosystems where they used to exist.

"They would be released into the wild and carefully monitored for their effect on the environment, and studied to fill in the many gaps that were left behind after they were hunted to extinction. From a scientific standpoint, there was a massive opportunity for gaining an understanding of one of the most amazing creatures on the planet. Even for the brief amount of time where the project was underway without hindrance, we found groundbreaking information related to their biology, physiology, and cognitive abilities.

"We discovered more about their social structure, behavior, feeding and mating habits, and relationships with species both of higher and lower levels of the food chain, so to speak. Let's say, in theory, if we released a certain number of non-harmful dragons into a region where there are known pests that plague the landscape. What happens? Will it strike a balance from where they had been a void? Our theory is that there are specific environments that would benefit from reintegrating dragons, particularly areas that lack natural predators due to various problems."

"Boy," Calloway mused. "Once you get him started, he's like the nerdy version of the Energizer bunny."

"Tell me about it," Agent Shannon groused. "It's gonna be a long night."

It took a lot out of Jack not to make a snide comment in return. He pushed forward through the lecture he'd all but memorized by now from various public speaking events and then started the Q&A session with the NDS members.

"Was there a particular species you were interested in cloning that you never got to clone?"

"Several," Jack agreed. "I had my eye on an aquatic dragon, as a matter of fact—the Nordic sea serpent. The one they attributed responsible for the Loch Ness monster phenomenon, or rather, one of the most famous sightings back before cameras were invented. Aquatic dragons were one of the scarcest breeds and there isn't a lot known about them. There were rumors that there was a deep-sea species swimming around down there with what I assume are Megalodons, giant squids, and Cthulhu."

Laughter rippled through the crowd before the next question. A guy stepped up to the mic. "What were you able to learn about Baba Yaga before you guys captured her?"

"That I honestly think she'd have made mincemeat of a T-Rex without breaking a sweat. I can't divulge details of the trip we took to capture her, but some of the information we learned will be published in an upcoming paper of ours. I can give you a small preview, though. Baba Yaga's level of intuition and intelligence is much higher than any of us predicted. She also displayed social behavior that's been argued against for decades. Scholars have said for ages that she's a lone wolf that attacks anything that comes into her territory and that she'd kill humans before she'd even look at them for more than a second, but Dr. Anjali was able to make brief contact with her that suggests that she might not be fully savage. The whole reason she went berserk in Tokyo when she escaped is the lack of maturation in her brain. Whoever cloned her used an illegal substance to grow her body to its adult size without taking into account the fact that there is a reason cloning in this fashion has never taken off. Our bodies and our minds mature at the same time as we age so that we don't have an adult body with an infant's brain. If we did, we'd never survive."

"Do you think we'll ever reach a point where she can be rehabilitated enough to exist alongside us?"

"That's a hard question, honestly. Worrisome too."

"How so?"

"Well, technically, yes. If they drained the sacs in her mouth so that she can't produce fire, then that would remove the biggest factor that contributes to why she's so dangerous. If they utilize some of the methods we've been able to implement to help get her used to human contact, then that also reduces the inherent danger surrounding her. However, it would mean that she could only be kept in captivity. She'd never be able to be released into the wild. She's just too dangerous. That's why she was never on the list of dragons we intended to clone. Baba Yaga predates the human race. She was never meant to be in the same time period as us. She's just too powerful. She thrived during a time when there were bigger, badder predators and a different kind of prey. By the time people were walking around, she was already on her way to becoming extinct."

Jack winced. "You also have to keep in mind that it would be too much to ask of people not to try and hunt her down if she somehow did get released into the wild. We know damn well that the black rhino didn't have to go extinct, but it did anyway, because the bastards hunting them for their horns simply didn't care about killing an entire species for profit. It's my theory that whoever cloned Baba Yaga, used her as a test drive. I think they intended to let her go at a time of their choosing and then show off how great they were by hunting her down. It would get them plenty of fame and money, and then they could repeat the process with other kinds of dragons. It's an old scheme, after all."

Jack checked his watch to see how he was doing on time just as the next attendee stepped up to the mic. "It sounds like to me that you regard these creatures as more than just animals. I wonder where you stand if it came down to us or them."

Jack shot a sharp look at the culprit. The overhead stage light was a bit bright, so his eyes had to adjust before he could see him properly. He spotted a tall Chinese man with slicked back hair. He had a scotch in one hand that he brought up to his smirking lips for a sip.

"I'm sorry," Jack said in a feigned calm voice. "What was the question again?"

"Hypothetically speaking," the man drawled. "If the world became overrun with dragons, would you hunt them?"

Jack had to unclench his jaw to answer. "Unless I woke up as a bald, overacting Matthew McConaughey, no, I would not."

"Not even if the country was in danger?"

"It's not in my job description. If that ever happened, there are people who are trained for that sort of thing that would handle it, not me. I have a doctorate in Biological Engineering. Nobody needs me out there in chainmail and carrying a sword, hunting dragons."

"Not even if your little honeypot Dr. Anjali was in danger?"

Jack bristled. "Excuse me?"

"Okay," Swati said, lowering her phone enough to glare at the man. "That's more than enough, Wei. Take a seat or you'll be asked to leave. Again."

Wei raised his glass to Jack before slithering away from the mic, the smirk still fully intact. Jack tracked the man intently as he slunk back towards the bar against the wall.

"I think we just found our first suspect," Calloway said mildly.

"No shit," Jack muttered under his breath, careful not to let the mic on the podium catch the sound. "I'll check the sign in sheet for a full name when I'm done, assuming I don't strangle him and steal his wallet instead."

"Easy, man. They arrest people for shit like that."

Jack finished up the remaining questions the NDS members had and left the stage to thunderous applause; not that he noticed much, as he made a beeline for Wei at the bar. He didn't quite make it, as Swati immediately intercepted him once she'd finished livestreaming.

"That was amazing, Dr. Jackson!" she squealed, trapping him in another rib cracking hug.

"Uh," Jack said through the remaining air in his lungs. "Are you always this friendly?"

She let go. "Yeah, why?"

"No reason. Remind me again when I agreed to this

meeting?"

She cocked her head to one side, confused. "I sent you the invitation back in January."

Jack eyed her. "Did you send it to me or Dr. Anjali?"

"Dr. Anjali."

"Ah. Mystery solved. She has to remind me to eat, sleep, and breathe. Thank you for having me. If you don't mind, I'd like to mingle a bit."

"Not at all. But first--" She yanked him down to her height by his tie and held up her phone. "Science selfie!"

Jack managed to slap on a smile just in time and survived one last suffocating hug before heading over to his intended target.

"Mr. Wei, was it?" Jack asked once he was within earshot. "Any particular reason for that question or should I just assume you're an asshole?"

Calloway made a choking noise over the comms. "Apparently, MIT doesn't teach people tact."

"Lower the hostility, Dr. Jackson," Agent Shannon said. "We can't get answers if you get yourself booted out of the meeting."

Wei chuckled as he finished off the scotch. "I was just curious, that's all. Nothing wrong with that, is there?"

"It came off like a threat, just so you know," Jack said through his teeth. "and I honestly don't take kindly to those these days."

Wei slapped his shoulder lightly. "Lighten up. They told me you were a do-gooder, but I wouldn't have thought you were this bad. Not after Aokigahara."

Jack narrowed his eyes. "And just what do you know about Aokigahara?"

Wei shrugged. "I just think it's interesting how you preach about conservation and yet you were on the first thing smoking to go take down Baba Yaga. A bit hypocritical, don't you think?"

"Do you know how many people she killed in the Tokyo attack?" Jack asked quietly. "I do. I've spoken to the families that lost loved ones that night. I wasn't going to let that happen to anyone else."

"So altruism, then? That's your angle?"

"It's not altruism. I may not have made Baba Yaga, but I am indirectly responsible for the technology that made cloning her possible. I hold myself accountable for every dragon that's been illegally cloned ever since and I try to do the right thing when possible."

Wei leaned an elbow against the bar. "So it's okay when you do it for the right reasons, huh?"

"Look, get to the point. What's your problem with me?"

Wei pushed the sleeve of his jacket higher up his arm. "Do you know what this is?"

Jack glanced at Wei's bared skin. There was a silver dragon with a purple hyacinth clutched in its fangs tattooed along the length of his forearm. "You're a member of the Silver Dragon clan. So what?"

"You'll hunt dragons to protect people, but it's really just for your own code of honor," Wei said, the smugness dissipating from his expression to be replaced with anger. "Why is it any different for the people in my clan who were born with the right to do the same?"

"Hunting dragons is not a sport," Jack snarled. "It's a bunch of people trying to validate themselves through the slaughter of creatures who have a right to coexist with the rest of the animals on this planet. It's a disgusting practice. I'll be damned if I ever let it resurface for any reason."

"You'll be damned alright," Wei sneered. "If you think you can stop us."

Jack stepped in close to him, his eyes glinting like amber fire. "Watch me."

He turned and left the ballroom, checking the sign-in sheet on his way out. He rode the elevator up to the lobby and headed outside. "Wei Zhang. Run the name."

"Well," Calloway said. "At least you didn't strangle him."

"Not for lack of trying," Agent Shannon said as Jack climbed back in the car. "Way to keep your temper in check, doc."

He tugged his seatbelt on and shut his eyes, breathing deep to calm his nerves. "Shut up and drive the goddamn car, Shannon."

The agent's dry chuckle could just barely be heard as he started up the engine. "You kiss your mother with that mouth?"

"No, but I kissed yours."

Calloway sighed again. "I swear to God, I'm going to go buy that tape measure on my way home tonight."

"What was that?"

"Nothing."


Kamala was standing in front of the mirror brushing out her hair when the door to the hotel opened. She glanced over to see Jack give her an exhausted smile as he let it swing shut behind him.

"Hey, angel."

She tilted her head up to accept a kiss. "Hello, my dragon."

She paused to let him kiss her belly. "I take it by that look on your face that everything went well?"

Jack sighed as he shrugged out of his sport coat and hung it in the closet. "Swimmingly. Before I get into that, how are you? Are your feet sore?"

"No, not this time. I sat for most of the shift today."

"Any more Braxton Hicks contractions?"

Kamala lifted an eyebrow. "You'd know it if I had, dear."

"Sorry," he said sheepishly. "You know me. I worry."

She reached up and undid his tie. "Don't. I've got it all under control. The baby and I were watching Animal Planet. You are welcome to join us after you give me a recap. What happened after I left?"

111

Jack folded the tie neatly and put it in the drawer, then started unbuttoning his dress shirt. "Calloway and Shannon teamed up to convince me to attend the D.C. NDS chapter meeting."

Kamala froze. Then she narrowed her eyes at him. "And did you?"

"Under protest, yes."

Kamala massaged the bridge of her nose. "*Jack.*"

"I know," he said. "I know. I told them no several times, but since we didn't have a lead because the lab got shut down, I didn't want us to fall further behind. Nothing happened, hon. I swear."

"That's not the point. What if something had happened? We wrote that contract for the express purpose of keeping the three of us safe from harm for the duration of this assignment. It becomes void if they can get you to crack under pressure. You have to stand up to them, Jack. You were willing to say no to the project at first. What changed your mind?"

"I don't know."

She drummed her fingers on the desk before continuing. "Did you at least find any suspects?"

"Yeah. Some little pissant named Wei Zhang said something that made me want to punch his head backwards and it was grounds enough for Agent Shannon to take a good long look at him. He's from the Silver Dragon clan and they've been stirring up trouble ever since Aokigahara."

"What did he say?"

"Some tired rhetoric about how it's hypocritical that we went hunting for Baba Yaga and yet they weren't allowed to in our place. Forgetting the fact that there were trained professionals out there and not just a band of violent nut-jobs. Though, to be fair, I'm not sure Juniper Snow wasn't the latter..."

Kamala eyed him. "That's not why you're so worked up."

Jack frowned as he unbuckled his slacks. "Who says

112

I'm worked up?"

"Jack, I know you. What's wrong? What did Zhang say that upset you?"

"It's nothing, Kam," he insisted as he put the pants on a hanger.

She crossed her arms as she watched him gather his undergarments. "He made a comment about me, didn't he?"

"Kam--"

"You have to learn to let that go. You can't go stomping around punching out everyone who flippantly mentions me. You're putting too much stress on yourself."

"Shouldn't I?" he asked. "I don't know what's out there. I don't know who wants to hurt us. I can't take that risk. We have to treat every threat like it's a credible one. That's the only way you stay safe."

She gripped his wrist as he tried to brush past her. "And having this level of anxiety and paranoia all the time is going to prevent you from keeping me safe. You can't fly off the handle at every provocation. I can take care of myself and our child without you bearing your fangs at everything that moves."

Jack stiffened a bit. "I never said you couldn't."

"You didn't need to say it. You've been like this for the past couple months. You have to learn to control your temper or you'll end up like--" She shut her mouth abruptly, as if rephrasing what she'd been about to say.

"Or what?" he asked. "I'll end up like my father?"

Kamala exhaled. "I didn't say that."

"You didn't have to." He strode past her and disappeared into the bathroom, slamming the door shut behind him. She sighed and climbed back onto the bed.

It was a long shower. He returned with damp hair and nearly pink skin; the water in this particular hotel could get blistering hot if one wasn't careful and he'd forgotten at first. He sat on the bed, his back to her, gripping the edge of the mattress.

"Sorry," Jack mumbled. "I just...I wasn't in the right

113

mind a little while ago. There's no excuse. I shouldn't have snapped at you."

"You didn't mean anything by it," Kamala said softly. "Your heart is always in the right place. It's your head and your mouth that get you into trouble."

Jack almost smiled. "My mouth is a part of my head, Dr. Anjali."

She swatted him with one of the smaller pillows. "Smartass."

He flopped onto his side facing her. "Well, I do have a PhD. Technically, so does my butt."

Kamala rolled her eyes. "Such high brow conversation. Weren't you apologizing?"

"Yeah, you're right." His hand found her belly and began rubbing it in gentle circles. "I am sorry. I'm sorry I put myself in danger and I'm sorry for what I said to you."

Kamala nodded. "I accept your apology. That being said...I want to talk about where that came from in the first place."

Jack frowned. "Sorry?"

"You're still working out issues that you have with your father. I think that's why you were so touchy. Talk to me. What's going on there?"

"I...the last time I talked to him was after that scare with your Braxton Hicks contractions. He sounded about as torn up about Mom splitting as I was when I found out. She's still not talking to either of us. My grandmother called and said she'd tell her you're alright and so is the baby."

"Are you angry that your father couldn't bring her back?"

"Not really, no. My mom is the epitome of stubborn. She's not going to come around until she wants to, doesn't matter what anyone else does. She's been like that my whole life. However, she was sort of the interpreter between my dad and me when I was a kid, so that's why things are so stressed between us right now. We don't really know how to communicate without her."

114

"And you're worried it will be that way between you and our daughter?"

Jack winced. "Yeah. I don't want to repeat history."

"Jack, there is so much time between now and when our little one will start to retain and understand the things that you say."

"I know. But, my mind keeps running all these scenarios. Like, it's quizzing me to know how I'll react once she's old enough to talk and make decisions for herself. I'm just worried about blowing it. There are so many small things a parent can do that the kid never forgets and that shapes their confidence, their sense of being."

Kamala rubbed his wrist. "Like what?"

He thought it over. "It wasn't about when my dad accidentally broke my arm. It was smaller things. He was dismissive of my thoughts and opinions. He always had a snide or a passive aggressive comment ready. It made me retreat a lot. Most things he handled on a practical level, almost never an emotional one. I felt like I couldn't tell him anything personal without getting some kind of judgment passed. You'd think I'd be able to shrug that off more than ten years later, but here I am, a nervous wreck a month out from my kid's birth."

"You're right. Small things our parents do shape us into who we are. However, it's not the final say. In the end, it'll be her choice of who she becomes when she grows up, just as it was yours. I don't think you'd ever do something harmful to her psyche because you're so aware of what your father did that upset you when you were a kid."

He almost smiled. "Yeah, I'll just find all new ways to screw her up."

She shook her head. "She'll be stronger than that. Trust me. The only time that history repeats itself is when we don't learn from it. You've made it a point to never stop learning for as long as I have known you. You won't hurt her, Jack. And if you do, I know you'll make it up to her."

He nodded solemnly. "I'm also sorry about back there

in the hangar. What Agent Shannon did, keeping you from seeing Pete."

Kamala scowled. "Don't be sorry. It's not your fault. It's just another burden to bear."

"Hey," he whispered. "Come on. Don't dismiss it like that. Talk to me. I know you're still upset."

Kamala lay there for a long moment, soaking in his loving caress, allowing the words to surface on their own. "It's as if this baby has canceled who I am in the eyes of certain people. Like I'm no longer Dr. Kamala Anjali. I'm just a vehicle for a baby. As if it's all that I am for as long as I'm carrying her. I wanted to throttle him for exerting that kind of control over me. For erasing me. For seeing me as some pathetic, weak creature that should be protected. To him, my mind, my beliefs, my profession, my skills no longer matter with this child inside me. How does someone become that way? To think a child invalidates the woman carrying her?"

"I think he's more than a little sexist," Jack said. "And I also think he's sweet on you."

Kamala glanced at him sharply. "What?"

"Not in a sexual way," Jack clarified. "I think you remind him of someone. It's in his actions. It's clear he doesn't want either of us here, but now that we are, I'm starting to read between the lines. He's taking that security thing way too damn far, but I don't think he even realizes he's doing it at all. I think it's subconscious."

Jack kissed her stomach lightly. "And I think some guys can't help it, when they see a pregnant woman, regardless of their own relationship with their parents. It's sort of a knee-jerk reaction. Even if the guy hates his own mother, on some level he still acknowledges that mothers are something special. Doesn't excuse him for how he's been treating you though."

He scooted a bit closer and brushed a lock of hair away from her cheek. "You are more than a mother, Kamala. You're the best person I've ever met. If there's ever anything I can do to help you feel more like yourself, then tell me and

116

I'll be damned sure to get it done. It's been rough and you've been strong this whole time, strong for both of us. I appreciate that, but don't hold it all in. If you need to be honest with me, then do it. Doesn't matter if it hurts my feelings. I told you, I'm in it for the long haul. I meant that."

She touched his hand where it rested on her face, her eyes wet. "Rhett Bartholomew Jackson, you are going to make one hell of a father."

He kissed her gently in thanks. "God, I hope so."

# CHAPTER SIX
## LULU'S BACK IN TOWN

If there was one thing that could get Faye Worthington to stop thinking about her stalled investigation or the two loves of her life running off to hunt killer dragons, it was the beach.

Clearwater Beach had become a favorite of hers and Kamala's in their time together as roommates. They had always booked a trip every ninety days—about the amount of time it took for their respective careers to drive them crazy—and went to the same hotel each time. It was one street away from the beach, giving them a gorgeous view of the sparkling water and white powdery shore, which was one of the highest rated beaches in the country thanks to its uniquely fine sand and location not far away from the Tampa area, meaning there was plenty of entertainment.

The city of Clearwater itself was small and largely communal, with the majority of its attractions within walking distance of the coastline. The two of them had made a regular habit of going jet-skiing to release some tension and cut loose followed by frozen margaritas at sunset after a day of baking in the Florida sun. It was one of her favorite quarterly trips.

Although she went alone this time, Faye still rented the suite instead of a simple room so she'd feel a little more comfortable and so she could keep food in a full fridge rather than a tiny one. The apartment styling of the room reminded her of her old place in some ways and helped keep her mind off her current sources of stress. Any normalcy was welcome.

The door swung shut on its own as Faye stepped into the heavenly air conditioning, having spent the last couple hours of the morning getting a head start on what promised to be an amazing tan. She nearly regretted going steady with Jack and Kamala, since she always seemed to become even more irresistible to men when she had a nice even tan. She knew her paramours would appreciate it nonetheless, Jack in particular.

She set her purse, sunglasses, and half-full water bottle down on the breakfast nook counter and noticed she had a new item, a vase of bright blue Forget-Me-Nots. She leaned in and smelled them, smiling warmly at the thoughtfulness of the hotel staff. They'd honestly always gone above and beyond her expectations and that was why she always booked with this particular local place.

Even more surprising, she found a little note taped to one side of the glass vase. Faye tugged it off and unfolded the small card.

*Turn around.*

Heart hammering wildly in her chest, Faye whirled around to see a man sitting in the blue linen chair of the den.

The man had plain features aside from a slightly crooked nose. His hair and brows were darker than the last time she had seen them — a deep brown rather than a sandy color. He sported an even closer haircut than before, only about an inch from a true buzz cut. His skin had a healthy tan to it, as if he'd been out on the beach as well for a few weeks. His build hadn't changed — compact, thick muscle that reminded her of a Navy Seal. Blue eyes sparkled up at her this time instead of brown. He wore a baseball cap, plain white polo, khaki shorts, and tennis shoes, which let him blend in with every other tourist in the town.

"Welcome back, Blondie," Winston, hitman extraordinaire, said. "How was the beach?"

Faye's eyes immediately snapped down to his hands. He held a Beretta .9mm in the right one that sat on his thigh, casually aimed at her upper torso.

The blonde balled her hands into fists and glared at him. "Really? After all this time, this is how you wanted our confrontation to go down? I'm in a bikini, for God's sake."

Winston lifted his eyebrows and the smile split into a grin. "Expect the unexpected. I thought you'd have learned that by now."

She waited for his gaze to make the eventual path down her lithe, half-naked upper torso to the floral-print wrap loosely draped around her hips, but it didn't. It was a first for her. She'd been rejecting men left and right ever since her sandals hit the doorjamb when she'd left that morning. Winston seemed immune to her looks. Or he was just an excellent actor.

"I've learned a lot since the last time we saw each other," Faye said, easing the tension out of her spine one second at a time. "Care to find out?"

"You know I do," he murmured, and a dark hunger crept across his face. He hadn't moved a muscle, and yet her belly tightened with fear. Adrenaline flushed her skin from head to toe and her breathing picked up as she got ready to fight.

A second later, the pleasant smile flicked back across his mouth. "But not right now. Let's not be premature. We need to talk."

"I'm done talking," she snarled. "I've been waiting for this day for months. There is nothing I have wanted more than a second shot at taking your sorry ass down."

"Believe me, we'll get to that, but it's not why I'm here." To her shock, he replaced the Safety on the gun and settled it on the arm of the loveseat. "I'm here to help you."

Faye stared at him. "What?"

He held up his hands in surrender. "Honest Abe, Blondie. Not here to threaten."

She let out a derisive laugh. "Let me see how many different languages I can recall to tell you to go fuck yourself."

Winston rolled his eyes. "I mean it. No tricks."

"I don't want your help. Now get out of that chair so I can tear you limb from limb."

Winston sighed. "So hardheaded. I'm a lot of things, but I'm first and foremost a man of my word. That's the only way you get ahead in the killing-people business. Hitmen have trust issues."

"No shit, Sherlock. Forget it. No deal. I want no part of whatever the hell you're trying to drag me into."

"Look, what do you want from me? I'm offering nicely and everything."

"You tried to kill me and my best friend!" Faye shouted. "You kidnapped me and chained me to a bed like a wild animal. Do you know how much therapy it took for me to be able to go out in public again? I'll send you the bill, asshole. I've spent the last six months looking over my shoulder just to make sure you weren't there breathing down my neck. Now, you finally show up and we're just supposed to exchange witty banter and team up like this is some kind of Saturday morning cartoon? No thanks. Here's my deal, you get up out of the chair and we settle our account."

He stared at her. "You know I could just shoot you, right?"

Faye strode towards him. She got a single step before the Beretta had returned to his hand with the safety off once more.

"Don't," Winston said tiredly. "You're right. This isn't a cartoon. If you force my hand, I will kill you out of self-preservation."

"Do it," she whispered, her blue eyes glowing like the inside of a blazing inferno as she crept closer one step at a time. "I fucking dare you to do it, Winston. Because if you do, I guarantee you'll see my face every time you close your eyes for the rest of your miserable life. You don't want me dead and we both know it."

Winston scowled. "That's a bit of a reach, Blondie."

Faye let out a low laugh and leaned over him until the muzzle of the gun pressed between her breasts. "Fine. Let's find out, shall we?"

She flattened her hands on the arm of the loveseat. "Point blank range. I won't even feel a thing. Go ahead, Winston. Kill me."

He stared up at her, unflinching, his gun hand steady, breathing slowly as she penetrated him with her fearless stare. She waited.

Winston kept the gun where it was and lifted his other hand, which held a manila folder.

"Someone's been hired to kill your friends."

Faye's heart rate tripled. "You're lying."

"I'm not. You know I'm not."

Faye's gaze wandered over the folder and then back over to his impassive expression. She plucked it from his fingers and backed away, flipping it open as she went. She kept him in her peripheral vision and scanned the document inside. It was a screenshot of an exchange in some kind of encrypted chat room. The names and dates were all blacked out, but the conversation hadn't been redacted.

*Hotel. India. Tango. Two. Sam's friends. Quatro. Fortnight doubled.*

"When it's not word of mouth, most hitmen communicate through this secured channel," Winston told her. "The access codes change on an hourly basis. I was offered this contract at midnight. I turned it down and the assignment disappeared from the site at about six o'clock this morning. That means someone else said yes."

Faye flipped the page and saw snapshots of Jack and Kamala walking into a government facility. It appeared to be from far away, maybe a few buildings over. Ice slid down her spine as she thought about the two of them in the scope of a rifle, blissfully unaware that their lives were in danger. She turned to the next page and saw a profile on the man she knew to be Agent Shannon—height, weight, hair color, eye color, professional and military background, weapons of choice, and even his most frequently used transportation.

"That's the profile they compiled on the guy heading up the dragon recovery project," he continued. "Whatever's going down is supposed to look like an accident."

"If what you say is true," Faye said, her eyes frosted over. "Why are they still alive?"

"Whoever placed the hit wants the dragons to kill them. That way it has poetic justice." He paused to roll his eyes. "Sounds like they're going to wait until your friends catch up with the dragon-fighting ring and they'll lay a trap."

"It won't work." Faye said. "Neither of them is doing fieldwork. That was the only reason they agreed to the assignment in the first place."

"Accidents happen, Blondie. Someone's moving chess pieces to get the two of them out in the open for the hit. It'll be loud and nasty and they will die."

Winston stood from the chair slowly. "Unless you help me save them."

"Oh, so now the Grinch suddenly has a heart?" Faye shoved the folder against his chest. "I'm not buying it."

"Don't worry, I'm as heartless as usual," Winston said. "But I also know for a fact that if the beanpole and the little doc die, you don't have anything else to live for. If you don't end up swallowing a bottle full of pills, you'll get yourself killed trying to avenge them. We're going to stop the hit and find out who called it in. Once it's over with, then we'll settle our account."

"That's dangerous, stupid, and unnecessary," Faye shot back. "They're already working with the government. They have more men and more resources. All we have to do is give them this information and they can stop it."

"Not if they're the ones who put out the hit."

Faye swallowed hard. "What?"

Winston flipped the folder open and pointed to the chat room. "Hotel India Tango. That's the military alphabet. Normal hitters don't use that when they communicate. We're looking at spooks here, Blondie. If we tip them off, they'll just work even faster and forget the 'make it look like an accident' thing. They'll just take out the whole building with a block of C4 and blame it on domestic terrorism."

"I'm not going to fall for this. You're a professional killer. There is no reason to endanger myself off of something you can't prove."

"You think I dragged my ass out here to God's Rubber Room just to play with you? I've got a life, you know. I had to turn down another assignment just to get this crap and fly out here to give it to you."

"Cry me a fucking river, Winston. You're full of shit. You just want to string me along for whatever sick, demented reason you took an interest in me to begin with—"

Before she could blink, his massive hand was on her throat and he'd shoved her up against the wall, squeezing hard enough to seal off any oxygen. Her skull throbbed where it had thudded into the drywall. Winston peered down at her cheeks as they reddened, his blue eyes flat and dead.

"Do you have any idea how boring it is to be unchallenged?" he asked quietly. "To realize you've conquered just about every challenge that you can possibly imagine and find that the world has nothing left to offer you? Honestly, it's the next best thing to madness. Think of the hardest, scariest kind of person that you can and I've killed them all. I'm walking in a world full of ghosts."

His lips quirked up at one corner slightly. "And you're the first thing I've seen with a pulse since I started this gig. You don't have to trust me. You don't have to believe me. Look at me, Faye. You know damn well I'm telling the truth. I have no reason to lie to you. If I wanted you dead, you'd be dead. If I wanted your friends dead, they'd be dead. If we let them die, you'll be just another ghost."

"There...is...no...we!" Faye broke the choke-hold and drove her elbow into his temple.

Winston hissed and jerked back on impulse, and it was all she needed. She landed a brutal jab to his solar plexus and twisted his gun arm to one side. She slammed her arm down on his shoulder and he grunted, losing grip on the Beretta. She caught it and swept his legs out from under him. He hit the floor and she pinned him there with her forearm, pressing the gun to his forehead. She flicked the safety off with her shaking fingers and towered over him, breathing fast and hard.

Winston didn't move. Her elbow had split the skin

124

over his left brow and blood trickled down one side of his head onto the tile.

"Well," he drawled. "That was anticlimactic."

Faye dug the muzzle into his skin harder. "Tell me why I shouldn't do it."

"Because you don't want to go to jail for the rest of your life."

"I could claim self-defense, asshole. You broke into my suite with a gun. I'm gorgeous and blonde, you're tall and creepy. Do the math."

Winston smirked. "Alright, point taken. We both know that this is your crossroads moment. You can kill me and live with the consequences. You know you'll be safer if I'm dead. You know that I'll just keep creeping back into your life like kudzu if you don't kill me first."

He reached up and fingered the lock of her blonde hair that had spilled out of the ponytail. "But you could have killed me back in that house when you broke free. No one would have blamed you. You're a different person now. I can see that. I'm not going to pretend like I know you inside out, because I don't. However, you know that if you kill me, the spark I lit that night is going to become an inferno and you will set aflame every good thing in your life if you do it. That's the difference between the two of us. My world is embers. Yours is still green. You're not holding a gun, Faye. You're holding a match."

Something soft entered his eyes for just a split second. "Besides, you can't kill me. I bought you flowers."

Faye stared at him. He stared right back. Her chest shook with a laugh. Then her shoulders. Then her whole upper body. He joined her a moment later.

Faye lifted the gun away and flopped down beside him. She hit the release along the side. The magazine popped out, revealing that it had been empty the whole time. Faye popped it back in and handed him the gun. "Winston?"

"Yeah?" he said as he sat up with a pained groan, clutching his chest where he felt a bruise already forming from her fist.

"When we're done with all of this mess," Faye said, her blue eyes sparkling, her mouth still curled in an utterly beautiful smile. "I'm going to bury you."

Winston's smile was dark and eager. "Looking forward to it, Blondie."


"First things first," Winston said after shoveling the remaining half of a shrimp po'boy into his mouth. "No cops."

Faye narrowed her eyes at him. "They can help."

"They can try," Winston corrected. He picked a bit of lettuce from between his teeth and finished chewing before continuing. "From what I gather, Carmichael and Houston are stand up guys through and through, but they would only be able to take the investigation so far before having to call the top brass. Whoever tried to hire me would get tipped off and they'd kill Jack and Kamala outright to avoid any other complications."

"Or," she countered. "You know that Carmichael and Houston are good enough cops to figure out who you really are and you don't want to be directly involved with them."

Winston grinned. "Well, that's just an added bonus."

"Speaking of which, what's to stop them from throwing me in jail? If I help you, I'm an accessory to a murderer, for God's sake."

"Not really," Winston said. "Hostage situation. It's survival. I told you to do what I say and you obeyed so I wouldn't kill you. If they get hold of my rap sheet, they'll believe it, trust me. That brings me to my second point."

He popped a fry into his mouth and fixed her with a steady stare. "You don't tell either of the docs that they're targets."

"What?" she demanded. "Why?"

"Someone's probably already keeping tabs on them, if these photos are any indication. If they find out you know, they'll blow the whistle early. Then, once those loose ends are

126

tied, they'll come after you as well and they won't stop until you're six feet under. They need to stay in the dark until the contract is terminated."

"I can't do that," she growled. "These are people I care about. People I am sharing my life with. I'm not going to lie to them."

"Don't have to lie," he said frankly. "Just omit it."

"That's the same thing."

"Splitting hairs, Blondie. My point is that if you tell them, the deal's off. I'll come after you proper and you'll just have to see if you're as good as you think you are. The two of them will be on their own and I doubt they'll last long without professional help."

"This is bullshit. If we tell them, they can be ready. They can prepare and look out for a trap someone tries to spring on them. Every time someone tries this stunt, it backfires. We have to tell them they're in danger. Kamala is pregnant, for God's sake. She's due in a month."

"Then she shouldn't have said yes to this assignment. She made her choice. So did the beanpole. Choices have consequences."

He wiped his mouth with a napkin. "This isn't a negotiation. If I find out you tried to tell them behind my back, you'll regret it. Don't test me, Faye."

The threat was somewhat undermined as he slurped his soda through a straw until it was empty. Faye swatted the cup aside in annoyance and he chuckled.

"Fine." Faye hissed. "I won't say anything for now, but if we have no choice, I'm telling them the truth, regardless of what you do to me."

Winston snorted. "Stubborn woman. We're leaving as soon as I'm done. Keep your hotel reservation and we'll leave your stuff in there as an alibi so they think you're still here. I'll clone your phone so if anyone tries to ping it, it'll show you were still at the beach the whole time. We're going to D.C. to pick up on the trail and see if we can beat the spooks at their own game."

"How? If we fly up, they'll know it's me."

Winston reached into his wallet and handed her a fake I.D. She frowned at him. "Seriously? You just had this made beforehand off the assumption I'd cooperate?"

He winked. "Does it scare you how well I know you?"

She rolled her eyes and examined the card, weirded out to see the photo from her actual driver's license and the new name he'd given her. Only, she had brown hair, eyes, and brows. "Bobbi Morse? Really?"

Winston shrugged and burped, though he politely hid it behind his fist. "If they're savvy enough to get that reference, they deserve to catch us. Don't look so surprised. I was underground for a while after our last confrontation and I had some free time to read."

"Fine. Let's say for the sake of argument that I believe you. What are we going to be doing?"

"We keep an eye on your friends and figure out where they're headed. We get there first, take out the people laying the trap, get them to talk, and take out whoever put out the hit."

"If it's an inside job like you say, then you're talking about the assassination of government operatives. Are you insane?"

Winston just arched an eyebrow. She sighed. "Yeah, I guess that was a stupid question. Insane or not, you're forgetting the fact that it's just the two of us and I'm not going to help you kill any criminals. Maybe the cops will believe you took me hostage, but not if I pull the trigger."

"Capture is not going to be good enough, you know," he said evenly. "They're smart. Connected. They could plead their sentences down to a slap on the wrist or just pull a jailbreak."

"Then we'll beat them again. You said so yourself. Once I start down that path, there is no going back. Or do you want me to end up just like you?"

Winston clenched his jaw slightly. "I'll take it under advisement, alright? Just remember that they might not give you a choice. If it's you or them, then choose yourself. Survive. Nothing else matters."

"That won't be a problem, trust me."

Winston grinned and took his cap off, tugging it low over Faye's forehead. "Then saddle up, Blondie. We've got a plane to catch."

"So," Winston said as he unzipped his duffel bag on Faye's bed and started withdrawing items. "One of the first rules to being a hitman is to blend in. I've already got my boring persona perfected, so we have to work on yours before we catch our plane to D.C. It's time to knock you from a ten down to about a five, Ms. Worthington."

He handed her a sealed plastic bag with a brunette wig inside it and a small liquid bottle of dye. "Blondes and redheads draw more attention. We need you average white girl coloring first off."

He then handed her a contact lens case and a bottle of solution. "Those'll feel weird at first, but you get used to it after a while. Just takes practice putting them in and taking them out."

Last, Winston drew clothing out of the bag. "Clothes will stay bland and unremarkable like your persona. Nothing tight, nothing glamorous, nothing noticeable."

Faye eyed the lingerie lying across the shirt. "A sports bra? Really?"

"You've got great tits," Winston said frankly. "The key is to be unnoticed, remember?"

Faye rolled her eyes and headed for the bathroom. "Have I mentioned how much I hate you?"

"Four times already."

Faye kicked the door shut behind her and muttered insults as she pulled her hair back into a bun so that the wig would fit. She brushed it out first, surprised that it was real human hair instead of synthetic. He'd obviously shelled out for something of high quality. It wouldn't have been cheap, either. She slid it on and made sure it fit securely, tucking stray hairs until every blonde strand disappeared. She almost smirked to herself. Jack liked brunettes. He'd have flipped his lid if he saw her this way.

A pang of guilt poked a hole in her stomach. She tried not to think about him as she uncapped the dye and went to work on her perfectly arched eyebrows. To distract herself, she lifted her voice enough for Winston to hear it through the door. "What else should I know about hiding in plain sight?"

"Let people do the work for you," Winston said. "The average person will talk themselves right out of something they see with their own two eyes if you give them just the right misdirection."

"What about the assassin who took the assignment?"

"They'll be playing a similar game. Staying on the outskirts. We'll be looking for someone related to the agency, but with a comfortable spot to blow the whistle if it goes sideways."

"Any lead suspects?"

"I thought maybe we'd start with Agent Shannon. Guy's got a strong motive. Wants things run his way and he'd definitely want Jackson and the little doc out of the way."

"But I thought that profile for the hit had his information in it?"

"Doesn't mean he didn't do it. It's possible to set it up to look that way so you have an alibi, so to speak. No one thinks you did it if it looks like you're one of the targets."

"Makes sense, in a really messed up way. Who else?"

"Possibly the same clowns who hired me to abduct you, the Yamaguchi-gumi. However, I highly doubt it. The yakuza like to be careful, but not this careful. A bullet from a rifle would serve their needs just fine. No need for the irony of the dragons being the one to kill them. They're out."

Faye breathed out slowly as her heart rate rabbited for a moment. She'd never met Aisaka Tomoda, the woman who had hired Winston to kidnap her, and she never would.

Aisaka had died in the Suicide Forest, shot by Juniper Snow. She was also the reason Jack had that nasty bullet scar in his side. Anger flooded through her. She'd have liked to make Aisaka pay if she could have.

She paused as she mulled over what he'd just told her. "You sound like you know them."

"Well enough, I suppose."

Faye nibbled her lower lip and took a chance. "So you've worked with them before, even before Aisaka hired you to kidnap me?"

"I try to stay stateside when I can, but yeah, I've worked Japan before. It's not that lucrative, though. I stick out too much when I travel through Tokyo, even with a subdued demeanor."

"When's the last time you were there?"

"I think January of last year? Where did the time go? 2016 went by in a blink, I swear."

Faye changed out of her clothes and into the drab, oversized ones he'd given her. There was an excellent chance Winston was still manipulating her, but they had a rapport. If she played her cards just right, there was a chance she could extract something she could give to Carmichael and Houston to investigate, assuming she lived through this mess. She couldn't press too hard or he'd notice. She'd have to be careful.

The contact lenses frustrated her, as she struggled to get them into her eyes, she kept wanting to close them as her fingertip neared her cornea, but she got them in eventually. She rinsed the dye off after it had set and opened the bathroom door in a red flannel shirt, baggy cargo pants, and Dockers. Winston glanced at her and smiled.

"You look terrible."

"Thanks," she groused, tossing her former clothes into her own bag. "Do I get a pair of Clark Kent glasses while I'm at it?"

He produced a pair of black-rimmed bifocals. "As a matter of fact, you do, Ms. Morse."

Faye groaned and snatched them out of his hands. "I swear, if I find out this is all fake and you're just screwing with me, I am going to chop off your balls."

Winston clucked his tongue. "So hostile. That's our next thing to address. You're about as Type A as a person can get, so you're going to have to dial it down. Think Type B."

She slipped the glasses on and scowled. "You're getting off on bossing me around, aren't you?"

Winston smirked. "Blondie, if you had even the slightest inkling of what I got off on, you'd head for the hills and never look back."

Faye rolled her eyes. "I'm in a polyamorous relationship with both of my best friends. I'm way past the point of being shocked by anything people are into these days."

"Oho?" Winston crossed his arms. "So you did listen to me after all."

"Blow me," Faye replied with a sneer. "It wasn't because of you. Jack and I dated for a bit after that incident in the Suicide Forest and while we got along, we were both miserable without Kam. So Jack suggested that I tell her the truth and we see what happens."

"And how did that go?"

"None of your goddamn business, that's how."

Winston touched his chest. "Damn, Blondie. I'm invested in this shit. Throw me a bone here."

She glared. "Don't we have a plane to catch?"

He zipped the duffel bag up again and slung it over one broad shoulder. "It's a long drive to the airport from here. We've got time."

"Fine," Faye said. "I'll make you a deal. I'll tell you what happened if you tell me what you were doing in Cambridge this past week."

Winston frowned. "And just how did you know about that?"

"Because I'm goddamn amazing."

Winston shook his head. "Boy, the ego. I don't know

how either of your significant others put up with it."

"I'm seriously phenomenal at sex."

Winston barked out a laugh. "Why does that not surprise me? Alright, Blondie, you've got yourself a deal."

He opened the bedroom door. "Ladies first."


*Faye was close to chewing a hole right through her lower lip by the time the front door opened and she heard the faint footfalls of her former roommate. Kamala rounded the corner, a neutral expression on her lovely features, and Faye's stomach did a backhand spring.*

*"Hey, Kam," Faye said softly. "Like your hair."*

*Kamala touched the curled edges slightly, as if on reflex. She'd probably heard the compliment quite a few times lately. She'd let it grow another two inches since the last time they'd seen each other. "Thanks."*

*Jack appeared, having shut and locked the door behind her, and came to stand a little off to one side so they could both see him and vice versa. "Thanks for coming, Kam. Really."*

*She nodded and took a deep breath. "What did you decide?"*

*"Before we go down that road..." Jack walked over and held Faye's hand. Kamala didn't exactly tense, but her posture shifted to slightly more defensive. "Faye has something to tell you."*

*The blonde swallowed, glancing furtively at Jack for a second, but he just nodded. "I, uh...I should have told you this ages ago, but...Kam, I think I might be in love with you."*

*Kamala froze. "You...what?"*

*Faye nodded, trying to smile. "Have been for a while now. Ever since that night we fooled around. I didn't say anything because I value our friendship and because you're important to me. Because you and Jack started up and I didn't want to complicate things. But now everything's complicated and I shouldn't keep lying to you about the way I feel if I ever want to regain your trust. So there's the truth."*

*She lifted her gaze reluctantly, expecting abject horror mixed in with the shock, but instead she only found a soft look of*

133

concern.

"Faye," Kamala whispered. "All this time...I had no idea. I didn't know that night had affected you that much."

Faye shrugged. "It's not your fault, Kam. We both had way too much to drink, but that's what set everything off. I've never respected someone the way that I respect you. I've never had a better friend or roommate, hell, even a boyfriend who supported me and cared for me the way that you do."

She nudged Jack's shoulder. "And your idiot boyfriend here said that it's unhealthy to keep that sort of thing bottled up forever. I only listened since he knew from experience."

"All too well," Jack agreed.

Kamala sent him a searching look. "How long have you known she felt this way?"

Jack scratched the back of his neck. "Since that night at the bar. Faye confronted me about how I felt about you and I returned the favor. We both kept our mouths shut because we were afraid of making things too awkward. I mean, it's a lot to find out both your best friends want to get in your pants."

Faye smacked him in the stomach. He grinned as he caught both of them trying to hide smiles. Kamala folded one arm over her slightly protruding pregnant belly and studied Faye for a moment. "So...have you ever been with a woman before that night?"

"Once," Faye admitted. "A threesome back in my undergrad years. Not sure where that fits in in terms of sexuality spectrums. You're really the first woman I've found myself attracted to, honestly. Maybe it's a one-and-done type thing, if that's even possible."

"Any chance you want to fill in the details on that threesome?" Jack asked hopefully. She glared and he held up his hands in surrender. "Kidding. Mostly."

"And...you would want to be with me that way?" Kamala asked softly. "More than friends, I mean."

Faye swallowed hard, blushing and rubbing her arm self-consciously. "Maybe? I've never given it much thought. I was sort of just admiring you from afar. I never thought I'd get the guts to say something until Stilts brought it up."

134

"And you, Jack?" Kamala asked. "Why did you push her to tell me now?"

"Because," he said slowly. "I thought it might make what I'm about to say a little easier."

"Which is?"

Jack licked his lips. "A month ago, you asked me to choose. I can't. I want you both in my life."

Faye gave a start, her jaw dropping open. "Wait, what?"

"Seconded," Kamala said, her dark-honey eyes wide.

Jack held up his hands again. "Before either of you gets the wrong idea, I'm not talking about sex. I'm talking about the fact that the three of us are already so completely woven into each other's lives that maybe it's not the worst idea in the world to just give it a shot."

He gestured towards Kamala. "Kam, it's been torture without you to come home to every night. We went out, what? A month and two weeks? I've been alive for damn near thirty years and I haven't been that happy in my entire life. Even seeing you at work isn't enough. I want to be there with you when you come home. I want to rub your feet and feed you every ridiculous vegetarian dish you can think up and I want to help you pick out baby clothes and do every last thing you ask me to while we wait for the little munchkin to arrive. I want to be a part of your life. I will do anything to make you happy. I don't care what it is. If you ask me for the moon, I'll find a fucking ladder right now and I'll get it. You're an incredible woman."

He turned to Faye. "Faye, you're by far the most aggravatingly complicated woman I've ever met. You know exactly how to get under my skin and you're one of the first people I've ever met to be able to do that. I don't know what it is about me, but I tend to build a wall around myself sometimes and you took a sledgehammer to that thing without even blinking. You damn near demanded that I take you seriously after we finally connected that morning after the bar fight. As much as we drive each other crazy, this whole month I've been thinking that whatever the hell we have, actually kind of works in its own way. Maybe this whole thing started up initially with the offer of sex, but it's more than that for

135

both of us. You're a hell of a woman and you amaze me every single day."

Jack ran a hand through his hair, searching for the right words. "Look, I know this is insane. I'm not trying to be indecisive here. I'm not trying to have my cake and eat it too. When you're a kid, you learn about the so-called American Dream. The house, the white picket fence, the wife, the dog, and two-point-five kids that you pile into the family minivan and drive off into the sunset. That's bullshit. Everyone's dream isn't the same. Maybe my dream isn't what I thought it would be. Maybe my dream is being with two people who care about each other and about me, where all of us want the same thing somehow. But more than that...I think we make each other happy. All three of us. I'm not saying it'll be easy, but honest to God, I think we can make it work. All I'm asking is that we give it a shot. If it doesn't work out, then I was wrong and I'll find a way to make peace with it."

He shut his eyes for a second, summoning the courage to speak again. "I just want to make you both as happy as you've made me. That's all."

"Goddess," Kamala muttered, absently rubbing her belly. "Of all the things I thought you'd say, that certainly wasn't one of them."

He smiled weakly. "Sorry. Didn't mean to sucker-punch you."

"No, I..." She shook her head. "I didn't expect this, but I'm not upset, I promise."

Kamala paced along the length of the couch for a while before she spoke again. "Truthfully, I hadn't considered polyamory as an option before. But, I dug a little further into my faith in the month we spent apart and to be honest, it's not the most radical thing I've ever heard. I believe that it's possible to love more than one person. That more than one person can complete you. That we meet our soulmates through each life cycle again and again in different forms."

She raked a hand through her thick, glossy hair. "I suppose I've been keeping Faye in a box, much like I did with you, Jack. It was easier to think of her that way, as a sister, not as a person. The attraction never really went anywhere; I just kept it to myself. I didn't revisit that night since I thought it was just a one time thing."

Faye almost smiled. "Yeah. Notice how I've never asked the literal translation for 'saheli'? I pretty much gathered what it meant by context."

Kamala winced. "I am sorry if that hurt your feelings, Faye. I didn't mean to."

"I know, Kam. You'd never do it on purpose. And I've missed you so damn much this month that it makes me sick."

Kamala smiled. "You're not the only one. My place feels so empty without you."

She glanced at Jack. "Both of you."

She took a long breath. "I'll say this. It's not the worst idea I've ever heard. I might be willing to give it a try. To examine how I've felt and see where it might lead."

Jack nodded. "Faye?"

"What are you asking me for?" she snorted. "I've wanted to bang you both the longest."

The pair of scientists burst into equally embarrassed laughter. "So I take it that's a yes from you, then?" Jack teased.

"Damn right. Let's get this threesome going as soon as possible. You, off with the pants."

Jack chuckled. "You're such a romantic, Faye."

She batted her eyelashes at him. "You have no idea, big boy."

"I don't know how you did it, Blondie," Winston said as he hit the parking brake on the car after they'd pulled into a space in the Tampa airport shuttle area. "But you somehow made polyamory sound positively adorable."

"Of course that's your reaction," Faye muttered as she undid her seatbelt. "There. Now you know. Your turn. What were you doing in Cambridge?"

Winston climbed out of the car, popping the trunk as he went. "Tying up a loose end."

"Meaning?" Faye demanded.

"Not everyone in Cambridge is as charmed by me as

you are," Winston deadpanned as he dragged the duffel bag out of the car. "I made a few enemies the last time I was there for my assignment with you and the beanpole."

"That must be par for the course with you, I imagine."

"For the most part, yeah. Had to set a few things straight after they sent someone after me."

"Wait," she said, holding up her hands. "Someone sent a hitman to kill another hitman?"

"Happens all the time, actually. It's a competitive business and some people hold grudges."

"I don't get it. Shouldn't the yakuza have sent someone after you failed instead of the criminals in Cambridge?"

"I managed to parlay with the Yamaguchi due to our history. This was something else."

"What?"

Winston eyed her. Faye fought to keep her face blank as she hastily elaborated. "Look, it's not like I can prove anything that you tell me anyway. Curiosity killed the cat."

"The driver," he said. "The one who was driving the night I came after you two. He was a loose end. We argued after I failed my end of the bargain and that meant we couldn't be paid. He forced me to act. Threatened me. I took care of him, but apparently he has mob ties, so they sent someone after me."

"And what happened then?"

Winston stared at her and then just smiled. Faye fought off a shiver. "Never mind."

"Anyway," he continued. "I went back to Cambridge to cut a deal. We negotiated. End of story."

He nodded towards the other end of the parking lot. "Shuttle's this way."

Faye fell in step with him, her mind whirling back to the anonymous man who had called her with information related to Winston. Maybe he actually had been a legit source who wanted to rat on him to get him out of the way. Still, if she was going to be stuck in Winston's company for the next day or two, she wouldn't get anything through to Carmichael and Houston to let them know what to investigate. The lead might dry up by the time this entire mess was resolved. She had to find a way to tell them.

But how?

# CHAPTER SEVEN

## FIELD TEST

"Have I mentioned this is the coolest fucking thing that's ever happened to me?"

"Yes. Several times, in fact."

"Just checking."

Jack smirked and drank his coffee. "Dork."

"Oh, don't even try it, man," Calloway said over the rush of the high winds. "You'd be saying the same thing if you were in my place right now."

"And you'd be calling me a dork if I were."

"Point taken."

Libby shook her head. "I smell a bromance brewing."

Jack flicked an annoyed glance at her. "Hey, watch it, little girl."

Libby grinned wickedly. "Or what? You'll spank me?"

"Libs," Calloway said, exasperated. "Can you not?"

"Stop cockblocking and fly the dragon, dude."

"I can do both," Calloway said defiantly.

"It's not cockblocking if you have no chance with me, you know," Jack said, eyeing her over the rim of his coffee cup as he took another sip.

"That's what they all say at first," Libby said with a haughty sniff as she adjusted the body-cam attached to Pete to expand its focus out further. "But we both know you can't resist brown sugar."

The coffee squirted out of Jack's nostrils. Libby burst into giggles as he coughed and wiped his face with a napkin and glared harder through a prominent blush. "God, you're easy. Walked right into that one."

"Can I ground her?" Jack asked.

"You have my full permission to ground her," Calloway answered.

Jack pointed at the door. "Go to your room."

Libby stuck out her pierced tongue. "Spoilsport. And no, I'm not leaving. He's testing my equipment and I need to be here for any adjustments."

"It's working great so far, honestly," Calloway admitted. "Even at this altitude."

The zoologist currently sat astride the dragon on a modified saddle that had magnetic footholds rather than traditional straps. He wore a monochrome-colored Kevlar-woven suit that was fireproof and tear resistant enough to stop a knife at close range, and gunfire up to a .38 caliber bullet.

His gloved hands currently rested atop two round control panels built into the saddle that were connected to pressure switches along small points on Pete's body that indicated which direction she needed to turn during their flight towards the dragon they were currently tracking. He wore a helmet modeled after a motorcycle helmet that had a heads-up display of various readings as well as a radio link and mic to communicate with base. He and the dragon had reached an altitude just high enough that any cameras wouldn't be able to clearly spot them, but low enough that they didn't run the risk of hitting a plane.

"We're getting some great footage," Libby said. "Bird's eye-view of things really puts it all in perspective. I can't wait to post this to Instagram once we're cleared."

"Assuming we ever are," Jack said. "That memo they sent out to the poor unsuspecting Philadelphia public to justify any sightings was pretty vague and I don't think they want to encourage the public to know we're out here doing this."

"True, but I think it'd be good damage control. After all, according to Agent Shannon, they've been collecting any firsthand accounts of the dragon-fighting ring and shutting them down. Paying people to keep quiet and not expose the fact that they're out there. Makes the government seem incompetent."

"Gee," Jack muttered. "Can't imagine anyone thinking

that."

"Hey," Libby said. "They are bankrolling us, after all."

"As much as I pay in taxes, Uncle Sam should be compensating us for once."

She chuckled. "Amen to that."

"About five miles to target," Calloway said. "At least that's what I'm showing on my end. I'm gonna switch lines to coordinate with Shannon real quick. You two behave, please."

"No promises," Libby said. "I'm wearing him down. He'll be in love with me by the time you get back on the line."

Calloway sighed. "Ugh, God help us all. Calloway out."

Libby chuckled. "It's so fun to mess with y'all."

"Glad to amuse you," Jack said mildly, holding one hand out for the tablet. "Do you mind?"

She handed it to him. "You've got to loosen up, doc."

"Probably should," he admitted, checking the readings. "Just a bit antsy now that he's catching up to our perps. Could be dangerous."

"I'm not worried," she said, plopping down next to him at the table. "Bruce can handle himself. Smartest guy I know."

Jack touched his chest and pouted. "I'm hurt."

"Well, I don't know you very well yet," she said, lowering her eyelashes. "But we can fix that easy enough."

Jack sighed. "Dammit. I keep setting myself up for these, don't I?"

"You really do, doc." She propped her head up on one hand, the smile softening. "Can I ask you something?"

"No," Jack said, but he was smiling.

She rolled her eyes. "What's it like having changed the world with your research? I mean, do you feel any differently than you did before this all happened?"

Jack blinked at her in surprise. He hadn't expected a real question. He sat a little straighter in the chair and thought it over. "Yeah, a lot differently, actually. It's kind of hard to put it into words, though. It's a little weird to have a spotlight on me even though I knew it would happen eventually once the project was successful. People know who I am now. I go out and it's like, 'Hey, look, it's that dragon guy' and it's kind of surreal since I've been flying under the radar my whole life. I'm not usually the kind of person people remember. Not like Kam."

Libby nodded. "Yeah, my brother said she's kind of known in the medical world. She was on track to do some big things if she'd followed in her parents' footsteps. So she's used to the spotlight more than you are, huh?"

"Yeah. I'm a pretty quiet guy and this whole thing sort of put me on stage. When that happens, it makes you think about who you really are. If you are who you think you are or if maybe you've just been who people want you to be."

"Who do you want to be?"

Jack winced. "I'll let you know when I find out."

"I think it's awesome what you're doing. I mean, you had every right to tell these fuckers to kiss your ass--" she said.

"Language," Jack chided.

Libby pursed her lips, ignoring the comment. "--but you still showed up to help anyway. I know a lot of people who wouldn't have done that. And, Dr. Anjali, wow, doing all of this crap while she's a month out from having a baby? She's even more badass than you are."

"She's always been more badass than I am," Jack said. "I'm the Robin to her Batman, honestly. If you want to fawn over someone, she's a way better choice."

"That's probably true, but I'm a sucker for a nice pair of broad shoulders."

Jack finally chuckled. "Alright, are you just pulling my leg?"

"Mostly just pulling your leg. Lab gets real boring when it's just me and my brother. Besides, if everything goes according to plan, I probably won't ever see you guys again. Might as well make it fun."

"What about Larry?"

She rolled her eyes. "Ugh, Lackey Larry is just about as frustrating and uninteresting as Agent Shannon. I can't tell you how many things he's mansplained to me since I started working here. He tries to pretend he's just some harmless lab rat, but he's got an ego as big as any jock."

Jack frowned. "Sorry to hear that."

She shrugged. "Comes with the territory. Not a lot of guys like getting schooled by someone younger than them, and then when you add in being a girl and black, it's just bad all around for someone like him."

"He ever say anything rude to you?"

"No. Not in so many words, anyway. I can handle microaggressions. Been doing it all my life."

"Mm."

Libby tilted her head to one side. "What?"

"Nothing," he said, sipping his coffee again. "How'd you get into the tinkering business?"

"My dad. When I was little, I used to watch him work. He repaired automated assembly line robots for cars. He used to take his work home a lot, he'd show me different things he was working on, and I picked up on it pretty quickly. I could disassemble a whole engine and put it back together by the time I was eight."

"Wow. I think I was still into dinosaurs when I was eight."

"Yeah, I might've gone into the automotive automation business before the accident happened."

Jack winced. "Oh. What happened?"

"Line broke down. It sparked a fire and then an explosion. My dad saved one of his coworkers, but he lost an arm in the process. After that, he sort of just..." She shook her head. "lost faith in himself. Building and tinkering was all he knew. He had a hard time finding work that was fulfilling, so my brother had to jump into the workforce to make up for what disability didn't cover."

"I'm sorry."

She shrugged again. "It's no one's fault. We turned out alright, and working for the government means those fat checks keep him taken care of for the foreseeable future."

Jack's intuition noticed the nonchalant tone in her voice. She'd told this story enough times not to let on how she actually felt about it. He'd met people who could distance themselves from something traumatic in their past. Hell, he wasn't all that different when he'd told Kamala about what happened between him and his father in early high school. It was also implicit that the Calloway's mother wasn't in the picture. If she'd died, he had the feeling Libby would have mentioned it. Either way, he thought it smart not to bring it up, not since he'd only met her yesterday. Though the lack of female role model might explain why she went overboard on flirting with older men.

"It's a shame he can't see some of the stuff you've designed thanks to that whole 'secret government project' thing."

"Might not be good for him anyhow. Could bring up some resentment, to be honest."

"Guess so. If it's any consolation, I'd love to take a look at the other equipment you've made for the project."

Libby grinned. "See? Told you I'd get ya."

"You wish, little girl."

Just then, the line clicked and Calloway's voice returned. "Still alive, Dr. Jackson?"

"So far," he said, and Libby stuck her tongue out at him. "What's Shannon's status?"

"He's not far behind me. We're en route. How are things coming with Kamala in the morgue?"

"I'm gonna go check on her and see what's she and Dr. Whitmore have found out. Baby sister will keep an eye out for you in the meantime."

"Good man."

Jack handed her the tablet and stood, taking his coffee with him. Libby made a wolf whistle. "I hate to see you go, but I love to watch you leave."

Jack grabbed his lab coat off the hook nearby. "Don't you have homework to finish?"

"As long as you stay with me after class, professor."

"In your dreams, Punky Brewster."

"Who?"

Jack grinned and winked at her as he opened the door. "Thanks for proving my point, young whippersnapper."

He headed over to the other side of the compound to the makeshift morgue and swiped his card to get in. Kamala stood at the exam table with her arm down the throat of a Hercules dragon. The dragon's corpse was eight feet long from snout to tail. Its scales were dark brown along its spine, but had lighter browns and gold along its sides and belly almost like a python.

"Now there's a sexy image," Jack said, shutting the door behind him and heading towards the corner of the room to put on gloves, a mask, and booties.

Kamala snorted. "How are you, my dragon?"

"Great, angel. How's it coming?"

"Slow," she admitted. "But I've learned a lot so far. We're on dragon number three."

"Where's Dr. Whitmore?" Jack asked as he crossed the room to the exam table.

"Stepped out to take a call," she said. "Frankly, I'm glad to have some space. He hovers. It's quite annoying."

"You're not the only one who's had to deal with that. Libby said she's had similar problems, and with added mansplaining on top."

Kamala rolled her eyes. "She's right. I had to tell him I've taken courses in dragon anatomy so he'd stop trying to name every single body part I touched during my exams. How are Calloway and Pete?"

"Right on schedule. He was five miles out before I left. Should be at the site soon."

"Is that why you're so nervous?"

"I'm nervous?" He glanced down at himself, confused.

"It's your posture, dear," she said simply. "You slouch

more when you're anxious. It'll be fine. They have backup and they're both professionals."

"You know all my tells. It's going to be impossible to lie to you, isn't it?"

Kamala smirked beneath her mask. "I can pretend not to know better, if it helps."

She nodded towards the other desk against the wall. "Take a look under the microscope. I've been studying samples to see if we can identify whatever serum they're using to clone these dragons at such an accelerated rate."

Jack loped over to the table and made a few adjustments to the microscope. "Did this come out of that Hercules dragon?"

"Yes. It was one of the earlier bodies they found, so it's suffered a bit of deterioration, but I still think it might shed some light for us. I put together a list of what I've been able to glean from the samples as well as what matched the lab reports. I'm just not sure what's missing."

"Chemical X," Jack mused.

"What?"

"Nothing, just being a dork." He reared back and read the lab report next to the microscope. "These active ingredients are something else. Rare. It's similar to a growth hormone, but you're right, there's a factor we can't account for just yet. Bet you a dollar who would be able to answer that question."

"Yagami."

"Bingo. Boy, what I wouldn't give to drag his ass in here and demand some answers. Let me ask you something, have they cross-referenced any of this stuff with the blacksite where they're keeping Baba Yaga?"

Kamala thought about it. "I'm not sure, but I can ask. You think it might be the same serum?"

"Or a similar one. Maybe Yagami and whoever else helped him figured out how to refine the serum to grow the dragons, but without the same side effect that made Baba Yaga go berserk. I think if we compare the two together, we might have a better chance of replicating that formula."

Kamala grimaced. "That is dangerous."

"I know." He passed a look to her over his shoulder and she nodded in understanding. She reached up and shut off the mic hanging over the exam table.

"You mean to say that if we do figure out the formula, we destroy the evidence," Kamala asked in a low tone. "That's risky, Jack."

"It is, but it might be for the best. Doesn't mean we'll have the opportunity to get to it first, but we should consider it. I don't think it's a good idea for the US government to have that formula either. There are way too many loose lips around here and people looking to get money or fame out of these dragons."

"Agreed, but if they find out, we'll be in a whole new world of trouble."

Jack snorted. "Like that's anything new."

The door to the morgue opened and Larry appeared. "Oh, Dr. Jackson. Didn't know you were joining us."

"Just checking in on my baby mama."

Kamala groaned. "I will pinch you so hard if you call me that again."

Jack waggled his eyebrows. "Promise?"

She glared at him. Jack scooped up the lab report and peeled off his gloves and mask. "No, I was just on my way out. Calloway's closing in on the dragon they're tracking, so I'm gonna head back over there for an update. I'll call you guys once they make it there."

"Alright, thanks. Oh, uh, Dr. Anjali, you might want to be careful with the mandible there."

Kamala glanced up at Jack, who stood behind Larry. Even with half her face covered with a mask, he knew that expression. Jack bit his lip to keep from laughing and mouthed. "You got this" before leaving the morgue.


Faye awoke to Winston's gravelly voice humming

148

show tunes.

She found herself surprised to be waking up at all. She thought she'd be too anxious to sleep. Yesterday, they'd taken an afternoon two-and-a-half hour flight out of Tampa to Washington National Airport. She'd been worried passing through the security checkpoint with her fake I.D., but whatever the hell it was made of had been legit and no one questioned her. After they landed, they caught an Uber to a cheap hotel where Winston paid cash for a three-day stay-- which he assured her was just in case--in a room with two Queen-sized beds. They split a pizza he ordered from across the street and he told her he'd wake her in the morning. She'd told him there was no way in hell she'd be able to sleep in the same room as the man who had tried to kill her, but Winston had simply smiled and promised her she'd be surprised that she could.

The blonde rubbed her eyes and rolled over to see Winston standing in front of his bed, already neatly made, its surface crowded with what appeared to be parts of a disassembled handgun. He picked up items one by one and cleaned them in slow, careful movements. He wore a pair of plain blue coveralls with a sewn-in company logo on the lapel. Odd choice, she thought.

"Morning, Blondie," Winston said without glancing up. "Sleep well?"

"No," she said groggily. "Because someone woke me up with their tone deaf humming. Didn't figure you for a Hamilton fan, Winston."

"I'm not made of stone. Helluva musical." He nodded to the package sitting on the table beside an old lamp. "Courier dropped that off a little while ago. It's the dragon tracker the feds wanted you to fix."

Faye tossed the covers back and shuffled over to it, popping the box open. "Just like them to seize something they have no idea how to operate."

"Pretty much. Hungry?"

"Not yet." Faye turned the tracker over in her hands.

149

"Got any tools?"

"Not here. We're gonna hit one of my safe houses shortly. Got some tools there. Your phone chimed a few times. I'm guessing S.O. numbers one and two want you to check in."

Faye narrowed her eyes at him and strode over to the nightstand, checking her phone. Nothing appeared out of the ordinary. "Do you want to check it before I send it?"

"Nah," Winston said. "I trust ya."

Faye scowled and read the texts from their three-person group chat. She nearly smiled as she answered them. It wasn't hard to pretend everything was totally fine in text form. She'd be in trouble once they called her. Faye could convincingly lie to pretty much anyone except Jack and Kamala.

She tossed the phone down. "So what's on the agenda for today?"

"Recon," Winston said. "follow the breadcrumbs to figure out where our hitter is."

"Where do we start?"

"First off, the site where your friends are. If the hitter's camped out to see when they leave, then we have an opportunity to intercept."

"Why'd you pick this place, by the way?" she asked as she went over to her duffel bag. She found a pair of coveralls that matched Winston's, neatly folded on top. "I'm surprised it's not like *John Wick* where you all congregate in one giant fancy hotel and pay with rare currency."

Winston chuckled as he began putting the handgun back together now that it was clean and oiled. "Well, such places exist, but definitely not in D.C. New York is a lot friendlier for hitmen, but D.C. has its share of problems so they're not easy to come by."

Faye stared. "I was just kidding, but good to know. How would you be able to tell if the hitter who took the contract is in town?"

"Looking for familiar faces. Not everyone does the

cosmetic surgery that I do. They find it too tedious, so they're just careful to avoid identification. However, the pool of hitmen isn't that huge in the U.S. You tend to see the same folks over time."

"How many hitters are there in the country?"

"At any given time? Dunno. Depends on your definition. From a business standpoint, it's easier to just hire some desperate mook to do the dirty work if it's just a basic hit with no mob ties or complicated organization behind it. If you're smart, the mook does the job, however neat or sloppy, and if they are caught, they can't rat you out because they don't know anything. Your client pays you and you give the mook a percentage for his trouble and keep the rest. Career hitters like me who do the job directly aren't numerous. By my estimation, there are less than fifty of them here. The world's a big place. If you want in on this job, you travel constantly so no one recognizes you aside from maybe other hitters and the industries who supply us what we need for a price."

"With that in mind, what if the hitter recognizes you first?"

"That's where you come in. I don't usually travel with a partner. It should help keep them off my scent."

"And what about their employer? Won't they just hand the contract off to a new hitter if we manage to stop this one?"

"Depends on their time table. Sometimes when a job goes south, they regroup and find a new way to accomplish their goal. Plus, word gets around. If a hitter dies on a job, most of the others take a wide berth around it. Particularly if the hitter was legit and not just some newbie kid, who didn't know the ropes. If we do this right, there is a good chance, they'll lay off your friends and figure out another way to fix their little problem. If I can manage it, we'll take this thing to the source and make them shut it down."

Faye crossed her arms. "And then we settle our account once and for all?"

Winston smiled. "Yes ma'am."

He popped the magazine inside the gun with a smooth, practiced movement. She didn't flinch as she heard the heavy, sharp click. Now that it had been assembled, she recognized the make and model, a Kimber Pro Carry II. "How are you able to talk in spite of how full of shit you are?"

"Talent, my love," he said with a grin. "Miles and miles of talent. Get dressed."

Faye grumbled insults under her breath and stomped into the bathroom with her clothes.

After she showered and donned her disguise, he offered her the Kimber he'd been cleaning. She didn't take it. "You'd trust me with that after I made my intentions clear yesterday?"

"You have the right to protect yourself," he said. "If something happens to me, you get clear by any means necessary."

"Is it loaded this time?"

"Yep. Carries nine rounds at a time. Don't forget that."

She snatched the gun and pointed it at his forehead. "So what if I hold you hostage and call the cops to come get your sorry ass?"

"Then your friends die and it's on your hands." He lifted a finger and pushed the barrel away from his head. "And let's be real here, Faye. You know I can take that gun away from you any damn time I want. This will go a lot easier without all the posturing."

"Try it," she whispered. "I dare you."

"Temper, temper, Blondie. Maybe later." He handed her an underarm harness for the gun. "Come on. We've got work to do."

To her surprise, Winston didn't take her to a rooftop somewhere nearby the government facility like she'd seen in spy flicks. Instead, he led her to a windowless van with a decal that proclaimed them plumbers. The back of the van had two desks built in with a network of monitors patched into various exits and entrances to the facility.

"How the hell did you manage all this?" she asked as she sat down, her eyes wide as she noticed just how many cameras he had set up.

"Fake I.D. can work wonders," he said. "So can making phone calls pretending to be someone else. I set these up about two hours ago."

She tried not to frown at the fact that she hadn't heard him leave their hotel room. It was definitely a missed opportunity to get in contact with Carmichael and Houston. She'd have to be more mindful next time. He always seemed a step ahead of her. "Don't they check for this sort of thing on a regular basis?"

"They do," Winston said, as he sat at the desk opposite her. "I just know all their blind spots. From what I can tell, your friends are already inside. I didn't see the fella who recruited them or their handler Agent Shannon, so my guess is they're out in the field. See if you can get that tracker up and running. For now, we're going to see if we can spot the hitter in the area."

"How long will that take?"

Winston shrugged. "Matter of hours. If we don't spot them by the time the little doc has to head home, we'll keep an eye on her rather than your boyfriend. She's the weaker link of the two. Easier to spot in a crowd."

"Is that what you'd do if you were the hitter?"

He sipped his coffee. "Yup."

Faye resisted the urge to draw her gun on him again. "Fine. Hand me the toolkit."

He passed it over to her. They'd stopped at a storage facility on the way here. She'd noted the address and the storage unit for future reference, but she had a hunch it would be empty by the time she could get a message out to the detectives. It had a ton of his gear, from firearms to surveillance equipment to fake IDs and passports. Everything a traveling killer needed to survive.

She'd been working on fixing the tracker for two solid

hours before Winston spoke again.

"Bingo."

Faye swiveled in her chair. "What is it?"

"Hitter has a spotter," Winston said, pointing to one of the screens to his right. Faye leaned over his shoulder and examined the tall, thin man in an overcoat who leaned against the wall outside of a coffee shop adjacent to the facility.

"How do you know it's a spotter and not the hitter?"

"No hardware on him," Winston said. "Hitters are always armed, even if they're not intending to engage at the time. He's been out here too long to be on a lunch break and he's checking out license plates on vehicles that are leaving the facility."

"So what do we do?"

Winston rubbed his chin. "I'll have a conversation with him, get him to tell me who he works for and then send him on his way. Spotters are usually just low-level thugs who need an extra buck and they don't really have any loyalties. You use them and throw them away. They often don't know enough to get you into much trouble if a cop catches onto them."

"It's broad daylight. You can't exactly just waltz up to him and hold him at gunpoint."

"No need. You catch more flies with honey than vinegar." Winston nudged the suitcase he'd brought with him from the storage unit. "That's what this is for. If I double what the hitter paid him, odds are his tongue will start wagging."

"What if he tips the hitter off that you sent him away?"

"Wouldn't be a smart move. Hitter will get suspicious and he'd be a loose end to tie off once the job is done. If he just ghosts on the hitter, he'll survive."

"Bribery," she said, shaking her head. "We're just stacking up the crimes, aren't we?"

Winston stood and grabbed his coat. "Hey, this is one

of the nicer parts of my job."

He knelt and unlocked the case, drawing a fat stack of hundreds and counting out a smaller stack that he stuffed into an envelope. "On the off chance this guy's actually loyal, we might have to get a little messier. If he doesn't flip on the hitter, we have to keep him quiet. I don't want you getting your hands too dirty, but just be ready to act. Trust your instincts."

"My instincts say I should shoot you."

"Trust your other instincts." He opened the door to the back of the van and hopped out first, offering his hand. She glared and climbed down by herself.

They crossed the street and made their way towards the spotter. As they neared, Faye could see him better; dirty blond hair, amber eyes, five o'clock shadow. His fingertips were yellowed from heavy cigarette use. He didn't look particularly muscular or threatening, but the air around him seemed dismal, as if he threw off an aura of "don't mess with me."

Winston took the lead once they were within earshot and offered the man a broad grin. "Morning. Nice weather we're having, huh?"

The man stared unblinking at him and just grunted. "Well, I've got a proposition for you, if you're interested."

"Don't swing that way, man."

"Funny. Not that kind of proposition, friend. Mind if we step somewhere in private to discuss it?"

"What if I do mind?"

Winston shrugged. "I might have ten thousand reasons for you to reconsider."

The man eyed him, then her, and nodded once. "I'll hear you out."

They walked back to the van and went inside. The man took Winston's seat while the two of them remained standing. He glanced at Faye again and smirked. "So what's with Velma here? Is she your intern?"

"I'm the muscle," Faye said with a straight face.

The man snorted. "You haven't got a single muscle on you, girlie."

Faye offered him a pointy smile. "Keep talking and I'll prove you wrong."

"Play nice," Winston chided her before returning his attention to the man. "You're a spotter. That much I know. What I need to know is who you're working for. Ten grand if you tell me and another five if you keep your mouth shut about our conversation and skip town. Keep in mind I don't like tattletales, so don't try for a double cross or you'll regret it. Easy money. What d'you say?"

The man sat there for a bit, seeming to mull it over. "I'd say you're shorter than I thought you'd be."

Winston frowned. "Excuse me?"

The man grinned. "She saw you coming from a mile away, dude."

The hitman stiffened. "Bullshit."

"No. Real shit. She paid me thirty grand, upfront, and she said you'd be coming."

"Shit!" Winston growled, turning away and running a hand through his hair. "Of course it's her. Like I don't have enough problems right now."

Faye tilted her head, keeping her voice low. "What's going on?"

"This just got a hundred times more complicated, is what," Winston said before turning back to the man. "So why'd you tell me instead of just taking the money and leaving before I found out it's her pulling your strings?"

The man stood and dusted off his knees. "She wanted you to know that she knows you're here. And because your reputation precedes you, Winston. You're a man of your word. Money's only good if I'm alive to spend it. I'd have to be pretty damn stupid to steal from a hitman."

"You're smarter than you look, then. I take it she's got eyes on us already?"

The man made a finger gun at him and pulled the trigger. Winston muttered another curse and shoved the

156

door to the van open. "Beat it."

The spotter winked at Faye before exiting the van. Winston shut it and Faye whirled on him.

"Okay, so what the hell's going on?"

Winston gestured towards the chair. "Sit. We need to relocate and ditch this van for something else. I'll explain later."

"You'll explain right now or I'm gonna shoot you."

He gave her an exasperated look. "No, you won't."

"Try me."

He rolled his eyes. "Our cover's blown. She was waiting for us the whole time."

"She who?"

"Stella. My ex-wife."

"...I'm sorry, *what?*"


"Closing in on the compound," Agent Shannon said as quietly as possible. It wasn't easy. He could hear the low growling hiss slithering out of the throat of the dragon standing several feet away, hidden in the brush. She hadn't taken her yellow eyes off him since he'd appeared. He felt her glare like razor wire raking down his skin. Calloway stood to her left, one gloved hand on the dragon's neck, the other holding a pair of binoculars.

The building had once been a Home Depot, if the lingering orange paint on the roof was any indication. The empty parking lot had grass poking out between the cracks in the concrete and an overturned cart that had been turned into a nest, perhaps for rodents of some kind. It was in a bad part of town on a long stretch of road in the backwoods, hence why the retail store hadn't survived in the long run. It sat on a couple acres of land as well, so it had no immediate neighbors and no houses across from it that would notice anything.

The only thing out of the ordinary was the semi-tractor-trailer parked at the loading dock behind the building.

"Four men," Calloway said.

"They armed?" Agent Shannon asked as he opened his equipment bag.

"Looks like handguns mostly."

"Right. Tether the dragon, will ya? Don't want her breathing down my neck while we get ready."

"Give her a break already," Jack said over the comm-link. "If she hasn't spat venom into your eyeballs by now, you're safe."

"You'd like that, wouldn't you?"

"I'd take a picture and get it blown up to a 24 x 36 print, then frame it on my wall."

"Guys," Calloway said as he set the binoculars aside. "Cool it. I know we're all a bit tense about catching these clowns, but we need to keep focused. Where are we at with SWAT?"

Shannon checked his phone. "ETA twenty minutes. They were running short on staff this morning. We'll maintain surveillance until they arrive—"

Before he could finish that sentence, the tractor-trailer rattled as a roar bellowed from inside it.

Two of the men came running down the ramp, shouting something at the ones standing at the top of the loading dock. Seconds later, a Highlander dragon came barreling out of the truck bed at full speed. One man had already begun sprinting across the empty parking lot; the other hastily climbed onto the loading dock and screamed for them to close themselves inside the garage. Unfortunately, the other two men got there first and locked the door on him. The dragon flapped its wings and landed on the loading dock. Its long, spiny tail lashed behind it as it crept towards the man, who drew a .9 mm Beretta and took aim at the dragon.

He fired. Both shots ricocheted. One hit the wall. The other hit his right thigh.

"Shit!" Calloway hissed, grabbing his helmet.

"Shannon, we gotta go!"

"Goddammit," Shannon complained. "I'll get the net launcher ready. You go."

"What's going on?" Kamala demanded.

"Highlander dragon's loose," Calloway said as he raced down the grassy hill towards the loading dock. "The crew bailed. He's got a guy pinned. I'm gonna intercept."

The man tried to crawl away from the dragon, his injured leg trailing blood in a long smear on the concrete. The dragon clamped its jaws down on his ankle and dragged him back. The man shrieked and kicked at it with his other leg in vain.

"Highlander dragons react to loud noises," Kamala said. "See if you can distract it."

"Hey, Lake Placid, over here!" Calloway shouted.

The dragon dropped the man's ankle and snapped its head in Calloway's direction. The man tried to wriggle out of range, but the dragon hissed and he curled into the fetal position to make himself a smaller target.

"What else ya got?" Calloway asked.

"Eyes," Jack said. "Got anything that can blind it?"

"Yeah, a flashbang." Calloway addressed the man. "Cover your eyes!"

He pulled the pin and flung it towards the dragon. The flash grenade bounced once, twice, and then ignited. The entire parking lot flashed with blinding white light for an instant.

The dragon roared in pain and backed away from Calloway, its head whipping to and fro in panic. Its deadly tail slashed at the air around it in erratic swipes, trying to hit something, anything, now that its vision had gone out.

"Calloway!" Agent Shannon barked as he approached with the net launcher in his hands. It was about the size of an automatic rifle with a wide, open barrel. He planted his feet and aimed as his partner moved over to one side.

Just before he could pull the trigger, the door to the abandoned building flung open and the dragon smugglers

159

opened fire.

Agent Shannon cursed and raced for the other corner of the building for cover. Calloway followed him and narrowly escaped the men's gunfire.

"This is going great so far," Calloway said, flattening himself against the brick as the shots continued tearing holes in the wall.

Agent Shannon handed him the net launcher and drew his gun, waiting for a pause in the gunfire. "I'll try and take them out. If I can't manage it, I'll see if I can lead them away from the dragon."

"Any chance you guys can request a chopper?" Jack asked.

"Wouldn't do us much good. There isn't one close enough to make a difference. We're on our own for now."

"I've contacted the incoming SWAT team," Libby said. "They're hauling ass now, but they're still ten minutes out even with their sirens going to cut through traffic. Be careful."

"No worries, little bit," Calloway said. "We got this. If we can manage to trap it, how the hell am I going to sedate it with scales that thick?"

"Underneath the jaw is a soft spot," Kamala said. "Inject it there."

"Gotcha." He glanced at Agent Shannon as they heard the telltale clicks of the smugglers' guns going empty. "Ready?"

Shannon nodded. "Follow my lead."

He gauntleted the Beretta in his fist and whipped around the corner, firing twice. One of the men cried out and hit the ground with a shot to the leg and another in the shoulder. The other one took cover behind the tractor-trailer. The first injured man had managed to wedge himself in a corner away from the snarling, blinded dragon.

"Listen up," Shannon said as he pressed up against the other side of the tractor-trailer. "I'm a federal agent. Lower your weapon and come out from around the truck with your hands up. I am authorized to use lethal force if you do not cooperate. If you fire on me or my partner, you will be shot."

"Federal agent, huh?" the remaining smuggler said, his voice heavy with a New York accent. "Killing you oughta make my rep forever, then."

"You sure you wanna go down this road, son?"

"Hell yeah."

The tires behind Shannon's legs abruptly punctured and deflated as the man ducked and tried to sneak a shot. Shannon knelt and held still as the truck groaned under the weight of the trailer as it shifted to one side. The smuggler closed in on him, all but emptying the clip in hopes of hitting him through the tire. A bullet grazed Shannon's shoulder, but he didn't budge.

Just as the smuggler got close enough for a point blank shot, Agent Shannon grabbed the man's wrist and jerked his arms up. He fired a single shot into the man's temple. Blood splattered against the side of the tractor-trailer and the man crumpled to the concrete.

Agent Shannon kicked the gun away from his twitching fingers just to be safe. "Clear."

Calloway rounded the corner with the net launcher as Shannon went to subdue the other smuggler with the two gunshot wounds. The dragon still couldn't see, but he could tell it knew where he was, based on scent and sound. It charged him each time he tried to get a clean shot, snapping its jaws or flicking its tail in his direction, missing him by a few inches. Calloway finally got just far enough away to fire, but then the dragon spread its wings and vaulted into the air.

"Son of a bitch," Calloway whispered. "This just went from bad to worse."

# CHAPTER EIGHT
## BAGGAGE

Calloway sprinted his way back up the hill to Pete. The dragon had seen its kin launch up into the cloudy sky moments before and had pulled the tether taut as she strained herself trying to go after it. He unhooked the tether and threw one leg over the saddle. "Let's go!"

He placed his hands on the panels connected to her pressure switches. Pete flapped her great wings and took off after the runaway Highlander dragon.

"Christ," Jack hissed as Calloway's helmet camera calculated the distance the Highlander dragon had already put between them. "How many freaking feet per second is that? It's already got a lead on you guys."

"It's panicking," Kamala said. "Fight or flight response. He's not as large as Pete and he doesn't have the added weight of a passenger."

"Shit," Calloway said as he read the altitude they'd reached. "From this high up, he'll die from the fall if I hit him with the net. Not sure Pete would be able to take the weight if we try to catch him."

"Check your pack," Libby said. "There's another net with a line attached. Then at least you can lower him to the ground."

"Atta girl." Calloway lurched to one side and reached into one of the large pouches over Pete's rear leg. "Steady, Pete."

He leaned the net launcher on one broad shoulder and took out the first net bundle. He fed the line through the launcher and secured it, taking aim at the fleeing creature.

That was when the helicopter loomed into view.

Calloway lowered the launcher. "*Fuck* me."

He slammed his hands down onto Pete's back and the dragon dove sharply down to avoid the helicopter as it roared past them.

"What the hell?" Libby screeched. "Where did that thing come from?"

"No clue," Calloway panted out, glancing over his shoulder. "But that ain't no coincidence. It's turning around."

"You've got to be kidding me," Jack was livid. "Cops?"

"No," Shannon said. "They couldn't scramble a chopper in time. Best guess is the smuggler that ran away called in a favor. As much as I hate to say it, we're out of options. Abort mission."

"What?" Calloway demanded. "I'm dead on this thing's tail, man. I can shake these clowns."

"Like hell you can," Shannon snarled. "We didn't hire you to be in a firefight, kid. I am ordering you to land that dragon."

"Why? So these assholes can catch it and put it right back in a goddamn death match?"

"You can't fight a chopper with a dragon. Land. *Now.*"

"I don't have to fight the chopper. Just the dudes flying it."

"Last warning, Calloway. Land the dragon or you and your sister are both fired."

Calloway fell silent for a moment. "Libby?"

His sister's voice didn't waver. "Kick their asses, bro."

Calloway grinned and shifted his hands in concentric circles on the controls. Pete banked around to face the chopper. He spotted the pilot and one passenger. The passenger hung to one side, dangling by a thick strap, aiming an assault rifle in their direction. Pete snarled in open challenge as the passenger opened fire.

The dragon pulled her wings in close to her body and went into a spiral. Bullets whizzed past the duo on all sides, never touching them. She snapped her jaws at the man on the first pass, but missed by inches. Calloway turned them around and aimed for the rear of the helicopter. Pete seemed to understand on intuition alone; she slammed her hind legs at the tail. Her wickedly sharp claws dug furrows into the metal and tore a chunk of something metallic and electronic out. The helicopter lurched into a tailspin and dropped several dozen feet below them, disappearing under cloud cover.

"Nice shot!" Jack, Kamala, and Libby all cheered.

"Atta girl," Calloway said, patting the dragon's neck. "Let's go!"

He guided her after the vague blob on the sun-drenched horizon. The Highlander dragon had been wheeling about in random, erratic directions before, but now its flight patterns had stabilized. Once they got within shooting range, the Highlander dragon whipped its head around and growled. It banked and headed straight for them, its deadly jaws aiming at Pete's throat. She evaded the first bite and ducked as the Highlander dragon's tail took a swipe at her belly.

Calloway molded himself against her back and narrowly avoided a swipe from the dragon's claws. Instead of turning again, he had Pete pull straight up and then he turned in the saddle, aiming the launcher at the Highlander dragon. Just as it reached up to bite Pete's tail, he fired.

The net deployed and wrapped around the creature. It tightened immediately once it made contact with the dragon and it dropped out of the sky like an anchor in a Looney Tunes cartoon.

And so did Calloway and Pete.

"Holy shit!" Calloway almost flew off the saddle completely as the dragon's weight yanked them out of their skyward climb and sent them plunging towards the ground.

"You've got to even out," Kamala said urgently. "She can't take the whole weight of it."

"I'm trying!" Calloway attempted to haul himself onto the saddle with just his legs as they spun closer and closer to the grass below.

"Don't try to catch the dragon," Jack said. "Pete's not strong enough. Glide! Now!"

Grunting with effort, Calloway wrenched one hand

164

away from the launcher and spread his fingers out over the panel to Pete's controls. The dragon spread her yellow wings out all the way this time, and they went from a free fall into a hard, sharp arc towards the ground. The Highlander dragon hit the ground first, rolling, but not at lethal velocity. Pete reversed the direction of her wings to compensate and they jerked to an unsteady, but safe halt next to the wriggling captured dragon.

"Yes!" The lab crew cheered.

Calloway slumped forward on the dragon's neck and caught his breath. "I owe you a few dozen buckets of fish, lady."

He reached down and patted her snout before dismounting and grabbing the tranquilizer gun. He eased over to the struggling dragon and carefully rolled it onto its back, keeping clear of its tail. "Easy, fella. It's all over."

He found a small circular scale at the edge of the dragon's jaw and inserted the syringe near a crack between the scales. The dragon stopped thrashing after a moment or two and settled into a deep sleep in the meadow.

"He's out. Sending coordinates for pick up. It's been nice working with you, folks. Looks like you'll be on your own from here on out."

"The pleasure's been all ours, Calloway," Jack said. "Helluva job, man. Sorry it turned out this way."

Calloway glanced over at the dragon curiously pawing the daisies at her feet and smiled.

"It was worth it."


"You were *married?*"

Winston arched an eyebrow. "Is it really that hard to believe, Blondie?"

"You..." She pointed at him, then herself, then couldn't seem to form words for a second. "You *kill* people for a living. How the hell were you ever *married?*"

"I'll have you know I'm quite the romantic. More than

165

she ever was, if I'm being honest." He brushed past her and climbed into the front seat. The old van sputtered to life and pulled into the street. Faye stumbled into the passenger's seat and kept staring at him with her mouth open. "But--you--and the killing--and she--what the *hell*--"

"Breathe. I can't answer questions if you're not making sense, you know."

Faye finally just pressed her fingertips to her temples and took several deep breaths to clear her thoughts. "How? When? Why?"

Winston heaved a sigh. "I was younger. Met Stella in Atlantic City on an assignment. We were both after the same guy. Double bookings don't happen often, but this one schmuck had pissed off two different outfits and they both wanted him dead to set an example. We made a move on the target and instead found each other. We hit it off. Simple enough."

"So *Mr. and Mrs. Smith* but without the secrecy?"

"Guess you could say that," Winston said with a chuckle. "We dated. Got married. Then about three years in, Stella said she wanted to put down roots in New York."

"Roots?"

"Like I told you, if you're a career hitter, you never stay in one town. Always stay mobile. It's how you keep from being caught. Stella got an offer to be a personal hitter for the Harlem outfit at the time and she wanted to say yes, but only if I agreed to move to New York with her. I told her no, that it was too dangerous, and there was too much competition in New York. We got a divorce and I agreed not to work New York out of respect for her and she promised not to ever see me again."

"So why break the truce? Why come after this assignment specifically?"

Winston fell silent for a while. Faye noticed an almost imperceptible wince around his eyes. "This would've been our ten year anniversary if we were still married."

Faye shut her eyes for a second. "Son of a bitch. So,

instead of getting you something tin or aluminum, she took your assignment just to screw with you. Great. She sounds like a darling woman."

"That she is."

Faye scowled at him. "If I find out we look anything alike, I'm gonna shoot you."

"I'm not looking for a second wife, Blondie, relax. You're not my type."

Faye crossed her arms and sank down into the old velvet chair, muttering. "I'm everyone's goddamn type" under her breath before buckling her seatbelt. "If she's just doing this to get back at you, what can we do to stop her?"

"Well, she's a diva, for one thing. I know her habits. Instead of guessing what a normal hitter would do, we're going to scratch that and narrow down to what Stella would do."

"But isn't that a double edged sword? She knows that you know that she knows. She'll just do the same thing to you."

"Yeah, and that's where you come in. Stella doesn't know you. She knows me. She won't be looking for you."

"The spotter saw me."

"The spotter saw you in your disguise," he corrected. "We'll ditch this one and get you in another one. Stella might have eyes on us now, but we can lose her. I'll just have to take myself out of the spotlight, so to speak."

They drove in silence for a while before Faye asked the heavy question. "Is she going to try to kill you?"

"We were married, Faye."

The blonde breathed out through her nose, her voice soft. "Dammit."

"Don't get your panties in a bunch," Winston said. "I ain't easy to kill. You'll still get your shot."

"I don't want you dead, you son of a bitch. I want you rotting in a jail cell until Doomsday. So between now and then, tell me everything I need to know about Stella so we can keep you alive."

He offered her a perfunctory smile. "Aw, you really do care about me, Blondie."

"Don't make me shoot you."

"How about another compromise, then? I'll tell you about Stella if you tell me about what went down that got you into this polyamory thing."

Faye leaned her head back and suppressed a groan. "You are so goddamn nosy."

"What can I say? I ship it."

Faye strangled a laugh in her throat. "Fine. What do you want to know?"

"Did you and the beanpole sleep together when you were dating for that month?"

Faye's cheeks flushed. "Not exactly."

*"You've gotten better," Jack said, sucking in quick breaths as he ducked under the combination of punches Faye threw at his head. "You're actually a legitimate threat to my person. Well, more than usual, anyway."*

*"Thanks," she said brightly. "Does that mean you'll let me break your nose?"*

*Jack batted her punching glove to one side in a parry. "Sorry. I can't pull off the Owen Wilson look."*

*"Aw, I think you'd look rugged." She tried to catch him with a left hook his time. "Manly, even."*

*"Kam did say you like tough guys. Didn't know she meant that literally."*

*Faye's smile wilted at the edges. Jack winced. "Sorry."*

*"It's okay," she insisted, rolling her shoulders. "Shouldn't keep walking on eggshells about her anyway. Not healthy, from what my therapist says."*

*Jack lowered his hands. "How's that going so far?"*

*"I hate it," she admitted. "God, I hate it. Who the hell wants to spend an hour talking about their goddamn feelings?"*

*"Uh, normal human beings, Ice Queen."*

*She scowled. "Normal is overrated."*

*"Maybe so, but recovering after what you went through requires that you occasionally talk about your feelings, you know.*

168

The memories can't just sit there burning a hole through your brain and dripping acid down into your heart."

"Visceral, but not inaccurate." Faye stretched her arms. "I think my therapist hates me."

"Male or female?"

She narrowed her eyes at him. "Why does that matter?"

Jack just stared at her pointedly. She hit him in the ribs. "Ow. Low blow, Faye."

"Female, if you must know," she sniffed.

"Well, that means you're out of your comfort zone this time," Jack wheezed. "Most men you can have wrapped around your pinky in about five minutes. Women are harder for you to crack."

"Tell me about it," she grumbled, sinking into her defensive stance. Jack started throwing combination punches for her to dodge, block, or counter. "She says I'm not in denial, but I'm not dealing with what happened either. I'm in Purgatory, so to speak. Neither heaven nor hell."

"What do you plan to do about it?"

"Dunno. Still don't see how spilling my guts to a stranger is going to help."

"It's because you see that as a weakness. It isn't. Think of it this way, when you're throwing these punches at me, you're releasing kinetic energy, right?"

"Yeah."

"That's therapy. Instead of kinetic energy, it's...personal energy. You have all that anger and fear and whatever else you're feeling bottled up inside and therapy helps you release it one session at a time so you don't explode."

Faye eyed him. "I've...never heard anyone explain it that way before."

Jack shrugged. "It's the way that made the most sense to me. Hiding from yourself isn't going to do you any good. Pretending to be alright so you can get through doesn't either. I would know."

"That bad, huh?"

"Worse," he admitted. "Kam told her parents about the

169

baby. She's not letting me in right now. Doesn't want to talk about it. I only see her at work and it's killing me."

Faye hesitated. "Do you...know if you're ready to make a choice yet?"

"No," he whispered. "I'm still pretty torn, to be honest."

"I'm sorry."

He smiled. "Don't be. I like being with you. And that's the truth. I promise."

She smiled back, but he saw something awfully leonine in it this time. "Really?"

Faye hooked her leg behind his ankle and yanked hard. Jack toppled over backwards onto the mat he'd placed in the middle of the den with an oof! Faye pounced and landed on top of him, the feline smile melting into a simmering smirk that made Jack's blood race southward all at once.

"Couldn't tell on my end," she said, nonchalantly unstrapping her gloves as she straddled him. "I mean, we've been hanging out for, what? Almost a month now? Are you going to make a move on me or should I just go join a nunnery?"

Jack adopted a disarming look as he popped off his own boxing gloves. "You do realize it took me over a year to 'make a move' on Kamala, and I'm in love with her. Hell, you had to tell me to do it in the first place."

"Exactly," she said tartly. "You should have learned better by now."

Jack flipped her over easily and pinned her wrists, grinning down at the genuine surprise on her face. "Who says I didn't?"

He kissed her. Faye sighed into his mouth, mumbling something that sounded like. "damn you" and slipped her tongue past his lips. She looped her long legs around his hips and pulled him down to her, swallowing the groan he released upon the contact of their lower bodies. She twisted her hands free and ran them up his back beneath the shirt. She raked her nails over his spine and made a path towards his shorts, but he broke the kiss before she got there.

"Easy," she murmured, noticing how hard and fast he'd started breathing. "Easy, big guy. What's wrong?"

170

"Sorry," he said. "It's...been a while."

Faye read his expression. "And you still feel like you're cheating on Kam."

Jack winced. "Faye, I...it's not that I don't want to."

She almost smiled then. "Yeah, don't worry; I got that memo."

She snapped the band of his shorts against his narrow hips with one finger and he blushed. "I just...I'm worried sex is going to make it harder to know what I want in the long run. I imagine it had to be that way for you when you and Kam hooked up."

"It didn't get that far," she said. "Second base. We sort of just laughed it off the next morning, but I never got over it. I was too scared to ask her if she felt the same way."

"You should tell her, Faye."

"Things are screwed up enough. I can't. I shouldn't."

"Not knowing is worse than her saying no," he said gently. "I promise you it is. You'll spend the rest of your life wondering what could have been. At least if you tell her, then you can heal from it if she says no. For all you know, she was too scared to tell you if she reciprocated."

"Jack--"

"Faye, she won't abandon you. Neither will I. I'll be there with you if you need me to be."

Her breath caught. "You...would?"

"Of course I would."

Her eyes stung. She hated that. Why the hell was he the only guy she'd ever met who somehow knew what to say at just the right moment?

Faye cleared the lump out of her throat. "Fine, so we're on a sex embargo until I get up the nerve to talk to her. Can we at least compromise on second base?"

Jack pretended to think about it. "A beautiful blonde begging me to feel her up...gee, I just don't know what to say to that."

Faye rolled her eyes as she tugged him back down to her lips. "Jackass."

"Yeah, but I'm your jackass."

*She grinned up at him before kissing him again. "I guess you are."*

"You told me what went down after she found out," Winston said. "So what'd you do then?"

"She and I made a date to see if the mutual attraction was still intact."

"How did that go?"

Faye gave him her best Poker face. "Tit for tat, Winston. I showed you my tat, so show me your tit."

He rumbled with a short laugh. "Fine. I'll give the skinny on Stella. She's a bit old school. Big fan of revolvers, for instance, instead of automatic weapons. She likes to be seen, which you'd think is counterproductive for a hitter, but she uses it avert expectations. Came from a broken home, so she started right out of the gate with a chip on her shoulder. Orphan. Mother died of an overdose at birth, never found out who the daddy was. She's a survivor first and foremost. Everything comes second to that. After she got passed around in the foster care system, she swore she'd never let anyone control her life again. She didn't want to become a prostitute, so she made a name for herself taking on contracts. She's good."

"Better than you?"

Winston shrugged a shoulder. "Depends on who you ask."

"I'm asking you," Faye pressed, narrowing her eyes.

He didn't say anything for a while as they drove. "Let me say this, our strengths complimented each other when we were still together. I'm tough. Can take a lot of punishment, as you well know, and I can blend in to the point of near invisibility. Stella is creative. She can come at you sideways and you'll never know what hit you. She's a wild card. That's why she's survived this long."

Faye mulled over his words, his tone, the vacant expression on his face. "You still love her?"

"Don't have much of a heart, Blondie. Thought you knew that."

172

"You didn't answer my question."

He still wouldn't look at her. Finally, he answered. "No."

Faye examined his slightly weathered features, his posture, the steady way he drove while scanning their surroundings for danger. Everything about him from head to toe confirmed the simple word. And yet, something in Faye's gut knew there was more to the story. She would never assume that she knew him, but she'd managed to at least peel back one layer of the onion. Plenty more to go.

Winston parked the van inside a parking garage beside a '67 Impala, gathered their things, wiped the computers clean, and then they switched to the new vehicle. By now, she'd fiddled with the dragon tracker enough to coax it into working, and he'd agreed to let her drop it off to FedEx later to make it seem as if she'd sent it from Clearwater. Winston switched on a receiver that had been planted at the government site and they listened in to get caught up on current events.

"Alright," he said. "Deadline for the hit is four days. We're on Day One. If I were Stella, I'd be looking for a stoolie to figure out just what the plan is for their field agents so I could manipulate the odds in my favor to get Dr. Jackson and Dr. Anjali out in the open for the kill."

"Is it that easy to bribe someone working for Washington?"

"Easier to bribe politicians. Workers, not so much. They're under a microscope pretty much twenty-four seven, but not all of them. You aim for the people on the lower end of the spectrum janitors, lunch ladies, and administrative staff. People who are disgruntled and largely ignored. Plus, the government doesn't pay shit, so they're always needing extra cash."

"So you think Stella's already made contact with one of those kinds of people here?"

Winston nodded. "More than likely. We need a man inside."

"How do we get one?"

Winston offered her the kind of grin she felt a Great White shark would have. "By asking nicely."

"You're not fired."

Calloway and Libby pushed off from the wall outside of the conference room Agent Shannon had just exited, scowling hard enough to create a maze on his forehead.

"What?" Calloway asked.

"In light of your successful capture of the Highlander dragon, my superiors turned down my recommendation to fire the both of you," he continued, every word dripping with bitter disgruntlement. "consider today, strike one. There will not be a second or third. You do what I say when I say it or I won't give a damn what my superiors tell me, I'll escort you both off the premises. Do you understand me?"

"Loud and clear," Calloway said, though he was unable to keep the grin off his face, Libby high-fived him, as well as Jack and Kamala. Agent Shannon rolled his eyes so hard it was a wonder they didn't eject from his skull.

"In the meantime, you all have work to do. Libby, get back in the lab and sort through the footage. Comb through every single second and see if there's anything that can help us identify, whoever the hell, was in that chopper. Calloway, go write up your field report and have it on my desk in an hour. Dr. Jackson, you and Dr. Anjali will join Larry in the lab to see what you can learn about that Highlander dragon. I want results by lunchtime. Dismissed."

"Where are you going?" Jack asked.

"I have witnesses to interrogate." He turned on his heel and headed down the hallway alone.

"Why do I get the feeling he prefers the Jack Bauer approach to interrogations?" Jack wondered aloud.

"Wouldn't surprise me," Calloway said. "Thanks for your help back there, you guys. We couldn't have done this without you."

"You were outstanding," Kamala said. "It took courage to do what you did. I'm glad it worked out for you."

"For now," Calloway said, glancing in the direction Shannon had gone in. "Don't think he won't find a way to get even since I disobeyed a direct order. Guy can hold a grudge until the end times."

"Let him. You did the right thing. Come down to the lab as soon as you're done with the report. Hopefully, we'll get some good results right off the bat."

"Sounds good to me." He offered Kamala and Jack both a fist bump, gave his little sister a kiss on the cheek, and headed towards his office.

Jack and Kamala made their way towards the lab. "Any idea of what to expect?" Jack asked.

"Brahma knows," Kamala admitted. "With any luck, the dragon is still sedated."

He snorted. "When have we ever been lucky?"

"Point taken."

Just as Jack swiped his card and reached for the doorknob, they both heard a resounding thud as well as the clatter of something being knocked onto the tile. He sighed. "We really need to switch careers. Mind if I go in first?"

She smirked at him, her brown eyes sparkling. "Be my guest, Sir Gawain."

He scowled. "Hardy-har, baby mama."

She pinched his backside as he slipped inside the door and he yelped. Rubbing his butt and grumbling, Jack took brief stock of the state of the lab. There were two scientists in lab coats standing on either side of a large exam table, both trying desperately to pin down the wriggling, snarling Highlander dragon. Larry stood a few feet away, a bit pale, a tranquilizer gun in his hand. The Highlander dragon's tail had been heavily wrapped in cloth, but it thrashed violently as it tried to get free from the net still tangled around it. It had managed to swat nearby chairs over and by the exhausted, pained look on one of the scientist's face, it had landed a blow or two on them as well.

"So this is going well," Jack said over the dragon's furious growling. "Need some help?"

Larry cleared his throat and edged towards the exam table. "It's not as bad as it looks."

"Yes, it is," one of the scientists said.

Jack nodded to Kamala and she stepped inside all the way as well, letting the door slide shut behind her. Jack shrugged off his lab coat and folded the sleeves inward after he took the remaining items out of the pockets and handed them to Kamala. "Do you mind?"

Larry shrugged. "Have at it."

Jack walked towards the front of the exam table and wrapped the lab coat around the dragon's head completely, until only its snout poked out. He gestured to Kamala, who found a roll of electric tape in one of the cabinets, and then he taped the coat in place. Within a minute or so, the dragon quit flailing and went still with an annoyed, but subdued hiss.

The scientists cautiously let go of the creature. Its breathing gradually slowed and it twitched its tail a bit, but made no other violent movements.

"God rest your soul, Steve Irwin," Jack said. "You're still helping us from beyond the grave."

Larry leveled a confused look at him. "How'd you—"

"Highlander dragons have a common ancestor with alligators and crocodiles," he said. "Blinding them is sort of like hitting a reset button. Out of sight, out of mind."

"Wish you'd been here ten minutes ago," the male scientist said ruefully as he rubbed one side of his ribs. "This fella woke up while we were trying to administer another dose of sedative and basically went berserk."

"How long will you need him out for the initial analysis?" Kamala asked.

"Couple hours or so."

"Were you able to complete any initial tests regarding his metabolic rate?"

"What little we have is here," the female scientist said,

handing her a file folder. Kamala flipped through it and nodded. "Until we have something more in depth, I'd go with the dosage that Calloway used when the dragon was captured. Has it been fed yet?"

"No," Larry said.

"I'd do that beforehand so it has something in its system and isn't running on fumes. It also might have been acting out because it's simply hungry."

The female scientist nodded. "Diet?"

"I'd start with venison if possible. If you can't get that, fish should do the trick." The two scientists nodded and headed out of the lab.

"What else can you tell us about him?" Jack asked.

"He's definitely been used in the fights more than once," Larry said, grabbing a pointer from the chalkboard behind them and indicating different spots on the dragon's body. "He's got missing scales and scarring all over."

"Any sign of a tracker implant?"

"We won't know until the X-rays come back, but if he's anything like the others, yes, he'll have one."

"Is there any way to reverse engineer them?" Kamala asked.

Larry snorted. "This isn't like the movies, miss. That sort of thing doesn't work in real life."

"Doctor," Kamala said. "Not miss."

Larry cleared his throat. "Right. Sorry. The trackers we've collected are high grade, but they come from a third party tech company overseas. They've located the manufacturer, but so far there's no lead on who ordered them."

"Aren't you guys worried about the bad guys knowing where your site is with these trackers?" Jack asked.

"We always pass an EMP over the dragons before they're brought to the facility to deactivate them offsite. The ones we collect are always torn apart to make sure they're not active. We take security very seriously here."

He put the pointer aside. "To that end, have you

heard back from Ms. Worthington about the status of the dragon tracker?"

"Not yet," Jack said, checking his watch. "She should be up by now. I'll give her a call and see if she's made progress."

"Tell her she owes me baby names, by the way," Kamala added, to which Jack grinned.

"Will do, angel."

He went out into the hallway and dialed Faye's number as he paced. It rang for a bit, and then she answered, sounding a bit sleepy. "Hello?"

"Alas," Jack said wistfully. "The dulcet tones of my beloved. I've been without for too long, my lady."

Faye snorted. "How much coffee have you had this morning?"

"A fairly large amount. How's that tan coming along?"

"Beautifully. I'm like a bronze goddess."

Jack laughed. "Pics or it didn't happen."

She returned the laugh, albeit with more seduction in it. "Since when are you a fan of sexting? You told me you almost crashed the Mazda the only time I ever sent you one."

Jack blushed profusely. "Point taken. Glad you're having fun, though. You needed a break."

"That I did. So what's up, Stilts?"

"The good ole government is leaning on me to ask where you are with fixing the tracker, despite the fact that I told them you're on vacation."

"Actually, that's the good news. I need to run a couple more diagnostics just to be sure, but I think it's back in tip-top shape. I can FedEx it over to your hotel room sometime this afternoon."

"Thanks, Faye. Seriously. It's going to be a huge help. It'll take some of the strain off of relying on Pete to track."

"How's that going?"

"A lot better than I expected, knock on wood. We're about to run some tests on the dragon we captured

178

yesterday. Assuming your girlfriend doesn't tear Lackey Larry in half."

"She does have super strength now," Faye agreed. "It's kind of terrifying."

There was a pause and Jack heard a muffled voice, as if Faye had put her hand over the phone for a moment. "Babe, mind if I call you back later?"

He felt a tug of old insecurity in his gut, but forced himself to keep his voice the same. "Yeah, sure. Text me when you get the tracker in the mail, and don't forget that you owe Kam some baby names. Thanks again, gorgeous."

"Always, handsome. Give Kam and the baby a kiss from me. Bye." She hung up.

Jack frowned down at the phone for a moment. Something was off. He knew it in his gut. Her tone had switched from amiable to cautionary right before she'd hung up.

He glanced at the door to the lab and chewed his lower lip, debating if he should tell Kamala. He didn't want her to worry, but she had the uncanny ability to get through to Faye when he couldn't. Jack pocketed the phone and swiped his card to get back in.

"Hey," he said. "Faye's got the tracker working. She just needs to do a few initial double checks and she'll send it back sometime today."

"Good," Larry said. "Dr. Anjali and I were about to start the physical."

Kamala eyed her boyfriend as his mouth flew open. "If you sing one lyric of 'Let's Get Physical,' you're sleeping on the couch tonight."

Jack shut his mouth and then muttered. "Spoilsport."

He then nodded to one side and she followed him until they were out of Larry's earshot. "Do me a favor later and please call Faye around lunchtime. She sounded a little...I don't know. Tense."

Kamala frowned. "Like she's in trouble?"

"Don't think so. She'd tell us if she were. Just see if

179

you can get her to talk about whatever's bothering her. I'm a little worried, that's all."

Kamala squeezed his hand. "Try not to. She's tougher than both of us. She'll be alright."


"You're sure this bribe is going to work?" Faye asked as she trailed Winston back down the hallway towards their hotel room.

"Usually does," he said. "And you were very convincing."

"Still, though, should we be doing this now? Aren't you worried we'll miss something while we're here packing up?"

"Shouldn't take more than a few minutes, and we're close by. Trust me, you don't want Stella to find us first. We'd better switch hotels just to be safe."

"Since when are hitmen ever safe?"

"Heh. Point taken, Blondie."

She nearly jumped as her phone buzzed and belted out the bubblegum pop song "Let's Be Friends (So We Can Make Out)." Winston arched an eyebrow at her wordlessly.

"It's Jack," she said. "I haven't spoken to him since before I left. He might get suspicious if I don't answer."

Winston eyed her, but nodded before continuing down the hallway. "Go ahead."

She answered the call, doing her best to sound drowsy, since it was only a little after eight o'clock in the morning. "Hello?"

"Alas," Jack said wistfully. "The dulcet tones of my beloved. I've been without for too long, my lady."

Faye snorted. "How much coffee have you had this morning?"

"A fairly large amount. How's that tan coming along?"

"Beautifully. I'm like a bronze goddess."

Jack laughed. "Pics or it didn't happen."

She returned the laugh. It was surprisingly easy to slip into their usual banter despite the circumstances. "Since when are you a fan of sexting? You told me you almost crashed the Mazda the only time I ever sent you one."

She could practically hear the embarrassment in his voice. "Point taken. Glad you're having fun, though. You needed a break."

"That I did. So what's up, Stilts?"

"The good ole government is leaning on me to ask where you are with fixing the tracker, despite the fact that I told them you're on vacation."

"Actually, that's the good news. I need to run a couple more diagnostics just to be sure, but I think it's back in tip-top shape. I can FedEx it over to your hotel room sometime this afternoon."

"Thanks, Faye. Seriously. It's going to be a huge help. It'll take some of the strain off of relying on Pete to track."

"How's that going?"

"A lot better than I expected, knock on wood. We're about to run some tests on the dragon we captured yesterday. Assuming your girlfriend doesn't tear Lackey Larry in half."

"She does have super strength now," Faye agreed. "It's kind of terrifying."

The two reached their hotel room and Winston opened the door. He took about three steps into the room and stopped dead. Faye bumped into his broad back, confused. She put her hand over the mic and said. "What gives?"

Then she peeked around his shoulder.

There was a black woman sitting on the second Queen-sized bed closer to the far wall. She was voluptuous, but with evidence of firm muscles beneath the copious curves. Her hair was black except for the swoop over her eye, which had been colored with white, pink, and light blue streaks. Pinkish-silver eyeshadow glinted over each eyelid. She wore a burgundy leather jacket that was cinched and had her knee-high boot-clad legs crossed. Light from the mostly closed window glinted off her white-gold hoops in her ears.

And off the .44 Magnum in her right hand.

The woman smiled and dragged her gaze over Winston slowly before her lips parted and a resonant purring voice slithered out.

"Hello, Pooh Bear."

Winston spoke, but didn't move a muscle.

"Hello, Stella."

# CHAPTER NINE
## STRANGE LOVE

There was enough tension in the air to choke a blue whale.

Winston didn't say another word, but he reached back and simply gripped Faye's wrist. She remembered to breathe and lifted the phone back to her bone-dry mouth. She did her best to keep her voice level as she spoke. "Babe, mind if I call you back later?"

"Yeah, sure," Jack replied. "Text me when you get the tracker in the mail, and don't forget that you owe Kam some baby names. Thanks again, gorgeous."

"Always, handsome. Give Kam and the baby a kiss from me. Bye." Faye hung up and slipped the phone into her pocket. The door had already closed behind them on its own. Cold sweat gathered along her spine and in her armpits as she calculated how many seconds it would take her to open it and run down the hallway towards the car. Winston had angled his body so that she was almost entirely behind him, perhaps for that very reason, but touching her had been a cue for her not to run. As much as she didn't want to do it, he'd silently told her to trust him.

Stella cocked her head to one side. "You look good. I like the extra bulk."

She wrinkled her nose. "Wish your hair was longer, though. Not a bad color this time."

"You should talk," Winston said, matching her conversational tone. "Thought you were done with the sew-in weaves."

"I thought so too," she said, brushing her swoop from her brow. "But then I found this really gorgeous hair that I like so I decided to go back."

"Brazilian?"

Stella's brown eyes sparkled. "You remembered my

183

preference. I'm surprised."

Winston shrugged. "I try."

Stella gestured with the Magnum. "Take the mag out of your gun and put it on the bed. Nice and slow."

Winston let go of Faye, removed the gun from inside the shoulder holster under his coveralls, and popped the ammo out, tossing them onto the bed. He removed the bullet from the chamber and set it next to the gun as well.

"Now the cutlery."

Winston knelt and pulled up one pants leg, revealing the eight-inch knife strapped to his calf, and dropped it to the bed as well.

She gestured again. "There. Now we can have a civilized conversation."

Almost immediately, Winston's posture relaxed. Faye nearly did a double take. It was as if Stella had spoken a code word of some kind. He strode over to the desk to his right and leaned his backside against it, his hands on the tabletop. Faye swallowed hard and eased to her left until her back was against the wall closest to the door. Four and a half steps to the door. Then another two steps to get out of Stella's line of sight.

After Faye had settled into her new spot, Stella's eyes tracked lazily over her. She smirked. "So who's the tart?"

"Needed some cover," Winston said. "I usually travel alone, if you remember."

Stella snorted. "You're still a shit-ass liar, Pooh Bear. I know covers when I see them."

She squinted at Faye. "Most covers you can mold in your hand like Play-Doh. She's a diamond. Have you taken on an apprentice?"

"Not hardly," Winston grunted. "Too much goddamn work."

"Got that right." Stella suddenly grinned. "Don't tell me she's your sugar baby."

Winston rolled his eyes. "Gimme a break, Stella."

"Just how long do the two of you plan to continue

talking about me like I'm a slab of meat?" Faye demanded finally.

Stella sent her a bored look. "Look, sweetie, the adults are talking. You'll get your turn soon enough."

"Adults, huh?" Faye said, crossing her arms. "Is that why you took this assignment so you can get back at him like a high school prom date that got stood up?"

Stella blinked. Just once. Slowly. She cut her eyes over at Winston. "Is this basic bitch for real?"

Winston smiled. "Why don't you ask her?"

"Fine." Stella tossed her hair a bit. "So why don't you tell me why you're here in your own words?"

"I'd love to. None of your fucking business."

"Ooh, she's feisty," Stella chuckled. "Must be giving you trouble."

"Like you wouldn't believe," Winston said. Faye glared at him and he just shrugged.

"You don't have to tell me, baby girl," Stella said. "I see you anyway."

"Really? Is that why you asked for his weapons and not mine?"

Stella offered her a catty grin then. "You can't pull fast enough to shoot me, sweetie. Might as well keep the gun on you. Might make you feel safer."

"I'm traveling with a hitman," Faye said. "Safe isn't what I'm about."

"Guess not. But let me see if I can paint the picture." She scrutinized Faye for a long moment. "You're gorgeous, and you carry yourself like you've been this way for a long time. You got that pretty in early middle school, probably in seventh or eighth grade when the PMS fairy landed early. Probably got it from your mother. Mom and Dad were, what? High school sweeties? The prom queen and the all-star quarterback, right? And not the kind they write about in Hallmark and Lifetime movies; the kind where the girl figured out too late that she hitched her wagon to a loser, but he got her pregnant too soon to break it off so she stayed to raise the kid. I'd take a guess to say they separated after you graduated high school. By then, you were tired of being a beauty queen. Got tired of people thinking you were a blonde bimbo, so you graduated salutatorian and went into some kind of complicated subject, maybe engineering or programming, to subvert everyone's expectations. You're great at it, but deep down, you know it's just for show. It's not what you really wanted to do, but it was the only way to get the world to take you seriously. Anna Nicole Smith the Brain Surgeon."

Stella glanced at Winston. "And you were skipping happily along in your delusional bubble until Pooh Bear went and popped it. It was probably the first time shit got real for you. Then you dropped the façade and had to figure out what you were really made of."

She returned her gaze to Faye. "It's interesting. The vibe I'm getting from you two is that it's not sexual…but it's also not-*not* sexual. He's hung up on you. But then, he's always been the sweet one. *Hitman with a heart*. Should be his tagline."

Stella smiled sweetly. "So how close did I get, boo boo?"

"Not bad," Faye said. "Mind if I return the favor?"

Stella shrugged. "Take your best shot, Becky."

Faye perfectly mirrored Stella's condescending smile. "The foster care system treated you like shit. After all, black women are some of the most underrepresented, mistreated people in the country. You got bounced from place to place because they couldn't handle you, and it wasn't the attitude. It was the anger. The anger that your mother left you. That she was so selfish that you never even got the chance to meet her face to face because of her addiction. You saw what other girls had to do to survive on their own, and you saw what most of their fates were too.

"So you decided that instead of finding a place in the world, you'd make one instead. You made the underworld your bitch because men never expect a gorgeous black

186

woman to be smart enough to kill them. I'm betting that's what caught Winston's eye. How effective you were. How ruthless you were. You matched him. I think he made you happy. Actually happy. And you didn't know what to do with it. You kept expecting life to take him from you, looking over your shoulder constantly for that rotten nightmare to snatch him away. But it didn't. So, you got comfortable. You let yourself fall for him. Then you got that job offer and you got your feelings hurt that your Pooh Bear didn't want to settle down with you. So you split. Now you're realizing that the Queen isn't the same Queen without her King. I don't think you're here to kill Winston. I think you're here to try and win him back."

Faye's smile stretched wider. "And you can have him back when I'm done with him."

Stella raised her arm, aimed the gun at Faye's head, and pulled the trigger.

Winston's hand lashed out and knocked the barrel of the gun up just in time for the bullet to punch a sizeable hole in the wall five inches over Faye's head.

Faye didn't even flinch.

Stella ground her teeth and glared at Winston, who put himself between the two women. "Ladies. Play nice."

She exhaled hard through her nose and snatched her arm out of his grip. "You better check the little bitch before I do."

"Look, as fun as this reunion has been, get to the point, Stella," he growled. "What do you want?"

"This is a courtesy call," she said, pushing to her feet. She was nearly his height in her boots, which made Faye estimate she was at least 5 '11" or taller. "I'm only gonna ask you this once. Drop the tart off and go home. Let me do my job. If you don't, I will go through you."

"Wouldn't be the first time we disagreed on something."

"But it'll be the last."

"I suppose it will. The answer's no. Do what you gotta

do. So will I."

Stella's fingers tightened around the Magnum. Winston didn't move. "Either use that thing or walk your pretty ass outta here."

The two assassins glared at each other for a handful of seconds. Then Stella chuckled softly. "Damn, boy. You always were good at the alpha male shit."

She got up on her tiptoes and kissed him, then wiped her lipstick off his mouth. "See you around, Pooh Bear."

Stella stepped around him and strutted towards the door. She paused to give Faye the evil eye. "You owe me a bullet, bitch."

Faye batted her eyelashes. "Keep talking, and you might just get your wish."

Stella left without another word, slamming the door shut.

Faye let out a long, shaky breath. A caustic silence descended for nearly a minute. Then, Faye let out a soft snicker.

"Pooh Bear?"

Winston didn't exactly blush, but it was a close thing. "Shut up and get packing, Blondie."


"Alright, folks," Agent Shannon said, unbuttoning his suit jacket as he sat down at the head of the conference table in the team's usual lab. "Updates."

He glanced at Libby. "What did you find on the footage, kiddo?"

"Still not a kid," Libby said crossly. "But I was able to get a look at the serial number on the side of the chopper. I sent it on up the ladder to see if they can get a bead on it. I also contacted air traffic control for the area to see if they can find out where it took off from, but it's probably a dead end. At best, we might be able to ask around to see if anyone spotted it en route to where you were."

"Good." He nodded to Calloway. "Your field report

was adequate. I turned it in to my superiors to go over it. The next thing I want from you is an assessment of how the prototype suit held up."

"Got it," Calloway said, winking at his sister.

"Larry, how far have you gotten with the Highlander dragon?" Shannon asked.

"Some new pieces to the puzzle," Larry said. "Biologically speaking, it matches the other remains we've found, but with Dr. Anjali and Dr. Jackson's help, we've identified some elements that help us account for their seemingly impossible growth rate."

"Which is?"

"Radiation," Kamala said. "In addition to whatever kind of cocktail of a serum and growth hormone these dragons are being given, they're being exposed to radiation to correct whatever glitch occurred when the Sugimoto organization engineered Baba Yaga."

Shannon frowned. "In that case, do we need to quarantine it?"

"No," Jack said. "From what we can calculate, the combination of the radiation and the serum, means these creatures reach their adult size within 90 days to six months. By the time they're awake, it's no longer emitting from their bodies. We've added an extra screening process for the ones we bring in just to be safe."

"Alright. Behaviorally, how is the subject?"

"Foul-tempered," Kamala said, wincing a bit. "But that's to be expected from so much abuse. However, we were able to find something rather interesting."

Jack handed her the tablet and she turned on the projector. She swiped over to newly acquired footage. The camera showed a part of the facility that was largely unoccupied grass that stretched out several acres. The Highlander dragon had been tethered to a bolt set deep into the ground where they usually allowed Pete to stretch her wings and get some fresh air. The poisonous spikes on the dragon's tail had rubber tips, as did its claws, and it wore a

Nylon band to keep its deadly jaws shut. The dragon's eyes were fixed straight ahead where Jack and Pete stood a few yards away.

In the footage, Jack reached into his lab coat pocket and hit a button on his phone. Soft orchestral music filled the air. He patted Pete's neck and nodded towards the Highlander dragon. Pete fell in slow, steady steps with him as they approached the new dragon.

The Highlander dragon's upper lip curled back in a warning hiss and it retreated to as far as its tether would allow. Jack nudged Pete forward and the dragon lowered her head in the new dragon's direction, her nostrils flaring. The Highlander dragon's hissing increased in volume and it sank onto its belly, still trying to tug at its leash.

Jack stepped a few paces away from the pair. Slowly, the Highlander dragon's hissing decreased in intensity. It switched its gaze to Pete and then snorted once.

Pete took a few steps closer, her forked tongue flicking out every so often. The Highlander dragon slowly rose from the grass and shook itself, flapping its wings a couple times. It didn't move towards her, but it also didn't try to get away. She inched her way over until they were a foot apart and then sat back on her haunches in front of it. The Highlander dragon cocked its head to one side. Pete mirrored it. The two stared at each other as if trying to figure out what each was seeing.

Then, the Highlander dragon settled down in the grass and kept a calm, but wary gaze on Pete, its hissing retreating to placid silence.

Kamala stopped the footage. "As you can see, we've got some very interesting results here."

"Definitely," Calloway said. "I would have expected it to immediately try to fight her like it would have seeing any other dragon."

"We had a theory," Kamala said. "Pete is a pack animal. However, she's also an anomaly. Her species only reach about the size of an iguana, but she grew to her current size due to an unusual gene when we cloned her. She inherited some traits from the Komodo dragon we spliced into her DNA, and so we had a theory that she became an alpha based on her size and behavior. The Highlander dragon is a solitary creature, but if its captors also spliced her with another type of reptile, it too has pack behavior. Based on its wounds and age, we believe this dragon has only been in a few fights, so it hasn't completely associated other dragons with violence yet. It associates people with violence instead. Have you ever seen that show with Cesar Milan?"

Calloway grinned. "I'm a zoologist. Of course I have."

Kamala smiled. "Good, then you're familiar with the concept. We might be able to use Pete like a rehabilitation dog. She seems to have a calming presence. It's possible the dragon might see her as its pack leader, so it might reduce hostility if we keep her around while we interact with it. More testing is of course necessary, but this method looks promising for now."

"Where is it now?" Agent Shannon asked.

"They set up its enclosure next to Pete's. It's resting."

"Alright, keep me updated on its progress. For now, we have a new assignment. I was able to extract the next site for one of these death matches from one of the suspects."

Jack blinked at him. "That fast?"

Shannon gave him a thin smile. "I'm very persuasive."

"Uh-huh," Jack said, not hiding his skepticism. "Just how many of their fingernails did you pull off?"

"Enough," Shannon said, his tone far too casual. "Calloway and I are heading to Alexandria, Virginia, but this time the asset stays behind since we don't need her scent tracking. The match is supposed to start at nightfall, so I want our equipment ready in an hour. We're wrangling for a SWAT team to meet us there."

"What else did they tell you? Anything about the organization?"

"That's classified," Shannon said in a bland tone.

"This entire outfit is classified," Jack said, exasperated.

"We can't exactly be a team if we don't have all the information."

"You have what is relevant to your assignment, doc. I don't work for you. You work for us. Keep your eyes on the prize."

Jack clenched his jaw. "Oh, trust me. They are."

The older man snorted and rose from the table. "Get to it, people."

He left. Larry excused himself a moment later as well. Calloway stood and stretched, shaking his head. "The fun never ends."

"Tell me about it," Libby sighed. "If this keeps up, we'll all die of stress before the week is out."

Her brown eyes brightened then. "Hey, why don't we all go out for drinks after my brother gets back? You know, decompress."

Kamala pointed at her belly. Libby bit her lip. "Oh, right. Drinks and maybe some sparkling soda?"

The little doctor laughed. "Actually, that sounds lovely. It would be good for us as a team."

"As long as Shannon's not invited, count me in," Jack said mildly.

Libby groaned. "Oh my God, just marry him already."

Jack threw a pen at her head and she cackled, ducking. "I'm gonna revoke your phone privileges if you keep it up, whipper snapper."

She grinned. "Why don't you skip that and just—"

Calloway clapped his hand over her mouth and glared down at his sister from where he stood behind her. "If you say 'spank me' again, I am going to murder you."

"You're no fun," she whined from around his fingers.

Calloway rolled his eyes and let her go. "There's a pool hall about three blocks over. Nice spot, pretty quiet, no smoking. Sound good?"

"Hell yeah," Jack agreed. "I could use a beer. Or three. Or ten."

"I would love to see what this man looks like drunk,"

Calloway said. "It's got to be hilarious."

"You'd better hope the pool hall doesn't have karaoke," Kamala warned him. "Jack only sings when he's drunk and it's quite horrifying."

Jack pouted. "You said you love it when I sing."

She patted his thigh. "Of course I do, darling. I love laughing at you."

He sighed. "Shoulda known. Either way, yeah, we're in. In the meantime, let's get going."

They split up to go their separate ways. Jack and Kamala headed back towards the lab. Kamala glanced up at her boyfriend and cocked her head slightly, which caught his attention.

"What?" he asked.

"Something on your mind?"

"What makes you say that?"

"Instinct. Is something bothering you?"

Jack allowed the frown that had been threatening his features to finally creep onto them. "Sort of. I didn't want to say anything in there, but...I don't know. I don't like that Agent Shannon got those smugglers to crack so fast. It doesn't feel right to me. This is a very secretive operation. It's making their organization rich beyond their wildest dreams. Why would they give up the information in only a matter of hours?"

"He does look as if he's quite...effective at intimidation," she replied. Then she too frowned. "But you're not wrong. It does make me hesitant as well to believe they would roll over so easily."

"Exactly," Jack murmured as he hit the elevator button. "It feels too...easy. Maybe I'm just paranoid, but my gut doesn't like it."

Kamala winced as she felt the little one shifting in her belly, rubbing the tender spot. "Me neither. However, both of them are highly trained. You saw how they handled the Highlander dragon. They'll be fine and we'll help them as best as we can if the worst should happen."

They stepped inside the elevator. "I hope I'm wrong."

Kamala slipped her fingers between his and squeezed lightly. "Me too."


"What's our next move?" Faye asked as she watched Winston hang up his burner phone.

"Our inside man says your friends are on the move," he said as they turned the corner towards the parking lot. "Shannon and the dragon's handler are heading out of town. Virginia. We've got to beat them there."

Faye frowned. "I thought we were trying to protect Jack and Kamala."

"Exactly," he said, tucking the phone away. "Those two agents are heading for a trap. My guess is they'll walk into a firefight and be put out of commission, and then the government will be forced to ask Dr. Jackson to be their replacement. It's all downhill from there to manipulate both of them to be attacked by the dragons."

"Jack wouldn't say yes to that," Faye insisted. "He's got a kid on the way, for God's sake. They're consultants only."

"That's what it says on paper. Doesn't mean he can't be persuaded otherwise through extenuating circumstances. Look how personally he took it when Detective Stubbs died. If something happened to their team members, I don't think it's unreasonable to assume he'd want to avenge them, even at the risk of his own life."

Winston turned his steady gaze. "Think it over. What kind of a man is your boyfriend?"

Faye started to protest, but then just grimaced. "I saw him shortly after Stubbs died. You're right. We have to get there first and shut the smugglers down before anyone gets hurt."

"Yup." Winston set his duffel bag down next to a burgundy Dodge Charger and withdrew a small kit with equipment to break into it.

194

"What are you doing?" Faye demanded, jabbing a thumb behind her. "Our car's on the other side of the lot."

As if on cue, an explosion rocked the entire parking lot.

Faye shrieked and ducked as bits of glass and blasted car parts flew past her; not close enough to graze her, but she watched open-mouthed as they scattered to the concrete. Winston hadn't even flinched. He calmly stuck a wedge into the car door and used a small pump to push the edge of it away from the car to allow him to pull it open.

"Not anymore, it isn't," he grunted.

"What the hell was that?" Faye said, dusting herself off as she watched plumes of black smoke billow up from the remains of the Impala.

"I told you, Blondie," he mused, yanking the car door open. "Stella's creative."

He yanked the steering wheel panel out. "Now be a dear and hand me the pliers."

# CHAPTER TEN
## UNTOUCHABLE

"So let me get this straight," Jack said in a facetiously even tone over the comm-link. "You guys know this is probably a trap, but since the bad guys don't know that you know, so you're still going to raid the joint anyway?"

"Correct," Calloway confirmed.

Jack paused for an additional second. "This may be the single dumbest plan I've ever heard."

Calloway snorted. "Thanks for the vote of confidence, bruh."

"Hey, I calls it like I sees it."

"That would be why we brought SWAT and a bomb squad," Calloway said. "Should cover all our bases depending on what type of trap this might be."

"What type of trap this might be," Jack muttered, shaking his head. "What is even my life right now?"

"Oh, quit whining," Libby said as she passed him a can of Coke and sat down beside him at the conference table. "He's the one in mortal danger, not you."

"I'm concerned," Jack insisted. "I complain when I'm concerned."

Libby popped her Sprite open and propped the chair up on two legs, propping her own up on the table. "You must be concerned twenty-four seven."

Jack casually stuck his shoe under her chair and tipped it further back an inch. She flailed her arms to maintain balance and then shot a glare at him. He just grinned and drank his Coke.

"Doing alright, Kam?" he asked.

"Just ordered room service," his girlfriend said. "This hotel has surprisingly good vegetarian options."

"Save me some dessert."

Libby waggled her brows. "Bow chicka wow wow."

Jack rolled his eyes. "That wasn't a euphemism."

"It wasn't?" Kamala said, feigning disappointment. "Am I no longer appealing to you, Jack?"

Libby cackled. Jack sighed. "Look, don't encourage her, hon."

"Sorry. Couldn't resist."

The door to the lab opened and Larry came in. "Sorry I'm late, guys. Are we about to be underway?"

"Yep," Jack said. "SWAT's doing the perimeter check. They should be breaching soon."

"Good," he said, sitting next to Jack at the table. "Are we live?"

"Live and in color," Calloway confirmed as he tugged on his helmet. The projector in the lab blinked to life with a pale green night vision heads up display. "Well, sort of."

He stood to one side of an old, greying brick building that had once been part of a train yard. The trains had long since stopped going through the area, so its streets were blocked off and the buildings were abandoned. Most had broken windows and faded, cracked bricks. The police usually had to come by every so often to drive out the squatters and homeless population. Aside from that, it would be the perfect place for the illegal fights, since it was closed to the public and was far enough away from the city that no one would likely hear the noise.

The main center of the train yard was down a long, sloping gravel path. The building had three floors and had been used for train repairs as well as construction. None of the agents of SWAT were in plain view; rather, they had used the surrounding buildings for cover and approached in pairs.

The gravel to Calloway's left crunched as someone approached. "They finished the area sweep. No trip wires or explosives around the buildings. I want you flanking me when we go in."

"Gee, Shannon, I'm flattered, but I think we should just stay friends," Calloway replied mildly.

"I'm not your friend, kid," Shannon said. "Lose the

197

sarcasm and follow me."

"Bundle of joy, that man," Libby said. "Good luck, bro."

"Thanks, little bit. Standby."

Calloway and Shannon took positions behind the two SWAT officers standing on either side of the back door to the building. Shannon nodded to the one on the right who had a tactical camera mount reading heat signatures.

"What have we got?" he asked.

"Heat sigs," she confirmed. "Six."

"Human?"

She shook her head. "Doesn't appear to be. I think we might have found a facility where they store the dragons in between matches."

"No shit," Calloway said, shocked. "Seriously?"

He glanced over her shoulder to see the screenshot she'd taken. The dragons were in cages lined up against the walls of the building opposite each other. None of them were standing nor seemed alert. They were curled up, sleeping. It explained why they hadn't heard any noise just yet.

"They might be sedated," Calloway noted. "What else did you see in there?"

"A shipping container, but there's no heat signature. Whatever was in there is gone now."

Calloway frowned inside his helmet. "Yeah, that's not foreboding at all."

The SWAT officer snorted in amusement. "I like the way you think."

He chuckled. "Once we breach, I'll do an analysis of the species and then call in the cavalry while you guys make sure there aren't any other surprises. We're going to need some semis out here to get them all taken back to the facility."

"Keep a close eye on them," Shannon said. "I don't want another fiasco like last time."

"Hey, that fiasco was successful, you know."

Shannon rolled his eyes and just gestured towards the

door. The female SWAT officer set the camera mount aside and returned to her position by the entrance. Her partner used a small torch to melt the padlock and chains off. She counted down and then kicked in the doors.

The metal doors screamed in protest as they wrenched aside to reveal the innards of the old building. It had thick cement floors that still had bits of debris from its decaying walls and busted windows. Not everything inside was as old as the building; there were wooden boxes stacked in the center of the factory floor, some of which were open. As the SWAT officers swept inside with their flashlights on, they spotted supplies as well as a few hay bales near the boxes.

There were freezers to one side of the room. A peek inside revealed frozen meat, cow, pig, chicken, fish, and venison.

The dragons in the cages lining the walls didn't move even as the SWAT officers called out police just to be sure there were no people inside. Most of the cages had hay laid out beneath the creatures with large, deep water bowls and discarded parts of past meals. Calloway waited until he got the all clear and walked over to the nearest one, which contained a live Hercules dragon, its brownish-golden scales glittering under his helmet light.

He whistled lowly. "God, it's beautiful. Got to be, what? Nine feet long?"

"Maybe more," Kamala said, awe in her voice. "Look, next to it. The cage isn't the same as the others. It looks refrigerated."

Calloway stepped over to the next cage, touching two fingers to the iron bars, which had beaded with condensation. "Yeah, it's reading at below forty."

His flashlight spilled over an albino dragon with deep blue spines down the length of its back. It was eight feet long from snout to tail. Like the Hercules dragon, it had a band holding its jaws shut. Its breaths plumed into cold vapor.

"Holy *shit*," Jack said. "That's a freaking arctic dragon. They are one of the scarcest dragon species on the planet.

Historians only found about a hundred of them in the wild. Where the hell did they get a DNA sample to clone one of these things? Is there just some kind of dragon remains supermarket we don't know about?"

"These people are seriously connected," Calloway agreed. "In ways we underestimated."

The third cage contained another Chinese dragon, so he moved to the cages along the opposite wall. The fourth held a Highlander dragon while the fifth and sixth held two Netherland forest dragons. The forest dragons bore similarities to Pete, with long, tall bodies and green scales, but theirs were darker green and they had no spines.

"Something's not adding up," Libby said. "The smugglers said there'd be a match here tonight. They were wrong. This is a storage facility. Why would they surrender the dragons like this?"

"That's the million dollar question," Kamala agreed. "What's their end game? If this is a trap, then where's the actual trap?"

Calloway felt something prickle along his spine and the nape of his neck. He turned towards the shipping container at the end of the building opposite the back entrance. "Good question, Doc."

He strode over to the shipping container to find the female SWAT officer he'd met a moment ago burning through yet another padlock and chains. "Whoa, are you sure that's a good idea?"

"No heat sig, remember?" she said. "We might be able to recover some samples of whatever used to be in here. Should help you guys find out what to anticipate in the future."

"Alright," he said, eyeing the container. "Just…take it slow. Be careful."

She had goggles and a mask on, so he couldn't see her lift an eyebrow, but he heard the indignation in her voice. "You sayin' that because I'm a girl?"

Calloway sighed. "Because we're in a dragon-infested

200

den that a bunch of criminals told us about. Not because you're a girl."

"That's better," she said, popping the padlock off and tossing it to him. "Stand back."

She unlatched the heavy door and creaked it open about an inch. To her surprise, water rushed out and splashed over her boots. "The hell?"

She shone her flashlight. "Couple inches of water. Nothing near the door. I'm gonna open it. Gimme a hand."

Calloway helped her pull the enormous door until it was partially open. He shuddered. "Damn, it's cold in here. Didn't think this thing was refrigerated like the arctic dragon's cage. Must be a thermostat in here."

The pair swept the front half of the container, finding only cold water, and then their flashlights created dual spotlights on an enormous pool. It had a ladder that led up to the rim, which was over eight feet high.

"Uh," Calloway said. "Remember when I said something wasn't foreboding at all?"

"You said it," the SWAT officer muttered, drawing her Sig Sauer from her hip. "Screw this horror movie bullshit. Should we check it?"

Calloway sighed. "I think we're obligated."

She shook her head. "This is stupid. So stupid."

She grabbed her walkie-talkie and radioed for a couple of her companions to join them. "Go. I'll cover you. If there's anything in there, don't even stop to identify it. We'll close the door and see how it likes trying to get through four inches of solid steel."

Calloway let out a weak chuckle as he set one foot on the lowest rung of the ladder. "Just remember, lady. The black dude always dies first in these movies."

She echoed his nervous laugh. "Well, don't worry. I'll keep an eye on that nice ass of yours and make sure no one takes a bite out of it."

"Hey-o," Libby teased in his ear. "Big bro's got a fan."

"Shut *up*," he hissed into the link as he climbed the

ladder. He went slow, listening for any sign of disturbance in the pool, but he didn't hear anything. When he was one rung from the top, Calloway took a deep breath and hauled himself up.

The pool was easily thirty feet in diameter and was indeed circular like he'd suspected rather than ovular. He could see bits of salt dried along its rim, meaning that they'd been stepping in ocean water. Unlike ocean water, though, it was completely black as if someone had dumped ink into it.

"The hell," Calloway muttered, staring at the unbroken surface of the water. "What did they put in this thing?"

"Oh my God," Jack whispered in recognition. "Calloway, kill the light and get the *fuck* out of that container right now."

Calloway froze. "What?"

"Go!" Jack shouted. "Get everyone out of that building now!"

Before Calloway could move, bubbles frothed beneath the inky water, swirling into a small funnel. A huge spray hit him in the face and then something emerged.

Calloway jumped down from the pool and waved at the SWAT officers who had begun to enter the container. "Close the door! Now!"

Seconds later, a Nordic sea serpent came screeching out of the giant pool.

The dragon grabbed its webbed feet, tipped with three-inch long claws, onto the rim of the pool, and hauled its heavy body from the water. It was jet-black with two burning, bright blue eyes that matched the bioluminescent color along its back in wide fins much like a moray eel's. It stood on all fours at over eight feet tall and over twenty-feet long from snout to tail.

"Shit!" The female SWAT officer opened fire as she backpedaled towards the shipping container's entrance. "Calloway, get clear!"

He raced towards the door while she kept firing until

her Sig clicked empty. Divots appeared in the dragon's thick black skin, but it didn't bleed. It screeched and charged her, swatting her to one side like a rag doll. She cried out and hit the side of the container, crumpling into an unconscious heap.

"Shit!" Calloway swore, dodging a swipe from the dragon. He threw himself into a roll and grabbed the fallen officer's arm, hefting her as he headed for the door. He squeezed his way out as the other officers swung it shut and latched it.

The sea serpent let out another ghostly wail from inside the container and threw its huge body against the door. An enormous dent appeared.

Calloway shook his head. "No way that's gonna hold. Evacuate."

Shannon shoved his way over to Calloway, carrying the net launcher. "Don't panic, son. Everybody stay calm."

The container's door buckled another couple of inches as the dragon rammed it again.

"Shannon, don't be an idiot," Libby snarled. "The net's not going to hold something that size."

He gritted his teeth. "I thought you said this thing is made of diamond wire."

"It is, but it's designed to catch anything the size of Pete or smaller. That dragon has to weigh a ton, maybe more. My brother's right. Get those officers out of there and regroup."

"Negative," he said, slinging the launcher onto his back. "Give me that shotgun."

The SWAT officer next to him obeyed. "You, you, and you, we're gonna hold the line. Get everyone else out of here and get me a goddamn chopper now."

The door crunched outward with another blow. "Now would be the time for one of you egghead dragon experts to offer some advice."

"Listen to Calloway," Kamala said. "Bullets won't penetrate its skin. Its got literally inches and inches of blubber that protect it from the cold. Not even the shotgun shells will hurt it. If you leave its territory, you have a chance to survive."

"It's an aquatic species," Jack continued. "Even if it chases you, it has to eventually go back to its water source."

CRUNCH went the door. "How long can it survive outside of the water?" Calloway asked.

"Hours. Think penguin or frog."

"See?" Calloway snapped to Shannon. "You can't do anything. You're going to get these people killed for no reason."

CRUNCH. CRUNCH. "And what if this thing goes stomping around a nearby neighborhood looking for another food or water source?" Shannon shot back.

"Shannon, you hired us to advise you," Kamala said, not hiding the fury and frustration in her voice. "We're fucking advising you to run."

CRUNCH. CRUNCH. CRUNCH.

Shannon ground his teeth and then growled out. "Everyone, fall back! Get to a safe distance and wait for my word."

The SWAT officers, Calloway, and Shannon had made it halfway to the exit when the container door knocked free and the sea serpent came wriggling out of the darkness like a wraith.

The stragglers opened fire on the dragon, hoping to slow it down, but it only drew the creature's attention instead. It snapped up one man in its jaws and ate him in two quick chomps, still screaming on his way down the dragon's throat. It batted another man aside with its long, heavy tail and he flew several feet before he hit one of the dragon's cages. It cornered another officer and slammed one massive clawed foot down on him, crushing his chest in seconds and then biting his head off.

While it fed, the rest of the group slammed the door shut and headed up the gravel hill towards the police vans.

"Where's my goddamn chopper?" Shannon snarled

into the link.

"ETA ten minutes," someone answered.

"We're gonna be sushi in ten minutes," Calloway said, checking over his shoulder to see the entire building shuddering from the force of the dragon ramming its way out. He glanced down at the unconscious woman still draped over his shoulder and sighed internally just as he reached the police van. The other men helped lay her down safely inside it just as the rear door to the building slammed into the ground.

The sea serpent sent another chilling siren's call out into the night air and barreled its way up the hill towards them, its eyes glowing like twin points of Greek fire.

Shannon grimaced and took a stance between himself and the vans as the dragon approached. "Get them out of here, Calloway."

Calloway snorted. "Yeah, right, old man. Like I'm going to let your crusty ass die a hero."

He tilted his head slightly. "Hey, docs. What'll *really* piss it off?"

Kamala sighed before reluctantly answering. "You're in a train yard, right? There's got to be fuel and lighter fluid around. Sea serpents hate fire."

Calloway felt a wolfish grin spreading over his lips. "Sounds like my kind of party. Shannon, see what you can get going. I'll keep it distracted."

He reached back and pounded his fist on the door of the nearest van twice. The three police vans peeled off up the hill and safely out of sight. Shannon handed him the shotgun. "Don't do anything stupid, kid."

"Would I do a thing like that?" Calloway said, cocking it and taking aim at the creature's front legs. Shannon kicked the door to a nearby building open and ducked inside just as Calloway opened fire.

The first round of buckshot tore a hole in the serpent's chest no more than about two inches wide. It still didn't bleed, but he could see puckered flabs of blubber poking out from the wound. The dragon snarled and launched itself at him in a pounce.

Calloway threw himself to one side and pumped another round in, firing at its back leg. Another hole appeared and the dragon swung its tail at his head. He ducked and retreated still facing the creature, this time heading downhill. "Any ideas, crew?"

"Those things can't climb well, right?" Larry asked. "Can he get up high?"

"Yeah, and put himself in perfect biting distance," Libby said tartly. "That thing can push a tree over easy. I know these things like the cold, but do you think a freeze bomb might slow them down?"

"*Freeze bomb?*" Jack and Kamala asked in unison.

"Yeah, they're weaponized liquid nitrogen capsules. Figured he might need them for the fire-breathing dragons."

"Smart. That might slow it down," Kamala said. "Aim for one of its limbs."

"Got it," Calloway said, grabbing a couple pellets from the fourth pocket on his belt. He aimed and launched one at the dragon's right front leg as it made another charge towards him. The capsule burst and sent a cloud of vapor up into the air, and then the substance instantly hardened over the dragon's elbow. It stumbled in mid-gait and landed hard, the momentum taking the dragon right into a roll headed straight for Calloway. He cursed and took off in a sprint, sliding to one side as the dragon's titanic form smashed into the side of the building at the bottom of the hill.

"Nice shot!" Libby said. "One down, three to go."

Calloway eased to one side as the dragon struggled to rise and hit it a second time with another pellet. It froze part of the dragon's webbed foot to the ground.

"Calloway, wait," Jack barked. "Don't get too close or it'll—"

Before he could finish the sentence, the dragon opened its jaws and spat a thick black liquid. It splattered over his helmet and drenched his upper body, blinding him.

"Shit!" He wrenched the helmet off just in time to see the serpent rise and swing its massive tail again. It hit him in the midsection and sent him flying head over heels several feet away. He landed in a heap towards the other end of the building and didn't stir.

"Bruce!" Libby screamed.

"Shannon, get over to Calloway now!" Larry shouted. "He's down!"

"I'm coming, kid," the agent said in between breathless pants of exertion. "Calloway, do you copy?"

The lab team couldn't see, but they heard the impact tremors and the shifting gravel as the dragon slithered closer to the unconscious Calloway.

"Calloway, do you copy? Answer me, dammit!"

"Bruce!" Libby cried. "Bruce, say something!"

The dragon let out another undulating hiss and then the link abruptly went silent.

They'd lost the feed.

# CHAPTER ELEVEN
## QUEEN'S GAMBIT

"So...Pooh Bear?"

Winston sighed as he slammed the Dodge Charger's trunk shut. "I knew you were going to ask about that."

"It's too weird not to ask," Faye insisted as she picked up the other equipment bag he'd taken out of the car. "Spill."

He grumbled something under his breath as he hefted his duffel bag and the two of them started up the hill into the thick wooded area. "We used our professional names for the first few months of dating. She went from Winston to Winnie the Pooh. Thus, Pooh Bear. Happy?"

"There is absolutely nothing cute or likable about you," she said frankly. "But the fact that she calls you Pooh Bear might be the funniest damn thing I've ever heard. Pooh Bear the hitman."

He tossed a glare at her. "And I suppose your own pet names from either of your S.O.'s are any more dignified?"

"Jack just goes with the usual for a guy his age, beautiful, gorgeous, etc. Before Kamala knew about my feelings, I was *saheli*. Now I'm *alabeli*."

"Translates to 'charming young woman,'" Winston said, nodding in appreciation. "Cute."

Faye blinked at him. "You speak Urdu?"

Winston just smiled. She rolled her eyes. "So since Stella basically declared open season on the two of us, why are you so calm while we're walking through the woods at night like we both have a death wish?"

"Told you," he said. "Not her style. She's not cold enough for a high-powered rifle to take me out from a distance. She'd want it to be personal for both of us."

"Then exactly what is waiting for us down there in that train yard?"

"Bad things."

"No shit, Sherlock. Maybe you want to give me some specifics?"

"In chess, you make moves to deceive your opponent, eliminate their resources, and then isolate them before the takedown," Winston said. "In a proper trap, you lure them into a false sense of security and then strike when they least expect it. I don't expect there'll be men down there. Men can run their mouths and blow your whole operation. That's likely why the smugglers they apprehended gave them this cock-and-bull easy clue. Let your opponent think he's won and he'll start playing right into your hand because he doesn't know any better."

"You think it'll just be a trap laid with dragons."

"Yup."

"Where does Stella come in?"

"If for some reason they do get away in the end, she'll rig something to take them out as a backup. As you saw with our poor Impala, she's a master with explosives."

Faye shuddered. "How do we stop her?"

"Keep 'em alive," he said, drawing a couple pairs of night vision goggles from his bag and handing them to Faye as they closed in on the compound. She slipped hers on and got used to the odd light green coloring that illuminated the forest around them. She could see possums skittering away, an owl, and even a snake curled up the roots of trees.

"Sounds easy enough—"

Winston grabbed Faye's arm and jerked her backward abruptly. She stumbled into his arms and froze, bewildered. "The hell's the matter with you?"

He covered her mouth with one big hand and put a finger to his lips. He then moved her to one side and knelt as he dug a pair of pliers out of his bag. She watched as he snipped a tiny wire she'd almost walked right through. Cold fear flooded through her.

"Tripwire," Winston whispered. "She knew we'd approach from the woods."

Faye swallowed hard. "Have I mentioned how much I

wish your ex was a ballerina or something?"

Winston snorted softly and hit a button or two on the side of his goggles. "Me too, Blondie."

He paused, his lips moving, though no sound came out, and stared about the forest floor. "I count six charges and three bear traps. She's not trying to kill us yet. She's stalling us."

"Can we go back up towards the car and find another way around?"

He shook his head. "Take too long. I'm betting they're already there, then, if she's done this to us. She wants us to arrive too late."

"Is there anything else we can do?"

He grunted. "Not really. Cut the wires and keep moving."

Faye ground her teeth. "No offense, but your ex-wife sucks. Hope the sex was good."

Winston's chest rumbled with a laugh. "Bet your pretty ass it was."

He went ahead of her, snipping the wires carefully one at a time. With every wasted minute, Faye's anxiety increased. There was no telling what was happening now and how far into the trap they'd gotten. Maybe she'd been wrong about doing this with him. Maybe she should have bitten the bullet and turned what she knew over to Carmichael and Houston, or to the people Jack and Kamala were working with. What if she couldn't protect them? Hell, what if she couldn't protect herself? She was damned tired of playing catch up.

Winston cut the final trip wire. No sooner than he did, an eerie wail filled the air. The entire forest went dead silent —no crickets, no frogs, nothing.

"What the hell was that?" Faye breathed.

"Dunno," Winston said, pushing to his feet. "But it sure as hell ain't good. Stay close. Keep up."

There was a grassy hill between the forest and the train yard. They descended as quickly and quietly as possible and found themselves along the back entrance to the main building. Faye stubbed her toe on something and cursed. Then she paled.

"What the hell is big enough to do that?" she asked, pointing at the twisted, crumpled metal door that had once been attached to the wall.

"*That*," Winston said, pointing.

Faye glanced up enough to see a thick, black tail whipping around the corner, its tip a glowing blue fin the size of windshield.

"Holy hell," she muttered. "We're too late."

"Like hell we are," Winston said, dropping his bag and rooting around inside it. "Any chance you recognize what that thing is?"

Faye peeked around the corner, her heart in her throat as she watched a man in an odd-looking armored suit firing a shotgun at the dragon as it wriggled uphill towards him. "Y-Yeah, uh, it's a Nordic sea serpent. Used to live in the coldest waters of the Arctic Circle and in the Norwegian Fjords of its namesake."

"Those shotgun rounds doing any good?"

Faye shook her head as she watched. "Looks like it's just pissing the thing off."

"Well, I ain't equipped for freaking sea serpents, so we're going to Plan B." Just as he stood, she shoved him to one side to press into the wall as the dragon went rolling past them and hit the side of the building. The ground shook violently and the creature roared in pain.

"Here," Winston said, handing her something. "You'll know when to use it."

"But—" He slipped around the other side of the building before she could get another word out. Faye gritted her teeth and watched as the man in the suit tossed something at the dragon that froze one of its feet, but then its tail swung around and knocked him in a tumbling roll several feet away.

"Shit!" She watched, eyes wide, as the dragon shoved

itself to its feet and slithered towards the unconscious man. His helmet cracked in half under one of its enormous clawed feet and she saw its huge jaws with deadly black teeth open to bite his head off.

"Screw it!" Faye slapped the flare against her knee and bellowed. "HEY, FUCKHEAD!"

Bright red light burst to life from the end of the flare. The dragon's head whipped around towards the light and it hissed, seeming to dislike it intensely. It crawled towards her with menace as she waved the flare back and forth before launching it into the forest behind her. She dove into the bushes and lay as still as possible as the dragon went after the flare, its shrill cries filling the area. Cold sweat beaded along her back as she heard it claw and stomp the flare until it sputtered out.

Then the dragon started searching for her.

Air shifted and brushed over the nape of her neck. She forced herself to keep still and prayed it wouldn't find her.

Just then, she heard a loud whistle.

The serpent snarled and turned its head to see Winston standing at the bottom of the hill.

With a flamethrower in his hands.

He smiled, winked at the dragon, and then drawled. "Get fucked."

The dragon charged him. He squeezed the trigger. A column of fire ten feet long licked out from the muzzle of the gun and engulfed the dragon. The sea serpent howled in pain and stumbled to one side to avoid the explosion of light and heat. Its thick skin didn't catch, but the wounds where the buckshot had torn into its blubber suddenly caught like Roman candles. The creature flopped onto its belly, screeching wildly, as the layer of fat inside its skin began to burn with an intense white-hot flame. Winston edged away from it as its own flesh scalded it to death. In only minutes, the dragon curled on its side and died with a whimper, still burning like a meteor entering the earth's atmosphere.

He walked over to Faye and offered her his hand.

"Note to self, sea serpents are extremely flammable."

Faye took his hand and hauled herself out of the bushes. "Understatement of the century."

Winston squinted up into the night sky. "Sounds like a chopper's en route. We'd better get scarce and keep an eye out to see if Stella gets cute and tries to--"

He quit talking mid-sentence and stared at her chest. Faye frowned at him.

"What's with the pervert act?"

"Ah, hell," Winston muttered. Then he grabbed her shoulders and yanked her to one side.

She had only a split-second to see that there had been a red laser spot right where she'd just been standing.

Two bullets took Winston right through the abdomen.


Jack hated hospitals.

He'd been in his fair share by now thanks to Kamala's pregnancy, but he still never really cared for them. As much as he'd anticipated the arrival of their bundle of joy, something always felt mildly upsetting about hospitals. New life and fresh death walked hand in hand with hospitals, especially the emergency room. Some people were experiencing the best moment of their lives, others, the worst. Memories would be created whether people wanted them or not. Perhaps it was the lack of choice that unsettled him the most about them.

He sat in one of the uncomfortable chairs of the Inova Alexandria Hospital in the lobby of the emergency room. Libby sat to his right, his sport coat draped over her shoulders, one shaky hand clutching it absently, the other wrapped around his fingers. The fearlessness in her eyes had given way to bone-deep weariness and worry. She'd long since cried off all her eyeliner and sat silent, twitching at the sound of every door that opened, hoping the surgeon would appear to give her a status update. Kamala sat on Libby's other side, one arm around the girl's shoulders rubbing in slow, soothing circles. Kamala's eyes were closed in concentration as she prayed to Ganesha to remove the obstacles in the way of the surgical team and to guide their steady hands through the procedure safely. Larry stood pacing back and forth along the length of the lobby, chewing on his thumbnail. Agent Shannon had been taking near non-stop calls since the helicopter had landed. They hadn't seen much of him once he'd checked him in and made sure they were all safe.

"It's my fault," Libby whispered mournfully. "This is all my fault."

"Hey," Jack said gently. "No, it's not."

"It is. I should have told him not to take this assignment. I read the file. I've seen how many people have gotten hurt or died over this mess."

"Libby, look at me."

Tears welled up in her eyes, so she shut them and stubbornly shook her head. He squeezed her fingers. "Your brother is about twice as stubborn as you are. Do you really think you'd have been able to talk him out of it? Seriously? I've known him barely a week and I can tell you that's bullshit."

A tiny ghost of a laugh left her lungs then. "He made his own choices. So did you. This isn't on you. It's on the people who made that dragon and the people who are running this illegal fighting ring. No one else."

"But I--"

"You're not responsible," he said firmly. "I know how you feel. You keep thinking about all these decisions you could have made to stop it from happening. It sounds simple, easy even, in the hypothetical. That won't help you and it won't help him either. Focus on the now. Not the past."

Libby sniffled and finally looked at him. "So when were you on the other side of this?"

Jack sighed. "The detective who caught our case back when Pete was stolen. His name was Colin. He...got killed in the crossfire when the yakuza busted their boss Okegawa out

214

of police custody."

She tilted her head slightly. "And you felt that was your fault too?"

Jack nodded. "Couldn't help it. The project was my idea. None of this would've happened if I hadn't based my entire career around dragon resurrection."

Libby thought it over for a while. "How did you get past it?"

"I didn't," he said. "I just learned to carry it around. Made sure to keep fighting to find the men responsible and bring them to justice."

"Did you?"

Jack's features darkened. "Some of them. Not all. But you're damned right I'll keep at it until they're all behind bars."

He exhaled and released the anger in his tone. "I haven't met anyone as tough and smart as your brother before. He'll pull through. You'll see."

She gave him a little watery smile. It looked awful, but he saw a touch of hope in it. "Thanks, Jack."

She leaned her head on Kamala's shoulder and closed her eyes. A while later, she fell into a light sleep. They moved the chairs around to let her stretch out and rested the girl's head in Kamala's lap.

Jack settled next to his girlfriend and leaned his head against the wall. "How goes the prayer?"

"Laborious and intense," Kamala said, gently running her fingers over Libby's short hair.

"Is it working?"

She gave him a ghost of a smile. "Well, no one's said otherwise yet. Perhaps."

He kissed her forehead. "Thank you."

"For what?"

He gave her a small smile. "For having faith enough for the both of us."

"Always, my dragon."

An hour later, the doors parted and the head surgeon

emerged, pulling off his mask. Kamala gently shook Libby awake and they walked over to him, anxious.

"How is he?" Libby asked.

"He pulled through," the surgeon said. "He's not going to be up and about for a while, but he's out of danger. That armor he was wearing likely saved his life. We were able to stop the internal bleeding, but he's banged up pretty good. Eight broken ribs, punctured lung, bruised internal organs, and a fractured collarbone. He'll be on bed rest until the swelling goes down, but we're very optimistic about his recovery. You'll be able to see him in about half an hour. I'll make sure the nurse gives you his room number once he's settled."

"Thank you so much, doctor."

He gave her a pat on the shoulder and returned through the double doors.

"You hear that?" Jack said, nudging her. "You saved his life, whipper snapper. Now you can rub that in his face for all eternity."

She smiled, and it was a real one this time. "Point taken. Who wants to go find Agent Shannon and give him the good news?"

"I've got it," Larry said. "You guys get some food and some coffee and then tell me which room they send him up to."

"Thanks, Larry." He nodded and left.

"Cafeteria food," Libby sighed, her shoulders slumping. "What I wouldn't give for some Popeyes right now."

Jack's stomach gurgled in protest of her words. "Oh, don't say those words or I'm gonna start crying soon."

Kamala arched an eyebrow. "Why are you both longing for a 1930's cartoon character?"

Libby's jaw dropped. "You've never had *Popeyes*?"

"She's not Southern," Jack explained. "And there aren't any in Cambridge. Plus, she's vegetarian, remember?"

Libby shook her head. "As soon as we're all clear of

this mess, we're going on a road trip to fix that problem. Unacceptable, honey. Unacceptable. You can at least try the sides."

Kamala snorted. "If you say so. Come on, let's go."

The three of them ate and then checked in with the nurse at the desk to find out where Calloway had been taken. Jack and Kamala took seats nearby while Libby went in alone first.

She shut the door behind her and took a deep breath as she turned her eyes on her brother. His bed at least looked plenty comfortable and he wasn't completely reclined. There was a small cut high on his cheekbone, but his face hadn't suffered any other damage. She could see the bulk of bandages underneath his hospital gown as well as bruises along his bicep.

Libby touched his wrist gently. He stirred, opening his eyes. He smiled slowly. "Hey, little bit."

"Hey, bro," she said softly.

He pursed his lips at her. "You been crying?"

A stubborn look crossed her features. "No."

He grinned. "Good. I didn't raise no weak-ass sister."

She snorted with laughter and pulled up a chair. "Damn right."

"You call Pops yet?"

"Yeah, called him when I was on the way here. He's getting his stuff together and he'll be here first thing in the morning."

He nodded. "What about the rest of the family?"

"He said he'd make calls. Wanted me to just keep an eye on you. He knows you're just faking it for attention."

Calloway tried to laugh, but mostly just winced. "Damn, sis, don't make me laugh. Ribs are killing me. Doc said I broke, what? Eight? Christ. That dragon was a bitch."

His brown eyes glinted then. "Speaking of which, what happened?"

"We haven't gotten much out of Agent Shannon yet," she said. "He's been running back and forth trying to clean up this mess. I'll find out for you once we catch up with him."

"Anything on the news about it?"

"No, we're in the clear. No one was around. At most, maybe some of the neighborhoods nearby heard the noise but I doubt anything else got reported. If it did, I'm sure they'd suppress it."

Calloway sighed as he glanced down at himself. "Shoulda stayed my ass in Brazil, huh?"

She squeezed his hand. "It could be a lot worse. So much worse, Bruce."

"I know munchkin." He glanced at the door. "The docs outside?"

"Yeah."

He shook his head. "Not good for Kamala to be out all night. Send them back to the hotel."

"They just wanted to see you first. I'll go get them." She leaned over and kissed his forehead before she went to the door to call for them.

Jack and Kamala appeared, both with tired but genuine smiles. "Well, if it isn't Thing One and Thing Two. You look like hell."

"Great, 'cause you look like shit," Jack said cheerfully. "It's a tie."

Calloway grinned. "Smartass. Sorry about keeping your girl out here all night. You two should head back and get some rest. I'm alright."

Kamala sat next to him on the bed. "How long do they want to keep you?"

"Depends on how fast the swelling goes down. My guess is a week minimum, unless I sneak out of here. They just need to make sure there isn't any more internal damage."

Kamala nodded. "I'll see if I can sweet-talk your physician into letting me take a look. If there's anything I can do to help speed up your recovery, let me know."

He squeezed her hand. "Thanks, doc."

Calloway nodded to Jack. "See if you can get Shannon or Larry to tell us what went down after they got me out of there. Even if I can't be out in the field right now, it's still my case. We need to know where we stand from here on out."

Jack nodded back to him. "Will do."

He offered his fist. Calloway reciprocated. "Glad you're alright, man."

Calloway sucked his teeth. "Don't go mushy on me, Jackson."

"Yeah, yeah," Jack said, rolling his eyes. "You're not fooling anyone, dude."

Calloway scowled. "What's that supposed to mean?"

Jack did a passable imitation of his voice. *"Like I'm going to let your crusty ass die a hero.* We all know you're a big softie."

"Well," a female voice said from the doorway. "That's a relief."

They turned to see the female SWAT officer that Calloway had saved standing there. With all her tactical gear removed, they could see her clearly now, a short, stocky light-skinned black woman with her dreads back in a messy ponytail. She had a cast on her right arm, but didn't look much worse for wear otherwise.

"Hey," Calloway said. "Look who it is."

"Yes," Libby said, obnoxiously loud and suggestive. "Look who it is! Well, we'd better get going."

Calloway gave a dirty look, but she just winked and followed Jack and Kamala out into the hallway. She stuck her head in enough to waggle her eyebrows at her brother before closing the door, just to annoy him further.

"Man just got himself a date off of a killer dragon rampage," Jack said, smiling and shaking his head. "I only wish I had game like that."

Libby patted his shoulder sympathetically. "Maybe someday, doc."

She checked her watch, frowning. "Sheesh, what's taking Larry so long?"

"No idea. Maybe he stopped to mansplain something to one of the nurses."

She snorted, but then spotted Agent Shannon walking towards them with a brisk gait. "Finally. Look, what the hell happened out there?"

Agent Shannon nodded his head to one side and they trailed him to a small alcove of the hospital away from prying ears and eyes. "We have a problem. There's a second player in the field."

"What?" they asked in unison.

"Calloway went down and you guys called me over. I was on my way over to him when someone shot a flare to distract the dragon. It went after them while I dragged Calloway to safety. The chopper arrived and after I got him loaded up, I did an area sweep. That sea serpent was somehow burned to a crisp. None of my team members were in the vicinity. Someone else is out there that knows about this assignment."

Agent Shannon made a face as if he tasted something disgusting. "They are the reason your brother is still alive, not me. We need to find out who the hell was out there tonight."

"I don't understand," Kamala said. "Who would be trying to help us in secret? Who would have access to this kind of confidential information?"

"It gets better," Calloway said. "When we started digging into the financials of the smuggler who told us about that train yard, something came up. Guy got paid twenty large shortly before we had our conversation in interrogation. I think someone paid him to give us that location. It wasn't just a trap. It was an assassination attempt."

"Someone paid that creep to try to kill my brother?" Libby questioned. "Did you find out where the money came from?"

Shannon shook his head. "It routed through about ten different foreign banks. I've had someone looking into it. It could be that whoever is organizing this fighting ring has an inside man. We have to keep this quiet and between us. No one else needs to know until we find the mole."

His frown deepened. "Where's Dr. Whitmore?"

Jack blinked at him, confused. "What do you mean? We sent him to go find you earlier."

Shannon shook his head. "No, he never came to see me. I had to ask the nurses where you went."

All four of them stiffened at once.

"Son of a bitch," Jack whispered, his eyes wide. "It's *him*."


Winston woke up inside his own storage unit.

He was surprised to be waking up at all, and he wasn't exactly happy about his current state. A steady burn had made a home in his chest. One below his left pectoral, the other not much higher than his right kidney. Heavy bandages adorned his upper torso. His shirt had been cut off. He had an I.V. hooked up to one arm and there was an empty bag of blood beside it that he suspected had been recently used. His brain felt foggy from the pain, but things cleared after a moment or two.

"Welcome back," Faye said.

He tipped his head slightly to one side to see the leggy blonde sitting in a fold out chair next to him, idly flipping through one of the many medical books he'd kept in the unit. He was no stranger to self-surgery by now, so he kept himself current on all things related to the subject.

Winston licked his dry lips and croaked. "How?"

Faye stood and reached into a small cooler at the far wall, returning with a bottle of water. She handed it to him and he slowly took a sip. She capped the bottle and set it on the floor.

"It's just going to make you angry," she said frankly.

Winston scowled and repeated. "How?"

Faye sighed. "After Stella shot you, I dragged you behind a tree. She took a couple more shots, but then the police helicopter landed and she made tracks. I dragged you back to the car and went through your phone—"

"Bullshit," Winston interrupted. "It's password protected."

"You've used the phone several times in front of me," she said. "I kept watching until I memorized your finger movements to unlock it."

He frowned. She spread her hands. "Told you it'd just make you mad. Anyway, I went through your contacts until I found a doctor. He wasn't in the area, but he told me who to call for emergencies of the illegal variety in this part of town. I drove you here and the doctor operated and then closed you up. I paid for it with the money in the briefcase you had intended for the spotter. By the way, you really should use different passwords for things, but I'll cut you some slack since you're old."

Winston glared. "How bad?"

"Your heart stopped. Twice. Some serious organ damage. You lost a shitload of blood on the way here."

He kept a steady stare on her and then glanced at the clean floor. "I take it you found the number for a cleanup crew?"

She nodded. "The doctor gave it to me."

"What about the car?"

"Once you were stable, I drove it to the parking lot of an old Blockbuster and then torched it."

Winston sipped his water again and mulled over what she'd told him for a few stagnant minutes. "Could have let me die. Why didn't you?"

"We're not done," she said simply.

Winston eyed her. "Mm-hmm. You see anybody following us?"

"No. The best thing to do is act like it worked. If Stella thinks you're dead—"

"Stella didn't do this to me."

Faye froze. "Um, what?"

Winston shook his head. "Told you, Blondie. Stella wants to make it up close and personal."

222

She exhaled through her nose and tried to reel in her temper. "That's a stupid assumption."

"Faye, look at me."

"I am."

"Am I still breathing?"

"Yes."

"Then that wasn't Stella. First off, whoever shot me wasn't very smart. They used a laser scope at night like a rookie. Tipped me off. Second off, they were a bad shot. Should've gone for my head, but they took the sloppy way out with two plugs to the body. Third off, they got spooked by the cops instead of staying to confirm the kill. All signs point to another party's involvement."

"How is that possible?" she demanded.

"Might've been someone the smugglers hired to tie off loose ends. Might've been that the fellas I went to see in Cambridge went back on their word and put out a kill order on me. Folks in the Boston Mob can be a little touchy sometimes, and I apparently whacked one of the Mafioso's cousins when I did that drive-by on you and Jackson. Nothing we can't handle."

"Nothing we can't handle." Faye echoed incredulously. "Winston, I just watched you die tonight. Twice. What's it going to take for you to admit you're in over your head?"

"No such thing, Blondie. Still alive, ain't I?"

She stood then. "Because of me. You're right. I could have left you there, bleeding out, but I didn't. I dragged you out of that forest and got you to safety. You're not invincible, Winston."

She let out a harsh noise. "Hell, I could kill you right now if I wanted to. You can't even get out of that bed."

Winston gave her a crooked smile. "Just you try it, Blondie."

She crossed her arms. "I'm not scared of you."

"Then you're dumber than you look."

Faye kicked his cot over onto its side.

Winston hit the ground. He braced himself with one arm and grabbed the IV pole with the other, hefting it at her like a club. She'd moved to one side with the Kimber Pro pointed dead center between his eyebrows. The only sound either heard for several seconds was their harsh breathing.

"Don't," Faye whispered. "Call me dumb *ever* again. Do you hear me, Winston?"

He stared up at her and then nodded once. "Fair enough."

Winston straightened the I.V. pole and the cot and then lurched back into it with a groan, grimacing as both bullet wounds yawned wide with pain inside him. Faye returned the gun to its holster under her arm and sat down. "I'll give you this much, you may be crazy as a fruit bat, but you're a tough old bastard."

Winston shut his eyes. "How 'bout you get my old ass some painkillers while you're at it?"

She snorted and stood up, fiddling with the third bag attached to his I.V. "I've got something better."

He groaned happily. "Hello, morphine, my old friend."

Faye's lips twisted with the threat of a smile as she sat down again. "So what's the plan?"

"I'm benched until further notice," he said. "But you aren't. Your inside man should be able to give you a status update on who made it out of there alive. Once they do, we'll cover the docs for Stella's endgame attack. It'll be soon. Won't be easy to stop her, but we can do it."

The hitman pulled the blanket up over his midsection. "For now, get some rest."

"You're the one who got shot. *You* get some rest."

He snorted softly as he started to drift off on the wings of an exhausted slumber. "Blondie?"

"What?"

He cracked one eye open to look at her. "Did you cry when they shot me?"

"Go to sleep, you asshole."

Winston fell asleep with a chuckle on his lips.

# CHAPTER TWELVE
## SICILIAN DEFENSE

"What do you mean 'it's him'?" Libby demanded. "You mean we've been walking around listening to his bullshit all this time and he's been a snake in the grass?"

Jack nodded, licking his lips as he started connecting the dots in his head. "Think about it. The smugglers been a step ahead of us this whole time, and the information they would have to know in order to set us up had to be within our inner circle. Not many people know what the six of us know. He's the only one with the right access and he's appeared the least suspicious the whole time. Why else would he cut out of here like that? He must've realized that Shannon noticed something was off tonight."

Shannon ground his teeth. "Let's say for argument's sake that you're right, Jackson. What's his motivation?"

Jack ran a hand through his messy hair. "How long has he been working for you?"

"Seven months."

"And in that time, has he contributed any real big breakthroughs to your investigation?"

Shannon paused for a while. "Not exactly. We've mostly had him in the lab doing analysis on the dragons we recovered from the fights. We didn't recover any alive until you two came along."

Kamala nodded, catching on. "Jack and I are a threat. We came up with outside-the-box thinking. If we continued intercepting the matches and found more evidence to convict the smugglers, is it possible you would have considered him obsolete?"

Shannon's eyes narrowed. "You're not entirely wrong, no."

"There's more," she continued. "It might be a similar scheme to what we thought before, where someone in the smuggler's organization contacted him to keep you chasing your tails. Give you just enough evidence for a case, but not enough to stop them. It would divert your attention from where it might need to be placed. He could misdirect your energies so that you never came close to the real parties responsible. He could also give them a heads up if we were getting too close."

"This operation is run by a government agency," Libby said, aiming her furious gaze at Shannon. "You're telling me we're all not under heavy observation that would tip you off to something like this?"

"We don't have the resources nor the time to devote to watching every single person who works in that facility," he answered as he withdrew his cell phone. "If someone exhibits suspicious behavior, then yes, they get flagged by Internal Affairs."

He dialed Larry's number. A moment later, he swore. "The number's been disconnected."

Libby turned on her heel and marched down the hallway. Shannon called after her. "Hey! Where do you think you're going?"

She didn't answer. Shannon grimaced and nodded in her direction. "One of you deal with the kid. The other keeps an eye on Calloway. I have to lock down the hospital and get a bead on Whitmore. He can't have gotten far."

He headed towards the stairwell, already barking orders into the phone. Kamala touched Jack's arm. "Go. I'll keep an eye on Calloway."

He started to leave, but she squeezed his arm. "Be gentle, my dragon. She's young, scared, and hurting. Think with your heart, not your head."

Jack kissed her forehead. "I'll do my best, angel."

Thanks to Jack's long legs, he made it down to the lobby of the hospital quickly and spotted a blur of pink hair at the hospital's front entrance. Cold rain slapped down over the city of Alexandria. The darkness seemed thicker, more impenetrable, with the onslaught of bad weather. Jack broke into a jog until he caught up with her. Libby's shoulders were hunched, her arms at her sides, ringed fingers clenched into fists. She didn't look at him even after he fell in stride next to her on the sidewalk.

"And you're going where exactly, whipper snapper?" Jack asked in a tone he hoped was harmless.

"Go back inside, Jack," Libby said quietly.

"Libby," he said. "Easy. Talk to me. What's going through your head right now?"

"You're not my fucking therapist, Jack. Go. Back. Inside."

Jack stepped in front of her. "Make me."

She finally stopped and aimed a nasty glare up at him, not even flinching as the rain dripped down over her face. "Go to hell. Just because I cried on your shoulder doesn't mean you get to tell me what to do, alright?"

"And just what is it that you plan to do, huh?"

She clenched her jaw for a moment. "I've worked with these people long enough to know what's going to happen. If they catch him, Whitmore will cut a deal. He'll rat out the organization in exchange for amnesty or a reduced sentence. He's some white-bread Ivy-League asshole with a favorable background, so the judge will go soft on him. He might not even see the inside of a jail cell. My brother is in that hospital right now with broken ribs and internal bleeding and yet Whitmore is just going to walk like none of that happened?"

She shook her head. Water sluiced off her bright pink locks, now curly and flat to her head. "Not on my watch, man. Not on my fucking watch."

"So you're going to find him yourself and what? Kill him?"

Libby glared harder. "Tell me you wouldn't do the same goddamn thing if it was Kamala lying in that bed right now."

Jack stiffened. He swallowed hard before answering. "What do you think your brother would do if your plan somehow succeeded and you went away for the rest of your life for killing Whitmore?"

She didn't quite flinch, but he could see something unsure flit across her expression. "Do you think he'd be okay with that? With you, throwing your life away, over some coward who betrayed you? He told me he practically raised you, Libby. You're the apple of his eye. He'd do anything in his power to protect you, and this is what you want to do with that life? Go on some half-cocked revenge scheme to try and prevent something that you don't even know will happen?"

She shoved him. "Shut up! You know I'm right, Jack! You know that's how this godforsaken system works. My brother could have *died*."

Her shoulders shook harder. Her breath came in fast, trembling gulps. She bowed her head and clutched her arms. "He could have died, and I wouldn't have even gotten to say goodbye."

She covered her eyes with one hand, her voice a raw whisper. "I was supposed to protect him."

"Libby," Jack said softly. "You did protect him. You've been doing that all along."

She shook her head even as he pulled her into him, wrapping his arms around the crying girl. "Yes, you did. It's not your fault. If you want Whitmore to pay for what he did, then you're going to have a little faith. Not in the system. Agent Shannon may be a sour, cold, dispassionate asshole, but do you really think for one second that Whitmore pulling this shit under his direct supervision means Whitmore will get away with it?"

Libby sniffled and answered in a small voice, slightly touched with hope. "No."

"Exactly," Jack said. "The man hates my guts and all I did was punch his lights out. Whitmore is a dead man walking. It's just a matter of time."

He pulled back and leaned down to her height to meet her eyes, his words reinforced with steel conviction. "We *will* find him. Together. And, when the time comes, I bet Shannon himself will let you lock the son of a bitch in a cell and throw away the key. The man holds a grudge better than anyone I know."

She almost smiled. "Of all the things you've said, that was the most believable."

He rubbed her shoulder. "Good. Now can we get out of this freezing cold rain, please?"

Libby shrugged. "I don't mind so much. After all, your shirt's completely see through."

Jack sighed and hung his head. "Goddammit, Libby."

She giggled. Jack fought down a smile and looped his arm around her neck as he led her back towards the hospital. "Come on."


"Let me get this straight," Calloway said in a measured tone. "You're telling me that you guys think Lackey Larry is responsible for this shit?"

Kamala gave him a solemn nod. He exhaled hard through his nose. "Boy, y'all be better be happy I can't get out of this bed."

"Shannon went after him. I don't exactly think highly of Shannon by any means, but something tells me it won't take long for him to get a lead. As you said, the man is a bloodhound out in the field."

Calloway frowned suddenly. "Where's Libby?"

Kamala cleared her throat. "With Jack."

He eyed her. "Doing what exactly?"

She winced. "He's talking her down. She didn't handle the news well."

"Shit," he grumbled, tossing the covers to one side. She stood and held up her hands. "Jack can handle it."

"This is Libby we're talking about," he insisted, trying to hide a grimace as his entire upper body screamed with pain as he tried to pull his legs over the edge of the bed. "She's the most hard-headed, impulsive, foul-tempered girl I've ever met."

"Gee, bro, tell me how you really feel."

Calloway glanced up to see her at the door with a scowl on her lips. He sighed in relief and sagged back to the bed. "Thank God. Sit your five dollar ass down before I make change, girl."

Libby snorted and held the door for Jack. "Yeah, right. You haven't been able to take me since elementary school, punk."

He arched an eyebrow at the pair as they steadily dripped puddles onto the linoleum. "Went for a walk, I see?"

"Yeah," Jack said ruefully. "I'm the winner of the wet t-shirt contest."

Kamala grabbed the extra blankets in the corner of the room, draping them over the soaked pair. "It's late. We should all head back to get some rest. We'll be up early to help Agent Shannon locate Whitmore."

"I'm fine," Libby said stubbornly. "I don't need sleep."

"Little girl," Calloway growled. "Sit down before I make you sit down."

She just crossed her arms. Jack rolled his eyes, picked up her overnight bag, and shoved it into her hands before pointing at the bathroom. "Change into something dry. We don't have all damn night."

She glared at him next. He glared right back. "Don't make me carry you in there."

Libby grumbled uncharitable things about him under her breath as she stomped over to the bathroom and slammed the door shut.

Calloway sighed. "Hardheaded heifer."

"I heard that!"

Jack snorted. "You got it from here?"

Calloway flashed him a smirk. "I'll get her to rest if I have to have the nurses sedate her. You're good, Sir Gawain. Thanks for talking her off the ledge."

The smirk faded, replaced with concern. "Look…are you sure you guys want to stick around? Things just got a helluva lot more dangerous, and I know you only took this assignment on the grounds that you'd be safe. I don't want anything to happen to you while I'm stuck here in this stupid hospital bed. Maybe we should just call the whole thing off. Find someone else to take over."

Jack and Kamala shared a look. Kamala spoke for them both. "If we really are targets, we'd be safer surrounded by government agents than back home in Cambridge. We're staying."

"Then be careful. We might have an idea of Whitmore's endgame, but things could get real nasty if he tries to get rid of the rest of us to cover his tracks. Watch your backs out there. I'll see you guys first thing in the morning."

He offered them both fist bumps. The bathroom door opened a moment later and Libby reappeared in fresh clothes with a towel around her neck and another in her hand. She tossed it around Jack's neck and then hugged him fiercely. "Stupid jerk."

He grinned. "You love me."

"Shut up." She hugged Kamala just as fiercely. "Get out of here. Be careful."

"You too." Jack and Kamala waved and left the hospital room.

Kamala reached out and caught Jack's hand as if out of habit alone. He closed his cold fingers around hers and squeezed gently. "Are you alright, my dragon?"

"Feel like my head's going to explode," he admitted. "Other than that, I'm great. Christ. Can't believe Lackey Larry sold us out like that. What the hell is the matter with people?"

"They are the worst," she confirmed with a wise nod. "Still, what Shannon said about there being another player on the field is even more shocking. Why would this ally be helping us from the shadows? Why not come to us with what information they have and share it? Why hide?"

"God, who knows? It could be anyone. My money's on someone like the woman I met in Tokyo when Yagami

232

had me brought over to Sugimoto Pharmaceuticals."

"Minako?"

"Yeah. Or someone working for her. My gut said that she wasn't about what the Sugimoto siblings want to get out of this whole thing. She seemed to be interested in the conservation aspects of dragon resurrection, same as us. Trying to understand them in order to open the door to something even greater."

"Agreed, but perhaps we've picked up a Good Samaritan. Maybe someone who found out about what they were doing, felt bad, and wanted to help."

Jack nodded. "Also possible. Still, though. The fact that they were able to kill the Nordic sea serpent suggests someone closer to home. Someone with an X-factor, if that makes any sense. Hopefully, we'll have a comprehensive list of potentials by morning. We need to put this all to bed soon before things get out of control."

He held the towel out over their heads as they climbed into the limousine he'd called. The limo pulled off into the wet, inky night. Jack checked his phone. "Haven't heard from Faye since this afternoon. Did you get through to her?"

She shook her head. "Went straight to voicemail. She might need some Me Time. Being in a relationship with two people at once can get overwhelming."

"Especially when those two people run off on dangerous secret government missions," he said, leaning his head back on the seat and closing his eyes. "We've got to talk to her soon so she doesn't worry so much. You know she never likes to let anyone see her sweat."

He kissed the back of her hand. "Just like someone else I know."

"I'm fine."

Jack opened one eye. "You sure?"

"Well, not entirely."

He lifted his head, worried. "Why? What's wrong?"

Kamala gave him a wicked little smile. "Well, you are soaking wet and we're in the back of a limousine in the middle of the night, driving to our *hotel room.*"

Jack blushed madly. "*Kam.*"

"What?" she said, her tone innocent as she started rolling up the tinted partition window between the two of them and the limo driver. "You asked."

He shook his head. "Sometimes I really think you only want me for my body."

She caught his soggy tie and tugged him down towards her lips. "Only sometimes?"

*"Is it weird that I'm more nervous with you than with Jack?"*

*Kamala shrugged one shoulder. "To be fair, we've known each other longer and we used to live together. Not that many people start out friends, roommates, and then move toward romance. After all, you learn the person's bad habits."*

*"Point taken." Faye twirled her fork in her fettuccine alfredo and took another bite. She closed her eyes for a moment. "Mm, this is great, Kam. My fave."*

*"Thanks. I was torn between making this or vegetarian curry, but the latter isn't exactly conducive for first dates. Tastes amazing, but it makes your breath strong enough to knock out an ox."*

*"Tell me about it. Is it even a first date when we pretty much know everything about each other?"*

*"Not everything," Kamala said, her tone softer, more cautious. "You did hide this from me for a couple of years. You and Jack may be oil and water sometimes, but in that, you're awfully similar."*

*Faye's cheeks flushed a bit as she stared down at her plate. "Yeah. I think you underestimate just how amazing you are. That's why both of us wanted to keep our mouths shut. Didn't want to ruin things when they were working out so well."*

*Kamala sighed. "I understand what you mean, but it still bothers me that you held your feelings in for such a long time. It's not healthy to pine over someone. Rejection is terrifying, but it's* better to know than not to know."

"Well, in that case, why didn't you say anything after that night?"

Kamala chewed her lower lip. "I admit part of it is my background. I thought the alcohol was the catalyst, for lack of a better word, to us fooling around. I hadn't really had any attraction to women up until that point. Sort of like one of those things that had to be experienced for you to know it's there at all. You're also much bolder than I am in the dating world, so I had assumed it was something you'd done before and this was no big deal."

"Meh. Not so much. That threesome in undergrad was really more of me impressing some stupid guy that I liked at the time, than exploring my sexuality. The girl I was with was nice enough and we had good chemistry. We felt more comfortable with each other than I would have thought. At the time, it wasn't something I felt I would want to repeat and so I let it go. After I met you, I didn't realize that what we shared was more than just friendship. It had an intimacy to it that I've always sort of unconsciously looked for in relationships. I can trust you. That's rare for me. It's probably what motivated me to kiss you that night."

"You were the first long term positive relationship I'd been in since my ex," Kamala agreed. "So you're right. I shouldn't place the blame with you. I wasn't honest with myself either."

Faye exhaled and grabbed her wine. "Phew. We need to open a window. It's getting too cloying in here."

Kamala grinned, rolling her eyes. "Sorry, but you do realize if we start dating, you will occasionally have to share your feelings with me and Jack."

"Oh, please, he's easy," she said, dismissing the comment with a wave of her hand. "I take my shirt off and he'll forget all about talking."

Kamala giggled. "He is rather partial to a nice pair."

"My God, if we ever do have a threesome, I think his head will explode from overstimulation."

Kamala sent her a mysterious smile. "I wouldn't mind seeing that."

*Faye's cheeks deepened to a rosy hue. She cleared her throat. "What did the OB-GYN say at your last checkup?"*

*Kamala touched her stomach absently. "We're right on track. Little one is growing at a normal rate, and consequently, driving me crazy already. The morning sickness and constant urination are my particular favorites. Then there's the neurotic urge to clean all the time, fretting over saving money for her first years of infancy, making sure my maternal leave will cover the new apartment, figuring out when to tell my bloody family – "*

*Faye blinked. "They don't know already?"*

*"My parents do. The extended family doesn't yet, but I'll start showing soon enough, so I'm going to have to tell them."*

*"You told your parents when you went to see your mother last month."*

*She nodded. Faye bit her lip. "Christ. How did that go?"*

*The little scientist pushed both hands into her thick, glossy hair and rubbed her forehead. "My mother managed to handle it with her usual grace and understanding."*

*"And your father?" Faye asked gently.*

*"We got into a screaming match and had to be separated."*

*Faye swore under her breath. "I'm sorry, Kam. Did he try to disown you?"*

*"After we had our knockdown drag-out, my mother took him for a drive. The next morning, he apologized and explained that his anger was mostly out of fear for me and the baby. He certainly has made no bones about the fact that he doesn't like Jack, but he bears no ill will towards the baby. I don't think it'll ever be possible for him and Jack to be in the same room anytime soon. He promised that he will come to town for the birth to give his blessing and he'll support me whenever I need it."*

*"Wow. Your mom changed his mind in just one night?"*

*Kamala snorted. "No. She probably threatened to divorce him unless he behaved himself. I'm sure he's still angry and resentful, but he didn't want to do the same thing to me that his family did to him when he married my mother."*

*"So when will you tell the rest of the family?"*

*She rolled her head back against the chair and groaned.*

236

"My mother wants me to tell them at Thanksgiving. We only celebrate the big two American holidays in my family. We usually have my mother's side over at my parents' place for Thanksgiving and then spend Christmas with my father's side. Some of my relatives fly over from Bangalore and Islamabad."

"I hate to ask, but does that mean you're not going to say anything about being bisexual?"

"It'll be hard enough for them to accept that I'm having a child with someone outside of our faith and either of my racial backgrounds. For now, I'm not going to double up trying to explain that I have two significant others."

Kamala paused. "But I hope you know that doesn't mean I'm going to hide the relationship or act as if I'm ashamed of how I feel about you. I won't. I would never do that to you."

Faye's shoulders relaxed a tad bit. "Oh. Thanks, Kam. I'm sorry this all got so complicated. If I could give you non-caring parents like mine, I would."

"Collette and Brad won't care if you tell them you're dating me and Jack?"

"Pfft, yeah, right," Faye said, draining the last of her wine and taking her and Kamala's now empty plates to the sink. "They'd have to take their heads out of their asses long enough to listen to me. I think we're safe."

She dusted off her hands as she returned from the kitchen. "Now then, why don't we get this Netflix portion of Netflix-and-chill underway?"

Kamala laughed and stood. "Subtle."

"Always," Faye said with a wink, plopping down on the couch and firing up the television. Kamala crawled next to her and reclined the seat. The two sifted through until they found something they liked and turned it on. Faye dragged the couch blanket across them and settled in for the night.

The strange part was that it wasn't that much different from things they had done before, and yet the atmosphere had changed. Faye's heart thrummed in her chest, somewhere between anxious and excited, with the kind of jitters she hadn't felt in years. Kamala had been right. Maybe because they'd known each other for *so long, the prospect of being close to her with everything out in the open made her nervous; not with the fear of rejection, but with the trepidation of traveling through mostly unknown waters. Jack had teased her before, that she could wrap most men around her pinky without thought, almost as if it were reflex, and yet women gave her pause. She liked Kamala. She respected her. She felt the need to protect and nurture her, an impulse that was largely foreign to her with the exception of Jack.*

*Faye kissed the top of Kamala's head. The dark-haired pixie glanced up from where her head rested her shoulder. "You okay?"*

*"Never been better."*

*Kamala smirked and lifted an eyebrow. "I might be able to fix that."*

*She kissed her.*

*Faye hadn't really ever melted before when someone kissed her.*

*First time for everything.*

*"Wow," she murmured once they pulled apart. "Yep. I'm bisexual as fuck."*

*Kamala burst into light, almost musical laughter, and that was the moment Faye knew that for better or worse, everything would be alright between them.*

Faye woke up as someone brushed a cloud of fallen golden hair away from her forehead to tuck it behind her ear. Automatically, she slapped the wandering hand away and wrenched her heavy eyelids open to see Winston standing in front of her chair.

"Morning, Blondie."

"Get back in the cot," she growled hoarsely at him.

Winston rolled his eyes, but lowered himself down onto it anyway. Faye yawned and stretched, pushing the blanket off her body. Odd. She hadn't fallen asleep with it on her. She scratched her head and stared blearily at him, noting that some of the color had returned to his skin. A glance at her phone revealed it was half past six o'clock in the morning. She suppressed a groan of annoyance at the fact before returning her attention to the assassin.

"How do you feel?" she asked.

"Like I've been shot twice," he grunted. "The hell do you think I feel?"

"Complain, complain, complain," she said, folding the blanket and tossing it at the foot of the cot. "Did you tuck me in last night?"

Winston just looked at her. She smirked. "You're getting soft, Pooh Bear."

He mirrored the smirk. "Well, I can't get hard. Not enough blood in my system for that yet."

She kicked his ankle and he chuckled before nodding towards the duffel bag. "Get dressed. We've got to get over to the facility to see what's what with our inside man."

"We nothing," she snapped, pushing to her feet and tugging her blood-stained t-shirt off. "You have two holes in your chest. You're staying put. You can advise me over the phone."

"I've been shot before. A lot. I'll be fine."

She squatted and pulled clothes out of her bag. "Look, save the tough guy act for someone who will buy that shit. I've lived with a doctor for almost two years. I know all about the human body and how much punishment it can take. You need to stay in that cot until you're healed enough to move around or your stitches will tear, you'll bleed out, and be completely useless to me."

He glared at her. "And what if Stella makes a direct play for your friends? You think you can take her on your own? You're greener than a lizard's ass, Blondie. She'd eat you alive."

Faye hopped into a pair of jeans and raked her hair off her brow. "Oh, is that right?"

"You know it is."

"Then why did you take an interest in me to begin with, Winston? You said you saw something in me. Maybe I'm not Mrs. Smith, but I'm not going to let that bitch kill the people I love. I will find a way to protect them or die trying. You're no good to me dead, so shut up and stay in the cot until you heal."

The two stared each other down for a long moment. Winston put his back to the wall of the storage unit and crossed his arms. "Now, sweetheart, you wouldn't happen to want me to stay here so that after you somehow stop Stella, you can tell the cops where I am?"

"Blow me."

He bared his teeth. "You're smart. I'll give you that. But I know how you think. I'm sure the doctor would've given you the location of a safe house. You took me back here because it's small and hard to leave without being seen, and the cops could surround me. I'd have to either give up or kill myself. Either option gets you what you want in the end, technically. So what's to stop me from waltzing right out of here once you head over to the facility?"

Faye took a deep breath and bent over until their heads were level. "Winston, this stopped being about me chasing you a long time ago. You and I both know it. I'm not stupid. I know that you saved my life last night. Those bullets would have hit me if you hadn't moved me out of the way. I'd be dead right now if you hadn't done that. Whether you want to admit it or not, you care about me in some fucked up sort of way. For that reason, you get one and only one pass. You're going to leave me in the lurch. I already know that. Survival first."

Her blue eyes frosted over. "But rest assured, I will find you again and I will bring you to justice for what you did."

Winston nodded slowly. "As long as you know where we stand."

Then he leaned forward and kissed her gently.

Faye's mouth dropped open in complete shock.

Winston grinned. "Relax, Blondie. That was for luck. Get going. We're wasting daylight."


*"Mommy, what's this one?"*

240

A little dark-haired, brown-skinned girl around five years old, plucked a brilliant yellow-and-peach colored flower with brown spots from the garden and tottered over to the blanket where Kamala sat.

"This is called a tiger lily," Kamala said. "It's named that because it's the same color as a tiger."

"It's pretty," the child said, beaming. She held it out to her mother. "I want you to have it."

"Why thank you, my little flower," Kamala said with a grin, tucking it behind one ear. "Go pick another one for me."

Her daughter wandered back towards the garden. The backyard had now become one of Kamala's favorite things about the house she and Jack had bought. It had a porch with two round glass tables with umbrellas and chairs, a stone path that bisected the yard, a couple of steps, and then a patio with a fountain at the center. She'd had the gardener surround the fountain with all kinds of bright, vibrant flowers to fill the air with their sweet scents. Often, when she needed a break from work, she'd put down a blanket and sunbathe. Jack would join her sometimes, but he knew when she needed some alone time to clear her head, like now.

"What's this one?" her daughter asked, returning with a light purple blossom with five petals.

"This is called a mayflower. It's actually the state flower for Massachusetts."

"What's a state flower?"

"All the fifty states in the country each chose a flower to represent them. This is the one for where we live."

Her daughter flopped down in her lap and rolled her head back to look up at her. "What's your favorite flower, Mommy?"

"Aside from you?" she said, kissing her daughter's forehead. "Hmm...I think I'm partial to marigolds. They're very friendly looking flowers."

"I like that name. It's nice." The child began plucking petals off the mayflower. "I like our garden, Mommy."

"So do I, sweet pea."

A shadow swept across the sun. Kamala raised a hand above her brow and noticed a formation of angry grey clouds sliding over it. She frowned as she recognized the shelf formation they made. A storm was imminent.

"Alright, sweet pea, it looks like it's going to rain. We'd better head inside."

"Aww!" the little girl complained. "Do we have to?"

"Yes, we do. Come along now." She set her daughter on her feet and nudged her towards the house as she stood and began folding the picnic blanket.

Just then, a crack of lightning licked overhead and thunder barked sharply. Instantly, rain slapped down onto Kamala's head, soaking her in seconds. She groaned in annoyance and tucked the edges of the blanket in faster.

Once finished, she turned towards the house. The folded wool slipped out of her wet hands.

A Nordic sea serpent stood in front of the patio, its eerie blue eyes glowing mad with hunger as it stared down at the little girl petrified before it.

"Goddess above," Kamala whispered, her eyes wide, ice water in her veins.

"M-Mommy," her daughter squeaked. "Mommy, I'm scared."

"It's okay, baby," Kamala said, struggling to breathe past the overwhelming panic as the deadly creature crouched motionless, enormous, and threatening against the sudden rainstorm. "Listen to me. I want you to very slowly back away and come towards me, okay?"

The child shook her head wildly. Rainwater sloughed off her short, matted curls. The dragon's upper lip slid away from its jaws. Black, curved fangs dripping with saliva glinted in what remained of the sunlight.

"Come on," Kamala whispered hoarsely. "Sweet pea, please, come towards Mommy."

Shaking violently, the little girl stumbled backwards one step at a time. The dragon hissed and took one gigantic step towards the small child. Kamala's eyes darted around for something, anything resembling a weapon, but she didn't have anything within reach. The dragon only had to lunge a couple of *feet to be able to reach her daughter. She was helpless.*

*The scientist sunk down on one knee and gripped the blanket in her cold hands. "Sweetie, when I tell you to, I want you to run inside. Don't look back. Just run as fast as you can and hide under your bed."*

*"I can't! Mommy, I can't! I'm scared!" the child wailed as the dragon's deadly hiss increased in volume. Its shoulder blades moved beneath its pitch-black rubbery skin as it readied itself to attack.*

*"Be strong, baby. I won't let it hurt you. I'm going to count to three."*

*Kamala unfurled the blanket between her trembling fingers, her eyes never leaving the dragon as its jaws spread wide, exposing its pink gums and razor-sharp teeth, preparing to bite.*

*"One...two...three!"*

*Kamala launched herself at the dragon with the blanket and wrapped the thick cloth around its head. She closed her arms down around its jaws tightly and screamed. "Run, baby! Run!"*

*Her daughter screamed and fled inside as fast as she could, stumbling over the dragon's tail.*

*The sea serpent screeched and worried Kamala like a Barbie doll, tossing her off. She flew in a short arc and slammed into the wooden fence beside them, the breath knocked out of her.*

*Then the dragon's clawed foot sliced through the air and impaled her through the chest.*

*White-hot pain seared through Kamala's upper body. Blood oozed from the puncture wounds and dribbled down her blouse, staining it along with the rain. She gasped for breath, half blinded by the rain, as the dragon's foul-smelling breath filled her nostrils. The last thing she saw was its hellfire eyes when it opened those monstrous jaws once more to eat her.*

Kamala jerked upward in bed with a short cry.

The second she did, she became aware of a sharp, pulsing pain in her lower abdomen, not far from her pelvis. She clutched her oversized belly and groaned, shutting her eyes to the sudden discomfort.

"Kam?" Jack muttered behind her, stirring. The

mattress lurched for a second and then he appeared to her right, mussed, disheveled, and worried. "Baby, what's wrong?"

"I..." she gasped, trying to focus. "I don't know. Bad dream."

"Where does it hurt? Are they contractions? Are you bleeding?"

Kamala slid her legs over the side of the bed and concentrated to locate the origin of the pain, but then as soon as she did, it vanished. She tried to slow her labored breathing, wiping cold sweat from her brow. "N-No, there's no bleeding. I think the nightmare just agitated me."

He rubbed her shoulders gently. "Get dressed. I'll take you to the hospital to get checked out."

She shook her head. "I've had the phantom contractions before. Jitters. Nothing more."

"Kam--" he protested.

She squeezed his knee. "I'm fine, Jack. Please, just get me something to drink, you great useless *pagal*."

He reluctantly stood and went to the sink, running her a glass of cold water. She drank the whole thing and sat still with her eyes closed, practicing her Lamaze breathing until her pulse slowed and her joints loosened one at a time. Jack remained at her side and ran his hand up and down the length of her spine in soothing circles.

"No one would blame you if you want to hang back today," he said quietly. "It's been crazy. I can stay with you, if it helps. Spend the day pampering you until you're sick of me."

"I'll never get sick of you." She leaned her head against his neck. "We have work to do. The sooner we finish our assignment, the sooner we can go home."

Jack slipped his arm around her. "Is that what's bothering you? Homesick?"

"A little," she admitted. "I just want this little cretin out of me before she drives me off the deep end."

Jack winced. "Pregnancy nightmare?"

244

"Close," she whispered, shuddering. "I'm not...ready to talk about it yet."

"Don't have to, angel." He kissed the crown of her hair. "Anything I can do to help?"

She thought about it. "Don't suppose you can switch bodies with me for the next thirty days?"

"I'll see what I can do," he said mildly. "I meant aside from mad scientist experiments that spit in the face of God. We've already got one of those going already."

Kamala glanced at the ancient but functional alarm clock on the nightstand. "We only have another couple hours until we have to head over to check on Calloway and Libby. Maybe just rub my belly and tell me a bedtime story."

"I think I can manage that." He slid the sheets back and she wriggled beneath them. He spooned her and settled one hand over her swollen stomach. She shut her eyes and concentrated on the familiarity of the gesture. She'd gotten so used to his embrace, his touch, that some part of her would miss their pregnant routine once the baby was born. Maybe she'd convince him to keep up the tummy rubs. She rather enjoyed them.

"Once upon a time," Jack said. "There was a princess and a dragon..."

Time dripped off the clock as Kamala relaxed against her lover, listening to the steady, pleasant rumble of his voice as he made up a fairytale on the spot. Her anxiety unraveled one minute at a time, but one thread remained and twisted its way around her throat as she considered perhaps the scariest part of her nightmare.

Why hadn't Jack and Faye been in it?

# CHAPTER THIRTEEN
## ASTRAY

"Alright," Shannon said as he shut the hospital door behind him. "Here's where we are."

He stalked over to the small gathering around Calloway's bed, hands in his pockets, his usual scowl firmly in place. "We've transported all the dragons to the facility, as well as the corpse of the Nordic sea serpent. Dr. Anjali, I want you running point on the autopsy. Unfortunately, though, it's not going to be possible to achieve completely sterile conditions right now--the damn thing's too big to fit in the cadaver lab. We had to rent out a meat locker in town to at least emulate an environment conducive to studying the creature."

Kamala nodded. "Understood. I'll be as careful as possible."

"Good." He glanced at Jack. "Dr. Jackson, I want you to do a full run up on the dragons we recovered. I want to know every damn thing we can about these creatures since there are a couple of new species we weren't even aware that they were cloning. We need to draw a line back to where they might have gotten DNA samples for the dragons."

"A good place to start is that ice dragon," Jack said, blowing on his coffee before taking a sip. "They are extremely rare. It's probably our best bet to find something out of all the species we saw. If I recall correctly, there are only a handful of museums that ever recovered intact remains. I also had a thought on who might know something about where and when these matches take place."

"Oh?"

"Wei Zhang. Call it a hunch, but the smug, confrontational thing made me think that he knows more than he's letting on. I think it might be a good idea to shake the tree, so to speak."

Shannon eyed him. "What makes you think he'd betray the smugglers if he does know something?"

Jack shrugged. "No one's perfect. Apply pressure in the right place and we might be able to get him to roll over on them. Doesn't strike me as the type to take a bribe, not with all that honor nonsense he was spitting, but if we find some leverage, we might be able to break him."

"We?"

"You," Jack said, rolling his eyes at the correction. "Whatever. Think you might have any grounds to bring him in for questioning?"

Shannon offered him a shark-like grin. "I'm sure I can dig something up."

The agent nodded to Libby next. "You feel like coming in today, kid? Or would you rather keep an eye on your big brother?"

She glowered at him for the "kid" epithet before answering. "Are you saying I have a choice?"

Shannon shrugged. "There is a such thing as personal days."

She glanced at Calloway, who shook his head. "Dad's already here, squirt. No need to babysit. Just keep me updated and I'll be alright."

Libby squeezed his hand. "Okay, count me in. What do you need from me?"

Shannon's expression darkened. "Those men that died in the shipping yard didn't have to die if I had known what was in there. I want a full-on arsenal of weapons for every identified species of dragon that has viable remains on the planet earth."

Libby's jaw dropped. "Shannon, that's...that's a *tall* order. We're talking thousands of dollars worth of equipment and a ton of labor--"

Shannon withdrew an envelope from his suit jacket and handed it to her. She opened it to find a letter inside that made her eyes widen. "Jesus *Christ*."

"What is it?" Kamala asked.

"After last night's fiasco, I had a meeting with the boys upstairs about our operating budget," Shannon said. "Particularly for equipment. They just tripled it. Anything you need, ask and I'll get it for you. Those were my men. I am responsible for their deaths. As long as I'm still breathing, no one is going in unprepared like that ever again."

Libby swallowed hard as she handed the letter back to him. "Okay. I'll have some blueprints and specs ready for you by the time we leave tonight."

"What's the word on Larry?" Kamala asked.

"So far, we don't have anything just yet. Larry's been contracted with the government for a while, so he knew what initial steps we'd take in order to find him. Nothing on his credit cards or accounts, aside from a previous withdrawal of about ten grand. If he was a plant by the smugglers, odds are they have him holed up somewhere."

Jack licked his lips. "Uh, that's not a good thing. If his cover's blown, won't they want him dead in order to tie up loose ends?"

"Depends on how vital he is to their operation. If he's been supplying them with valuable intel, they'll keep him alive. If not, though..." Shannon rubbed his chin. "Might be an angle to pursue. If he runs back to them and finds out they're trying to kill him, he might return to the fold for protection. It's been several hours since he went on the run. Something will pop by the afternoon."

"Find anything on our mysterious Good Samaritan?" Jack asked.

"Nothing that makes sense," Shannon admitted. "We've got a blood trail leading back to where we think they parked a car. A *lot* of blood. Found a couple .38 shell casings, too. Someone obviously didn't like that they were out there helping us."

"You think someone killed them?"

"Hard to say. We're checking hospitals for gunshot victims, but I doubt we'll find anything. I've assigned someone to check for any unusual 911 phone calls that correspond with when we think it happened. Whatever the hell our Good Samaritan is into, its put them in the line of fire as well."

"You let me know if you find anything," Calloway said, idly rubbing his bandaged ribs. "I owe them one helluva thank you."

"Noted. In the meantime, I'm keeping a couple beat cops here to babysit you until we've got everything in the investigation stabilized. If anything feels off, call me immediately."

Calloway smirked at the older man. "Aw, I didn't know you cared."

Shannon rolled his eyes, ignoring the comment. "Since we still don't know that the leak in the facility is plugged, plan to meet back here at noon for updates. Unless it's absolutely necessary, don't openly discuss what we're up to while we're on the grounds. I've got Internal Affairs questioning staff as we speak. Sooner or later, someone will spill. Until then, assume they're all compromised and keep your mouths shut. Understood?"

They all nodded. "Lastly, you're each getting a security detail until further notice, so don't do anything stupid. They report straight to me."

Jack scowled. "Why'd you look at me when you said that?"

Shannon just arched an eyebrow. Jack sighed. "It's really too early for your bullshit, old man."

The agent grunted. "I call it like I see it. Get moving, troops."


"Forgive me a terrible pun," Jack said. "But this is the coolest thing that's ever happened to me."

He adjusted the goggles resting on the bridge of his nose slightly and zoomed the streaming camera in on the slumbering ice dragon lying on the lab table before him. Under the bright fluorescents, its pearly scales showed a slight iridescence that sharply contrasted with the deep blue spines running down its back as well as in its folded wings. It had taken the largest exam table just to fit atop it, and its thick tail trailed onto the floor, twitching every so often as the reptile slept.

"The subject is a member of the *gelus serpens* species of dragon. Male. Measured at six feet and five inches from snout to tail, standing three-foot-four-inches at the shoulder, wingspan of twelve feet. Obviously a cold-blooded reptile with a record low body temperature. Pun intended. Body maturation and blood samples suggest it's in its early adult stages."

Jack peeled back its upper lip and carefully measured the length of its protruding fangs. "Incisors are approximately two-point-three inches."

He inserted his thumb in the groove of the creature's jaws and pried them apart, revealing a long, black forked tongue. He flicked on the bright LED light on the goggles and peered into the creature's mouth. "Aside from some serious fish-breath, looks like its mouth and throat are indeed coated like the history books say to protect it from the mythical ice breath. I'll confirm that momentarily with a sample."

He grabbed a long Q-tip and carefully examined the lining of the dragon's lower jaw until he found a tiny puckered hole near its mandible. He swabbed the rim and a little of its interior, and then walked over to the microscope on the counter across from the exam table. Once he'd applied it to a slide, he examined it. "The prevailing theory that corresponds with firsthand accounts is that this dragon secretes a gas that can freeze anything on contact. It's considered to be a defense mechanism rather than a method for catching prey, like those freaky little lizards that shoot blood out of their eyeballs. Based on what I'm seeing here, it's not truly an ice breath like Superman or something. It seems to be a liquid, much like some fire-breathing dragons. However, it might appear like a cloud since ice dragons lived in freezing climates and maybe that's how the rumor got started."

Jack placed the slide inside a secure capsule and paged someone to take it down to the lab for analysis before returning to the dragon. He did a thorough physical before continuing. "No obvious marks on its scales, so I'm guessing our fella was slated to be in his first match pretty soon. Tracker's been deactivated and removed already by one of our super helpful lab techs. Radiation levels were faintly detected, but non-harmful just like the other species."

He settled his gloved hands on his hips, tilting his head a bit as he observed the sleeping dragon. "What's truly distressing to me is that like some of the other dragons we've recovered, it doesn't appear to be spliced with another living species or relative the way that we spliced Pete. Lab results will confirm as much, but the question remains how the hell they've found intact DNA samples enough to clone the dragon without splicing it. The best theory I've got so far is that the species that were discovered closer to before all the dragons were hunted to extinction had less deterioration than some of the more ancient species like Baba Yaga. The ice dragons were among the last ones to be exterminated along with certain forest dragons as well. They were highly coveted since their skins can withstand insanely low temperatures and are impervious to all kinds of blunt force as well as several kinds of weapons. They're extremely tough and wickedly fast. They were responsible for a lot of foolish knights never returning home, as a matter of fact."

He continued through his usual process of taking samples of its scales, saliva, blood, excrement, and tissue one by one before sending the creature off with a small team of lab techs to get its X-rays. "I'm definitely interested to see the dragon's temperament. Ice dragons are of the solitary breeds. I'd assume it would be relatively hostile towards us, since we'd be viewed as just another predator, but he might hit it off with Pete like the other dragon did. Doesn't help being cloned by a bunch of violent criminals, either. We'll run the first trial with our subject awake in a couple hours. Moving on to our next newbie."

The lab assistants wheeled the Netherland forest dragon. It had longer limbs than the arctic dragon and its snout was narrow with thin, needle-like teeth reminiscent of a Cayman. However, unlike the ice dragon's unmarred seaweed-colored scales, there were scars scored along its side, belly, neck, and forearms. Its leathery wings appeared untouched, rustling every so often as the creature slept.

"Our lovely lady here is *perfossoris nigrum* or the Netherland forest dragon," Jack said. "They are nocturnal dragons that based most of their diets around woodland creatures that they dug out of the ground and devoured. Our initial observation is that this one and her brother are of the same clutch of eggs, so they are the same age and possibly the same height and weight as well. Of the species we've seen so far, they're one of the most non-aggressive dragons ever recorded in history. Rumors of domesticated dragons are largely centered around them. Some people even said they could be taught to herd sheep and other beasts of burden, but nothing's ever been completely confirmed."

He performed a full physical once again. "Measured at eight-feet from snout to tail, four feet at the shoulder, wingspan of eighteen feet. Fangs are only an inch long. Claws are a hell of a thing, roughly two inches long. There's no doubt in my mind she could probably tear right through a wall, metal or otherwise, in a matter of minutes."

The dragon snorted and flexed its claws. Jack jumped backward and clutched his chest for a second. He kept an eye on the reptile, but it didn't wake. "Thanks for the free heart attack."

The outer lock to the door beeped and Agent Shannon strode in, looking annoyed. "Got a moment, doc?"

"I am legally obligated to answer yes," Jack said dryly.

"Stash the sass. There's a matter requiring your presence."

Jack paused and saved the streaming recording and

took off his gloves, goggles, and coveralls. He paged one of the lab assistants to return the dragon to its cell. "Which is?"

"While my team was going through the financial transactions from the guys we picked up at the previous fighting ring, a familiar name popped up."

"Let me guess," Jack said as they exited the lab and started down the hallway. "Wei Zhang."

"Bingo," Shannon said. "I had someone pick him up half an hour ago. He's in interrogation."

"Good times. And you need me why?"

"You're not good at much, but you are intensely irritating. Zhang's clammed up and I have a hunch you can kick the hornet's nest hard enough for something to fall out of him."

Jack did a double-take. "Wait, you want me to interrogate him? I'm pretty sure that's not even legal. It's not like in the Old West where you can appoint me as a deputy or something."

"There are loopholes. Typically, if you agitate a suspect enough to let one small thing slip, then they cave in and tell you the rest in the hopes that cooperating lessens their sentence. You loosen the lid and I'll take it off."

"What do you have on him?"

"We were given one of the offshore accounts where they aggregate the cash they get from these death matches. Zhang has contributed to said account every month for the past six months, always on the fifteenth."

"How much money are we talking here per contribution?"

"Five grand."

Jack whistled. "Guy's not hard up for cash, it seems."

"That's just the traceable money. My hunch is that it's like a subscription fee. You contribute to their cause and then place cash bets at the fights. The house takes a certain percentage, but you keep the rest of your winnings. Based on how much we found in the account, they have over twenty contributors in the area."

"Twenty people contributing five grand a month? Christ. That's a hundred grand minimum."

Shannon nodded. "Which is why we need him to spill his guts. Stop the cash flow and that's one way to disorient them. The account's been frozen, but if he gives up any information about how these things get organized, we've got them in the bag."

"It does explain why he was so hostile, to some degree," Jack said, following the agent into the elevator. "You can shake it off if someone gets on your nerves, but when they start screwing with your financial livelihood, then you get antsy. I can press him about that whole 'honor' spiel that he's on and see if it gets us some results. He sounded hell-bent on the idea that they can bring dragon-hunting back, so maybe he's observing the dragons' various abilities for future reference. Still, though, if Zhang expects that he'll get to live out his delusional fantasy, he's not going to want to squawk."

"That's where your Jackson charm kicks in," Agent Shannon drawled with the utmost sarcasm. "Identify a weakness and exploit it. That's how you get someone to crack."

Jack crossed his arms and leaned against the wall opposite the agent. "And you know all about that, don't you?"

Shannon gave him a grim smile, choosing not to answer. "How'd you get this assignment? You give off a vibe that you should be working for Secret Services, protecting the Madam President. What happened? Just what was it that allowed you to grace us with your enjoyable presence? Did you step on someone's toes and get stuck with us?"

"My wife died."

Jack paled. He swallowed hard, trying to formulate a response, but nothing immediately came to mind. Shannon tucked his hands into his pockets and leaned against the wall, his expression and tone of voice unchanged. "Leukemia. Cammy was a bit of a free spirit, didn't like going to the doctor much. Started getting sick about a year and a half ago, but she just thought it was a regular illness. I worked too many hours to have the time to push her to take her health more seriously, so by the time we went to the doctor, it was too late. After she died, they put me on bereavement leave. When I came back, I told them I wanted something with less demanding hours, so they put me in charge of this recovery project."

"Shit, man," Jack murmured. "I'm sorry."

"Everyone's sorry when they find out. Doesn't make much difference. She's still gone."

Jack eyed him. "No offense, but you haven't been forthcoming with anything about yourself before. Why'd you tell me now?"

Shannon smirked. "Just wanted to see the look on your face after you realized you punched a widower."

Jack scowled as the elevator doors opened. "That might be the pettiest thing that's ever been said to me."

Shannon walked out first, a dark, victorious chuckle in his throat. He led the scientist through another set of locked doors to a small, barren office on the left side of the hallway. It had clearly been meant as a small conference room, but it had plain concrete walls with no warmth or charm, which made it ideal for interrogation. They passed the police officer who had retrieved Zhang, idling in a chair outside said office.

Wei Zhang sat inside the office with a sour expression, arms crossed, the chair leaning on its back legs as he rocked in it impatiently. He was facing away from the door, glaring at the wall as if it would make his situation any less stressful.

"Don't lose your temper again," Shannon warned him. "Keep the focus on him. I can hear you just fine from here, so if you get him to crack, I'll take over with the official procedures."

Jack blew a long breath out through pursed lips and rolled his shoulders. "What if he gets confrontational?"

Shannon snorted. "You've got a decent right hook.

You'll be fine."

"Thanks for the vote of confidence." Jack opened the door and walked inside.

Zhang craned his neck at the sound of the door closing, an angry retort no doubt prepared, but it died on his lips as his brown eyes fell across the scientist. He clenched his jaw and launched a spiteful glare at him. "You."

"Yep," Jack said cheerfully. "Me. How's it hanging, Zhang?"

"Piss off, Jackson. I've got nothing to say to you."

"Awesome. I don't actually want to hear you talk, to be honest."

Zhang snorted. "Is that right?"

"You can just listen while I paint the picture of how utterly fucked you are right now, since apparently Shannon didn't reiterate it enough."

"I haven't done shit," Zhang spat. "All you've got are financial statements, nothing more."

"Exactly. They have enough evidence to get you charged for something. Just need the story to go along with it." Jack stroked his chin and wrinkled his nose in thought. "Let's see. I'm guessing you caught the scent of what was going on with the illegal cloning ring not long after Aokigahara. Maybe some old friends or a contact through the Silver Dragon clan who spoke with a member of the Red Fist. You kept your ears open for an opportunity and then found out about the fighting ring. You figured it would be a good opportunity to whet your knife and see just what the fuss was all about. Went to your first match and saw a bloodbath. Then you were hooked. You knew that the shit they were doing was real. It wasn't empty promises and rumors like with the Sugimotos, the Yamaguchi-gumi, or the Inagawa-kai. You also knew how much money there stands to be made from this little endeavor, which was why my lecture put a metaphorical bee in your bonnet. Thanks to your ego, you became a person of interest to us. If you'd have kept your mouth shut, you might not have landed yourself in hot water."

Zhang clenched his jaw harder as Jack spared him a patronizing smile. "And you know how to get out of this, but you know it means you're done for good. If you give up the illegal ring, you'll just get banned if you're lucky and you're dead meat if you're unlucky. These criminals are well-connected. Someone's bound to have seen you get picked up by the cops. I'm betting you'll be shut out if you try to go back. You have two choices left. One, take your chances on your own and hope that they don't want to spare the resources to find you, torture you, and kill you. Two, tell us who these people are, get a lesser sentence and some protection until the agency shuts them down."

Jack paced the length of the small table. "But you and I both know you've never had it easy your whole life, so why would you choose the second option? You know people. You have friends you can turn to that will help you, right? Your clan, for instance."

Jack snapped a finger. "Oh, right. You're a liability now for getting busted. My guess is they'll make you an outcast once this all goes public and you're on the list of perpetrators. Well, no big deal. You might know someone in the Red Fist who will provide protection for a price. Except you'll be viewed as a rat and they won't trust you, let alone hear your sob story. Meaning you have to navigate this mess by yourself. If you've got five grand to throw away once a month, I'm guessing you're probably not in a financial bind, but if this mess goes public, you might lose your job. I mean, who's going to want a trust someone who gambles and cavorts with violent criminals? Then again, you might look pretty good in one of those paper hats at a Jack-in-the-Box—"

"You don't know shit, Jackson. Tell all the wild stories you want. Doesn't make it the truth."

"The truth is a matter of circumstance," Jack said with a pointy smile. "And circumstances point to the fact that you're up shit creek without a paddle."

"Really? Is that what my lawyer's gonna say when he

gets here?"

"Buddy, this is the U.S. government. You really think that's going to fly here? If they want something, they get it. You can kick and scream all you want, but they'll still drag you off."

"You think I'm scared of you? Or that old bastard? Or this sham of a government?"

"That's exactly what I think. I think you're a scared little boy deep down and you haven't got the guts God gave Scooby Doo."

Zhang leapt to his feet and slammed his palms down on the table. "If my stomach was strong enough to watch a Highlander dragon tear another one in half last week, I think I'm strong enough to survive on my own."

A Cheshire cat grin stretched Jack's lips wide.

"What?" Zhang snarled.

"Agent Shannon," Jack called in the direction of the door. "Was that admittance of witnessing illegal activity?"

Shannon pushed the door open. "I do believe it was, Dr. Jackson."

Zhang shut his eyes. The agent closed the door and tossed a clipboard with paperwork between his outstretched hands. "Game's over, son."

"He tricked me," Zhang growled.

"You spoke of your own free will. Not his fault you have an even worse temper than he does." Shannon pulled out a chair and sat down, unbuttoning his suit jacket as he went. "Dr. Jackson is right. If you cooperate, you'll get a slap on the wrist, tops. We'll keep the big bad wolves from tearing you into lamb chops, but I want substantial proof of this organization if you want to avoid a trip to Club Fed."

Zhang worked his jaw, still seething. Shannon flicked a pen into his lap. "Let me be clear, this offer expires in exactly ten seconds. After that, we'll find out just how good your lawyer really is."

"Ten," Jack said helpfully. "Nine. Eight. Seven. Six. Five—"

"Fine!" Zhang shouted. "I'll cooperate as long as it shuts him up."

He lowered his gaze to the statement, read it, and signed it. Shannon withdrew a recorder and set it on the table in front of them. Zhang read his information aloud, albeit begrudgingly.

"State for the record how the dragon fighting ring works. Start from the beginning."

"Pricks," Zhang muttered under his breath. "About two weeks after the Baba Yaga incident in Aokigahara was resolved, I got a tip from an associate of mine in the Red Fist —"

"Name?" Shannon demanded, frowning at him over the clipboard, pen raised.

"Li Xing. He told me about what went down in the woods and the Red Fist was still able to recover something from the entire debacle. They had stolen some tech and DNA samples from one of the Sugimotos' labs in Tokyo and had undergone initial cloning trials that were successful. He told me a date and time for when the first dragon fighting ring would reach the states. I met him there and he told me the details of membership. Cash onsite only. Pay an upkeep cost via wire transfer for unlimited access to any one of the fights. The house keeps ten percent of anything you make, but the rest is yours. Cash for the bet has to be on hand or no entry. That way you can't skip out if you lose."

"How much money would you calculate that you've made off of these fights?"

"I do a standard bet of ten-thousand per fight. Sixty-grand."

Jack shook his head in disbelief. "Sixty-thousand dollars to watch innocent animals slaughter each other."

"They're hardly innocent," Zhang sneered. "You're a bleeding heart, Jackson. A broken record. You had the balls to bring them back to life, so have the balls to deal with the consequences."

"I hope that's the thought that comforts you while you

rot in a jail cell, asshole."

"Jackson," Shannon said in warning. "Cool it."

"You should have been there, Jackson," Zhang continued, smug malice dripping from every word. "That first match? It was a headliner to attract as much attention as possible in the dracology community. They bred a massive Australian horn-nosed dragon and pitted it against an Egyptian desert dragon. I was standing right there when that Australian dragon rammed his horn through the Egyptian dragon's throat."

He closed his eyes, as if recalling something wistful. "There was *so* much blood. I could have painted myself with it."

Zhang opened them again, his smile full of violent satisfaction as he saw the slowly building rage on Jack's features. "By the time the horn-nose was done, there wasn't enough of the Egyptian left to fill a teacup."

"You son of a — " Jack lunged at him, but Shannon shoved him back to the wall, using his large, stocky frame to block him.

"That's enough," Shannon barked. "You've done your job. Take a walk."

Jack took a deep breath and let the anger drain out of his body. He wrenched the door open and walked out into the hall in the wake of Zhang's low, mocking laughter.

He didn't really pay much attention to where he was headed, he just needed to be out of Zhang's vicinity before he did something reckless. A few minutes later, Jack ended up outside of Libby's lab.

"Hey, doc," she said without looking up as he walked in.

Jack blinked. "How'd you know it was me?"

"Calvin Klein cologne," Libby said, waving a hand dismissively. "No one else in on this floor wears that but you. What's up? I thought you were doing an analysis of the new dragons."

"I was, but then Shannon had me interrogate Wei

Zhang."

Libby glanced up then, one pierced eyebrow raised. "Did he now? I bet that went well."

"I got him to talk. I just..." He ran a hand through his dark hair and sighed. "Need a minute to collect myself. Guy's a major asshole."

"And your baby mama's busy at another site," Libby concluded, nodding. "Right. Well, take a load off. I'm sure I can find something to distract you."

"Thanks, Libs." He plopped down on the stool next to her. She stood at one of the counters where there were papers scattered all over. Some Jack noted were updated schematics of her brother's suit, while others were of complex weapons similar to the net launcher and the magnetic saddle equipment. She'd glance at one, scribble something down, and then turn to her laptop where there was a 3D image of the equipment in some sort of design program.

"Do you always do this?" Libby asked.

"Do what?"

"Hang out with girls when you're stressed out."

"Huh?"

"Oh. You don't notice that you do that?"

"Apparently not."

Libby giggled. "You're clueless, Jack."

"Probably," he agreed.

"You might have picked up the habit if you're close with your mom," she explained. "I've noticed you seem to relax a little more around the fairer sex. When my brother or Shannon are around, your posture is different. You're more...defensive? I guess? But when it's just me and Kamala, you're less tense."

"I...absolutely haven't noticed that at all, but now that you mention it, it makes total sense."

"You don't have any guy friends, I take it?"

"Colleagues and associates, sure. Friends? Not so much. Better run that past my therapist, if she hasn't already noticed."

Libby snorted. "See? Female therapist. You definitely have some sort of complex about women."

"Sorry."

She flicked him in the ear. "Ow!" he whined.

"That wasn't an accusation, stupid," she said, rolling her eyes. "Just an observation. Now talk to me. Why did Zhang get under your skin?"

He scratched the back of his neck and shifted in the stool. "You really want to hear this? I don't want to distract you."

"I can multitask. Now spill."

Jack raked his hand through his hair again. "If I had to put a word to it, I think my problem is responsibility. It's been almost a year since I began the resurrection project and shit went sideways on such a massive scale that I don't know what to think anymore. If this is all my fault or if it's someone else's or if we're both to blame. All I wanted was to give us the chance to understand these creatures, and yet history is repeating itself. They're right back to be violently exploited and killed as if they don't have a purpose aside from that. If I could change the past, I'm starting to think I shouldn't have done it at all."

"Hindsight is 20/20," Libby agreed. "But you couldn't have known history would repeat itself. We're in an entirely different era. Human nature has changed, even if the same dregs still exist in every culture. You're focusing too hard on the negatives here, Jack. You've seen the effects your project has had on the scientific community. There are, what? A couple dozen new projects that have properly utilized your cloning technique for other extinct species? They're in the infant stages, yes, but you unlocked a door that could lead to repopulating animals that were destroyed entirely or are on the brink of extinction. Who's to say that might not lead to repairing ecosystems and reversing some of the damage we've done to the environment?"

"That's above my pay grade," he said flatly. "But I guess it's still a good point."

"Exactly. This is the long game, Jack. The stuff we're seeing now is short term. They're bumps on the road. Things will stabilize."

"Maybe. With my daughter on the way, I'm not sure I'll be around to see it. I'm worried about the world we're making for her. I won't be around forever and there's so much out there that will affect her life."

Libby studied him for a moment. "Jack, I think that's where all of this is stemming from. Your daughter."

"How so?"

"All this guilt you feel is compounded on the fact that you're worried about her. Probably Kamala too. Being a parent is a big deal. You've sort of had to put it on the back burner because of this recovery project. She'll be here in a month and maybe you don't feel prepared for it."

"How can I?" Jack asked. "It's a *baby*. A whole person. A person who is going to depend on me for basically eighteen years of her life, and still depend on guidance after she's self-sufficient. It's…frankly, it's terrifying. What if I screw up?"

"Jack, you're not going to screw up," Libby said softly. "Not only are you one of the nicest guys I've ever met, you have an amazing mother to help you raise your daughter."

"I know. I'm just worried I'm not enough to make this work. To help Kam and not be a burden to her too. I feel like everything I touch goes to shit eventually."

"Everyone feels that way. If they don't seem like it, they're just faking it. None of us knows what the hell we're doing. We're just doing it. Look at me. You think I have a single clue what's going on right now? Hell no. I stopped questioning how things in life are supposed to work when my dad had the accident. Things change. We're all scrambling to adjust. As long as you recognize that you're struggling, at least it means you can work harder to stay afloat."

He let that sink in and then gave her a little lopsided smile. "You're awful smart for a whipper snapper."

"I am a genius," she said, pretending to polish her nails on her lab coat. "Now if you're going to stick around, you might as well help. Grab my brother's suit out of that bin over there and help me start on the repairs."

# CHAPTER FOURTEEN
## INSURRECTION

"I take it you have a strong stomach, Dr. Anjali? No pun intended?"

She offered the lab assistant, Ethan, a thin smile. "I was Internal Medicine."

"Ah," the sandy-haired man said in confirmation. "Good. This thing is...pretty grisly, honestly. I've seen a lot of shit working this job, but never a crispified freaking sea-dragon. Guess I can mark that one off the Bucket List."

He reached for the set of keys at his hip and undid the padlock. "I'm standing by to run interference to make it easier on you. Once your initial autopsy is done, we can discuss storage of the internal organs and any other delightful memorabilia we find in that thing."

"What are your thoughts on what to do with its corpse?"

Ethan wrenched the heavy iron door back and pushed hard to slide it open. "Guess it depends on what the agency wants done with it. My hunch is they'll remove the remaining tissue and muscle for research purposes and then possibly donate the skeleton to a museum once we've gotten all the data we need. It'll do nobody any good rotting away in a facility somewhere. Might as well let the world admire what's left."

"Won't that raise a lot of questions in the public eye?" she asked as they entered the freezer. She finished snapping on her gloves and tugged her mask up over her nose and mouth just in time to avoid the bulk of the strange, fishy stench of the cadaver waiting underneath the black tarp several feet towards the far end of the room.

"It will, but no one'll be asking the right questions, probably," he admitted, crouching in front of the gigantic dead creature. "They'll ooh and aah over it and forget all

265

about asking where it came from. Besides, you know the government. We can fabricate a story like nobody's business. My guess is they'll create some story about a civilian stumbling across the body in the middle of nowhere and people will buy it."

"Sounds realistic enough."

Ethan took a deep breath. "Well, let's get the horror show over with."

He peeled off the tarp. The Nordic sea serpent had curled into a ball upon its death, and therefore appeared not unlike a giant dead fetus. Its rubbery skin had become hard and cracked like asphalt melting under an oppressively hot day. Its jaws hung open, the inside of its mouth scorched to the point of its tongue and teeth were merely melted bumps. Vacant sockets where the eyes used to be stared up at Kamala like two empty voids.

It looked like it had died screaming.

"There's really not a whole lot to salvage, but we still have to go through the motions — "

Kamala lurched to one side, pulled down her mask, and vomited.

It happened so quickly that she just barely managed to miss the corpse. Worse still, she couldn't stop shaking. Her breath came in panicked gulps of air, her eyes tearing, throat burning from the stomach acid, her belly tightening into a knot. Cold sweat popped up along her forehead. Something was wrong. She'd seen mangled bodies before, more times than she cared to count, and yet something about those vacuous eye sockets scared her to the core.

"Dr. Anjali?" Ethan said, jumping up, his features etched with shock and concern. "Christ, are you okay?"

Kamala shook her head. "I...please, excuse me."

She hurried out through the door and fled to the nearest bathroom down the hall.

Still shaking, she ran cold water into a sink and rinsed out her mouth, then splashed it on her face. The image of the dead dragon wouldn't leave her. Why couldn't she stop thinking about it? Why couldn't she breathe?

Then the image switched to what she'd seen in her nightmare before — the serpent crouched in front of her daughter, seconds away from killing the frightened child.

Kamala fumbled for her cell phone and dialed without thinking.

"Good morning, my flower," Sahana Anjali answered. "How are you?"

"Mother," she choked out. "I...I think I'm having a panic attack."

"Oh, dear," Sahana said. "Where are you right now?"

"Bathroom."

"Are you alone?"

"Yes."

"What are your symptoms?"

"Can't breathe right. Shaking. Cold sweat. Stomach hurts."

"Did something trigger it?"

Kamala gritted her teeth. "I had to do an autopsy on a dead Nordic sea serpent. The one that nearly killed my friend last night. I..."

She struggled past the lump in her throat that felt as if it were growing in size every second. "I had a nightmare that it killed me last night while trying to save my daughter."

Her mother whispered a curse in Kannada. "Kamala, listen to me carefully. Close your eyes. Stand as still as you can. Breathe. Breathe with me. In. Hold it. Out. In. Hold it. Out."

Kamala clutched her quivering gloved fingers around the sink and followed her mother's instructions. Her lungs didn't cooperate at first, but after the tenth repetition, she could draw a full breath into her chest.

"Good," Sahana said. "Now try to relax your muscles. If you're holding onto something, release your grip. Don't rush. Gradually let go."

Kamala uncurled her fingers from around the rim of the sink and focused on the tightness in her shoulders and

267

rigidness of her spine. She moved aside and turned, placing her back to the wall, and then eased the tension from her limbs one at a time.

"Don't think about the dragon. Don't think about the dream. Focus only on yourself. Focus only on the little one inside you. She knows what you're going through. She wants you to be safe. Think about how she'll smile when she sees you face-to-face for the first time. Think about the warmth you'll feel when you hold her for the first time. Think about her tiny hand around your index finger. She's beautiful, isn't she?"

Kamala sniffled and smiled faintly. "She is."

"There we go, my flower. Keep thinking about her until your heart rate is normal. Breathe."

After a minute or so, Kamala settled down completely. She heard a knock at the bathroom door and Ethan's worried voice spoke. "Dr. Anjali? Are you alright? Talk to me, doc."

"I'm okay," she called to him. "I'll be out in a few minutes."

"Are you sure? I can call an ambulance if you need it."

"It's not the baby. Thank you. I just need a moment."

"Okay. I'm here if you need anything." His footsteps echoed away.

"Now," Sahana continued. "Talk to me about this nightmare. What happened? Don't try to visualize it; simply tell me the events in order."

Kamala took another deep breath. "My daughter and I were out in the garden picking flowers. A storm came on overhead and then it started raining. The sea serpent appeared and tried to attack my daughter, but she ran inside before it could get her. It killed me in the process."

Sahana sighed. "A common nightmare for a first time mother. I had some like it, but not nearly as colorful or direct. Being confronted with such a creature so soon after it hurt your friend is exactly what agitated you into the panic attack."

"But why?" she demanded, wiping away her smeared

268

mascara with a damp paper towel. "I've never had one before, not even in medical school. Not even last year in Aokigahara."

"This is different. You are a brave girl, Kamala. There is no doubt in my mind about that. You're strong. But, you're human, sweetie. If I remember my dracology studies correctly, the Nordic sea serpent was among the deadliest dragons. It would pull entire ships into the deep, killing dozens of sailors without mercy. What may help is if you focus on your faith. There are many serpents and reptiles that are helpful, divine beings. Perhaps positive association might help keep you calm. You also might consider not doing this autopsy. I'm sure there is someone else who can perform it. Jack, I'm sure, would have no trouble—"

"He's busy enough," she said softly. "And he was there when I had my nightmare. I don't want to worry him further."

Sahana clucked her tongue. "Kamala, what have I told you about hiding things from him?"

Kamala sighed. "Mother, I know. I don't mean to do it. It just…happens."

"I know you don't intend to get married, but I know you intend to spend the rest of your life with him. You must share both your fears *and* your victories with him. It is, as they say, a package deal. You won't be able to grow as a couple without letting him know when you are scared or in need of help."

"Jack struggles with so much already."

"And he will continue to, because he is a human being. So are you. Share with him. If you start keeping secrets now, the two of you won't make it in the long run. Trust me. I've been married to your father long enough to know better by now. Your house must be built on a solid foundation, and that only happens with trust, dear."

"I'll…try to do better," Kamala conceded. "I'll see him after the autopsy. We can talk over lunch. He can be frustrating when he worries, though."

"It comes from a place of love. You'll find the patience for it. You two are meant for each other."

*Two,* Kamala thought wryly. *Wait until she finds out it's actually three.* "Thank you, Mother."

"Of course, my flower. Do you feel alright enough to give it another try?"

She chewed her lip. "I think so."

"Give yourself a few more minutes. Meditate if you can. Take it slow and don't be afraid to ask for help. I love you."

"I love you too. Bye." She hung up and stared at herself in the mirror. She didn't look quite as shaken as she had when she came in. Absently, she rubbed her belly in the spot where the baby had settled. The child had stirred and fidgeted during her episode, but didn't feel any different. There had been some discomfort during the panic attack, but it had subsided by now.

"Sorry, my love," Kamala whispered to her baby. "I'll keep you safe. I swear it."

She straightened her shoulders and strode out of the bathroom. Ethan leaned against the opposite wall in the bathroom, chewing on his thumbnail, brown eyes immediately locking on her as she exited. "You okay?"

"You asked me that already," she said mildly.

He eyed her as she headed back in the direction of the freezer. "Look, if you want me to do it—"

"Thank you," she said. "But no. I'm terribly sorry I threw up. I'll clean it up."

"I already did. Are you sure about this? I'm not trying to get fired for freaking the pregnant lady out with a dead dragon."

Kamala chuckled. "I promise I won't let that happen. I didn't 'freak out' exactly. Last night was extremely traumatic and I didn't realize I'd have an adverse reaction to seeing the creature up close. I've dealt with it now."

She pulled her mask back up as they entered the freezer and closed it behind them. This time, as she looked at the corpse, she felt a slight flutter and tugging in her stomach, but nothing more. It didn't seem as monstrous as it had before, perhaps because the initial shock was gone. Kamala took a deep breath and clicked her brain over into medical mode.

"Let's get started."


*"Agent Shannon to interrogation. Repeat. Agent Shannon to interrogation."*

Libby frowned up at the loudspeaker in the lab. "Wasn't he already there?"

"Must be on break," Jack said as he pried yet another broken armor plate out of Calloway's suit and dropped it in the pile.

"Yeah, but who else does he have to interrogate? Didn't he say an hour ago that he got everything he was going to get out of Zhang since homeboy's lawyer finally showed?"

Jack paused. "Yeah, that's true. And he's already sent the other stoolpigeons up the river."

Libby's brown eyes widened. "You don't think it's—"

"Libby," he warned. "Don't start."

She set her jaw. "It might be Lackey Larry and you know it."

"He'd have told us already."

"Bullshit," she growled, setting her tools aside and heading for the door.

"Libby! If you don't get your short ass back here!" Jack yelled, but she disappeared into the hallway. Growling, he darted after her. She was quick for someone only five-foot-five and the hallway had enough people walking through it to give her a head start. He made it down the stairwell still threatening the twenty-one-year-old and spilled out onto the level with the interrogation office not a moment too soon.

Larry hadn't been having a good day, apparently— there was a sizeable bruise on his forehead and a cut to one

271

side of his lips. His mousy hair was haphazard and sweaty and some blood had crusted on his beard. The cop who had been watching the room was hauling him forward towards it, but didn't look up in time.

Libby roared and smashed her fist right into Larry's nose.

Larry cried out and hit the ground in a heap.

"Libby!" Jack shouted.

"Son of a bitch!" she bellowed, kicking him in the ribs once, twice, for good measure. "You sorry fat bastard! Do you know what that dragon did to my brother?"

She landed another vicious kick to his groin before Jack got his arms around her and picked her up off the ground entirely. She flailed in his grip, still reaching for the groaning, injured man, so he dragged her several feet away. The startled cop opened the door to the interrogation room and ushered Larry inside once he was on his feet again.

"Easy, *easy*, Mike Tyson!" Jack said, holding her against him. "Jesus Christ, Libby."

"Five minutes," she snarled. "Just give me five minutes with that fucking creep."

"In five minutes, you're going to be in jail for assault. Calm. Down."

She huffed and puffed for a moment, still high on the adrenaline, and then settled down. Jack kept an eye on her until he felt the tension leave her muscles. "You good?"

"I'm fine," Libby grumbled. "Unless you're gonna buy me dinner, hands off the merchandise."

Jack rolled his eyes and let her go. "Yep. You're back to normal alright."

She shook out her hand and winced as she noticed her knuckles had split. "Ow. Why does no one ever tell you how much that hurts?"

"You smashed your bony hand into someone's cranium," he chided, examining the injury. "Of course it hurts, dummy. S'why you aim for the soft targets."

He paused. "To be fair, you did exactly that. Caught

him right in the babymaker. I'm a little proud of you for that one."

She snorted. "Thanks. Anything broken?"

"Possibly his nose, but you're alright. We'll go to the cafeteria and get you some ice. Once the swelling's down, we can check with Kam to be sure."

Just then, Agent Shannon stepped out of the elevator and stopped dead as he spotted them. "The hell are you doing down here?"

"Nothing," Jack lied, attempting to shove Libby behind him, but she dodged to his other side instead.

"When the hell were you going to tell us you caught Lackey Larry?" she demanded. "After his trial?"

Jack pinched the bridge of his nose. "Goddammit, Libs."

"I've told you before that things are on a need-to-know basis, kid," Shannon said coldly. "And you didn't need to know yet. Last thing I want is not one but two loose cannons around here."

Jack glared. "I got Zhang to talk, didn't I? Don't knock it 'til you've tried it."

Shannon scowled and then noticed Libby's bloody knuckles. "What's that about?"

"What do you think it's about?" she said tartly.

"Did you assault my goddamn witness, little girl?" he snapped.

"He's a lying sack of filth."

"He's a *valuable* lying sack of filth," he corrected. "And that just cost you your pay for the day. Go back to the hospital. You're done."

"Go to hell."

"That's two days." He jerked his head at Jack. "Get her out of here."

"I'm not your fucking stooge," Jack shot back. He took Libby's uninjured hand and spoke in an infinitely softer tone. "Come on, let's get some ice."

She glared daggers at Shannon until he was out of her

sight as the elevator doors closed. Jack blew out a breath as he watched the numbers tick down one at a time. "Anyone ever tell you you've got a temper?"

Libby held her hand up as if she were talking on the phone. "Hey, pot? It's kettle. You're black as fuck right now."

"That's racist," Jack deadpanned. Libby covered her mouth, trying her hardest not to laugh, but a snort erupted from her all the same.

"Jerk."

"Eh, you love me. Now if you're done punching criminals, I think I've got an idea on how to find out what Shannon gets out of Larry."

She shot him a disbelieving look. "Uh, how exactly are you going to do that?"

"Got a twenty?"

"What do you mean you've got nothing for me?" Faye demanded into the borrowed burner cell phone.

"Internal Affairs is here stomping around," the informant said, her voice not much above a whisper. "All calls incoming and outgoing are being monitored. They're tearing through everyone's stuff trying to find out who the leak is and I'm risking my ass just by telling you right now."

"We paid you," she said through her teeth. "We expect results."

"I can't give you results from a jail cell. If you want your money back, fine. I can't do any more than I've already done. If you want intel, come get it yourself."

The informant hung up. Faye wrung the phone between her fingers for a few seconds and then forced herself to calm down. Didn't want to attract attention to herself.

"Not going well, huh?" Winston rumbled from the link in her ear.

"The informant chickened out," she said, leaning back against the headrest. "We're back to Square One."

"Not unusual. Means there's been a big break in their case, I'd imagine, if I.A. is up everybody's ass," he mused.

"Think that means they found out about the hit on Jack and Kamala?"

"Possibly, but I doubt it. That'd be quite a reach."

"What, then?"

"Maybe a big break while digging into the smugglers. By now, they've also combed the train yard. Would've found the blood trail I left behind and the tire tracks. Might know there's another player even if it's no more than that."

She mulled the thought over. "Then our next plan of action would be to get me inside."

"Whoa there, Blondie. Baby steps."

"She's gonna hit them soon, Winston. I'm not waiting any longer. She might already be inside while you're wasting my time arguing with me."

"And just how the hell do you expect to get in there?"

"By using my best attribute."

"Don't see how your tits play into this."

"Shut up. I meant my brain, you asshole. The informant gave me her employee number, right?"

"So?"

"So," she continued. "Those ID badges don't have photos for the department she works in since she's just an admin. She's got enough clearance that I can at least have a look around for Stella without anyone noticing if I stay out of her department."

"And then what? You gonna confront her in a freaking government facility surrounded by expertly trained agents? Maybe have a little showdown? I'll buy ya some tumbleweeds if you want."

"Screw you."

"Look, I know you want to help, but that idea has more holes than Swiss cheese. That shit only works in the movies. If there's a security guard, which I guarantee you there is, he'd notice you're a new face. He'd stop you, run your employee number, and they'd have photos in the database."

Faye gritted her teeth. "Then what's your idea, smart

guy?"

"She give you her employee number and password?"

"Yeah."

"You weren't that far off. You want to look for new hires aka people who may not have ID badges yet. Nothing's slower than HR, no matter what industry you're in. Log in to their system and see if there are any new people this week. You're a good enough actress that if you tell them you left your temporary access card at home, they'll probably let you in and the person is too new to have a photo taken yet. Just make sure it's someone low on the totem pole, like maybe janitorial staff or an intern. The less clearance, the less suspicious they'll be. If you find Stella, then you can threaten to expose her and she might back down."

"Might? What if she doesn't?"

"Then you've got a hard choice to make. You can cause an incident, but if they detain you, then they'll find out you were impersonating someone to get into their facility and that's no walk in the park. Plus, the little doc and the beanpole are going to be plenty mad you've been doing this behind their backs. Even if you can prove that there was a hit out on them both, you'll still be in a world of trouble."

Faye drummed her fingertips on the steering wheel. Unease knotted up inside her. She'd risk her life in a heartbeat for Jack and Kamala, but her future? Not much scared her, but rotting in a jail cell sounded like hell on earth for a free spirit. Winston certainly wouldn't come to her defense. She could certainly afford a hell of a lawyer, but escaping without at least some jail time was unlikely. Winston was right. She couldn't do this lightly.

But if Jack and Kamala died...she'd lose it all.

"So what's it gonna be, Blondie? You can't unring this bell once it's rung."

"I wouldn't have started this journey if I didn't have the balls to finish it," Faye said quietly. "If that's how things end up for me, so be it. I love them. I will protect them no matter what the cost."

"I was afraid you'd say that," Winston sighed. "You got grit, girlie. No sense, but plenty of grit."

"And sometimes that's all you need." She opened Winston's laptop and found the facility's website, then the employee page. She signed in and searched until she found the employee database, scanning it for the most recent hires. "Got it. Amber Carter. Hired three days ago. New intern."

"Good. Therefore, you're going to do the opposite of what I told you. Find a department store and buy a low cut top and some business casualwear. Time to put those acting skills to the test. And to hope the security guard's your typical guy who gets easily distracted by a nice pair."

Faye shook her head as she started the car. "Men are idiots."

"Yep, that's why we always die first."

She found a nearby shop, bought a light blue scoop neck blouse and a black suit, and then found a parking garage a few blocks from the facility. She dug up the layout of the buildings from their website, psyched herself up, and headed into the security checkpoint. Fortunately, Winston had been right — there was a male security guard, and as soon as she turned on the charm, she was granted entry.

As with most busy workplaces, no one paid her any mind as she entered the main building. The floor she'd been admitted on was full of cubicles and offices for the administrative and accounting staff members. She snuck a notepad and pen from the front desk, then began making rounds searching for Stella by asking for drink orders on the pretense of making a coffee run. No one gave her a second look, so she finished checking the entire floor in just under fifteen minutes. No sign of Stella.

Once finished, Faye waited for a lull and got onto the elevator alone to inspect the other floors. The administrative suite, cafeteria, and parking deck were easily accessible, but the research and development floors as well as the agents' floors required a card to get clearance inside. She met up with the informant to borrow her key card and rode up to the next level.

One thing she'd picked up over time was that acting confident and as if one belonged somewhere tended to work on the average person. She followed one of the lab techs inside a nearby lab, grabbed a coat and goggles, and a clipboard, and then made the rounds as if she were observing or inspecting on the peripheral. It wasn't until she was halfway done with the first R&D floor that she got a lead.

One of the janitors emptying the trash had mentioned to a coworker that his friend called in sick and that there was someone he hadn't met before picking up the shift.

"Excuse me," she said innocently. "I think I might know her. Can you describe her?"

"Tall gal, black, late forties, body like Pam Grier in her heyday."

Faye's heart rate sped up. "Does she have a little bit of color in her bangs?"

"Yeah, think so."

"Where'd you last see her?"

"Other building. The one where they keep the live subjects."

She thanked him and tried her best not to sprint towards the elevator. The earpiece had been in the lining of her bra so as not to be detected, and she fought not to put it in to update Winston.

"C'mon, c'mon, stupid," Faye muttered, glaring at the changing numbers above the elevator.

Finally, it dinged and the doors parted.

To reveal Jack and a pink-haired black girl she'd never seen before.


"Excuse me, Keiko-sama. You have a visitor."

Keiko Sugimoto shifted slightly on the stretcher until she faced the two massive doors where her assistant, Kenji, stood, calm and attentive as always. "I do not want to be disturbed."

"It is an urgent matter. It's Minako-san."

She sighed. Her long, bare, back lifted and made the tiny acupuncture needles wobble for a few seconds. The female acupuncturist paused in her work. "Very well. Show her in. Kaoru-san, please step out for a few minutes."

Kenji bowed his head and held the door open for a short Japanese woman with long black hair in a braid. She wore a navy suit and flats, and had a manila folder tucked beneath one arm. Kenji shut the door behind him after the acupuncturist left. Minako bowed her head before moving closer.

"My apologies for interrupting, Keiko-san."

"What is it?" Keiko asked. "News from abroad?"

"Among other things," Minako said, brandishing the folder.

Keiko pushed up on her elbows and accepted it. She flipped the folder open and read its contents carefully. "According to this, we've successfully diverted the attention of our government as well as the American government towards the illegal fighting rings, but we're still seeing some fringe interest from law enforcement."

"It's minimal," Minako confirmed. "But we should still keep an eye on it."

"Understood. It was a calculated risk, allowing the Red Fist and other parties to 'steal' our work. The government tends to focus on big picture issues. They miss nuances. Are we still on schedule?"

"Yes. As of this morning, there are twelve species that have been bred successfully, which brings us to a total of forty-eight dragons under the care of Dr. Yagami."

Keiko smiled faintly. "The bitter old goat hasn't been by recently. That explains why. He's been busy. When would they be ready for the grand unveiling?"

"If my projections are right, by summer's end. However, if we want a full understanding of their temperaments, I recommend we wait until the fall."

"I'll take that under advisement. The construction of the facility is actually ahead of schedule. I'll be conducting a site visit within the week, as a matter of fact. From the reports, you still feel as if we won't have the same incident as we did with Baba Yaga?"

"No. Dr. Yagami implemented my methods instead of his own. The dragons should be of stable mind and maturity once they are awake."

Minako paused. "There is another matter that concerns me. It's why I unfortunately needed to interrupt your spa treatment."

"Go on."

"We have received word that one of our insiders is cooperating with the American agency devoted to retrieving the rogue dragons. We worry he might divulge vital information that can eventually draw a path back to your organization."

Keiko narrowed her eyes. "Oh?"

"It's only a rumor, but I think it is worth an effort to investigate the matter."

She glanced at the clock on the wall. "Is it happening right now?"

"Yes."

"Your fears may be availed soon enough," Keiko said with another frosty smile. "I recently became aware that there is a kill order out on Dr. Jackson and Dr. Anjali that may neutralize the threat."

Minako stilled. "Keiko-san?"

"Rest assured, it's not from our organization. I wouldn't engage in such actions. As troublesome as they are, I still believe Dr. Jackson and Dr. Anjali have helped rather than hurt us. However, it's possible that in order to remove them from the equation without drawing too much attention, the assassin will instead strike the facility as a whole in order to mask their true intentions."

"You'll do nothing to stop it?"

"They are resilient people, especially for scientists. I

believe the plot will be foiled before it can happen."

Minako licked her lips. "Keiko-san...are you aware of the whereabouts of Kazuma Okegawa?"

Keiko lowered her lashes somewhat. "Why would I be?"

"It might interest you to know that he is no longer in Japan. He has been missing as of the last forty-eight hours."

"How do you know that?"

"One of Yagami's people told me. Forgive my impertinence, but you know Okegawa makes a mess wherever he goes. I implore you to find him. Soon."

Keiko pursed her lips, but nodded all the same. "I'll have Kenji reach out to some contacts we have. He's still an enemy of the Yamaguchi-gumi for being a sleeper agent for the Inagawa-kai. It's possible his comeuppance finally found him."

"In a perfect world, yes, he would be paying for his many indiscretions. In this world, however, good men die young and evil prospers. I don't feel confident, with his new enhancements, that the yakuza had him killed, and if they did, I believe they'd have made a public display of his remains."

"I trust your judgment. It will be taken care of. What else?"

"Baba Yaga may be pregnant."

Keiko froze. "What?"

"The dragon is still in cold storage and dormant, so we've been monitoring the changes in her biology as she continues to hibernate. We're starting to see early signs of pregnancy in her hormones. The labs are still attempting to figure out how to test for it, but the initial testing shows that she may have the same asexual reproduction trait as the dragon that Dr. Jackson and Dr. Anjali bred."

The younger Sugimoto sibling licked her lips. "How many eggs is the species known to produce if pregnant?"

"Between five and ten."

"Merciful gods," she whispered. "How many people

know about this?"

"Myself and Dr. Hudson."

"Keep it between the two of you at all costs. Do you understand me, Minako-san? No one else in that facility is to find out if the test comes back positive."

"Agreed."

Keiko frowned down at the stretcher in thought. "We'll have to adjust accordingly. Security is already at its height, but if anyone else becomes aware of the matter, it can spin out of control. If even one of her hatchlings is taken and raised, it would mean serious devastation. The Red Fist are bloodthirsty. They'd stop at nothing to replicate her again and again until the world is overrun with her kind. Even with technology and weaponry as advanced as it is, a rogue Baba Yaga would wreak havoc before it was taken down."

She glanced up at Minako. "This is your new priority. Keep a close watch. Notify me the very instant you are sure she is pregnant."

"Yes, Keiko-san."

"Your work is invaluable, Minako-san. Keep me apprised."

"Thank you." Minako nodded to her again, and then left.

She left the Sugimoto mansion and got into her car, immediately pulling out her cell phone. After some frantic searching, she found the number she'd been looking for and dialed it. A moment later, a throaty, slightly annoyed voice answered. "Fujioka Misaki speaking."

"Fujioka-san, I don't have time to explain, but you must contact Dr. Jackson and Dr. Anjali immediately. Their lives are in danger."

# CHAPTER FIFTEEN
## CHECKMATE

"For once in my life," Agent Shannon said as he pushed the door to the interrogation room closed. "Let's do this the easy way."

He flipped the lock and stuck one hand in his pocket as he leaned on the wall opposite where Dr. Larry Whitmore had set his chair up against. He'd always had a problem with slouching, and a solid wall kept him from doing so quite as badly. There was a damp washcloth clutched around a bag of ice pressed to his badly bruised nose. He took a breath and then spoke in a nasal, dispassionate voice. "What's the easy way?"

"Oh, you know," Shannon said. "Where I ask the questions and you just answer them. You don't lie. You don't dance around the subject. You don't resist. This whole thing can be over in an hour if we do it the easy way. Just a nice, quick chat, and then I send you on your way. No muss, no fuss."

Shannon scratched the back of his neck. "Most criminals opt for that, actually. TV dramatizes things a lot. Usually it's the fear. Sometimes it's the guilt, but that's more with the killers who got caught up in their emotions during a moment of passion. Good old-fashioned crooks spill 'cause they don't want to be locked up for longer than they can bear. It's hell on a man, telling him what to do, where to go, how to dress. Any sliver of a chance to lessen that time and —"

He snapped his fingers. " —they crack like an egg."

"And what's the hard way?" Larry asked.

Shannon heaved a sigh. "Intimidation, at first. I do the bad cop routine. I stall your lawyer with a bunch of phony paperwork or dismiss him entirely with some idiotic but legal loophole. I transfer you to another site and then all the bad shit starts. Nothing dramatic like bamboo slivers or a knotted-up rope to the bare genitals. We don't leave marks. It's unprofessional, and it's evidence. Human bodies are terribly fragile, you know, so it doesn't actually take that much to make you uncomfortable. Not always about pain. The illusion that the intense discomfort will never stop is often what gets the bad guys in the end. The thought of suffering for hours, days, weeks, years…it can get to them."

He picked at his fingernail. "That's why I never went the terrorism route. The hardcore Gitmo shit is the stuff of nightmares. Once a man's no longer afraid of death, then you have to get creative to torture him. I lack imagination."

He flicked his gaze up at Larry. "Me? I like to be straightforward."

Shannon withdrew a ballpoint pen and set it down next to the neat stack of stapled papers on the desk in front of the scientist. "We worked together for, what? Almost eight months? Side by side at first. Just you and me. We had a rhythm. Almost a rapport, if I'm being honest. And then I come to find out this whole time you've been making me and my team run in circles. You are in bed with the vipers, and you thought you were one of them, but you were just a rat the whole time, and now they've come to swallow you whole, so you crawled back into the cage and asked the cat for protection."

Shannon offered him a thin smile. "Well, let's clear that right up. I know that you want to talk to my superiors and work out a deal. I know you want to roll on the smugglers in exchange for leniency or amnesty. They're the big picture sort, those suits up there, and they might even hear you out."

He pushed off from the wall and set his hands on the back of the chair, and the very last smidgeon of light died out in his brown eyes. "And you're not going to fucking get it."

Larry swallowed hard. "Shannon—"

"The only words I want to hear out of your mouth, you detestable little weasel, is information regarding the

284

smugglers, the dragons, and the assassination attempt on Bruce Calloway. That boy bled for me. For us. You are only alive because of what you know. Otherwise, I'd drag you to a blacksite with a handful of my old Navy Seal buddies and we'd take turns cutting strips of bacon out of your lard ass. So spare me the sob story and take the easy way out. Take it or I will do things to you that will make you renounce God and all his angels."

Larry licked his lips and reached a shaking hand for the pen. He scribbled his signature and initials on all the appropriate places before sitting back in his chair. "What do you want to know?"

Shannon pulled out a recorder. "Who made first contact, them or you?"

Larry winced slightly. "Them. I was given a tip that there was an upcoming joint venture between the FBI and CIA to shut down Jackson's project and they'd be hiring for an expert. The hiring manager owed them a favor, so he bumped me to the top of the list."

"What was the main objective?"

"To stall the investigation. Keep you chasing your tails. Give you information, but never the kind that could lead to shutting the organization down once the operation was entirely stateside."

"What were they paying you?"

"Hundred grand. Upon completion of a full year, it would've gone to two."

Shannon swore under his breath. "How did you make contact?"

"I was given an encrypted login on a site on the Dark Web. Instructions were given on a weekly or monthly basis. I gave progress reports with files and photos to substantiate my claims."

"Are you aware of who your employer is?"

Larry shook his head. "No names. All I ever heard the organization referred to was the Apophis Society. The only person I ever met was a go-between who ran the smuggling rings. Goes by the name of Fisher. He gave me the dates and times for some of the matches to allow it to seem as if the government was 'catching up' to the culprits, while they held the real ones elsewhere."

"Do you have any contact information from him?"

"Phone number. That's all. He called if we needed to meet or just to exchange information."

"Describe him."

"Caucasian, blond, tall, thin, forties."

"Is he the one that did that — " Shannon gestured to the large bruise on Larry's forehead. " — to your face?"

Larry grimaced, but nodded. "Walk me through what happened at the hospital that led to you being face-to-fist with Fisher."

"After Calloway's..." Larry hesitated, swallowing again at the livid expression on Shannon's face. "...incident, I was pretty sure you'd connect the dots, so I left and contacted Fisher to meet with me. We did. I told him I wanted protection provided by the smugglers, but he said no, and that if I'd be compromised, I was no longer of any use to the organization. He pulled a gun on me and I ran. He caught up and there was a scuffle, but I managed to knock him out and get away. I logged onto the Dark Web to see if I could finagle another contact, but they shut me out and put a kill order out for me. I had enough money to run, but by then, I knew you'd have a BOLO on me, and I didn't have enough resources to cobble together a fake ID. Sooner or later, someone from the Apophis Society was going to spot me. Better to turn myself in than to try and beat those odds."

Shannon paced behind the chair for a moment. "But why did they want Calloway dead? If you were already stalling our investigation, what's his significance?"

Larry exhaled. "It wasn't about Calloway. He was a pawn. They wanted to get to Jackson and Kamala."

Shannon froze. "What?"

"Calloway was too competent in the field. They knew that if he kept running point on the recoveries, there wouldn't be much of an opportunity to strike at the two of them. They had to make it look like it was the fault of the government's negligence so that the entire thing would get shut down for good. If the dragons appeared to have gone berserk and killed the doctors as well as some innocent bystanders, it would prove that you were in over your heads, and the higher-ups would simply put a kill-on-sight order for dragons. This furthered the organization's agenda. Plus, Jackson and Kamala have been effective at stopping them in major points of their progress."

Shannon batted the ice pack out of Larry's hands. "What the hell did you do?"

"They had me set up a bounty," Larry said hoarsely. "Forty-grand a head. Killed at the facility and the dragons had to be the triggermen. Two birds, one stone."

Shannon grabbed the front of Larry's shirt and shook him. "Dr. Anjali is *pregnant*."

"They don't care," Larry whispered. He then gave Shannon a pleading look. "I didn't know when I signed up for this assignment that this would happen. I didn't know she was pregnant. I swear to you, I didn't know. But if I backed out, they'd kill me."

"And what could be more important than your precious little neck," Shannon snarled. "I hope that I'll be the one to snap it someday."

He shoved him back into the chair. "When's the deadline for the bounty?"

"Shannon, I—"

"Tell me when or so help me God, I'll kill you myself!" Shannon bellowed.

"T-Tonight!" Larry stammered. "Tonight."

"For their sake," Shannon whispered. "You had better hope I find the killer first."

He stormed out of the room and pulled out his phone, giving a cursory glance to the cop posted outside. "Whitmore's on lockdown. No one goes in or out, not even his lawyer."

"Yes, sir."

Shannon lifted the phone to his ear. "I want full facility lockdown initiated immediately—"

*"Dr. Jackson to the animal pen. Dr. Jackson to the animal pen."*

Shannon frowned at the announcement over the intercom. He checked his watch. He knew Jack was supposed to be continuing the lab analysis of the dragons for the remainder of his shift. If anyone paged him, it should have been the labs, not the pen. A worm of doubt wriggled through his gut.

"Sir?" The person on the other line asked.

"Belay that order," he said. "I need to go check on something first."

"Question?"

"Yes, whipper snapper?"

"Why did you have two-hundred and eighty dollars in cash just sitting around in your wallet?"

Jack shrugged a shoulder. "We're out of town. I get antsy when I'm not in my own backyard, so I took a big lump out just to be safe. Better to have it and not need it than the reverse. Plus, it worked out, didn't it?"

Libby eyed him. "And how'd you know you could bribe a cop with coffee, a donut, and three hundred bucks?"

"You're too young to know this—" He grinned as she punched him in the arm. "—but cops don't get paid diddly-squat. They're barely above minimum wage, the poor bastards. Babysitting suspects has got to be a pain in the ass, and he's not getting well-compensated for it, so I figured he'd be interested in a snack and some extra cash if all he had to do was just listen to the conversation."

"How long do you think it'll take?"

Jack checked his watch. "Larry doesn't have the guts to withstand Shannon's interrogation. I'd guess an hour, if that."

"The cop might not pony up the info."

"Calculated risk."

She scowled. "You owe me twenty bucks if he doesn't."

"Fair enough." Libby snorted as she noticed the red-white-and-blue shield emblem on the face of his watch. "Could you be any more of a Captain America fanboy?"

"Excuse you," Jack said. "He's only the best Avenger."

"Not hardly."

"Oh yeah?" Without hesitation, he rattled off the various abilities and the compelling aspects of the character while Libby stared at him somewhere between disbelief and amusement. The elevator dinged and the doors opened.

" — and that's why Captain America is clearly the best Avenger."

"Puh-leeze," Libby replied with a roll of her eyes. "It's clearly Thor and you know it, buster."

"Blasphemy," Jack insisted.

A tall woman with brown hair in a bun, glasses, and a lab coat stood alone inside the elevator. She sneezed and covered her mouth.

"Bless you," Jack said, stepping to one side as she passed by. He and Libby went in and hit the floor for R&D, but not before Jack frowned hard as the doors closed.

"Something wrong?" Libby asked.

"No, just…that was…odd," he said, shaking his head. "Felt like I've seen that girl before somewhere."

"What? The girl with the nice rack?" Libby elbowed him in the side. "If I find out you ever even *think* about cheating on Kamala, I'll rip your kidneys out and stuff them into your ears."

"Wow. That was mean even for you. And no, I wasn't talking about her — "

*DING.* The elevator doors opened on their R&D floor. Just as they started to walk out, the intercom overhead clicked and then a woman's voice spoke.

*"Dr. Jackson to the animal pen. Dr. Jackson to the animal*

*pen."*

Jack glanced up at the speaker. "O-kay, guess this is just kismet, then. Go on. I'll catch up."

"Eh, I'm not supposed to be here anyway since Shannon kiboshed two of my freaking shifts," Libby grumbled. "Might as well tag along."

"Suit yourself." They returned to the elevator and rode down to the ground floor, then took one of the golf carts over to the building with the dragons were being held.

It was feeding time, so the staff in charge of upkeep were moving to and fro feeding the dragons inside their pens. Not long after being put in their enclosures, they had realized chaining the dragons would often result in the creatures twisting around and accidentally choking themselves on the tethers when they became upset or restless. The team would have to find a long-term solution to keep them controlled while inside the cage, as the dragons had a tendency to attack the glass if anything came within their territory.

Each dragon appeared to react slightly differently when the door slid open and the caretaker offered it something to eat. The Netherland forest dragons charged them, heads lowered, their sharp antlers ready to gore and maim. The Hercules dragon slammed its massive, heavy tail against the concrete floor, shaking the transparent walls of its enclosure, hissing and trying to make itself appear larger. The Chinese dragon clawed at the glass along the opposite wall as if trying to escape. The Highlander dragon roared, but did not move from its spot. The Arctic dragon remained peaceful and serene, seeming unbothered by the newcomer. Jack scribbled some notes as he observed the behaviors before searching for someone in charge.

Pete and the small flock of diamondback dragons had both been socialized by Jack and Kamala back when their project was still in full swing, and therefore accepted their food without much fuss. Pete remained cautious and suspicious of company, but she didn't attack. Jack also noted that for future reference, and then caught up with one of the caretakers he'd been working with, a short brunette who had been working on a timesheet and checking the next scheduled time for feeding the dragons.

"Hey," Jack said. "Someone paged me."

She blinked at him. "They did?"

He frowned. "You didn't?"

"Wasn't us, no."

"Huh. Weird." Jack glanced down at his pocket as his phone vibrated and began belting out the lyrics to The Tads' "She is my Dream." Libby sniggered into her hand while he stuck out his tongue and answered the phone.

"Hey, Kam. What's up?"

"Jack, find Agent Shannon and get somewhere safe. We're both in danger."

He froze. "What?"

"Someone has put out a contract on our lives. I've already got a security detail, but you need to get away from the dragons immediately."

He paled. "Oh, shit."

The lights in the building went out.

Then the screams started.


Faye was certain time had frozen once the elevator doors opened on her boyfriend.

She was also certain that God was real, and He hated her guts.

The doors had opened when Jack was in mid-sentence, his brown eyes locked with those of the girl, an easy smile on his lips. " — and that's why Captain America is clearly the best Avenger."

"Puh-leeze," the pink-haired girl replied with a roll of her eyes. "It's clearly Thor and you know it, buster."

Faye knew if he locked eyes with her, it was a done deal. Even with her contact lenses, dyed brows, wig, and bifocal glasses, Jack had seen her naked. There was no way he wouldn't recognize her if they met eyes. Heaven forbid if he glanced down at her cleavage; he might recognize her even faster that way. She had only a couple of seconds to come up with something.

"Blasphemy," Jack said, and then he faced forward.

"*Achoo!*" Faye said, tucking her head down and covering her nose and mouth.

"Bless you," he said politely, and stepped past her into the elevator, continuing to chat with the girl beside him. Faye darted out into the hallway as fast as her legs would carry her.

After she was around the corner, she clapped a hand over her chest and tried to breathe normally. She had just barely caught her breath when she heard the intercom overhead.

"*Dr. Jackson to the animal pen. Dr. Jackson to the animal pen.*"

Faye paled as she realized what that meant. "Shit."

She scurried over to one of the golf carts and hopped in, hauling ass over to the other building. She shoved the link back into her ear and switched it back on.

"I've got a lead," she said. "Someone spotted her where they keep the dragons."

Winston cursed. "Did you get a location on the docs?"

"Just bumped into Jack on my way out. I don't think he recognized me, but it was a damned close call. Someone just paged him over there, too. No sign of Kamala, but I might be able to send her an innocuous text to find out where she is."

"If Stella's already there, things have been set in motion. Your best bet is going to be to yank the nearest fire alarm. If they evacuate, they may stand a chance. She might not be able to act in the middle of the confusion."

"But then what? It's not like she's just going to give up."

"No, but it gives us time to think of something else. If we can't stop her outright, we have to stall her."

Faye gritted her teeth. "Winston, we need to tell the authorities. There are enough agents in this facility to subdue her. She can't kill anyone if she's in jail."

"If you blow her cover, she'll blow yours."

"This is life or death. I don't have a choice."

"You do have a choice, Faye. That's what this has been about the whole time."

She swallowed hard as she parked the golf cart and glanced up at the long, tall shed in front of her. Going into that building would change the course of her life. There was no way around it.

"Yeah," she whispered. "I guess it is."

Faye walked inside the building, head high, shoulders back, eyes forward.

There weren't many people inside. Less than twenty, she counted. Most of them were lab techs that were standing near the dragons' pens writing reports as the others took turns opening the cages to start feeding them. She kept to the outskirts to scope out the room without seeming conspicuous.

She spotted Stella in the corner of the shed, mopping a spot beside the Chinese bearded dragon's cage, her back to the rest of the area, head down.

"I've got eyes on her," Faye murmured into the link.

"Shit," Winston muttered. "She's gonna make her move."

"Not if I can help it," she growled, and marched right for her.

"This is a new look for you," Faye said, crossing her arms once she stood within earshot of the assassin. She kept a distance of several feet between them; close enough for her to hear, but not enough to reach her.

Stella chuckled as she squeezed the excess water off the mop in its dingy yellow bucket. "Really? Don't think I can pull it off, huh?"

"It's kind of hard for anyone to look good in coveralls, honestly."

"Tell me about it," Stella snorted. "And this thing doesn't fit. It's all kinds of up my ass right now."

She finished mopping the spot she'd been on and dropped the mop in the bucket, adjusting the cap higher over her brow to finally look at her opponent. "How'd you get in?"

"By having a great rack," Faye told her. "Men are idiots."

"Such idiots," Stella agreed with a shake of her head. "If you've got a nice pair, the world is pretty much your oyster. Seems unfair, but there it is."

She folded her hands on the mop handle and smirked at Faye. "What exactly can I do for you, Becky?"

"This can go a few different ways," Faye said quietly. "But you already know that. Do I really have to say something as trite and cliché as 'if you want them, you have to go through me' or is there some other way to work this out?"

"To tell you the truth," Stella drawled as she dragged her gaze over Faye. "I sort of want to see what you've got. There aren't a lot of women in this business, to tell you the truth, and you've got a bit of a swagger to you. Not enough to stop me, but I want to know why you turned Pooh Bear's head."

Faye's wintry eyes narrowed. "And what? You think killing me will make him love you again or something?"

Stella's smirk faded. "Boy, you got a mouth on you."

"You're threatening to kill the people I love," she hissed. "You're threatening to destroy their lives for money and because you've got a fifth grade lover's spat with your ex. I'm sorry that I can't have a sense of humor about it. You don't know a goddamn thing about what Jack and Kamala have been through, how hard they've fought to stay alive, how they've got monsters out there gunning for them, and all they want to do is work on what they love and be happy. They deserve to be happy. Not killed by some stuck up bitch with an over-inflated ego and a vendetta. So yeah. If you gotta kill me, fine. If I gotta go to jail, fine. I'm done sitting on the sidelines and I'm done letting people hurt my friends."

Faye took another step closer and lowered her arms, her voice raw and unafraid. "So make your move, bitch."

Stella stared right back at her, and then gave her a Cheshire cat grin. "I already did, toots."

Too late, Faye realized there was a reason they were in the back of the shed in the corner.

It was next to the fuse box.

Stella grabbed the mop bucket and slung its contents into the fuse box.

"No!"

Faye leapt for her just as the electricity fizzled, popped, and then cut the lights out.


Generally, Kamala didn't leave her phone on when she conducted lab work, but with what happened to Calloway and being apart from Jack, she made an exception. She'd been elbow deep inside the sea serpent's chest cavity, helping Ethan remove organs the size of small animals, when her cell began ringing...and ringing...and ringing some more.

"Gracious," she said, glancing at her vibrating pocket. "Where's the fire?"

Finally, she reached a stopping point, apologizing to Ethan, and stepped out of the meat locker to check the call. She found eight missing calls from Fujioka. The ninth one began just as she pulled off her gloves and she answered it.

"My goodness, Misaki, what's wrong?"

"Okegawa's coming after you."

Kamala froze. "What?"

"Minako called just now and told me someone put out a contract on you and Jack that ends tonight. The only person with the proper motivation to want you both dead would be Okegawa. Get yourself somewhere safe immediately and tell the authorities. I'll track down what I can for now, but do *not* go out in public. Is Jack with you?"

"Gods," Kamala whispered hoarsely, her throat tight. "No, I'm offsite today. He's back at the facility."

"Warn him. I'll get back to you when I've got something. Be safe, Kamala."

"Yes, you too. Thank you, Misaki." She hung up and dialed Jack, trying her hardest to remain calm as the phone rang, but her breathing had already turned ragged in mere seconds. Okegawa was coming for them. For her. For her child.

The line clicked as Jack answered. "Hey, Kam. What's up?"

"Jack, find Agent Shannon and get somewhere safe. We're both in danger."

He inhaled sharply over the line. "What?"

"Someone has put out a contract on our lives. I've already got a security detail, but you need to get away from the dragons immediately."

"Oh, shit."

The next thing she heard were screams and panicked shrieks. "Jack? Jack, talk to me, what's going on? Can you hear me?"

"Kam, something's happening. I'm--"

The call cut off abruptly.

Kamala stared at her phone, frozen in horror. She redialed.

It went straight to voicemail.

She tried again, two, three, four times. Each time, it went straight to voicemail.

"Goddess above," she whispered, bringing one hand up to her mouth.

Behind her, Ethan approached, sounding worried. "Dr. Anjali?"

"We have to get back to the facility," she said, stuffing her phone in her pocket and marching for the door. "Jack is in danger."

"We can't do that."

She whirled on the lab assistant, snarling. "Why not?"

"B-Because," he stammered, pointing at the puddle on the floor. "Your water just broke."

# CHAPTER SIXTEEN

# PANDEMONIUM

Chaos.

Pure chaos erupted inside the animal pen after the lights went out.

Libby had a death grip on Jack's lab coat. He felt her slender form to his right, pressed against his shoulder, using him as a human shield. It had been a smart idea; five seconds later, someone smashed into him and Jack hit the ground with a groan. The blow knocked the phone out of his hand, and he heard a sickening crunch after he'd fallen. Before he even rolled over to confirm, he knew he'd broken it.

"Jack?" Libby called, her voice high and tight with panic.

"Here," he growled out, patting the concrete floor until his fingers closed around his busted phone. He tried tapping the screen, but nothing happened. "Perfect."

Libby's cold fingers trembled as she whipped out her own phone and hit the flashlight function. A bright spot of white flooded the area around them. Jack hauled himself to his feet next to her. "You okay?"

"I'm fine," she lied. "What the hell just happened?"

She jerked hard as someone else bumped into her. It was the brunette lab tech Jack had addressed a moment ago. She had a cut on her forehead, her eyes too wide, her face bloodless. "Run!"

"What?" Libby demanded. "What do you mean run?"

"They're loose," she hissed. "The dragons are loose!"

Without waiting another second, she vanished into the dark.

"Holy fucking shit!" Libby ducked as one of the Netherland forest dragons came barreling from the darkness straight at her, its deadly horns aimed at her throat. It shot past her and the darkness swallowed it again, but she heard the creature's roar and its long talons scratching into the floor.

"Libby," Jack said. "Kill the light."

"What?" she shrieked.

Someone else screamed nearby. It got cut short and a wet splatter followed. The ground trembled as a body hit the ground. Jack couldn't see very far thanks to shed having no windows, but he counted five other flashlights dotted in the room, bobbing back and forth. One of them vanished with another scream of pain. He heard the dragon's cry as it proceeded to maul the fallen person.

"They're drawn to the lights," Jack said. "Turn it off."

"Jack, we can't see--"

"Libby," he said, catching her shoulders. "Just trust me. Do it."

She gulped, reading the deadly serious look on his face, and she turned off the light.

"Hang on." Libby clutched his hand and he pulled her down into a crouch alongside him. He squinted as his eyes adjusted to the dark again. The other lights in the room were down to just two of them. Footsteps echoed all around them, frantic, and uncoordinated. He could hear people tripping over equipment and each other as they scrambled for the exit. He and Libby had been towards the center of the shed when the lights went out. They had at least another eighty feet to cover before they'd reach the exit. Before she'd shut off the light, he'd gotten a quick glimpse of what direction they were facing and he concentrated on remembering what obstacles were between the two of them. The outer doors to the shed banged open and shut a few times, as people who had been closer to them when the lights went out ran outside. He could tell there had to be only a few people left, based on the noise.

"Come on," he whispered to her. "Stay low."

They crept forward carefully. Jack shuddered as he felt something sticky and wet beneath his dress shoes, but kept going anyway. The temptation to hold his hands out in front of him was nearly overwhelming, but he knew better. Instead, he just listened. They made it about twenty feet before he heard the slithering sound of scales on the concrete floor. He froze and squeezed Libby's hand. He could hear her sucking in shallow little breaths behind him as the leathery rasp got closer and closer to them.

Gently, Jack nudged her to the right until their backs were pressed to what had been a crate of supplies near the center of the room. He forced himself to breathe slower and waited silently while the unseen danger wandered by with a hideous *click-ssh-click-ssh* sound. A low hiss filled the area around them. Jack swallowed hard and held as still as possible. There was no doubt that the dragon knew they were there. However, if they appeared non-threatening, there was a good chance it would move on.

Something brushed his knee. Jack nearly shit his pants. Libby's fingers tightened on his so hard that his entire hand went numb.

Then, the *click-ssh-click-ssh* echoed away. The dragon had deemed them harmless and wandered off in search of something else.

Jack let out a long breath and tugged Libby up to keep going. He heard her muttering under her breath to stay calm as they moved. "It's just an animal. Not a monster. Just an animal."

They made it another forty feet closer to the exit. At least three bodies lay strewn in that distance, too still be survivors. The shed had been retroactively turned into the animal pen, so there were no backup generators installed yet. He could hear voices through the walls, probably of the lab techs telling the agents that the dragons had gotten loose. Worse still, he could hear more screaming and gunshots around the back. Some of the dragons must have gotten out already.

Jack stopped once again, as he heard a rumbling growl and wet, sloppy tearing up ahead. He spotted another dropped, cracked phone that cast up light enough to let him see that they'd crossed paths with the Chinese bearded dragon. Even with its crimson scales, he could see blood dripping down its jaws as it fed on an unfortunate bystander.

The phone's light illuminated an area of about fifteen feet. The dragon stood between them and the left exit, but there was a door on the opposite side that they could reach if the dragon stayed distracted by its meal. Jack jerked his head to one side and Libby nodded in understanding. They crept as quietly as possible with the widest berth possible between them and the hungry dragon.

Until Libby's phone rang.

The Chinese dragon's head lifted.

Libby cursed and hung up on the call, and the pair stopped dead to see what the creature would do. They'd nearly left its line of sight, but they could hear it hissing as it drew in a breath to smell them. It cocked its head to one side and its long pink tongue flicked out to taste the air. The dragon stared at them with its eerie yellow eyes turned demonic by the lone light.

"Come on," Jack growled under his breath, tensing for a fight. "Come on, ya pansy. Make a move."

The dragon rose to its full height and roared at them, flapping its enormous wings.

"Oh, you just *had* to say something, didn't you?" Libby snapped.

"Yeah, well, what would Captain America do?" Jack let go of her hand and rifled through his pockets until he found his keys. He'd been carrying a small canister of pepper spray on his key ring for the last year or so. It wouldn't do much to a two-hundred-pound dragon, but it was better than nothing.

The Chinese dragon lowered its head and snorted, its upper body coiling as it prepared to pounce. Jack gritted his teeth and forced out the next words. "When I say go, I want you to run for the door."

"Are you crazy? What are you going to do?"

"Don't worry about it. Ready?"

"No! Jack, don't do this--"

"We don't have a choice, Libby."

The dragon charged.

Jack shoved Libby towards the door and leapt to his feet. "Go!"

He aimed the pepper spray as the dragon's jaws parted to snap at his outstretched arm.

And then Pete came flying down from the rafters.

She slammed the Chinese dragon into the floor a mere three feet from where Jack had been standing, and let out a snarl into the pinned reptile's face. The impact cracked the concrete beneath them. The bearded dragon wheezed and tried to push to its feet, but Pete held it down and barked sharply. This time, the dragon stilled, its tail thumping against the floor in subdued annoyance.

"Oh my *God*," Jack gasped in relief. "I love you so much, you giant gecko."

Pete flapped her wings once before tucking them against her back, and then brought her bumpy, ridged forehead down against Jack's sweaty one. He patted her neck, smiling at the majestic animal. "Thanks, girl."

Just then, he heard the doors to the left fly open and spotted a pair of armed agents rushing inside, guns and flashlights held high. He quickly stood in front of Pete and called out to them. "Guys, it's okay, this one's a friendly."

"Ten-four," the agents said. "More agents are coming in behind us. Get clear."

Jack shook his head. "Don't want my dragon to get shot. Can I get some help with this one here?"

The agents ran over and jumped in shock of seeing Pete holding the bearded dragon down like a wrestler in a pro-match. "Holy shit."

"I know," Jack said, almost smiling. "It'd be cool if this wasn't a horrific nightmare scenario of epic proportions. There should be a tether in one of those cages against the wall."

One of the agents retrieved it. Jack knelt and carefully

302

tied the dragon's jaws shut, then its limbs, and the three of them hauled it back into the cage.

Jack winced as the sunlight pierced his pupils when he stepped out of the animal pen. He didn't get too long to notice; Libby almost tackled him off his feet in a hug. "You stupid asshole!"

He hugged her back. "It's depressing how many times I've heard that lately."

She hit him in the ribs, hard. "Don't you *ever* do that shit to me again, you hear me, Sir Gawain?"

"Yeah, yeah," he said, rubbing the sore spot. "We only found the Chinese dragon and the diamondback dragons inside after an area sweep. Does that mean what I think it means?"

Libby nodded gravely. "They've all escaped."

"Dammit," Jack swore.

"Exactly. Now what the hell are we going to do?"

"We've got to get them back. There's no telling how many people they can hurt before the cops get to them. Where's Faye's dragon tracker?"

"In the lab."

He nodded tightly. "Get somewhere safe."

Libby crossed her arms. "Excuse me? And just where do you think you're going?"

"I have to go after them."

"No, *we* have to go after them."

Jack gritted his teeth. "Dammit, Libby, I've got this."

"By yourself?" she demanded. "Really? You think you can fly a dragon and catch another dragon at the same time? You've never even tested this equipment out. You'll be dead in ten minutes, tops."

"No, I'll be dead in five if your brother finds out I let you catch a bunch of dragons with me."

"You are so full of shit, Jack. Don't try to pin this on Bruce. I made this equipment and I know how to operate it. You're being a stubborn idiot and you know it."

She stepped close and pointed a finger in his chest,

glaring. "I'm. Coming. With. You."

Jack dragged his hand down his face. "Are you this difficult with everyone or just me?"

She poked him again. "Pot."

Then she pointed at herself. "Kettle. Now get in the cart, Galahad."

Jack sighed in resignation. "I really should've retired when I had the chance."

They climbed into the only golf cart left as sirens wailed around them and more and more agents rushed into the animal pen to search for survivors.

"What did Kamala say?" Libby asked. "You just about turned white when you answered that phone."

"I am white," he said on reflex, earning himself another punch to the ribs. "Kam said someone put out a hit on the two of us."

Libby's eyes widened. "Jesus Christ. So it wasn't just my brother?"

"No. This whole damn thing stinks to high heaven, and what just happened can't be a coincidence. That was an assassination attempt. The hitter's already here."

"Shit," Libby said, grabbing her phone. "We've got to tell Shannon. Is Kamala okay?"

"Yeah, she's got that security detail with her. She'll be safe and that's all that matters." He parked the golf cart and the two of them raced for the elevators. Despite the general panic and evacuation going on, they made it to the lab quickly. Once there, Libby tossed Jack her brother's suit.

"Put that on," she said, opening a large, heavy-duty duffel bag.

He blinked at her. "Uh, it's not going to fit. Your brother's got me by like thirty pounds of muscle."

"It's adjustable, you caveman. You won't last very long without it."

He frowned. "What about you?"

"There are some prototype pieces I can wear," she said. "Hurry up. We haven't got all day."

Jack scowled as he shrugged out of his lab coat. "Fine, but no peeking."

She lifted her eyes to the ceiling in exasperation. "I swear, you are an eighty year old man in a twenty-eight year old body."

"Where my teeth at," he deadpanned as he unbuttoned his shirt. Libby snorted as she pulled on one of the incomplete prototypes. It had a dark grey finish much like her brother's suit, but it moved fluidly like a lighter version of chainmail armor. She cinched one of Calloway's backup utility belts to her waist and then reached for her phone.

Libby couldn't reach Shannon the on the first try, but by the time they'd loaded up a duffel bag of supplies in the lab, she got through. He met them in lab just as they finished dressing and grabbing everything they'd need.

"What in God's name happened?" the agent demanded.

"Someone's trying to kill me," Jack said. "Kam too. They're using the dragons to pull the trigger."

Shannon narrowed his eyes. "Who told you?"

Both Jack and Libby nearly dropped what they were holding. "Wait, what?"

"I've had that intel for a grand total of..." Shannon checked his watch. "Barely half an hour. How the hell did you get it?"

Jack gritted his teeth. "Why am I not surprised? So when were you planning on telling us?"

"When I had everything contained and you were no longer in danger," the agent said. "And just where the hell do you think you're going?"

"The dragons are loose. Where do you think we're going?"

Shannon stepped in front of him. "You just said someone made an attempt on your life using those dragons. Why the hell are you giving them exactly what they want?"

"I don't have time for this shit," Jack snarled. "You wanna square up again, go for it. The reason you brought me in is to recover these dragons so no one else gets hurt. If you've got a better idea, then please share it."

"The authorities will kill these things on sight."

"And how long will that take? You know it only takes a few seconds for a dragon to rip a person in half. The DC cops out there aren't equipped to handle those dragons. The dragons can cover distances that no one can keep up with except for Pete. They're scared. They've been hurt by bad people. They don't know any better, and they'll start the whole cycle of violence over again, but this time with innocent lives. We can stop this here and now. Haven't you seen enough bloodshed, Shannon?"

Shannon worked his jaw, but he didn't answer. He glanced at Libby, but she cut him off. "Oh, don't even try it."

The older man finally sighed and unclipped the walkie-talkie on his hip. "Call it in when you find them. I'll send agents to back you up."

"Thanks. Get Kamala somewhere safe."

Something fierce glinted in Shannon's dark eyes then. "Done."

Jack nodded and opened the door for Libby. Shannon called out to them before they left.

He gave them both a rare smile. "Don't die. It's a helluva lot of paperwork."

Libby grinned. "We'd never be such a bother, old man."

Jack and Libby returned to the animal shed and retrieved Pete from her cage. Libby strapped on the saddle and made sure everything was secure before they led her outside while Jack set up the new and improved dragon tracker.

"I drive, you shoot," Libby said, climbing onto the dragon's back. "Don't miss."

Jack smiled fiercely as he climbed on behind her. "I won't. Just make sure you fly straight, whippersnapper. Ready?"

Libby matched his smile. "Damn right I am."

Together, they took off into the troubled skies above
Washington D.C.


"*Dēvara pavitra tāyi mattu avaḷa ellā ailupaikeya
sahōdararu!*" (*"*Holy mother of God and all her wacky nephews!*"*)
Kamala snarled as she stared at the liquid that had just
poured down her thighs and effectively ruined both her
slacks and her coveralls. As if on cue, the stabbing pain in her
lower body started up with a vengeance.

The first set of contractions had begun.

"Now?" she bellowed at the baby in her belly.
"*Really?*"

"Dr. Anjali," Ethan said, still pale and worried. "We
need to call you an ambulance."

"Calm down," she told him. "Labor takes hours, not
minutes. I need to know Jack is safe. If anything happened to
him, then--aargh!"

She crumpled in half as another wave of contractions
hit, stealing her breath. Ethan steadied her as she leaned one
hand to the wall and sucked in shaky gulps of cool air. That
worried her. The phantom contractions she'd had before
hadn't been nearly this painful. Something was wrong.

"Dr. Anjali, please," Ethan said. "We need to get you to
the hospital."

He lifted his phone, but as he did, it rang. He kept one
arm around her as she worked her way through the wave of
pain and answered. "What is it?"

Kamala felt him go entirely still beside her. "What did
you just say? No...that...no, you've got to be shitting me, man.
Holy shit. Okay. Yeah. Got it."

He hung up. "Doc, you're not going to believe this,
but...the dragons have escaped."

"What?" she demanded.

"Something happened at the facility and they broke
loose. They've instructed me to get you somewhere safe until
the dragons have been contained. There's bound to be chaos

on the streets until someone finds them or takes them out. Maybe we should wait on that ambulance. There'll be car wrecks all over the place once someone spots them."

Kamala's gaze wandered over to the doors where the corpse of the sea serpent lay. "That is not an option."

"I'm sorry?"

She straightened as the contractions finally subsided and pointed to the meat locker. "That dragon is now a gigantic beacon for the other dragons that are loose. They'll smell it from miles away. Dragons are inherently drawn to each other. We have to get out of here."

"Holy hell," he said, swallowing hard. "You think they'll converge here and what? Try to eat what's left of it?"

"Among other things." She marched outside to where a black limousine waited. One of the tinted windows rolled down to reveal a black man in his late forties. He was tall with compact muscle and wore a plain black polo and khakis. He sat next to a stocky brunette woman in the same ensemble, and both had links in their ears.

"I take it you've been apprised of the situation at the facility?" Kamala asked.

Both of them nodded tersely. "Good. We have to go. Those dragons will make a beeline for this place. I need you to protect me long enough to get me to the hospital."

"What for?" the male security guard answered.

"Oh, nothing," Kamala said. "I'm just having a baby right now."

"You're *what?*" he sputtered, and then he glanced down at her ruined coveralls. "*Fuck me.*"

"Yes," Kamala said mildly. "I take it you're armed, yes?"

"Yes, ma'am, both of us are."

She exhaled. "Alright, then. Follow us closely. There may be trouble along the way."

"We've got your back," the female guard said.

"Thank you both." Kamala rapped her knuckles on the hood and turned to Ethan. "Call for the ambulance."

Just then, her phone rang. "Hello?"

"Dr. Anjali," Agent Shannon said. "Are you en route to a safe location?"

"Not yet, but we're on the way to the hospital. My water just broke."

"Your *what* just did *what?*"

Despite herself, she raised an eyebrow. "Considering how obsessed you've been with my pregnancy, I'd think you of all people would know what that means."

"Jesus tap-dancing Christ," Shannon groused. "Like we don't have enough on our plate. Your boyfriend just left, but I think I can get him back here in--"

"No."

Shannon paused. "No what?"

Kamala winced. Her insides wriggled, not only with the impending pains of the upcoming birth, but with guilt, worry, and fear. "I..."

"You what, doc?"

She rubbed her swollen, sensitive stomach. "No. We cannot call him now."

"What?" Shannon demanded. "Why?"

"If you call him, he will drop everything and rush to my side. Countless people will be hurt if he doesn't catch those dragons in time. We wait."

"Dr. Anjali," Shannon said, his tone strained. "It's your *daughter*. If he misses the birth--"

"He won't," she said gently. "Now promise me you will not tell him."

"I don't owe you a goddamn thing, doctor."

"No, you do not." She drew in a deep breath. "But somewhere in that trash heap you call a heart, you still care. So promise me you will not tell him."

He didn't answer her right away. She could hear him breathing for a while. "If he finds out later, there'll be hell to pay. And it'll be all on you. Do you understand that?"

"Yes, I do."

"Damn you. Fine. The second you arrive to the

hospital, call me. I'll send men ahead to meet you there for extra security."

"Thank you, Agent Shannon."

"John," he corrected her. "Any woman who tells me to lie to the father of her child about its impending birth calls me by my first name."

She huffed out a little cynical laugh. "Very well, John. Thank you. I will call you when we arrive."

Kamala hung up and exhaled. She said a short prayer for herself, her child, and Jack, and then headed inside to wait for the ambulance.

"Faye? Dammit, Blondie, talk to me! What the hell is going on?" Winston barked.

Faye couldn't see a damned thing after Stella slung the water at the fuse box and shut off the lights. She'd been seconds too late, evidenced as she slammed her shoulder into the wall after she'd missed grabbing for the assassin. Immediately, she threw her hands up in a defensive stance and flattened her back to the wall. The shed was pitch black. She couldn't even see her own hand in front of her face. Cold sweat beaded on her forehead, along the small of her back, underneath her arms. Stella could come at her from anywhere and she wouldn't be able to do a damn thing about it.

Faye gritted her teeth and forced herself to stay calm as she responded to Winston as quietly as possible. "She shorted out the lights."

She jerked as she heard the other people inside shouting in alarm. Footsteps thundered all over, drowning out what the people were saying at first.

"Run! Everyone get out of here! They're loose!"

Faye stiffened. "They" could only mean one thing.

The dragons.

"Shit," she hissed. "Winston, the dragons are loose. That's what she wanted all along. Jack's trapped in here with them."

"Can you get to him?" Winston asked.

"Not sure. It's too dark and--" She spotted a flashlight a few yards away and then heard claws scrabbling against the floor. A man screamed and then she heard the crunch of bones, and the thud of a body hitting the concrete. The light fell with him, and she caught sight of glittering dark-green scales. She could only see its wings and part of its neck as it lowered its head to begin eating its kill.

She shivered and glanced in the direction where the outer doors banged open and shut. People were evacuating, but some were being killed in the process.

Her eyes adjusted enough to let her calculate the distance between her and the Highlander dragon. Stella had left her high and dry, at least for now. The real danger was the dragon that could gore her in half.

"And what?" Winston asked, frustrated. "Come on, talk to me."

"Can't," she whispered. "Dragon's right in front of me."

Faye sank into a crouch and felt around the floor until her slender fingers wrapped around the mop. She hadn't caught its attention yet, not with a fresh kill nearby, but it wouldn't take long. She ran through the lectures she'd attended that Jack and Kamala had given, and ran through what she could remember. Sounds. Light. Those could distract it. Dragons were cautious by nature and only attacked perceived threats. She couldn't try to fight the dragon with a mop; that was suicide.

Instead, she took a deep breath, hefted it, and threw it as hard as she could in her opposite direction.

The mop clattered loudly when it landed somewhere out in the shed. The Netherland dragon snarled and darted towards the noise.

Faye held out her hands and shifted to her left, staying close to the wall. Her back slid across the Chinese bearded dragon's enclosure, and she kept feeling along, inching towards the far side of the shed where the doors were. She had to hurry. In all the chaos, Stella could slip away and go after Kamala. Or she could very well push Jack straight into the jaws of a bloodthirsty dragon under the cover of darkness.

*Focus,* she scolded herself. *You can't help anyone if you panic and get yourself killed.*

As she edged along, she spotted another fallen cell phone with its flashlight activated. It gave her a frame of reference, finally, that she was less than fifty feet from the doors.

Just as she neared it, a pure white dragon stepped right into her path.

Faye froze.

The light bounced off the dragon's nearly opalescent scales and deep blue spines and wings. It leaned down and sniffed the cell phone, pawing at the device curiously.

Then it turned its reptilian eyes on her.

Its sapphire irises narrowed and a low hiss filled the area. It sank down onto its belly and flicked its black tongue at her a couple times. Its shoulder muscles bunched. It was going to charge her. If it did, she'd be dead in seconds.

She crouched to make herself a smaller target, and to put herself on eye level with the startled creature, muttering furiously. "Think, Faye, come on, think! What calms these things down?"

It struck her all at once; a sudden memory of being in the shower with Jack, laughing as she smoothed shampoo suds out of his hair, the two of them caterwauling a duet that would probably make dogs howl, since neither of them could carry a tune.

If she was wrong...well, at least she'd die doing something no one probably ever had before.

"*Oh, Danny boy, the pipes, the pipes are calling...*"

The arctic dragon blinked at her and tilted its head.

"Wait, what the hell?" Winston muttered in her ear, baffled.

312

Faye swallowed and kept singing very, very softly to the dragon. "*From glen to glen, and down the mountainside...*"

The creature didn't move to attack. It just kept staring at her, as if somewhere between mesmerized and bewildered. Sweat leaked over her forehead into one eye and she wiped it away. She wasn't dead yet. Maybe it was a good sign. "*The summer's gone, and all the roses falling...*"

Little by little, the tension in the dragon's spiny back eased away. It settled on its belly and watched her sing with a strange sense of interest, like a cat experiencing something for the first time. She didn't dare stop for even a second, and as she noticed its docile behavior, she inched to the right of it one careful step at a time. The arctic dragon watched her go, its long, slender tail lashing behind it. Then it snorted and strode off in the direction of the doors on the right side of the shed.

Faye let out a rush of breath and hurried to the doors on the left.

She burst out of them into the throng of people yelling frantically into their phones or walkie-talkies. She started searching desperately for Jack. She spotted him near the golf carts, arguing with the pink-haired black girl she'd seen earlier, and breathed a sigh of relief. She didn't see any visible cuts or anything, and his dragon Pete stood behind him, protectively eyeing anyone who got too close. Faye kept her back facing them, but eased over until she caught the tail end of the argument.

"I made this equipment and I know how to operate it. You're being a stubborn idiot and you know it. I'm. Coming. With. You."

She heard Jack's exasperated response, but he didn't deny the girl. They were going to retrieve the dragons. Which meant he'd give Stella exactly what she wanted. Catching them could get him killed, easily.

Faye's instincts screamed at her to forget the covert bullshit. She wanted to grab him, shake him, and yell in his face that he was about to blow her entire operation. Damn the consequences. He'd promised he'd return to her safely, and now he was about to jeopardize it all. She'd worked so hard to keep him from harm, and here he was yet again, diving headfirst into trouble. Winston had been right all along. Jack couldn't help himself. It was just a part of him. He'd always put others before himself.

Faye clenched her teeth and held still, choking back frustrated tears. No. She couldn't stop him. He'd never forgive her if he found out what she'd been doing all along. She'd have to trust him. Trust that he knew what he was doing and that he could stay alive. She still had a job to do.

She watched Jack and the pink-haired girl get into a golf cart and gun it across the lot towards the lab building. She still had to find and stop Stella.

Faye slipped away from the crowd until she reached the trees surrounding that part of the estate where no one could clearly see her. "Winston? You there?"

"You gonna tell me what the hell all of that was about now?" he demanded.

Faye recapped the last several minutes. Winston stayed quiet, as if chewing on his thoughts and digesting what information he could in such a short amount of time. "Okay. Boyfriend's in the clear, relatively speaking. Stella positioned the pieces on the board to get him killed, but according to the contract, she can't be the one to do it. If the beanpole is half as clever as you say, he'll pull through and she'll have failed part one of her assignment. If she gave you the slip, that means we have a completely new problem. I think she's going after your baby mama."

"So do I," Faye said, trying her hardest to keep her voice steady as an icy pang of worry stabbed at her stomach. "But if Kamala's not around any of the live specimens, how is Stella going to stage it like one of the dragons killed her?"

"Haven't worked that out yet, but I'm gonna. Any chance you can figure out where she is?"

Faye cleared her throat. "Yeah. I...may have turned on her Find my iPhone setting before she left Cambridge."

"You sneaky devil, you," Winston drawled with a teasing lilt.

"Shut up. I'm not proud of it. I worry, okay?" She pulled out her phone and hit a few things until she discovered the location. "Headed there now."

"Godspeed, Blondie."

# CHAPTER SEVENTEEN
## STRAIGHTEN UP AND FLY RIGHT

The District of Columbia understandably hadn't taken the sight of living, breathing dragons very well.

Libby had coaxed Pete into an altitude that would keep them from being sighted too easily, but from their flight out of the government complex, it was immediately noticeable that people had seen the fleeing dragons. D.C. was notorious for bad traffic, but the pair spotted traffic accidents on a mass scale immediately surrounding the area, and spreading further out into the city. Sirens screeched all over the place, both police and ambulances, car alarms blaring frantically, and furious honks from trapped drivers on the streets.

"Where's the closest one?" Libby called over her shoulder to Jack.

Jack examined the dragon tracker. "Head northwest."

"Can you tell if it's airborne?"

Jack cocked his head and examined the green blob on the radar. "No, it's not moving fast enough. I think it's on the ground."

Libby guided the dragon northwest, using the heads up display on her goggles to be sure they were headed in the right direction. As the grey cirrus clouds parted, she noted where they seemed to be drawing near. "That's Rock Creek Park up ahead."

"Makes sense," Jack said. "Not sure which dragon we're chasing, but I'm seeing two signatures in the area. If it's the Netherland twins, then that's exactly where they'd head. They'd need familiar territory."

"Boy, will they be happy to see us."

"Ecstatic."

Rock Creek Park in mid-April meant all the trees, flowers, and shrubs were heading towards their spring splendor. From up above, most of it appeared like a thick, green carpet spotted with brilliant colors. The park sat upon over 2,000 acres and stretched out like its own tiny country before them, broken into various sections for both indoor and outdoor activities.

Once they got close enough to confirm, Jack grabbed the walkie-talkie and tuned in. "Shannon, we've got our first bogie in Rock Creek Park. Can you contact the rangers for an evacuation?"

"Will do," the older man said, and then he scoffed. "Bogie? This isn't a movie, Jackson."

Jack rolled his eyes. "Whatever, old man, just do it."

He returned his gaze to the tracker as the distance to their first target closed in. "Libs, I need your phone. I'm gonna try to figure out which section of the park we're in so he knows where to move the people."

She fished it out of one of the utility belt pockets and then offered it to him. "Don't get nosy."

"Hardy-har," he shot back, and then quickly brought up the park's information page. He found what he was looking for and hit the walkie-talkie. "Georgetown Waterfront Park. Get everyone out of there as fast as you can."

"Got it." He leaned over Libby's shoulder. "Any sign of it yet?"

"Oh, you're gonna love this." She pointed.

Georgetown Waterfront Park had served as a port in its establishment, and sat upon the Potomac River with a host of various attractions for visitors dotted along the riverfront. East of the park's infamous fountain lay a set of concrete steps absolutely crowded with people who had their cell phones pointed towards the center of the river. Jack could see huge ripples and splashing beneath its surface, which could only mean one thing.

"Any chance this suit is waterproof?" Jack asked dryly.

"There's no way you can take that thing underwater," Libby replied, guiding the dragon to circle around to get a better look. "We've got to get its attention and lure it out of there."

"I was afraid you'd say that." He glanced towards the river steps to see some people splashing their hands in the water, trying to get the creature's attention. It wouldn't be easy with so many distractions. The dragon appeared to be amusing itself with a swim, and it wouldn't stay there forever.

"Alright," he concluded. "Land her over there and we'll get these folks to scatter. Then we'll figure out how to get it out of the drink."

"Got it." Libby turned the dragon and dove towards the river steps. Immediately, the spectators' attention switched to them instead and they backed up, shouting and pointing in excitement. Pete landed neatly on the edge of the water and then shook herself slightly, casting a wary glance at the random assortment of strangers, and then directing her gaze towards the dragon in the river.

"Uh," Jack said as he climbed down. "Hi there. Crazy day, isn't it?"

Libby facepalmed. "I can't take you anywhere, can I?"

Jack ignored her and kept addressing the throng of people. "Okay, so, I know this looks amazingly cool and everything, but the dragon out there is a wild animal. It's been badly mistreated by some really awful people, and it's dangerous. I need you guys to please clear the area so no one gets hurt."

"Dude," one of the teenage boys in the crowd said in awe. "You're *riding* that dragon? Who the hell are you? Where'd you get a dragon like that?"

"Long story," Jack said. "Please, guys, this is for your own safety. I need you to leave."

"No way, man!" A forty-something guy said, gesturing towards Pete. "You kiddin' me? This is crazy! I mean, look at that thing!"

"She's not a thing," Jack said, an edge creeping into his voice.

318

"Can we touch it?" A little girl piped up.

"Sorry, but no. Look, the park rangers will be here any minute. For the last time, guys, I need you to clear out."

"Who are you, anyway?" The forty-something asked. "The dragon police?"

"Close enough," Jack snapped. "Come on, people, I can't do my job if you're in my way."

By now, the crowd had gotten a little bolder and inched towards him, asking more questions. Jack gritted his teeth beneath the helmet and finally turned his head towards Libby, who still sat astride Pete.

"So this is going great. Any ideas, whipper snapper?"

She grinned. "Not any good ones, but yeah."

"Go for it."

Libby reached out and tweaked a nerve in Pete's long, swan-like neck. The dragon twitched and let out a roar, her wings snapping outward to full height.

The crowd immediately scattered.

Parents scooped up their kids and booked it away from the river steps, swearing profusely along the way. The reaction appeared to be entirely knee-jerk, as if they'd found the fight-or-flight response for everyone present. Then again, Pete's roar was downright terrifying.

"Better?" Libby asked smugly.

"You're so mean," Jack said. He then patted her knee. "I love it."

He turned towards the river and then froze. "Wait, where'd it go?"

"Shit!" Libby turned Pete towards the riverfront as Jack checked the tracker again. "It's further down, following the current. Think it can still hear us from here?"

"Let's find out, shall we?" Libby popped open one of her pouches and withdrew a small, silver item, and then two discs. She gently placed the discs on either side of Pete's scaly head over her ears and then brought the little reed up to her lips. She blew into it. No sound came out.

Then, a second later, a Netherland forest dragon burst

319

from the surface of the water with an angry snarl.

"Is that a dragon whistle?" Jack asked as he unhooked the net launcher from his back.

"Not exactly," Libby said. "It's just a dog whistle, but dragons can hear in the same pitch, so I figured it might work."

"Hoo boy," he muttered as the creature flew high up and then tucked its wings in for a dive. "Did it ever. Give me some room."

Libby nudged Pete towards the far side of the steps as the Netherland dragon flew straight at Jack, its jaws open and ready to take a bite out of him as soon as it was within range. Jack held his ground and aimed carefully, holding his breath as the winged creature bore down on him.

At the last possible second, he fired.

The net shot out and wrapped around the dragon. It cinched its wings to its side and turned it into an enormous living missile. Jack rolled to one side as it shot past him, over the river steps, and landed in a heap of grass and dirt behind them on the hill.

"Nice shot!" Libby cheered as she hopped off Pete's back and grabbed the tranquilizer gun from a pocket on the side of the saddle. Jack joined her as they approached the struggling reptile, dodging its flailing tail and sharp horns. He grabbed it behind the neck and held it down while she sought out the soft spot beneath its jaws and injected the sedative. The dragon's movements slowed, and then it stilled after a minute or so.

Jack let out a long breath and knelt in the grass, relieved. "One down."

"Holy shit!"

Jack leapt to his feet, fists raised, only to realize the teenage boy from earlier had reappeared. "That was *awesome,* dude! Who the hell are you?"

Libby pointed a finger at Jack. "If you say Spider-Man or Batman, I'm going to break one of your ribs."

Jack sighed in defeat. "Killjoy."

He turned to the kid and said. "No comment" before hitting the walkie-talkie again. "We've got the first one. It's one of the Netherland dragons. We're on the river steps."

"I've got the rangers inbound as we speak. They'll keep the public from messing with it. Head on to your next target."

"Got it." Jack flipped the dragon onto its back and examined it closely. "This one's the male, which means his sister's probably around here somewhere. She wouldn't go too far. I think--"

Without warning, Pete hissed up at the sky. Jack turned just in time to see the female Netherland dragon drop out of the sky. It snatched him off the ground and swooped out over the lake.

"Oh, come on!" Jack snarled as he grabbed the dragon's talons that were currently clutched around his shoulders. "I'm on your side, you crocodile-faced asshole!"

The forest dragon dug its claws in tighter. The suit held, but Jack grimaced as he felt the pressure bruising his skin. He slammed his forearms against the dragon's limbs, hoping to knock himself free, but its grip only tightened.

"Jack!" Libby cried over the comm-link. "Hold on! I'm right behind you. Can you get yourself free?"

He jerked his head to one side as the dragon tried to bite him and then batted its jaws away when it tried a second time. "Not sure. She's got me pretty good."

Jack swung his legs in an arc, hard, trying to throw off the creature's trajectory, but it just held on harder and dragged him up into the sky. Even over water, if the dragon went much higher, he'd break his legs or die on impact. He had to get at a lower altitude, and fast.

One of the dragon's wings dipped into his line of sight just as they skimmed over the trees across from the riverfront. Jack seized it with one hand. The dragon shrieked in panic and tried to fly with just one wing, but couldn't. They dropped into the treetops and the reptile finally let him go so it could catch itself.

Jack wasn't as lucky.

He crashed through several branches, but got his arms out enough to catch onto one big enough to support his weight. Wheezing, he locked his arms around it and waited for the world to stop spinning. He'd brained himself pretty good during the fall, more than once, and his ribs ached from the impact. He dangled there for a moment and then hauled his body up onto the branch so that he straddled it.

"Shoulda been a farmer," he mumbled to himself.

The branch wobbled dangerously as the forest dragon dropped onto it with a bubbling hiss, its eyes locked on Jack. It crept forward, saliva dripping from its long, narrow jaws.

"Oh, you are just a peach, aren't you?" Jack growled.

The dragon lunged for his neck. Jack ducked and its snout smashed into the trunk a couple inches above his head. He shoved the dragon, hard, aiming for its chest in the hopes of overbalancing it. The dragon's talons dug furrows into the wood. It stayed put.

Jack threw his arms around its head, blinding it with his upper body, and clamping its jaws shut. The dragon worried him and flapped its wings, and the branch couldn't handle the strain any longer. It broke off and sent them both hurtling to the ground below. They hit the forest floor in a writhing heap. Jack rolled on top of the creature, still wrapped around it. "Libby! Could use some help, if it's not too much trouble!"

He winced as one of the dragon's claws raked down his side, but he didn't relent. He locked his legs around the creature's wings so it couldn't take off and bore down harder to keep it pinned. Seconds later, limbs and leaves fluttered to the ground in the wake of Pete's landing. Libby jumped off and hurried over with the tranq gun. Once more, the dragon twitched a few times and eventually relaxed.

Jack flopped off it onto his back and stared at Libby upside down, panting furiously. "What? Did you take the scenic route?"

"Man up," Libby chided. "I thought you were

southern. Never wrestled a gator before?"

"I ain't that southern," Jack corrected her with an intentional twang in his voice. "Okay. How about I drive and *you* catch these things?"

She patted his chest lightly. "No can do, Sir Gawain. Not in my job description."

"Right. I regret my life choices so much right now." He heaved himself onto his knees and accepted the tether she gave him. He tied the dragon's limbs together as well as its jaws and radioed their coordinates in to Shannon.

Libby offered him an arm as he stood up. "Well, if it makes you feel any better, you're already trending on Twitter."

"How on *earth* have you had time to check that?" he demanded.

"I'm Gen Z, remember?" she said, showing him her phone screen. He squinted at the feed, seeing several different videos of his first capture already posted. "Hashtag dragon hunter? Very original, Internet. Great. I'm going to be a meme by dinner time, aren't I?"

"And you'll have fangirls within the next ten minutes," Libby confirmed as she kicked a leg over Pete's back. "Well, more of them, anyway. Wonder if they'll come up with some kind of cutesy nickname for themselves."

"Do keep me posted," he said with biting sarcasm.

"Spoilsport." She handed him the recovered dragon tracker. "Two down. Five more to go."

He fired it up. "Next one appears to be airborne going towards West End."

Jack changed his voice to a dreamy, borderline eerie tone as he pointed. "He went...*that* way."

Libby shuddered. "You're such a weirdo, Jack."

"Move it or lose it, whipper snapper."

They launched into the air to set after the next dragon. West End rested a stone's throw away from the park, which couldn't have been a coincidence. The dragons had been in the middle of feeding time when all hell broke loose, so there was a good chance they were seeking out sustenance and shelter. Just as they closed in on the location, Jack's walkie-talkie squawked.

"I'm getting reports of an animal attack outside of a seafood joint in West End," Shannon told him. "You en route?"

"Yeah, we're close. Any cops arrived yet?"

"Yeah, looks like a patrolman is on his way over."

"Shit. This is gonna get messy." He patted Libby's side. "See if you can land on the roof. They might get twitchy seeing two dragons instead of just one."

"Roger that."

West End hosted a number of luxury homes and apartments, and with its location near the Rock Creek, there was no shortage of fine dining. The tracker indicated the dragon was near a seafood restaurant on the small pier by the water. As they approached, they could already hear the hubbub from inside. Things were not going well, from the sound of it.

Libby landed Pete on the roof and tied her to the air conditioning unit. "This thing got its name for being unbelievably strong. You won't be able to pull a Steve Irwin on it. What's the plan?"

"It should be susceptible to the cold," Jack said as he loaded the net launcher. "If we're lucky, they have a walk-in freezer. We'll try to lure it in there and let it get cold enough to be too slow to attack us. Then we can knock it out."

"And if they don't have a walk-in freezer?"

"Uh," Jack said. "I'll...work out a Plan B on the way. Come on."

He wrenched open the roof access door as Libby followed, shaking her head. "Whatever you say, fearless leader."

They made their way down a narrow flight of stairs until the shouts of panic were easily audible. The door to the stairwell opened right into the far end of the kitchen, and once again, chaos reigned supreme.

The Hercules dragon had backed up against one corner of the line of counters. It had bits of raw fish clinging to its lower jaw and its hiss spilled a foul stench into the air. A young male dishwasher curled up in a ball several feet away, trapped between it and the wall with nowhere to go. He had his hat clenched between both hands and appeared to be praying furiously as the creature eyed the other employees that stood ten feet away, banging pots and pans together in hopes of scaring it off. Every so often, it slammed its giant, thick tail against the ground and the employees flinched back, not daring to get any closer. White dust coated the floor in front of it, and Jack could see someone had hoped to frighten it with a fire extinguisher. Not a bad idea, if it had been any dragon other than one of the strongest, bravest species.

Jack and Libby made their way around the other side of the counter to the group of people. "Everybody, I need you to calm down. We're here to bag this thing. Can you guys please take a step back so we can take a look?"

"Who the hell are you?" someone demanded.

Jack turned his head towards Libby. "You know, we really should have badges."

"Badges?" Libby sneered with an accent. "We don't need no stinkin' badges!"

"Not helping," he said, but he had to choke down a laugh first. He addressed the frightened employees again. "We work for the government."

Everyone visibly relaxed. "Okay, now who's our friend over there?"

"Olly," someone told him.

"Got it. Please step away for me, alright?"

Reluctantly, the six people inched back towards the entrance to the kitchen and let Jack and Libby through. The Hercules dragon continued hissing and whapping its tail on the ground, refusing to move an inch.

"Olly," Jack called. "How's it hanging, pal?"

The little guy didn't move. He just kept praying. He

had a rosary dangling from his fingers. Jack winced. "Shit. Poor kid's scared stiff."

He tried again. "Olly, we're here to help. I need you to do me a favor, okay? We're not gonna let this thing hurt you. I promise."

At the promise, the little guy gulped and opened his eyes. He couldn't have been more than eighteen, Jack predicted, and there was no way in hell anything in his life had prepared him for seeing a reptile the size of a gator standing not eight feet from him. "W-What favor?"

"I'm gonna try to get this big fella here to follow me. I need you to stay right where you are. Don't try to run or he'll chase you. Got it?"

Olly nodded shakily. "Y-Yeah, man."

Jack motioned to the staff. "Someone prop that freezer door open and then all of you get scarce. If you see a cop, tell him not to come in here."

They nodded, opened the door, and then vanished through the doorway. Jack eyed the defensive creature for a moment and then asked. "Libs, is there anything on this nifty belt that'll dissuade him from biting me in half?"

"Your only choice is to try blinding him. There's nothing we have that'll penetrate his scales. His hide's damn near as thick as the Highlander dragon's."

He swallowed hard. "Goody gumdrops. Alright, on three, blow the whistle. It should make him charge and then I'll lead him in."

Libby eased her way until she stood in the doorway, safely out of reach, and put the whistle to her lips. Jack steeled himself and got ready to run.

"One...two...three!"

Libby blew the whistle.

The black spines on the dragon's back stood straight up. Its pupils narrowed and its deep-brown wings knocked items off the shelves as they shot out. The dragon bellowed and lunged towards Jack. Olly ducked as its tail punched a dent into the metal counter inches above his head and flattened himself to the floor.

Jack ran around the corner and headed towards the freezer.

He was halfway there when the policeman appeared behind Libby.

"What's going on--*holy fucking shit!*" The cop shoved the pink-haired girl to one side and drew his firearm without thinking twice.

"No!" Libby cried, but she couldn't warn him in time.

The cop opened fire on the dragon with his .38 and the dragon roared, locking its yellow eyes on him instead of Jack. The bullets ricocheted off its scales and punched holes into the walls, the counter, cracking the tile floors. The Hercules dragon seized the officer by the shin and dragged him backwards from the doorway.

"Shit!" Jack grabbed a hand towel hanging off an oven and threw himself on top of the dragon, blinding it. "Libby!"

"Got it!" She caught the officer beneath his armpits and pulled with all her strength, trying to get him loose from the dragon's jaws. The cop screamed as the dragon's sharp teeth dug into the meat of his calf muscle and thrashed harder to try and free himself. Dishes and pots clattered off the counters as the dragon slammed Jack into them again and again.

Jack finally landed a punch to the dragon's eye underneath the hand towel and it let go of the cop. He tumbled backward into Libby's waiting arms. The dragon bucked its upper torso and Jack went flying off its back to land behind it in a heap. The creature shook off the hand towel and snarled at the cop yet again, creeping forward just as Jack stood to try and distract it.

Panicked, the cop aimed between the dragon's eyes and pulled the trigger again.

The bullet bounced off and hit Jack squarely in the chest.

"Jack!" Libby screamed. Furious, she kicked the cop to one side and grabbed the whistle again, blowing it. The dragon's head whipped towards her and it ran at her. She swung around with her back to the walk-in freezer, and then dove when the dragon tried to bum-rush her. It smacked the far wall on the inside of the freezer, and Libby slammed the door shut and locked it. The dragon roared and the door shook, knocking plaster off the walls beside it, but the door held.

Libby raced over to the fallen Jack.

Only to find him lying there, wheezing in pain, but alive.

He had both hands clutched over a spot just below his sternum where the armor had cracked, but the crumpled bullet hadn't penetrated it. She let out a long, shaking breath of relief. "Oh, thank God."

"Why," Jack seethed. "Does everyone keep *shooting me?*"

Libby laughed hoarsely. "I don't know. Maybe you're just really annoying?"

"That's it. I quit. I'm going back to Greenville and I'm gonna be a fucking farmer."

"Oh, it's just one itty bitty gunshot," Libby said, plucking the slug out. "Big whup."

He groaned as the throbbing pain in his chest began to spread through the rest of his torso. "Go check on Annie Oakley over there, will ya?"

"One sec," she said, prying off the helmet. His dark hair was a haphazard, sweaty mess beneath it as she ran her fingers over his scalp to check that the helmet had done its job, and it had. She didn't feel a lump, which meant he probably didn't have a concussion. She breathed another sigh of relief, kissed his forehead, and rose to her feet. "Stay put."

He grunted and obeyed, too hurt to do anything else. The cop had managed to drag himself outside of the kitchen, and the restaurant's employees had already gathered around with a First Aid kit. They were in the middle of bandaging his calf when Libby stalked over.

"What part of 'don't let the cop in' did you not

understand?" she shouted at the small throng.

"We tried," one of them protested. "But he just barged his way in."

She massaged the bridge of her nose and addressed the cop instead. "You just shot the man who saved your life."

"What is going on here?" the cop demanded. "Why the hell did a goddamn dinosaur just take a chunk out of my leg?"

"You didn't listen to what these people told you is why," she yelled. "You shot my partner. If he hadn't been wearing that armor, he'd be dead right now."

"I was doing my job."

"Bullshit you were. If the bullets didn't work the first four times, why would it work a fifth fucking time?"

The cop actually turned red. "Look, I figured the scales might've been thinner on the skull than on the rest of it and--"

"Save it." She took a picture of him, and of his badge number, and tucked her phone away. "Make sure you get an ambulance over here stat. Help is on the way to transport the dragon out of here. Everyone just stay put."

Libby returned to the kitchen to see that Jack had managed to get on his feet, and he was helping Olly out of the corner. They exchanged quiet words and the kid came shuffling up to her with a tired, sheepish look. "Thanks, miss. Really. You saved my life."

She patted his shoulder. "I'm so sorry this happened. Are you okay?"

He nodded. "Good. Make sure you get looked at just in case."

"I will." He squeezed her hand and then headed out of the kitchen.

Jack leaned one arm against a nearby counter and radioed for Shannon, telling him where they were and that they'd need an ambulance and something to transport the dragon. Libby could tell he was trying to play it tough from the look on his pale face. He could barely stand at the moment, and a wave of worry rolled through her.

"So that was a shitshow," she said, crossing her arms. "Got the cop's name and badge number, if it helps. You should definitely sue him."

Jack snorted. "On a cop's pay? That'll get me the McDonald's dollar menu and nothing else."

He shook his head. "Guy was just doing his job. Didn't know any better. I'm not gonna push it."

"He just *shot* you."

Jack shrugged a shoulder, and cringed when it hurt, badly. "So have a lot of people."

"My God, you're infuriating."

He gave her a sickly little smile. "Yeah, I know."

Jack waggled the dragon tracker in his hand. "Three down. Four to go."

Libby sighed and opened the door to get back to the roof. "God help us all."


"Ethan?"

"Yes, Dr. Anjali?"

"Remind me never to have sex again."

Kamala clenched her teeth as her next set of contractions rose up and filled her body with sharp, agonizing pain. She concentrated on her breathing and gripped the edges of the chair that the lab assistant had gotten for her, and the arms of the chair strained under her powerful grip. She nearly laughed as she realized Jack's jokes about her superhuman strength had been right all along.

From her background in medicine, she knew she was still only in the early labor phases. She'd timed her contractions and they had steadily occurred. The duration of each was about thirty seconds, and they strengthened with each one, it seemed. She had a sinking feeling that the stress had not only induced the early labor, but had sped it along a lot faster than normal. The average time for early labor was supposed to be eight to twelve hours. It had only been about one, and yet she knew they were intensifying.

"I'll be sure to do that," Ethan assured her sympathetically. "Can I get you anything?"

"Morphine," she said blithely as the contractions finally subsided. "How long has it been since you called for the ambulance?"

Ethan sighed and checked his watch. "Too long. Since the city's under siege, they're likely stuck in traffic."

"Just my luck. If this keeps up, I'll bloody walk there myself."

Ethan eyed her. "You will do no such thing, Doc. It's not safe out there."

"It's not safe anywhere. I swear to you, I seem to just be a magnet for trouble."

"It can't be *that* bad."

Kamala scowled at him. "Oh, now you've done it."

"What?"

"The universe isn't deaf. And it has a very bad sense of humor."

Ethan opened his mouth to reply, but then the sound of glass shattering stopped him. He frowned and turned his head towards the meat locker where the noise originated. Kamala's eyes narrowed and she lowered her legs from the other chair they'd been propped upon to try to alleviate her back pain.

"Uh," Ethan said, clearing his throat. "That was probably nothing, right?"

"In my line of work, it's never nothing," Kamala said as she rose to her feet. "Get Sean and Viola to check it out."

"They're doing a perimeter check."

She cursed under her breath. "Of course they are."

"I've got this, doc, stay here." He strode down the hallway to the door, wrenched it open, and poked his head inside.

"Well?"

Ethan shut the door and locked it. "I owe you an apology, Dr. Anjali."

331

"For what?"

He turned to face her and swallowed hard, his face completely white. "You were right. The universe was definitely listening. There's a Highlander dragon inside the meat locker."

Kamala cursed in Kannada. "Get outside. Find our security detail. We'll have to risk the traffic. We can't stay here or that thing will rip us apart."

He nodded tightly and raced out the door. Kamala made sure the meat locker doors were secured and waited for Ethan's return. A minute later, he raced inside and slammed the outer door shut as well, locking it.

"What's wrong?"

"They're dead."

Kamala covered her mouth with one hand. "W-What?"

Ethan pitched to one side and vomited, breathing so hard and so fast it sounded like he had a bad case of the hiccups. "Oh, God, it *ate* them. Ate their throats right out. They're gone."

"Goddess," she whispered hoarsely. "Oh, those poor agents. It must've snuck up on them. We never even heard gunshots."

She fumbled for her phone and dialed Shannon's number, but he didn't pick up. She tried twice more, but he didn't pick up. "Dammit. Ethan, we have to go. Did you find their car keys when you found the bodies?"

He nodded weakly. "Y-Yeah."

She gripped his shoulders. "Ethan, look at me."

He wiped his mouth and met her gaze, finding it hard as steel. "We will get through this, but you must stay calm and listen to me. Do you understand?"

Ethan nodded. "Yes, doctor."

"Good boy. Let's go."

She opened the door to the outside.

And found a Highlander dragon sniffing the tires to their limousine.

"Go!" she shouted, shoving Ethan back inside and locking the door. Outside, they heard the dragon growl in startled warning. Gravel shifted beneath the door. She heard a snuffling sound, and then the scream of metal as the dragon's talons raked across it.

"What the hell?" Ethan said. "How is that possible?"

"Merciful Goddess," Kamala whispered, raking a trembling hand through her hair. "Ethan, there were *two* Highlander dragons at the facility. One we recovered during Calloway's first mission, and another we recovered during the raid last night."

The door shook on its hinges. The dragon had started to ram it down.

"Come on!" Kamala grabbed his wrist and hauled him to the opposite end of the hallway where the assembly line and small offices were. No sooner than she slammed the door shut did the outer door crunch in half and the second Highlander dragon stepped inside the building, letting loose a chilling howl that meant it was now on the hunt.

# CHAPTER EIGHTEEN
## DECATHECT

"Alright, whipper snapper," Jack said. "We're headed south to the Eastern Market on Seventh Street. Shannon said they've been getting reports of the arctic dragon causing a panic."

He grimaced as he slid into the saddle behind Libby. She steadied him, her brow furrowing beneath the goggles. "You okay, tough guy?"

"Never better," he lied through a shallow, pained breath.

"Oh, you're so manly, Jack," she teased as she led Pete towards the edge of the building. "I'm liable to swoon in a minute."

He chuckled and hung on. "Chicks dig scars."

She launched the dragon into the air. Pete's wings caught a stray upward draft and the trio rose over the warm air into the heavens effortlessly. Luckily, the southeast quadrant of D.C. wasn't terribly far, and they closed in within fifteen minutes. Along the way, Shannon had told them it had already been partially evacuated. The police had been instructed not to engage after Jack recounted their last encounter. So far, there were no casualties; only some injuries when people ran to take cover.

White tents dotted the exterior of the market. Some had been overturned with their products lying abandoned on the faded red bricks. Jack and Libby landed nearby where there were a couple of officers directing the patrons towards the exits and dispersing the crowds that kept trying to gather to see the creature.

"It's inside," one of the uniforms told them. "We got all the vendors, and the patrons out and we set up a perimeter in case it comes out again."

"Thanks, guys," they told the cops before heading

towards one end of the huge space.

Jack and Libby peeked around the corner. The ceilings were high and well lit for the most part, though there were some scattered busted hanging lights. Sunlight beamed in on either side. At the very least, it wouldn't be hard to spot the dragon.

"Alright," Jack said as they carefully made their way in. "So we really don't want to tangle with it up close. From what I can tell, its glands will produce a liquid that'll freeze damn near anything solid. We can split up and try to distract it, then hit it with the net."

He paused and stifled a pained groan as his chest stung sharply when he lifted the net launcher onto one shoulder. "I'll go first."

"Jack," Libby said sternly. "You're hurt. Let me take the lead on this one."

"I'm fine."

"You got shot in the chest. You're the opposite of fine. Just give it here. You can be the distraction this time. After all, you do have a big mouth."

"You're one to talk," he said mildly, but he thought it over and realized she was right. His reaction time had already taken a bad hit and he moved too stiffly now that exhaustion from the other dragon hunts began to set in. He'd possibly endanger them both at this rate. Reluctantly, he handed her the net launcher.

They heard a commotion near one of the booths that sold poultry and fell silent. Jack signed to her what he would do and she concurred, hanging back to let him go ahead. He stayed low and made his way down the center of the show floor until he reached the booth where the noise had originated.

The arctic dragon had knocked over several things and stood with its spiny back to Jack as it feasted on what it had found. Bones crunched under its sharp fangs. Jack tried not to think about how his own would do the same if he made a wrong step.

He checked over his shoulder and Libby had settled into place. He drew up his nerves and cleared his throat loudly. "Come here often?"

The arctic dragon whirled around and spat a gelatinous glob straight at his face.

"Whoa!" Jack ducked as the glob knocked over a few potted plants behind him. He felt a brush of freezing cold air and turned to see that a fine layer of frost clumped on the fallen pots. Clear liquid leaked from the dragon's jaws as it hunched low in attack mode and fixed its gaze on Jack.

"That's it, handsome," Jack said as he edged towards the left of the partially destroyed booth. "Nice and easy. This way."

The dragon followed him into the open area. The second it did, Libby fired the net launcher.

The dragon leapt ten feet into the air and curled itself around the rafters. The net narrowly missed Jack and bounced harmlessly onto the floor. "Shit!"

"Tactical retreat!" Jack bounded to his feet and Libby joined him, racing up the center of the floor room as the dragon spat three consecutive globs of frozen gel at them. Each one missed, but Jack felt some of it splatter against the back of his suit and it hardened into ice almost immediately. He and Libby ducked into a booth towards the end of the showroom and caught their breath.

"Okay," Jack admitted. "So this guy's a little smarter than the other ones."

"No shit," Libby said. "I need to get back outside for another net."

"He's really not going to like that." He dug a small flashbang out of his belt. "Last one. Better make it count."

She nodded tightly. Jack stuck his head out enough to see that the dragon had landed on the floor again and stalked towards them. He pulled the pin on the flashbang and covered his ears, shutting his eyes as it exploded a couple seconds later. The dragon screeched and thrashed wildly, knocking over food and collectible items.

Libby hurried out of the hall to the outside where Pete had been tied to a fire hydrant. The police had done their job keeping people away from her, at least. She grabbed an extra net from the saddle and loaded it as quickly and carefully as she could. Just as she returned inside, the blinded dragon launched itself through a window and took off into the sky.

"Oh, for Pete's sake!" Jack snarled. "I'm really starting to hate dragons."

He gave Libby a boost. They untied Pete, and took off after the fleeing dragon. It wasn't easy. The arctic dragon wasn't the same size as Pete, and didn't have two passengers. They could see it pulling ahead in distance and speed. An excellent flier even under duress.

"We're not going to catch him like this," Libby said. "We've got to get him to turn or dive. We'll lose him in just a couple of minutes, if that."

"I have an idea," Jack replied.

"Is it as shitty as your usual ideas?"

"Yeah, pretty much. I can shoot the net ahead of it and knock it off course."

"That's too much strain on Pete if you try to reel it in. She can't carry that much weight."

"I know."

She glanced back at him, shocked. "Are you saying--"

"Yeah," he said, his tone heavy. "I'm not sure we can save this guy. If I shoot this net, and it disorients him, he's gonna hit the ground. He'll be gone."

"Dammit."

"I know. I hate it, but if he gets away, there's no telling how many people he'll hurt. I wish there was some other way, but we don't have enough time for anything else."

Libby bowed her head for a reverent second. "Okay. I'll keep Pete on course."

She steadied the dragon's altitude and with every passing second, the arctic dragon became more of a distant figure before them. Jack lifted the launcher to his shoulder, aimed, and whispered. "God forgive me."

He fired.

The net arched up over the dragon's head and deployed roughly a foot ahead of the creature. It snapped down over the creature's face and it twisted in the air, its front limbs and part of one wing catching. The dragon spiraled down towards the grassy patch near Pennsylvania Avenue below. The sunlight shone off its brilliant scales. It looked like a teardrop shed by the heavens.

Neither Jack nor Libby had the strength to watch its death.

Jack took a deep, cleansing breath before reaching for his walkie-talkie. "The arctic dragon is down. Coordinates incoming."

He read them off and Shannon sent backup over to the area. Jack returned his attention to the dragon tracker and frowned at it. "That's odd. I'm showing another two dragons converging on the same location.

"Where?" Libby asked.

"The meat locker where they've been keeping the sea serpent carcass. The dragons must be drawn to the smell."

He shook his head. "Thank God Kam already left."


Six minutes.

That was about how much time Kamala predicted they had before the Highlander dragon would break through the door, smell them, and come after them from where they hid underneath the empty cubicles in the office section of the meat packing plant.

She had to come up with a plan in six minutes or she and her daughter would die.

"Okay," Kamala told Ethan in a breathy whisper. "I saw a floor map on the bulletin board. The door behind us leads to a break room. Then there is a long hallway that has an exit door to the south side of the compound and a second door that leads into the meat plant. We can circle back around to get to the limousine and escape."

Ethan nodded and wiped the sweat from his brow, his brown eyes nervously pointed in the direction of the approaching dragon. "So what's the catch?"

"The dragon will hear us moving in here. It's going to chase us."

He shut his eyes. "Great."

"I know," she said grimly. "Right now, it knows we're in here somewhere, but it hasn't figured out where, and our footsteps will tip it off. We also don't know where the other dragon is, so we run the risk of encountering it on our way out."

"So what do we do?"

"We need a distraction. I think if we turn on the assembly line, the dragons will investigate that instead of us."

Ethan frowned. "You know how to operate a meat packing plant?"

"No, but Jack's father showed me some automated processes on his farm, and I think perhaps I can at least get the thing running while you get to the limo."

"Dr. Anjali--"

She snorted. "Ethan, we might die here together. You may start using my first name now."

"Kamala," he said, narrowing his eyes at her. "You're in early labor. You shouldn't be sneaking around a meat locker trying to distract both the dragons."

"We don't have a choice. You won't know what to look for, and I need you to drive."

"Kamala, please--"

The door to the office splintered in half as the Highlander dragon tore through it.

Kamala set her jaw and stared intently into Ethan's eyes. He cursed under his breath and nodded. "Okay."

"On three, we run for the door."

Ethan squeezed her hand. "Be careful."

"You too. One...two...three!"

They bolted for the door at the far end.

The Highlander dragon roared and tore after them. Desks shattered in its wake. Papers flew. The very walls shook as it smashed through the room towards them.

The pair snatched the door shut behind them and darted through the break room. Ethan yanked the next door open and wrapped his arm around Kamala, helping her hurry through it as well. He gave her one last squeeze before heading on towards the exit door. Kamala threw open the door to the meat locker and slammed it shut behind her.

She sunk onto her haunches and tried to control her breathing. Her belly ached, and she felt the baby's distressed movements in response to the danger. Little by little, she also felt the child descending, which meant her birth was that much closer. She had to get out of this alive. She just had to. There was no other choice.

Kamala saw no obvious sign of the other Highlander dragon ahead of her, so she took small, quiet steps until she was away from the door she'd entered through. It wouldn't take long for the other dragon to break down the door to the break room and smell where they'd gone.

The center of the plant had a long, open space, and the machinery wound around it and eventually led to a dock outside where it would be boxed and put into trucks. She examined the flow of the machines until she concluded which side had the control panel and moved towards it. There was a large set of handles, levers, and buttons to one end. The place had been cleared out so that none of its workers knew about the dead dragon in storage, and had all been well compensated for their trouble. There were keys that were missing from the mechanism, but she remembered what Jack's father had taught her. She didn't need the thing to work properly. She just needed to turn it on. It still served its purpose even if it malfunctioned.

The door she'd entered through shuddered hard, once, twice. The other Highlander dragon had caught up.

Kamala gripped one of the levers and yanked hard. The conveyor belts coughed to life and a few orange lights dotted throughout the floor began to flash and ring. The metal door banged open and hit the wall as the dragon launched itself through. Kamala eased over into the far corner and watched underneath the machines. The dragon's talons scraped the floor as it walked inside, its black scales catching the light from the windows. It moved with deadly, sinuous grace over to the machine. It stayed there long enough that she gleaned it was distracted, so she eased her way towards the exit door.

And just as she reached it, the *other* Highlander dragon appeared.

Kamala and the dragon stood roughly twelve feet apart, with the exit door to the right in the exact middle of the distance between them. The dragon cocked its head to one side and its upper lip slid back from its long, white fangs.

Kamala calmly reached up and pulled a 3 1/2 foot combination wrench off the wall of tools beside her. She turned to the dragon and hefted the heavy hunk of metal in both hands.

"You want us?" she murmured. "Then come and get us."

"If I live a thousand years," Faye said as she threw the car in park. "May I never drive in Washington D.C. *ever* again."

"You said it, Blondie," Winston chuckled. "Even without the rampaging dragons, it's hell. Now tell me what you see."

"I'm around the back of the packing plant," she said, and performed a thorough check of the grounds. "No obvious signs of Stella, but of course there wouldn't be any."

"Naturally," he agreed. "What else?"

She frowned. "There...should be cops here. Or agents, at least. I don't see any here either."

"That's a red flag if I ever saw one."

"Damn right." Faye checked the magazine on her Kimber Pro before sliding out of the car. She peered at the rooftop first to ensure Stella wasn't sitting there with a high-powered rifle, and confirmed that they were empty. Despite the screaming sirens and disarray of the city, this place felt nearly abandoned. She kept the Kimber in her hand and started around the corner.

Then the smell of spilled blood and gore hit her.

Faye poked her head around the corner and saw two bodies stretched out on the ground; one woman and one man, one face down, the other face up. The man had been clearly mauled, but the woman's throat was simply gone, as if something had taken an enormous bite out of it. Her stomach rushed up towards her mouth, but she choked it down.

"God," she whispered hoarsely. "They're dead. I think it's her security team. Something...something *ate* them."

"Don't panic. Do a perimeter check. Put the pieces together."

She kept the gun raised and crept down the long, narrow outside of the building until she reached the front. She peeked around the corner.

There stood Stella.

With her .357 Magnum in hand.

Faye wanted nothing more than to keep her eyes on the assassin, but she had to be sure. She quickly glanced into the limo behind the hit-woman, and saw a young man slumped over in the driver's seat. He had a bruise on the side of his head, but he was still breathing.

"So," Stella smiled. "You finally caught up with me, huh, Becky?"

"Ah, hell," Winston hissed in her ear.

For a moment, everything around her fell away. Faye closed her eyes and let her mind focus on the scenario. She ran the numbers a few times. She came up with a percentage of the likelihood that she would survive a firefight with a trained assassin.

So she did what any sane, rational human being would do.

She cheated.

Stella pulled off her janitor's cap and let it fall against the gravel, shaking out her dark hair. "I was kind of hoping this would happen, you know. I wanted to go *mano y mano* with Winston's little pet. I only wish he were actually here to see you die, but I guess listening in will have to be—"

Faye whipped around the corner and shot Stella.

The bullet took Stella high in the chest, shattering her collarbone.

"You little cunt!" Stella snarled, her left arm limp and useless as blood poured down her coveralls and soaked into the fabric. Her Magnum roared twice, punching holes into the brick near the corner where Faye had taken cover. "I'll kill you!"

Faye flinched as the enraged assassin shot at her. She couldn't risk returning fire. Stella wouldn't miss. The shots were getting closer. End of the line. She'd have to make her final stand if Kamala stood a snowball's chance in hell of making it out alive.

Just as she readied herself to leap out for one last Hail Mary, an ambulance came screaming around the corner into view.

Stella cursed and spat to one side. "This isn't over, Barbie. Watch your fucking back."

The gravel shifted and slid underneath her shoes, and in seconds, Stella had vanished.

Faye nearly slumped to the ground in relief, but she didn't have the time. Instead, she ran inside the building to search for the love of her life.

She unlatched the door to the meat packing room and just as she did, an exhausted, bleary-eyed Kamala stumbled out into her arms. She bled from a cut on her forehead, but she didn't seem any worse for wear. She seemed deeply woozy as well, as she leaned hard against Faye's shoulder and squinted up at her. "Who the hell're you?"

Faye laughed, tears pouring down her cheeks, and hoisted her best friend up to take her to the ambulance. "No one special."

# CHAPTER NINETEEN

## DAWN

Jack had never run so damn fast in his entire life than after he'd gotten the call that Kamala had gone into early labor.

Everything after the call had been one big blur. He didn't remember much aside from handing Libby her phone back and telling her to fly to MedStar Georgetown University Hospital. Libby hadn't even hesitated. She flew them straight there and told him to take care of Kamala while she coordinated with Shannon to figure out the aftermath of whatever the hell had happened with the last two dragons. He didn't remember the nurses' faces. He didn't remember the hallway or the elevator. All he could think about was Kamala.

The entire world dissolved into nothingness when he found her in the delivery room.

Kamala's midnight hair had been pulled back into a loose bun at her nape. She had a small white bandage on her forehead. She already wore her hospital gown and her sienna skin glowed with perspiration, but she didn't appear any worse for wear. Just tired.

She opened her honey-toned eyes as Jack's hand slid across her wrist and then wrapped hers in warmth and gentle strength. She smiled up at him. "Welcome back, you useless *pagal.*"

Jack laughed hoarsely and pulled up a chair next to her. "Hey, angel. How are you feeling?"

"Like there is a chainsaw in my vagina. How about you?"

Jack choked. "Jesus, Kam."

She chuckled. "You asked."

A nurse drifted by and Jack introduced himself. "How far along is the dilation?"

"She's at five centimeters and counting."

"Already?" Jack asked. "I thought early labor is usually several hours?"

"It looks like our young lady is just ready to meet you," the nurse smiled, patting his shoulder. "We've got a close eye on her, so don't worry. Get comfortable and help her with her breathing exercises. We'll be checking in frequently until it's the magic hour."

"Thank you." Jack kissed the back of Kamala's hand. "What do you need me to do?"

"You're already doing it." She squeezed his fingers. "How did it go recovering the other dragons?"

"Before I left, we'd gotten them all except for the Highlander dragons, but Libby went to check on that after she dropped me off." He winced a bit. "We...couldn't save the arctic dragon, but the rest were captured alive."

Kamala tugged his hand closer. "It's alright, Jack. You can't save them all. Let it go."

"I'm trying," he admitted. "It's just...God, it's been a helluva day. Finding out someone wants both of us dead, not just Calloway, and they put things in motion to get us both killed. It's exactly the nightmare scenario I didn't want all along."

"And yet if we hadn't been where we were, countless people would have died," she reassured him. "Nothing is cut and dry anymore, Jack. All of it is messy. But, we're still here. That is what matters."

"I know. I thought I was going to have a heart attack when you called. All I could think about was getting here and making sure my girls were alright."

"That does not surprise me in the least."

"Were you able to get through to Faye?"

Kamala frowned. "Not yet, no, and it worries me. She's never been this distant before. Something is wrong. I know it."

"I felt that too," he agreed. "I'll keep trying her. What about your folks?"

346

"I called them shortly after they put me in here. They're on their way."

He hesitated. "I...guess that means I should let my folks know too, huh?"

"I know it'll be hard, but yes, you should."

"Okay. I'll be right back, angel." He stood, kissed her forehead, borrowed her phone, and stepped outside of the room.

Jack paced back and forth, gnawing his lower lip as the phone rang. A grizzled voice with a surprised tone answered a moment later. "Hello?"

"Hey, Dad," Jack said.

"Rhett?" Richard Jackson said. "Jesus, boy, I've been calling you non-stop for the last hour. There are dragons running amok in D.C. What the hell is going on?"

"Trust me when I tell you that's a long story."

"I've got time."

"No, you don't. Pack a bag and get on a plane to D.C. Kamala went into early labor."

"Holy hell," his father hissed. "Is she okay?"

"She's fine. We're already at MedStar Georgetown University Hospital in the delivery room. She's in active labor, but the baby's not coming just yet. It should give you some time to make it here for the birth."

"I'll be on the first thing smoking, kiddo." His father's tone then frosted over. "Any chance you've gotten through to Edie yet?"

"No," Jack sighed, pinching the bridge of his nose. "That's the next phone call I'm gonna make. She's probably still got my number blocked, but I can get through to Granny and leave a message."

"Son, I want you to listen to me. She's your mother. She's never gonna stop being your mother, and I know it hurts that she's been avoiding you. You can't let what's going on between the three of us ruin this for you and Kamala. That little girl is going to be just fine, you hear me? She'll be beautiful and healthy and she'll be all yours. Whatever happens, remember what's important, whether Edie decides to do the right thing or not. Okay?"

Jack swallowed past the lump in his throat. "Okay. Thanks, Dad. I'll see you soon."

"Damn right you will, kid. Be safe." He hung up.

Jack paused to get his heart rate under control before dialing his grandmother's number. She answered immediately, damn near as if she'd been anticipating the call. "Kamala! Sweetie, how are you? How's the baby?"

Jack couldn't help but smile. "Hey, Gran, it's actually Rhett. My phone's busted."

"Rhett, sweetie, dumpling, puddin' pie!" his grandmother cooed. "Oh, I've missed hearing your voice, handsome. What can I do for you?"

"I've got some unexpected news. Kamala went into labor."

"Oh my! She's a month early, isn't she?"

"Yeah. I guess the rug rat just got a little impatient. Can you make sure to tell everybody?"

"Of course, dear. What hospital?"

"Well, we were on an assignment in D.C., so we're at MedStar Georgetown University Hospital. If everything holds steady, the baby will be here by tonight."

"I'm so excited for you! My grandchild is going to be gorgeous. I just know she is. I'll make sure to pass it along to everyone and keep you updated on who can make it."

"Right," he said. "About that--"

"Rhett," she said firmly. "I will tell your mother the instant I hang up with you. And heaven help me, if that stubborn child gives me one cross word about it, she's getting a switch to her backside like when she was seven years old."

Despite his unbelievably high stress levels, Jack laughed. "Thanks, Granny."

"I will do everything in my power to get her there, sweetheart. Leave it to me."

"You're the best, Gran. I love you."

"I love you more, my darling puppy. Be safe and give

Kamala and the baby a kiss from me. Bye."

"Bye."

He hung up. Two down. One to go.

Jack dialed Faye's number. Like Kamala said, it went straight to voicemail. He pushed a hand into his tousled hair and decided to just go for it.

"Faye," he said. "I don't know what the hell is going on with you, but this is important. Kam just went into labor. I know you're in Florida and I know we had a fight before you left, but you can't pull this shit on us now, not when we need you."

He licked his lips, his eyes closing as something scared fluttered through his bruised chest. "I need you. I need you here with us. I know you're not entirely ready to hear it yet, but I love you. I love Kam. And I'm gonna love the shit out of that little girl when she gets here, and I want you to love her too. So don't do this. Get your ass on a plane to D.C. as soon as you get this message. Just...don't miss this. I'm not sure I'm strong enough to handle it if you're not here with us."

Jack hit End Call and headed back inside, his heart heavy and conflicted, but determined nonetheless.


"Well," Faye said, nudging the lone padlock on the floor of the empty storage unit. "Not sure what I was expecting, but somehow I'm still disappointed."

Faye had lost contact with Winston shortly after she helped Kamala into the ambulance. Following a hunch, she returned to the storage unit to see if anything had happened to him. Lo and behold, he'd done exactly what she suspected he would now that their mission had concluded.

She walked in further and noticed it wasn't completely empty. The fold out chair was still there, and Winston's burner phone lay on its seat. As she finished pulling the door down, it began to ring.

Faye rolled her eyes, walked over, and answered it. "What do you want, asshole?"

"Aw, don't be mad, Blondie," Winston said. "I warned you, didn't I?"

She sighed and plopped down in the chair. "You did. I'm not mad."

"You sound mad."

"I'm not mad. I'm tired." She exhaled. "So it's done, right? The contract should have expired at six o'clock."

"That it is," he confirmed, and tension she didn't even know that she'd been carrying flooded out of her entire body. "Stella won't be getting a dime for her efforts."

"Thank God."

"Don't thank that useless asshole. Thank yourself. *You* saved them, Faye. Doesn't mean they'll stay safe, but you still kept them alive. And you lived to tell the tale."

Faye frowned. "And that's what bothers me."

"You're bothered that you're still alive?" he asked with heavy skepticism.

"Stella is a contract killer. What are the odds that she missed when she pulled the trigger on that Magnum?"

"She was off-balance, Blondie. Angry. Smug. She underestimated you."

"But why run off? She could have tailed me here and killed me."

"Well, to tell you the truth, Stella's pretty dramatic. You tagged her pretty good, from what you told me. Stella doesn't get her ass handed to her often."

Faye pursed her lips. "So what you're saying is I now have two assassins hopelessly in love with me because I'm so ruthless?"

Winston laughed. Not chuckled. Actually *laughed.* She could hear the difference--the genuine surprise and amusement in the sound. She thought it over and realized she wasn't sure she'd ever heard him laugh before. She shouldn't have cared one bit, but something in her felt weirdly proud. "Boy, that ego is something else. Don't mean to break your heart, Blondie, but I ain't in love with you."

"Yeah, sure, as if you'd ever admit to it," she snorted.

"You did kiss me, remember?"

"I've kissed a lot of girls. You're not special."

"Uh-huh. Keep telling yourself that."

A sudden silence fell. Faye's heart rate sped up. She had no clue what caused it, but it felt as if they'd come to a realization at the exact same time somehow. A very startling, scary realization.

"Look, you don't have to tell me what this is all about," Faye said quietly. "You probably never will. I'm not worldly enough to figure out, not yet, anyway. But, we did something, Winston. Something important to me. Maybe important to you, somehow. And I still don't know what you want from me. I risked my life to save my friends. You risked your life to save me. I'm not going to thank you for it, ever, because you're the one who put me in danger in the first place. But..."

She licked her lips and sighed. "Any chance you can at least throw me a bone here?"

More silence. She expected that he would hang up, but he didn't. "I meant what I said back in that hotel room. I don't want to see you set fire to your life. This mission opened your eyes. Now you can see everything. Before, you'd just gotten a peek through the blinds. Now the window's open. You know what kind of threats are out there. And now you know that you're strong enough to face them."

"So does that mean you're still going to try to kill me?"

He sighed. "I never wanted you dead, Blondie. I wanted an equal."

She froze. He kept going. "Surviving this proved that you've got what it takes to become an incredible force of nature. Whether it's for good or for bad, you are forged in steel now, Faye Worthington. You proved that to me. You proved that to Stella. You proved that *to yourself*. The next time we come at each other, it'll be a fair fight. I haven't had one of those in...Christ. I don't know how long."

He let out a little snort. "And if I'm gonna die someday, I'd be damned proud if it was by your hand. There are worse ways to go than being killed by a beautiful Valkyrie like you."

Faye sat there, speechless. Winston sighed. "I gotta go, Blondie. You won't hear from me anytime soon. These bullet wounds are going to be a bitch to get over. There's a beach somewhere with my name on it. I'll have an iced tea in your honor when I get there. Keep your head on straight, y'hear?"

"I..." She swallowed hard. "Yeah. I will."

"Oh, boy, I've got you at a loss for words, don't I?" he teased. "Don't get sweet on me, Faye."

"Fuck off," she growled, blushing. "Don't get too fat lying on that beach, Winston. I'm going to get you fitted for a prison jumpsuit soon enough."

He laughed again, a little softer, a little fonder than before. "That's what I like to hear. *Vaya con dios,* Blondie."

"*Vaya con dios,* asshole."


"Jack!"

The scientist whirled as he heard a voice behind him. Just as he turned, Faye flung herself into his arms and hugged him tightly. He sighed into her golden hair and hugged her back just as hard.

"You made it," he breathed. "God, I was gonna be so mad at you if you didn't."

"Of course," she whispered. "Of course I'm here."

He drew back and fixed her with a glare. "What the hell is going on with you? Why did you ghost us while you were in Clearwater?"

Faye glanced down at her feet. "I...got a little scared. And petty. It was childish and stupid. I'm sorry. I didn't know something like this would happen. I won't do it again. I swear."

"I'll hold you to that." He handed her a small bundle of clothing. "There's a bathroom down the hall. Put these on. She's fully dilated and she needs all the support she can get from us right now."

She hurried off, changed, and entered the delivery room. It bustled with nurses and doctors checking in on Kamala and preparing for the arrival of the newborn.

"Hey, beautiful," Faye said as she reached her girlfriend's side. Kamala's eyes opened as Faye smoothed her hair away from her forehead.

"Faye," Kamala smiled. Then her expression switched to livid in the blink of an eye. She grabbed a handful of the blonde's scrubs and jerked her down. "If I call you, *pick up the bloody phone*, do you hear me?"

Faye gulped. "Yes, ma'am."

Kamala let go and collapsed back onto her pillow. "Glad we got that cleared up."

She clenched her teeth as another contraction seized hold of her. Faye caught her free hand and held on tight. Jack had the other one and helped her count down the seconds through the contraction. One of the male doctors had ducked underneath the sheet draped over her legs and the stirrups, examining closely.

"Alright, everyone, her contractions are officially a couple minutes apart. It's the magic hour."

He stood to full height and blinked as he noticed Faye. "Oh. Hi there. And you are?"

"Faye Worthington."

He eyed her. "And you are...?"

"Her girlfriend."

The doctor glanced at Jack. "Wait, I thought you were--"

"I am."

He switched his gaze to Kamala. "Okay, so what did I miss?"

"All three of us are dating each other," Kamala hissed. "Now get this child out of me before I do it myself."

The doctor cleared his throat. "Right. Well, Dr. Anjali, I'm going to give you cues. When I do, I want you to push until you hear me say stop, okay?"

"Okay."

He gestured to Faye and Jack. "Both of you, make sure she's breathing and keep her as cool as you can. This is gonna get a little messy."

Gradually, the contractions quickened until they were thirty seconds apart. Jack regularly changed out her cold compress and helped her shift and adjust in the bed while Faye helped her concentrate through the duration of each contraction.

"Here we go," the doctor said. "Push, Kamala."

Kamala squeezed Jack and Faye's hands and began to push. She tried her best to rely on what she'd learned from Lamaze, but the pain was simply *unparalleled*. It tried to steal her breath every time she inhaled. Her body twisted and rebelled with every second. She wanted so badly to give up. She was exhausted and her world felt like it was crumbling apart.

"You've got this," Jack assured her. "You're the strongest person I know, Kam. Come on, angel. You can do it."

"Oh, gods above, I am never having sex again for as long as I live!" Kamala wailed, collapsing just as the doctor called for her to stop. She glared daggers at Jack. "You will never touch me again, do you hear me?"

Jack hung his head in sheepish defeat. "Yes, dear."

Faye tried her hardest not to laugh. "Come on, Kam, focus. Breathe. Just breathe."

"Here comes the next one," the doctor said. "Push!"

She tried again, but fell just short of when the doctor called for her to stop. She shook her head frantically. "I can't. I can't do this."

"Easy, stay with me," Jack said. "I know it hurts now, but you're almost there. You're so close, angel. She's going to be so beautiful when you finally meet her. Come on. Don't give up. We're here. We're not going anywhere."

Kamala shut her eyes and tried to absorb his words. He was right. For all the things that had gone horribly wrong, she was right here with the people she loved most in a moment when it counted.

How many other people could say the same thing?

She gritted her teeth, took the deepest breath possible, and gave it her all.

A tiny cry filled the air.

When Kamala opened her eyes again, she saw her daughter for the first time.

And she was just as beautiful as she'd imagined.

"Hey there, little girl," the doctor smiled as he carefully began to clean her off. "Say hi to your family."

"Oh my God," Faye whispered, tears running down her cheeks. "Kam, look. *Look at her.*"

"She's perfect," Jack said, his voice thick, unable to look away from the small, wiggling bundle. "You did it, Kam."

The doctor got the baby's initial cleaning done and offered the scissors between Jack and Faye. "Who wants to do the honors?"

"Well, we're in this together," Jack said, grinning at his other girlfriend. "Same time?"

Faye smiled back. "Same time."

They cut the umbilical cord together. The doctor shook his head in amazement and brought the baby over to be weighed and given a brief exam. "Great news. She's four pounds and six ounces. She's underweight, but not dangerously so."

He returned with her swaddled up and gently handed her to Kamala.

"Hello there," Kamala whispered to her daughter, her own eyes blurred with grateful, amazed tears. "My little flower."

Jack kissed his girlfriend's forehead and stroked the baby's fat little cheek delicately. "So what are we going to name her?"

"Naila," Kamala said all at once, and with complete conviction. "Her name is Naila."

"Naila Sahana Anjali," Jack said slowly, reverently.

"It's got a nice ring to it, doesn't it?"

"Gotta say, kiddo," Richard Jackson said, gently bouncing the sleepy infant in his strong arms. "You made one gorgeous little girl."

"That was all Kam," Jack said, winking at Kamala. "I had nothing to do with it."

Richard chuckled. "Oh, don't worry. She's all her mother now, but wait until she starts talking. I'm pretty sure the sarcasm is just hereditary in our family."

"That'll be fun. She'll have Kamala's smarts and my big mouth. The teachers are going to have a field day with her, I bet."

"Yours always did," Richard admitted. "I can't tell you how many parent-teacher conferences I had to go to when you were about seven or eight, and you kept correcting your instructors' grammar or explaining something that was two grades above the one you were already in. Smart kids are a handful. You'll find out soon enough."

Naila yawned. Richard grinned and carefully handed her back to her mother. "Congratulations, you two."

"Thank you, Richard," Kamala said, squeezing his hand. "I appreciate you flying out to check on us."

"My pleasure. If you need a single solitary thing, you just ask me."

"Wanna babysit for the next..." Jack checked his watch. "...eight years?"

Richard rumbled with a good-natured laugh. "I'll clear my schedule, sure."

He bent and kissed Kamala's brow. "In the meantime, did they say you can eat yet?"

Kamala's eyelids fluttered in pleasure at the mere thought of food. "Please get me something. I'm starving."

"Mind if I borrow Jack, since he knows what you like?"

"Not at all. He needs to stretch his legs anyhow."

"Be right back, angel." Jack kissed her and followed his

356

father out of the maternity ward. They followed the signs to reach the cafeteria.

"So," Richard said as he tucked his hands into the pockets of his jeans. "Freaking out yet?"

"Oh my *God*," Jack moaned. "Since the second I got here. Is that normal?"

"Totally normal," his father assured him.

"Is it ever going to stop?"

"Nope," his father said cheerfully. "But it'll get better. At first, everything feels overwhelming. You're scared to touch her. You're scared to carry her. You're scared to take her home. You're scared to put her to bed. You're scared to feed her. All of it is like defusing an atom bomb for a while."

"Gee, thanks."

"Over time, you just find your rhythm. You learn her habits. You learn your own. You adapt quickly. Whatever is best for her, you do it, immediately, without question. That goes for Kamala too. Some stuff will come up and you'll fight about it, but in the end, you'll be able to tell what fights are worth it and what fights you should let drop."

Jack's gut twitched a bit. "What kind of fights?"

"Every couple's different. It can be all kinds of stuff, from what brand of baby food to buy, to if you want to get the kid christened." Richard glanced at him then. "Which reminds me. Got anything planned yet?"

"Yeah, actually. Kam and Sahana just filled me in about the naming ritual they want to hold for Naila in a couple weeks with her mother's side of the family. It's called Namakarana. She's got me doing a bit of reading on it so I'll be ready. You're welcome to join us if you want."

"I would, if they don't mind. It'd be a good opportunity to meet her family." Richard paused and glanced over his shoulder in the direction of the maternity ward. "Assuming they're not all like her father."

Jack blew out air between his lips. "She's assured me that Daeshim is the worst of her side. The others have been much more welcoming. I met some of them at the baby shower, in fact, and while they're not exactly in love with me, they don't hate my guts the way he does. But, what else is new? I kind of derailed the choo-choo train that Kam's father had in mind for her. After she quit practicing medicine, he thought she just had a breakdown and needed time before she'd return. She found my project and decided to stay out of medicine for good, and so he blames me. I...corrupted her, I guess?"

Richard scowled. "Want me to kick his ass?"

Jack chuckled. "No, thanks. I don't blame the guy. He knows almost nothing about me other than I get his daughter in trouble every five damn minutes. Then I went and knocked her up. Of course I'm Public Enemy Number One in his mind."

"Think he'll ever come around?"

"Probably not. Maybe if things calm down and stay quiet, he'll grow to tolerate me. Not a big deal. I don't need his approval. I like the missus a lot better anyway."

"You do have a way with women."

Jack snorted. "Since when?"

"Since always. You tellin' me you never noticed that?"

"Well, I mean, Libby brought it up recently."

Richard arched his eyebrow. "Case in point, kiddo. Even when you were little, you had maybe one or two male friends. You gravitate towards the fairer sex by default, even before that asshole in college cheated with your girlfriend."

Jack's throat tightened. It was an old, dull pain by now, but it still hurt nonetheless. He'd been slowly but surely working on it in his therapy sessions. The anger had simply faded, but it hadn't gone away yet. "Guess that's fair to say. We can't all be Rhett Butler."

Richard rolled his eyes. "Here we go again. You know, that wasn't the entire reason we named you Rhett, right? Sure, your mother likes the movie, but that's not all it came from."

"Oh, really?" Jack asked skeptically. "What's the rest of the reason?"

"Names mean things. Depending on who you ask, Rhett means 'passionate.' It can also mean someone who gives good advice, or is wise. Maybe you're not so much the latter, but you are the former, and you always have been. Kids grow into names. I bet your munchkin will do the same."

"She already has. Naila means 'success' or 'achievement.' She's definitely the best thing I've ever had a hand in making."

They reached the cafeteria and wandered around. Jack located the best vegetarian option for Kamala and also grabbed some chocolate for good measure. Richard paid for it and the pair headed back to the cafeteria.

"After your mom split," Richard said quietly. "I...haven't been there for you as much as I should have been."

Jack shrugged a shoulder. "You did your best. Can't expect you to be Superman."

"It's no excuse. Her leaving hurt. A lot. I didn't want you to worry about me, so I sort of kept to myself. I knew you were dealing with it too. I just wanted to tell you that I aim to do better. Not just with money or things like that, but being there for you when you need it. Without judgment and second-guessing and passive aggressive bullshit like I've done in the past. I looked at myself and how my dad raised me, and I realized I'd done the same damn thing. Buried everything I felt so I'd be an authority figure for you. A sort of distant North Star. You didn't need that when you were a kid, and you don't need it now. I won't be that anymore. You have my word."

Jack cleared his throat and blinked rapidly at his dress shoes as they continued down the hallway. "Thanks, Dad."

"You're welcome, son."

They turned the corner, and stopped dead.

Edith Jackson smiled faintly at her husband and son. "Evening, boys."

Richard took a deep breath and scooped the tray out

of Jack's hands. He continued down the hallway towards the door to the maternity ward. He paused and nodded to her politely, but his tone and expression were both icy and remote. "Edie."

"Rick," she nodded back. He went inside.

Edie returned her hazel eyes to her son. "Rhett."

"Ma," Jack said, tucking his hands into his pockets and giving her a cool stare. "Lost weight?"

Edie shrugged one shoulder. "Few pounds."

"Looks good."

"Thank you. You look like hell."

Jack also shrugged a shoulder. "I got shot earlier."

Edie gave a start. "You what?"

"I mean, just a little bit. I was wearing body armor at the time. My chest looks like a freaking package of ground beef underneath this shirt."

Edie narrowed her eyes at him. "So this is how you get back at me, huh? Making me worry about you even more than I already did?"

"Oh, this isn't even *close* to how I want to get back at you," Jack replied in a heated tone. "Six months, Ma. Six. Not a word from you in six months. Now the baby's here and so are you. Is that what I can expect for the rest of my life?"

"Watch your tone, young man," she threatened. "You're not ever going to be grown up enough to talk to me like that."

"Why shouldn't I be? You were punishing me for being who I am. It's not as if I wanted this to happen. I didn't want to bring my daughter into this world when half of it's on fire, but I didn't have a choice. You're blaming me for something I had no control over."

Edie marched forward. "This is not just about that little girl in there, and you know it. This is about the lifestyle you've chosen, Rhett. There are people constantly trying to kill you because you are so stubborn that you can't just let it go."

"Let what go? People are dying because of what these

pricks are out there doing. Illegally cloning those dragons and abusing them to the point where they attack anything they see. What would you have me do, Ma? Just sit on my hands?"

"Find someone else. Train someone else."

"We didn't have enough time to do that."

She let out a derisive laugh and shook her head. "The knight in shining armor, Dr. Rhett Jackson. Swooping in to save the day to thunderous applause."

"You think I give a crap what the public thinks of me? I'm not doing this for glory. I'm doing it because it's the right thing to do and I have to fix this until someone else can do it for me. I will *not* apologize for who I am, and you shouldn't ever ask me to in the first place."

"Why does it have to be you?" Edie shouted, shoving a finger in his chest and ignoring how it made him grimace in pain. "Why does my son have to be beaten and shot and ridiculed for trying to make the world a better place?"

Jack froze. A tear slipped down one side of her cheek. "You don't even think twice about it, do you? Your own safety. You just see other people and it all just flies out of your head, doesn't it? You have no idea what a void you'd leave behind if you died, Rhett. No idea."

She turned away. "Every single day, I waited for my phone to ring and some detective would be on the line telling me my son was dead. Every single day. For six months. Don't you dare assume that you know how I feel and what I have been through since the morning you told us Kamala was pregnant."

Edie wrapped her arms around herself and bowed her head. "I'm not proud of what I did. I ran because I needed to do it. I didn't want to start this fight with you and your father over again. I thought maybe it would give me some perspective, but...all it did was make me miss you both. So much. When my mother called to tell me, all I could think about was getting here. I just wanted to be sure you were safe and that my granddaughter was healthy. I've done that now."

She started to walk away, but Jack caught her arm, turned her around, and hugged her.

Jack buried his face in her hair and squeezed her tight. "Why are you so goddamn hard headed?"

Edie laughed into her son's shoulder and hugged him back. "Language, young man."


It was an understatement to say that Kamala was tired after a long day of fighting dragons. Her parents had been the first to arrive and had spent a few hours with her, checking up on her health and--as doctor-parents tended to do--questioning the MedStar Georgetown delivery staff within an inch of their lives to be sure everything had been done properly. They left shortly before midnight.

Jack's parents stayed a long while as well, and had wanted to make it an overnight visit, but Jack eventually talked them into going back to their hotel to sleep. They'd have plenty of time at a decent hour to watch over the small family and get to know Naila.

Naila had been awake and responsive for most of the night, and had no qualms about breastfeeding. The doctors wanted to get her weight up immediately, thanks to her premature birth, but since she was over five pounds, they wouldn't need to keep her for longer than two days, assuming all her tests came back fine. Naila fussed on occasion, but hearing Kamala or Jack's voice soothed the child almost immediately. She seemed especially fond of Jack, thus confirming that reading to the baby nearly every night had indeed made a difference.

The maternity ward quieted for good around one o'clock. The doctors and nursing staff, at her urging, decided they would only check in once per hour rather than as frequently as they had before so that she could get some rest. They'd asked if she was ready to let Naila sleep in the room with the other children, but Kamala declined. For now, she just wanted some quiet time with her daughter. After all, she'd fought tooth and nail to deliver her safely. She wanted all the time she could get.

Jack and Faye had curled up in the corner on a set of chairs and slept deeply, peacefully, their phones set on an alarm to wake up to check on the pair later during the night. They'd lucked out for once; there weren't any other new mothers in the suite, so it was peaceful inside.

She wasn't sure what woke her. Just an instinct, perhaps. Nothing had moved. No one made a sound. She just woke up.

A man in scrubs stood beside her bed. He wore a surgeon's mask and had appeared to have been there for a bit, watching her sleep. She rubbed her eyes as the cobwebs of slumber fell away and yawned, muttering. "Yes, doctor?"

"*Ogenki desu ka, ojou-sama?*"

Kamala's blood froze in its veins.

Kazuma Okegawa pulled off his hospital mask and aimed a .9mm handgun directly at Naila.

"Did you miss me?"

# CHAPTER TWENTY
## EMBERS

"Don't scream," Okegawa drawled, his baritone voice smug and only low enough for Kamala to hear it. "Or I will kill everyone in this room, starting with your daughter."

Kamala shielded the infant against her chest and swallowed hard, trying her best to stay calm when every single instinct in her body told her to yell for help. There was no doubt in her mind that between Jack, Faye, and the hospital staff, they could subdue the yakuza lieutenant, but at point blank range, she and Naila wouldn't live to see help arrive. Frustrated tears flooded her eyes, but she refused to let them fall.

Once upon a time, Kazuma Okegawa had been a tall, ruggedly handsome man. He had since survived a grenade explosion when he fought Fujioka, and time hadn't much changed that; shrapnel and burn scars bisected his face with splotched, ruined skin. His long hair was mostly combed back from his face, but some of it hung down over his right eye. She couldn't tell if he'd lost his sight in it, and it was probably intentional. The scars dripped down his neck and shoulder as well, but they weren't the most startling thing.

He had *two* arms.

When last she saw him, Okegawa's right arm had been blown off at the elbow. The hand holding the gun glinted silver in the low lights of the mostly dark room. A prosthetic arm, no doubt, but as she watched, she could see the joints and digits adjusting with small pressure changes as he held the gun steady. Something advanced, far more advanced than she had ever seen before. Where on earth had he gotten it?

Okegawa's brown eyes roved over the newborn. "*Kawaii desu.* What have you named her, *ojou-sama*?"

Kamala licked her lips. "Naila."

"Beautiful," Okegawa cooed. "Well chosen."

Kamala narrowed her eyes. "Whatever game you're playing won't pan out for you. Someone will see you. Someone will stop you."

"I expect they will, yes," the *shateigashira* sighed. His eyes then flashed with challenge. "But will it be you, *ojou-sama*?"

The gun didn't waver as he reached into his pocket and pulled out a syringe. It was empty of any liquid. Kamala knew that because it was the one she'd been carrying inside her purse since last November.

Since she'd threatened to kill him in cold blood.

"Does he know?" Okegawa asked, nodding towards her sleeping boyfriend.

Kamala shook her head, and shame filled her gut. "No."

Okegawa rolled the syringe between his fingers and clucked his tongue. "Shame on you. He should know what you've gotten him into with your cruel, cruel words."

He took a step closer. Kamala held her breath and braced herself to run. "Did you know that there is quite a debate going about whether someone in a coma can hear what is being said around them? It's interesting. Some people report that when they wake, they heard nothing, and yet they have memories and sensations not their own."

The feigned jovial tone evaporated. Okegawa's scarred face emptied of all emotion aside from hatred. "I heard every single word, *ojou-sama*."

"Is that why you put that hit out on us?" Kamala sneered. "Did I scare you, Okegawa?"

He smirked. "To my core. To my very core. But, to tell you the truth, it wasn't the whole story. You and your fool Jackson have a knack for survival. I knew there was a chance my plan would fail and you would emerge alive and in one piece."

The smirk widened into a smile that chilled her to the bone marrow "Just like I wanted."

The gun swung away from Naila, and a tiny part of Kamala breathed a sigh of relief. Instead, he stepped closer with the syringe and leaned until the ends of his dark, unkempt hair nearly brushed her forehead. The pointed tip of the syringe settled over her carotid artery. Naila slept on, oblivious to the danger, too precious and innocent to know any better.

"I could kill you right now," Okegawa whispered. "Steal your life away in an instant, and you couldn't do anything about it. You are a smart, strong woman, but you lack the one thing that I have in excess."

Kamala swallowed again and didn't break his hateful gaze. "And what is that?"

"Patience," the *shateigashira* said. "I will wait an eternity to punish you, *ojou-sama*. I will make you suffer. I will make Jackson suffer. I will make Worthington suffer. I will make Fujioka suffer. I will render your life into nothing but ashes and embers. I will do it slowly, so that you see my good work every step of the way. In the end, you will realize that you should have killed me when you had the chance. Even now, you are not willing to accept the consequences of your actions. You could go for my gun. You could call for help. However, you and your daughter would not survive it. Your taste for revenge isn't as ravenous as mine."

"I think you'll come to find that things change," she whispered back. "Because if you come for me and my family, I will destroy you and everything you ever loved. If you so much as touch my loved ones, I will scorch the earth until I find you and I will kill you myself. Do you understand me, Kazuma?"

He let out a dry chuckle and pressed the syringe flat against her breastbone. "I cannot wait to see you try, *ojou-sama*."

Okegawa kissed her forehead sweetly. "Sleep tight. I'll see you again soon."

With that, he rose and left the room, silent as a shadow.

Kamala held her daughter close and wept.
"What have I done?"

"Who's the sweetest baby in the whole world? Who's
the sweetest baby in the whole world? You are! You are!"

Jack stifled a laugh as Libby's babbling continued the
question a few more times as she cuddled the newborn
enthusiastically. He passed his coffee over to Kamala, who
drank it gratefully, watching the interaction with the same
amount of amusement.

"Oh, I just love her so much!" Libby said. "I'm going to
steal her. Deadass gonna steal this baby when you least
expect it."

Jack shrugged. "Hey, if you can afford to take care of
her, go for it."

Kamala slapped his knee. "Stop offering our baby to
people, Jack."

"What? I mean, we'd save money."

Libby handed the newborn back to her father. "So
compassionate."

Her brown eyes then twinkled wickedly.
"Bartholomew."

Jack blushed. "Who told you?"

Libby batted her eyelashes. "Bumped into your mom
in the hallway. Lovely woman."

He heaved a sigh. "Well, that's not going away
anytime soon."

"Not even close. Now then..." Libby sat beside Kamala,
her cheerful tone sobering. "You guys ready for the field
report?"

"No, but tell us anyway," Kamala said tiredly.

"The second Highlander dragon--" She paused and
winked at Kamala. "--the one this pregnant badass *didn't*
brain with a big ass wrench--escaped. I tried all night to try
and find him with the dragon tracker, but it looks like he just
cut and run. He's in the wind."

"Shit," Jack muttered, and then winced and glanced down at the baby. "Sorry, munchkin. I meant shoot. Any indication of where it was heading when you lost sight of it?"

Libby shook her head. "The damn thing could be anywhere. We've alerted everyone within a fifty-mile radius of D.C. to be on the lookout. The Madam President put out a state of emergency for D.C. and the surrounding states. Something will turn up eventually. I just hope it goes postal on some livestock, not in a heavily populated area."

"What about the others?"

"The other dragons are all accounted for and securely in their cages, sedated."

"Any clues as to who killed the lights in there?"

"Nothing yet, but Internal Affairs is going over every last thing with a fine toothed comb. They'll find something soon and bring it to us ASAP."

"Well, it's not all a bust, at least," Jack said, brandishing his phone. "The cop we, uh, persuaded to help us gave me some details about Zhang and his operation. They've sent word out to law enforcement and they've already busted three of these rings up overnight."

"So what you're saying is it pays to bribe cops?"

He winked at her. "I plead the fifth."

"How is your brother?" Kamala asked.

"Getting antsy. He wants to hop right back in the saddle, as per usual." She paused enough to roll her eyes. "But he won't be discharged for another three days, at least. They want to be sure the internal damage doesn't run the risk of worsening. His recovery will take weeks but at least he can do it at home."

"Who's going to be his replacement in the meantime?"

"Not sure yet. Shannon had a big meeting with the higher ups and it's still going right now. He'll be out by this afternoon to tell us if we're all out of a job."

Libby smiled sadly. "So if you need a babysitter, I might be available."

"Done," Jack said. "Just don't teach her any memes. If

368

her first word is 'yeet,' I'm coming after you."

Libby cackled. "I make no such promises."

The door opened and closed, and Faye appeared, carrying brown paper bags of fast food as well as a cardboard tray with coffees on it. Libby helped her pass them out. "Oh, I guess we haven't met yet. I'm Libby. I've been working with Jack and Kamala for the recovery project."

"Faye Worthington," the blonde said, shaking her hand. "Nice to meet you."

"Are you her best friend?"

"No, I'm her girlfriend."

Libby laughed. Faye arched an eyebrow. Libby then blinked at her. "Wait."

She stared at all three of them and then her jaw dropped. "Whoa, whoa, whoa. Have you been holding out on me?"

Jack pinched the bridge of his nose. "Thanks a lot, Faye."

"What?" Faye protested, digging a sandwich out of her paper bag. "She asked."

"You didn't have to tell her! You could have said 'roommate,' you know."

"I'm their roommate," Faye deadpanned.

"Oh, this is too good," Libby said, rubbing her hands together. She pulled up a chair beside Jack. "Tell me everything. Now. Have you had a threesome yet? Or is it just two-by-two sex?"

Jack nearly inhaled his coffee. "Libby, Jesus *Christ*."

She pouted. "Oh, throw me a bone here, stud. You've got two insanely gorgeous women dating you and each other. You drop a bomb like that and expect me not to be interested?"

"Mind your business and eat your breakfast, whipper snapper."

She sucked her teeth and pointedly stole his sandwich, stomping off to go find some sugar to go in her coffee. "Cockblocking scientist douchebag."

369

"I heard that!"

Faye shook her head in amazement. "Where do you find these people?"

"I don't know. Just lucky, I guess."

"Though I do suppose that's our next challenge," Kamala said. "How we tell people we're in a polyamorous relationship, raising a child between the three of us. Not everyone is as open-minded as Libby."

"I say we don't mention it unless they ask," Jack suggested. "Keep it simple. If the media gets wind of it, good God, it's going to be a nightmare. We'll have Bible Thumpers picketing our house twenty-four-seven."

"Remind me to have that electrified fence installed," Faye said offhandedly.

"Will do. I think it's nobody's business but ours."

"I appreciate the sentiment," Kamala said. "But what if you want to take Faye on a date? What if I want to take Faye on a date? What about when we want to kiss each other goodbye in public?"

He frowned. "Hmm, good point. There is a lot more to this than I thought. Okay, we'll put it on the community bulletin board to figure out how this is going to work outside of the house."

The door reopened and Libby returned. "Despite how stingy you three are being with the details, I'll still fill you in. The general public has pretty much gone berserk after what happened yesterday. Hundreds, damn near thousands of videos posted with the dragon sightings. As for me and Jack's shenanigans..."

She held out her phone. "Read 'em and weep."

"The D.C. Dragon Hunters?" Jack read aloud. "There's an unofficial Facebook page already."

"With one-point-five million followers in only half a day," Libby finished. "We'll be at five million by tonight, I bet."

"Oy," Jack sighed. "So where are we with damage control?"

"Might be tricky. Your face is hidden, but there might be someone who compares a recording of your voice with the footage and they figure out it's you."

"So what? Am I going to pull an Iron Man and say it was a training exercise that went sideways?"

Libby shrugged. "That's for the higher ups to decide, I guess. They may want you to come clean, but they may also try to shift the blame onto the smugglers and pretend like it was one of their agents."

"It won't hold water long," Kamala said. "We might as well clear the air. The people will want to know it won't happen again. Jack and I are at least somewhat friendly faces."

"Personally, I wouldn't mind becoming a dragon-hunting rock star. I suspect I won't have much of a choice. There aren't too many pierced, pink-haired black girls with bodies like Beyoncé out there. Someone from my past is bound to put two and two together."

"Pssh, Beyoncé," Jack said. "Keep dreaming."

She stuck out her tongue. "Anyway, I'll keep an eye on all the social media to see if someone figures it out."

"What's the room reading like?"

"It's sort of mixed. A lot of people think it's badass. Others, not so much, but I don't blame them. There were unfortunately a lot of casualties."

Kamala exhaled. "Is there a final count yet?"

"Eight," Libby said softly. "Another four in critical condition. Plenty of injured."

Jack nodded soberly. "When you can, get us names. We'd like to pay medical bills and funeral costs. Anything they need."

"Done. The public's not aware of them yet, but I expect they'll have to announce it whenever they make an official statement."

Libby straightened up in her chair. "But it could have been so much worse. I'm just glad we all made it out in one piece."

She eyed Jack's chest. "Well. Mostly in one piece."

"I'm fine," he told her mildly.

"*I'm fine,*" she mocked him. "I hope both of your girlfriends eventually smack some sense into you. And then film it and let me see it."

He scowled at her. "Do you want me to ground you again?"

"You should have seen him," Libby told Kamala, ignoring him. "He got so swole about it when I told him I was coming with him to recapture the dragons."

Kamala nodded wisely. "That is very like him. He's terribly protective."

"Hey!" he protested.

"I know, right? I've known him like four days and he's already ready to jump on a grenade for me. No wonder people have been calling him Sir Gawain. Maybe that'll be his codename."

Jack glared. "You start that and I'm gonna start calling you Penny."

She gave him a mystified look and he hiked his voice up to a squeaky little girl's voice. "Hold on, Uncle Gadget!"

"You wouldn't dare," Libby growled.

"Try me."

Faye glanced at Kamala. "Is this what you've had to listen to for four days?"

"Pretty much."

"You have the patience Lakshmi."

"You could at least give me Max Gibson from *Batman Beyond.*"

"Ha! You're not nearly cool enough."

"Whatever you say, *Barry.*"

"I'm gonna kill my mother."

## EPILOGUE

## PHOENIX

**One week later...**

"I can't tell you how happy I am that she took after Kamala's looks and not yours," Calloway grinned, gently tweaking the baby Naila's chubby cheek. The newborn gurgled and reached a tiny hand up to grip his index finger.

"I'm very secure about my appearance, I'll have you know," Jack sniffed, pretending to toss his hair a bit before pouring coffee into the other two mugs. He brought them over to the dining room table where Libby already sat, fiddling with her phone and chuckling every so often. He dropped a kiss to the top of Kamala's head before taking a seat beside her and watching Calloway make funny faces as he held the infant. Calloway looked worlds better than the last time they'd seen him; the color had returned to his dark skin and most of the bruising had begun to fade. He was a fast healer, it seemed.

"Besides, we can't all be strapping, handsome gentlemen." Jack then smiled over the rim of his coffee. "So how's the SWAT lady doing? Her name is Summer, right?"

Calloway glared at Jack. "None of your business."

Jack held up his hands in surrender. "Hey, just asking."

He nudged Libby with his elbow and said in a stage whisper. "Tell me all about it later."

Calloway rolled his eyes. "So what? You two have a knitting circle going?"

"Hey, you started it."

The doorbell rang. Calloway safely deposited the infant in her father's arms and answered it. Agent Shannon walked in. "Morning, son."

"Morning, Dad," Calloway said, heavy on the sarcasm.

"Coffee?"

"Yes. I take it black."

Calloway and Jack both chorused. "That's racist." Shannon just sighed and accepted the mug once they were done chortling in unison. He sipped it and glanced around the house as Calloway took a seat at the dining room table along with the others. Shannon had a thick manila folder tucked beneath one arm, his tie loose, no walkie-talkie on his hip this time, though he did still have his firearm.

"So what's this all about, Shannon?" Jack asked. "And why'd you ask us to meet here?"

"You have a newborn to worry about. Figured it would make life easier not to drag you all the way back to D.C. for a briefing. And they cover my travel expenses one-hundred-percent."

"Aw, that almost sounded nice," Libby said, batting her eyelashes. "I think he's coming around, you guys."

"Don't hold your breath," Shannon grumbled. "Anyway, we're also still trying to plug any leaks at the facility. This is an unofficial visit. Off the books. Anything I tell you is not to be repeated until you're given the go ahead."

Shannon set the coffee down. "For obvious reasons, the talk with my superiors took a long time and was very annoying. That being said, it was also enlightening. All they've done since they gave us this assignment was sit behind a desk and read reports and look at charts. They haven't understood the gravity of these events, and the assassination attempts on you as well as the dragons breaking out finally got through to them. They no longer are under any illusions about these creatures and what they can do."

Libby winced. "So I take it we've been shut down?"

"No. They want to extend the assignment. Indefinitely."

They all gawked. "What?"

Shannon tossed the manila folder down. "They want to offer you the positions permanently. For Calloway and

Libby, it'd be full time. For Dr. Jackson and Dr. Anjali, it'd be part time since you have a newborn, and your participation wouldn't begin until after your maternity and paternity leave have concluded. You'd still be able to continue working for MIT. The facility in D.C. will not be our HQ any longer. We'll be setting up shop elsewhere, at a secure location, and it'll just be us. No extra agents aside from security. That cuts down on the interference and potential leaks about our activities. I pitched them the reservation that Jackson and Anjali had been working on before we seized the project and they agreed to help you get it up and running. The intent is for the dragons to be rehabilitated and kept out of the public eye. This isn't *Jurassic Park*. Recover the dragons, teach them not to kill everything in sight, and maintain their health and well-being. If our operation is successful, then it will be expanded to a larger staff of trustworthy experts in the field of dracology."

He tucked his hands in his pockets. "Meanwhile, the investigation of the dragon smugglers and the illegal cloning ring will be instead handled by another department. It's too much to expect our team to be able to handle this problem on many fronts. I felt we were overextended to begin with, so I convinced them to continue the collaboration among the different agencies and only receive input from our team on occasion. We'd receive updates on the status of their investigation and nothing more. We won't be expected to turn in results ourselves since our plate is full enough as it is."

Shannon glanced at Libby. "You'll be pleased to know that Dr. Whitmore is set to be charged with criminal conspiracy, collusion with a foreign criminal organization, obstruction of justice, accepting a bribe, spying on government confidential information, and hiring contract killers. He's never going to see the light of day again. And not that Camp Cupcake Martha Stewart shit. He's going to federal prison and he's going to stay there."

Libby nodded. "Thank you."

"Good riddance," Calloway growled.

"There is an open investigation as to the perpetrator who killed the lights while the dragons were being fed. We have some suspects compiled, but I'll bring you in once we have something solid. Dr. Whitmore provided the method of contact and they're doing their best to try to decode everything. Contract killers don't like to leave loose ends, so he's also not going to be in the general populace for the time being."

He paused to let the information sink in. "None of you have to say yes. After the public found out about the dragons, we've had previous parties express that they'd like to apply now that they've seen us in action. I understand your reticence after what you've been through. I may not be your biggest fans, but I acknowledge that each one of you has worked hard and made the sacrifices necessary to reduce the loss of life and to ensure that these animals are given what they need to survive. However, I understand that you have more important things to worry about. Family. Safety. A life outside of this assignment. Once upon a time, I did too. Therefore, I won't need your answer right away. Everything I've discussed is right there in this folder for you to review. You get one week to think it over and then we move on with whoever is qualified."

Shannon waited for one of them to speak. Unsurprisingly, Jack was the first to go. "So...you're basically asking us to be the Ghostbusters, but for dragons?"

Shannon didn't blink. "Essentially, yes."

"Okay. Glad we cleared that up. I've got dibs on Venkman."

Shannon shook his head in exasperation. "Think it over. I'll be back in a week."

He turned to leave, but then stopped, glancing down at Naila. "Cute kid."

"One more thing before you go," Calloway said. "Jack and Libby ran into all kinds of authority problems when they were out there. Is this team going to have some kind of name the public can recognize?"

"Yeah." Shannon glanced at Jack and smiled a bit.
"They're calling it the Knight Division."


"I have to tell you something. It's not going to be easy
for you to hear. You're going to be angry with me, and I
understand completely, but it's worth the risk. I hope you
have enough faith in me to understand why I did it, but if
you don't, well, there's nothing more I can do. All I can offer
is the truth. What you choose to do with it is up to you."

Carmichael and Houston exchanged a look. Both had
their cop faces on, and thus the expressions were pretty
much unreadable. They'd known from the start that
something had been wrong in the first place, if only because
they were meeting in a small, private conference room at the
library.

"Alright," Houston said. "Go ahead."

Faye quit pacing and sat down. She set her phone
down in front of her and laced her fingers on the table top.
"The morning after I went to Clearwater Beach, Winston
showed up in my hotel suite with a proposition."

Both detectives stiffened in their seats. Houston
rubbed his goatee and sighed. Carmichael dragged one hand
down his face. She waited for them to recover before
continuing.

"He told me that there was a contract out on Jack and
Kamala. Forty grand a head. Deadline of four days. It had to
be made to look like an accident, so the hitter had to
manipulate the actions of the dragons and the smugglers so
that they would kill the two of them and no one would be the
wiser that it had been a contract."

"Why the hell would he tell you that?" Carmichael
asked.

"Because he passed on the assignment, and he wanted
me to come with him to stop it."

"Lord Almighty," Houston said, closing his eyes. "Tell

me you said no."

"I didn't have a choice. If I told anyone, he said he'd leave and let them get killed. I agreed."

"Faye," Carmichael snarled. "Why didn't you call us?"

"I couldn't," she said dispassionately. "Winston was with me every second of the day since I agreed to help him. He'd have known if I tried to contact one of you. Don't ask me how, but he'd know. He's too smart. Before I tell you the rest, I need to know that I can trust you. I'm not looking for amnesty or anything. If I surrender what I have, I need to know that you are willing to help me find him and stop him without involving your office."

"You've got to be kidding me," Carmichael said. "You want us to investigate a case off the books? That would be cutting off our resources at the knees. We'd barely be able to make any headway unless you've just got some kind of ace up your sleeve."

He sat back in his chair, shaking his head. "Ern, talk some sense into her, will ya?"

Houston held Faye's gaze. He studied her for a long while before speaking. "You've got something, don't you? Something big. Otherwise, you'd have kept this to yourself and hired a P.I. instead."

She didn't answer. Houston mirrored her, lacing his own thick fingers together. "So you want our word that we won't discuss this case with anyone in our department in case Winston or someone who is tight with the crowd that he runs with won't catch wind of it. You're talking about confidential information that could lead to his eventual capture."

Again, she didn't answer, and she didn't blink. Houston glanced at his partner. "This is different, Rob. This isn't like the drug den thing we busted her on. This is the real deal. We'd be hunting a contract killer. A career contract killer."

Carmichael ground his teeth. "Ern, this is a bad idea. You know how things end when cops try to solve cases under the table. They'll have our asses in a sling if they find out."

"Well, I won't be telling anyone. I know she won't. Will you?"

Carmichael carded a hand through his blond hair. "You're both crazy."

He sighed. "Fine. I made you a promise that we'd bag this guy. Guess you're calling me out on it finally. Yeah. We'll keep this quiet."

"Thank you." Faye took a deep breath and told them everything.

It took a while, nearly half an hour. They didn't ask questions. They just listened intently. Carmichael got up and paced, loosening his tie and a button on his dress shirt. Houston remained seated, waiting patiently for her to finish.

"Now, then, Ms. Worthington," Houston said, his brown eyes narrowing. "Can you prove any of what you just said?"

Faye exhaled. "Yes, I can. I recorded almost every conversation I had with Winston."

They both froze. "What?"

Faye tapped her cell. "I had my phone recording as many times as possible when he and I spoke to each other in person. I uploaded the files to the Cloud and erased them from the phone each time in case he tried to check my phone when I wasn't around or when I went to sleep. It isn't everything, but at the very least, it's a confession of the murdered driver you guys pulled from the river as well as pertinent information about him. If nothing else, you may be able to compare his voice to another sample someday and figure out his original identity. There is also some audio from the ex-wife, who honestly, is who I am more concerned about at the moment."

She shook her head. "I want Winston. Bad. But Stella is a thousand times worse. She's completely unhinged and there's a good chance once she heals that shoulder wound, she's gonna come gunning for me. She's vicious and resourceful. She will kill me if she gets the chance, and she'll probably try to kill my family too. We need to get to work finding her, and we need to do it quietly."

Faye swallowed hard to steady herself. "Do you think we can do this? Do you think we can stop her from hurting my family?"

Houston glanced at Carmichael. The blond cop just smiled. "Does shit run downhill?"


"Knock, knock."

Kamala glanced up to see her boyfriend standing in the doorway to the baby's room. His dark hair stuck up off his forehead like usual, he had bags under his eyes, and his bed clothing had more wrinkles than a Shar Pei. But his smile was warm and fond. "Hey."

"You're cold for that, you know."

She lifted an eyebrow. "How so?"

He shut the door and shuffled further into the room, keeping his voice soft so as not to disturb the nursing newborn. "You let me conk out on the couch. I thought it was my turn to change her diaper."

"You looked so cute," she confessed. "I didn't want to wake you."

Jack leaned down and kissed her. "You're way too good for me, Dr. Anjali. Don't deserve you."

"Nonsense."

"She eating okay?"

"Yes, thank goodness. She's ravenous, in fact. It's an excellent sign for a preemie."

"Good. Guess you've been here ruminating about Shannon's offer, huh?"

"The baby's been an excellent distraction, but...yes. It's a lot to absorb."

"Tell me about it."

Naila fidgeted and yawned. Jack handed her a soft drop cloth and Kamala nestled the baby against her shoulder, gently patting her. They both smiled when a miniature burp emerged.

"She really is perfect, isn't she?" Jack said.

"More than perfect."

"Can't believe I was so scared to meet her. But I won't be that anymore. I promise."

Kamala found his hand with hers and squeezed tight. "Neither will I."

She kissed his wrist. "Now be a dear, and go make me a chocolate shake."

Jack laughed. "Yes, ma'am. Anything for my angel."

He kissed her, and the baby, and headed back towards the kitchen.

A few minutes later, as she gently rocked the child to sleep, her phone rang.

"Yes?"

"Hey, it's Fujioka. The plane just landed."

"Good. I will see you at your hotel room in the morning."

"Are you sure about this, Kamala?"

She glanced down at her slumbering daughter. Steel entered her voice. "Okegawa threatened my family. And I want him dead."

To be continued in *Of Fury and Fangs*
Coming in 2020

# Acknowledgments

To my mother, after whom this book is dedicated. You have always been my pillar of strength and wisdom and sympathy. I don't know how you do it, but I am so grateful for your continued love and support. You are my source of light in the darkness.

To my father, who continues to inspire me to do my best and make my mark in this ridiculous little world that I live in. I appreciate everything you've taught me, as well as your patience.

To Bryan, who provides an excellent perspective to keep me grounded and make sure that every book is as good as it possibly can be.

To Sharon, who is nothing short of a saint finding time for my silly scribbles and for adding suggestions that make the story that much richer.

To my family, who gives me so much love and comfort as I struggle to be the best I can be.

To Andy Rattinger, who hides a cape underneath his clothes, for he is surely a superhero considering how many times he's saved this series and taught me how to write past my mental roadblocks.

To my friends, who keep me from drifting off the edge into the abyss and who encourage me during my darkest hours to hold on.

To my fans, who are the reason I haven't given up on this extremely tough career path.

To Marginean Anca, for knocking the cover art out of the park just like you always do.

To Fay Collins, for doing a fantastic job on editing this monstrosity.

To KBoards, for your assistance with facts and logistical things for my research.

To the new readers, for making it this far in our crazy

train ride and not hopping off yet even though you can clearly see the conductor is out of her freaking mind.

To the *Jurassic World* movies, for being so goddamn terrible that you pretty much fueled a good forty-percent of why I wrote this novel and the proceeding one as well, you pathetic ruination of something that I once loved.

To fanfiction, for being my glutinous comfort food during the long months it took me to write this novel. You are the cause of and the cure for all of my problems.

To Chris Hemsworth and Tom Hiddleston, who didn't do anything at all for me, but I'm just really happy that both of you exist.

To the Darkest Timeline, for forcing me to dive headfirst into the world of fiction to distract me from how the entire real world is on fire and yet I have to still live in it anyway, screaming into the void like a madwoman. Good lookin' out, fam.

## Author's Note

My God, it's been a helluva year.

At the time this Author's Note is being written, we're three years into the hellscape that is the Darkest Timeline, and yet it feels as if it's been thirty years. We all know where each other is, pretty much, though—I'm tired, you're tired, we're tired, and things ain't gettin' any easier anytime soon.

But at least we've got each other.

One of the most prominent themes for this novel has been the juxtaposition of light and dark moments in life. It's kind of infuriating that your life can't be neatly sectioned off into good and bad times and then distributed evenly. Sometimes good things last a long time and bad things are short-lived.

Unfortunately, that usually is not the case.

Usually, things suck and it feels like you're being suffocated. That's life. No one gets out alive, after all, and it's typically just random chaos. Within that chaos, we have to figure out what to do and how to weather the hurricane somehow. It feels impossible more often than not, and that's why it's important to remember the dawn. The world may be embers right now, but the sun still rises every morning regardless.

Besides, it could be worse. We could be on Earth 616 and have gotten Snapped.

The journey that Jack, Kamala, Faye, and baby Naila just went on is full of some very serious highs and very serious lows. It's an ongoing battle for them to stay together and in one piece when life is pretty much throwing everything at them but the kitchen sink. I have to admit I am surprised with how much I enjoyed the final product, which is a rarity for me. I doubt myself severely, and yet I already feel rather fond of this story. I feel that we were able to further open the door to a new world. There are some very scary but very exciting things on the other side. I can't wait for you to see what's in store.

Well. Yes, I can. Writing is hard. But I'm going to do it anyway.

I truly hope you enjoyed this novel and maybe even took something away from it, even if it's nothing but the idea that you're not alone out there. Fiction has this crazy way of connecting us to one another. I know for a fact it makes me feel less lonely and less miserable. No one's asking for my advice, least of all me, but I just want to stop and say that you are important and loved and special beyond measure, even in your darkest hour.

How do we survive the Darkest Timeline?

Find your dawn.

Your dawn can be anything you want it to be. It might be tough to find it, and it might take a long time, but it is out there, waiting for you to grab it and hold it tight. Find the reason you're here and focus on that to get through the rough seas ahead. You're definitely not the only one struggling, so take comfort in that, if you can.

Hopefully, I'll see you on the other side.

If not, well. At least the sun's still shining.

Love always,
Kyoko

Graves, Robert. *Collected Poems.* "Mermaid Dragon Fiend," 1961. Public domain.

Made in United States
North Haven, CT
29 February 2024

49406237R00212